Zenescope Enterta

Grimm Fairy Tales
Volume 11

Grimm
Fairy

Zenescope Entertainment presents:

Grimm Fairy Tales Volume 11

Jack The Giant Killer 6
The Gates of Limbo 30
Lost Souls 54
The Immortals 78

The Arena 102
A Drink and a Tale 128
Cover Gallery 152

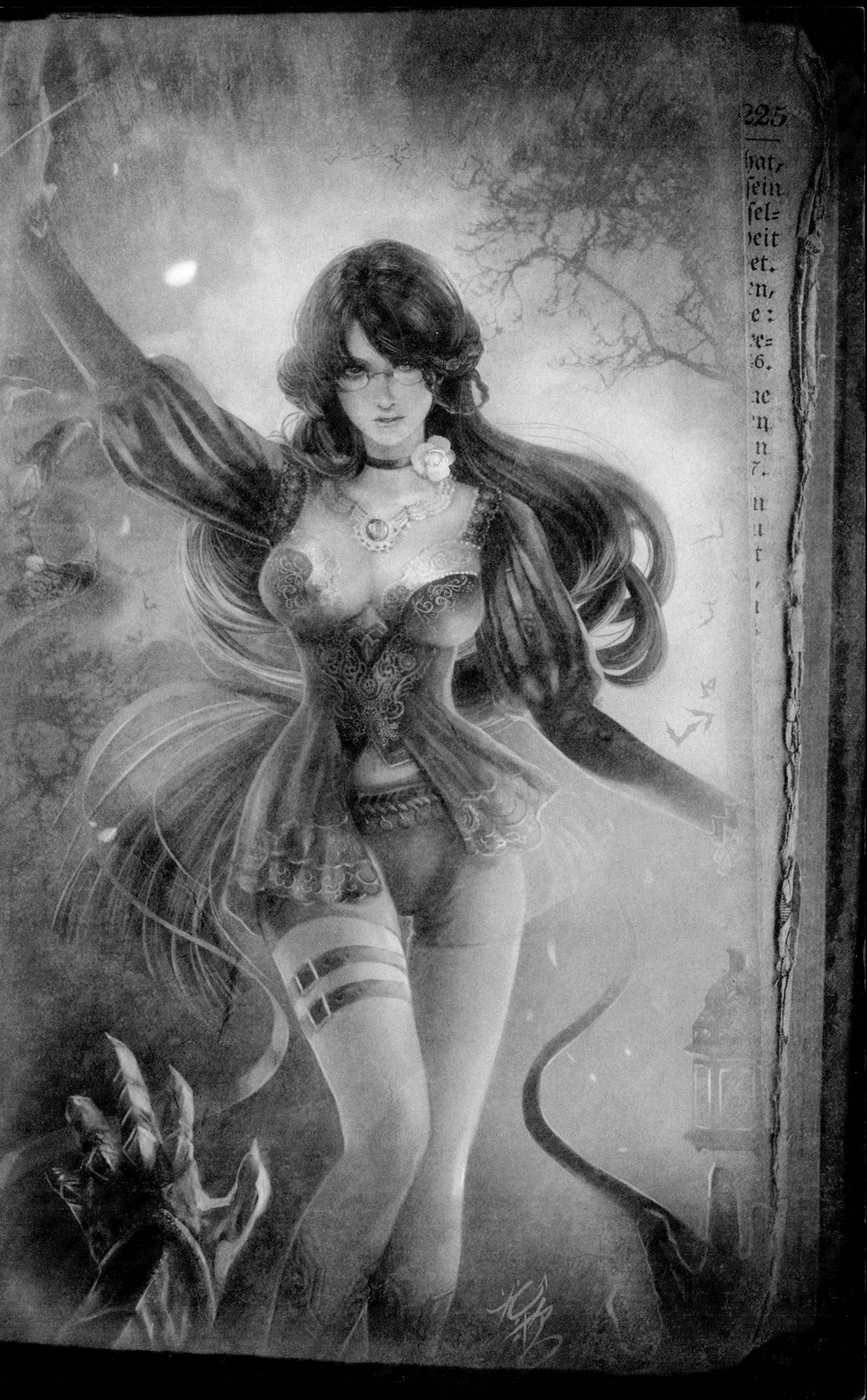
225
hat,
sein
sel=
heit
et.

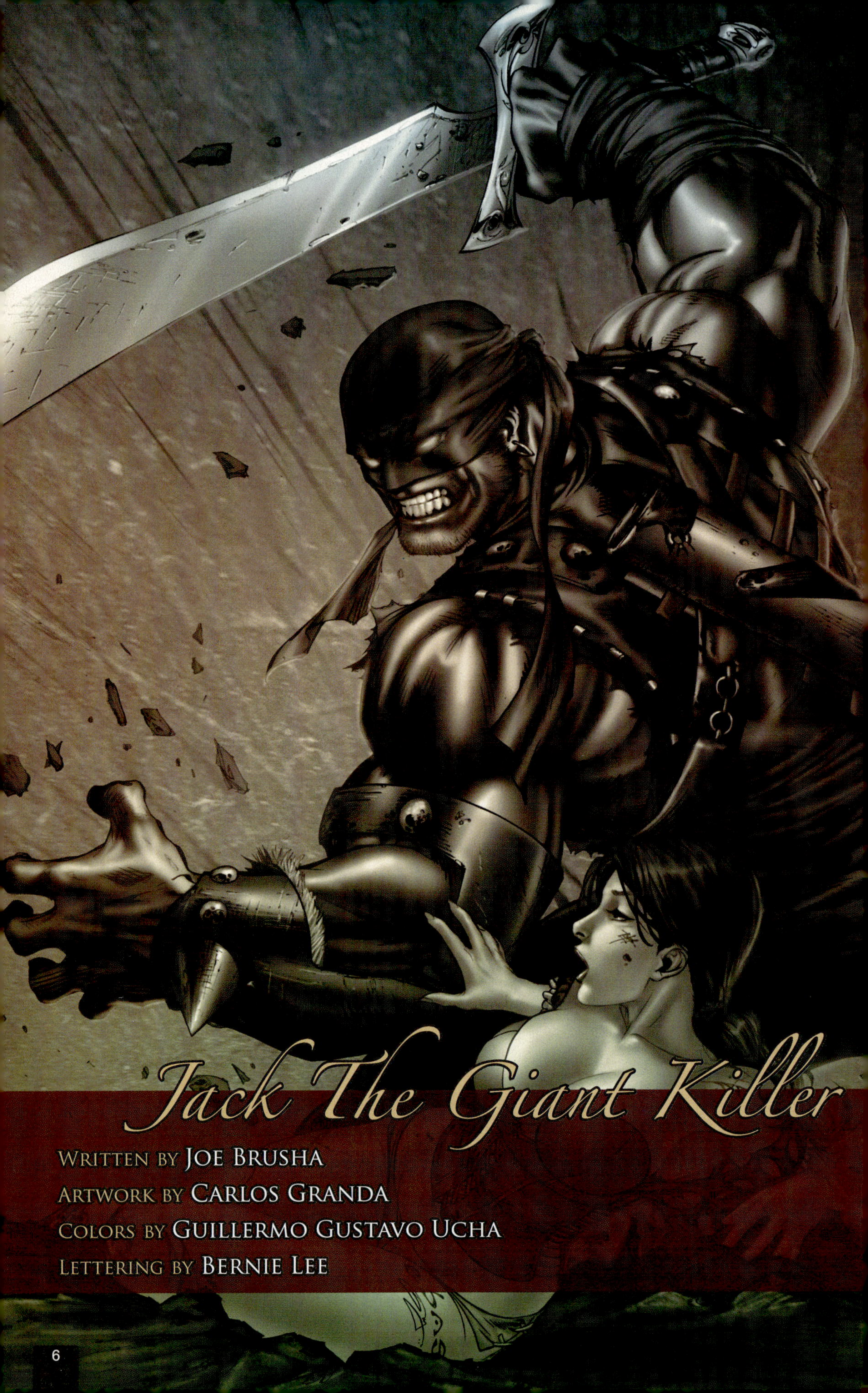

Jack The Giant Killer

WRITTEN BY JOE BRUSHA
ARTWORK BY CARLOS GRANDA
COLORS BY GUILLERMO GUSTAVO UCHA
LETTERING BY BERNIE LEE

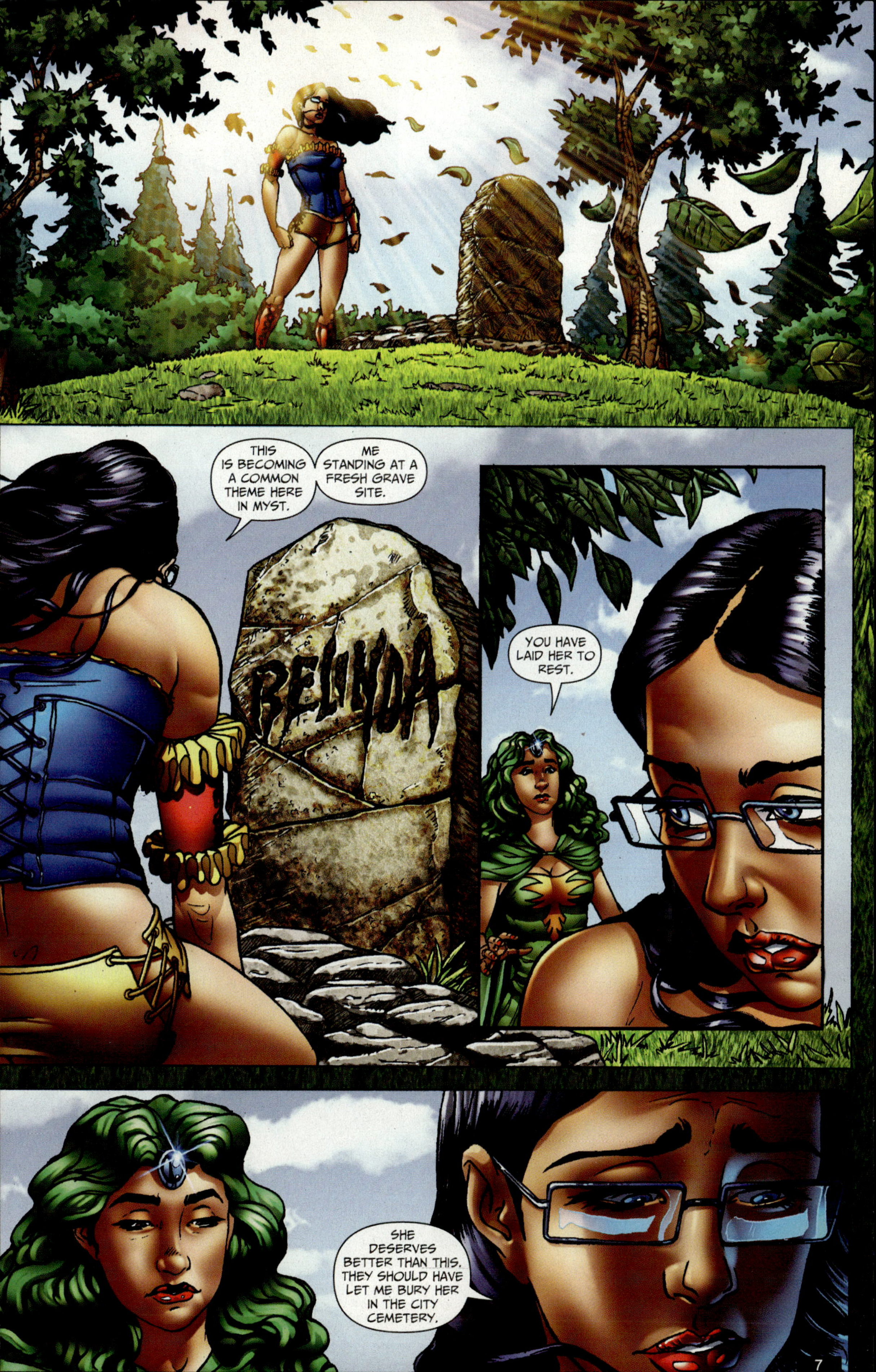
THIS IS BECOMING A COMMON THEME HERE IN MYST.
ME STANDING AT A FRESH GRAVE SITE.
BELINDA
YOU HAVE LAID HER TO REST.
SHE DESERVES BETTER THAN THIS. THEY SHOULD HAVE LET ME BURY HER IN THE CITY CEMETERY.

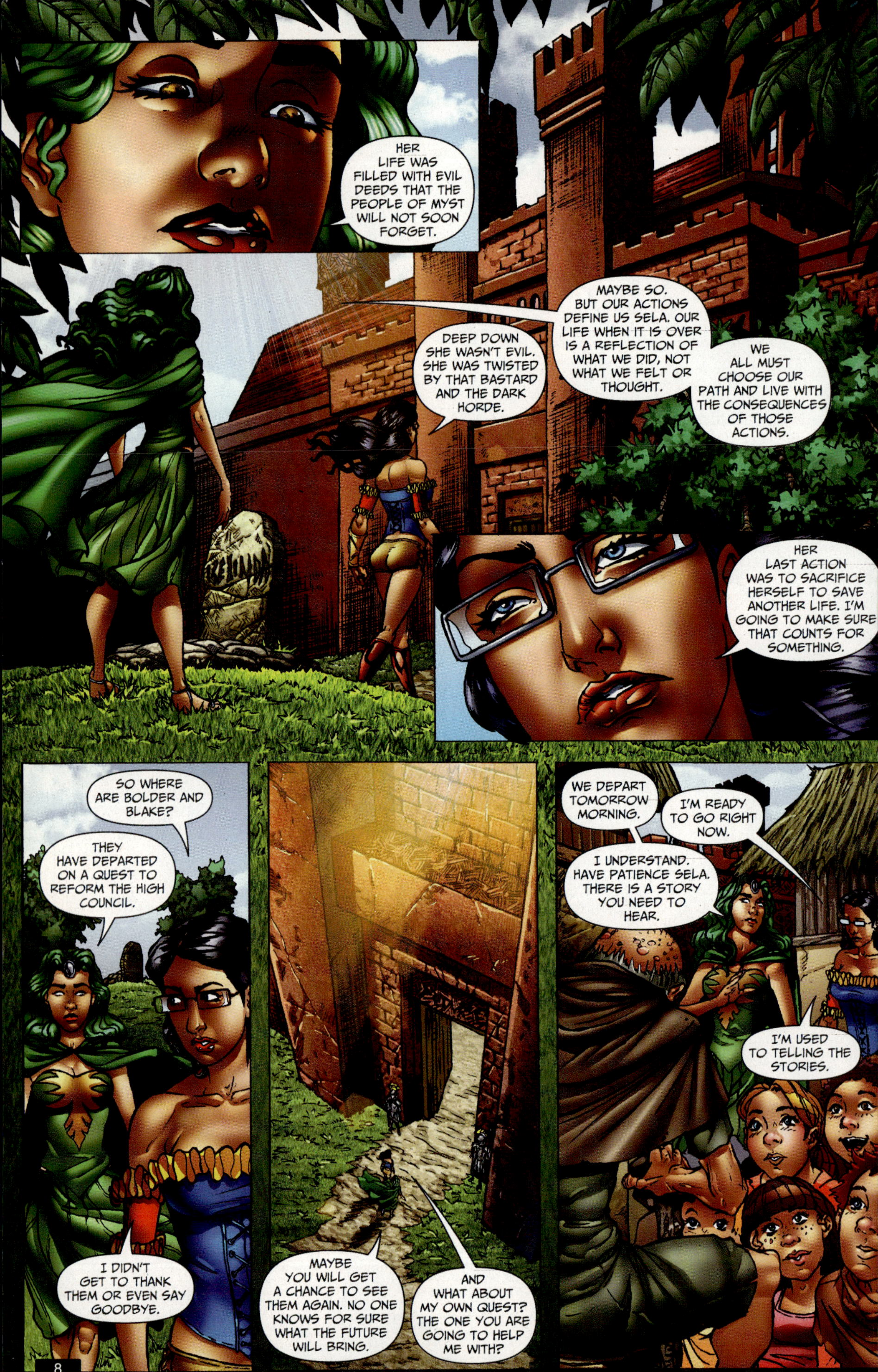
HER LIFE WAS FILLED WITH EVIL DEEDS THAT THE PEOPLE OF MYST WILL NOT SOON FORGET.
DEEP DOWN SHE WASN'T EVIL. SHE WAS TWISTED BY THAT BASTARD AND THE DARK HORDE.
MAYBE SO. BUT OUR ACTIONS DEFINE US SELA. OUR LIFE WHEN IT IS OVER IS A REFLECTION OF WHAT WE DID, NOT WHAT WE FELT OR THOUGHT.
WE ALL MUST CHOOSE OUR PATH AND LIVE WITH THE CONSEQUENCES OF THOSE ACTIONS.
HER LAST ACTION WAS TO SACRIFICE HERSELF TO SAVE ANOTHER LIFE. I'M GOING TO MAKE SURE THAT COUNTS FOR SOMETHING.
SO WHERE ARE BOLDER AND BLAKE?
THEY HAVE DEPARTED ON A QUEST TO REFORM THE HIGH COUNCIL.
I DIDN'T GET TO THANK THEM OR EVEN SAY GOODBYE.
MAYBE YOU WILL GET A CHANCE TO SEE THEM AGAIN. NO ONE KNOWS FOR SURE WHAT THE FUTURE WILL BRING.
AND WHAT ABOUT MY OWN QUEST? THE ONE YOU ARE GOING TO HELP ME WITH?
WE DEPART TOMORROW MORNING.
I'M READY TO GO RIGHT NOW.
I UNDERSTAND. HAVE PATIENCE SELA. THERE IS A STORY YOU NEED TO HEAR.
I'M USED TO TELLING THE STORIES.

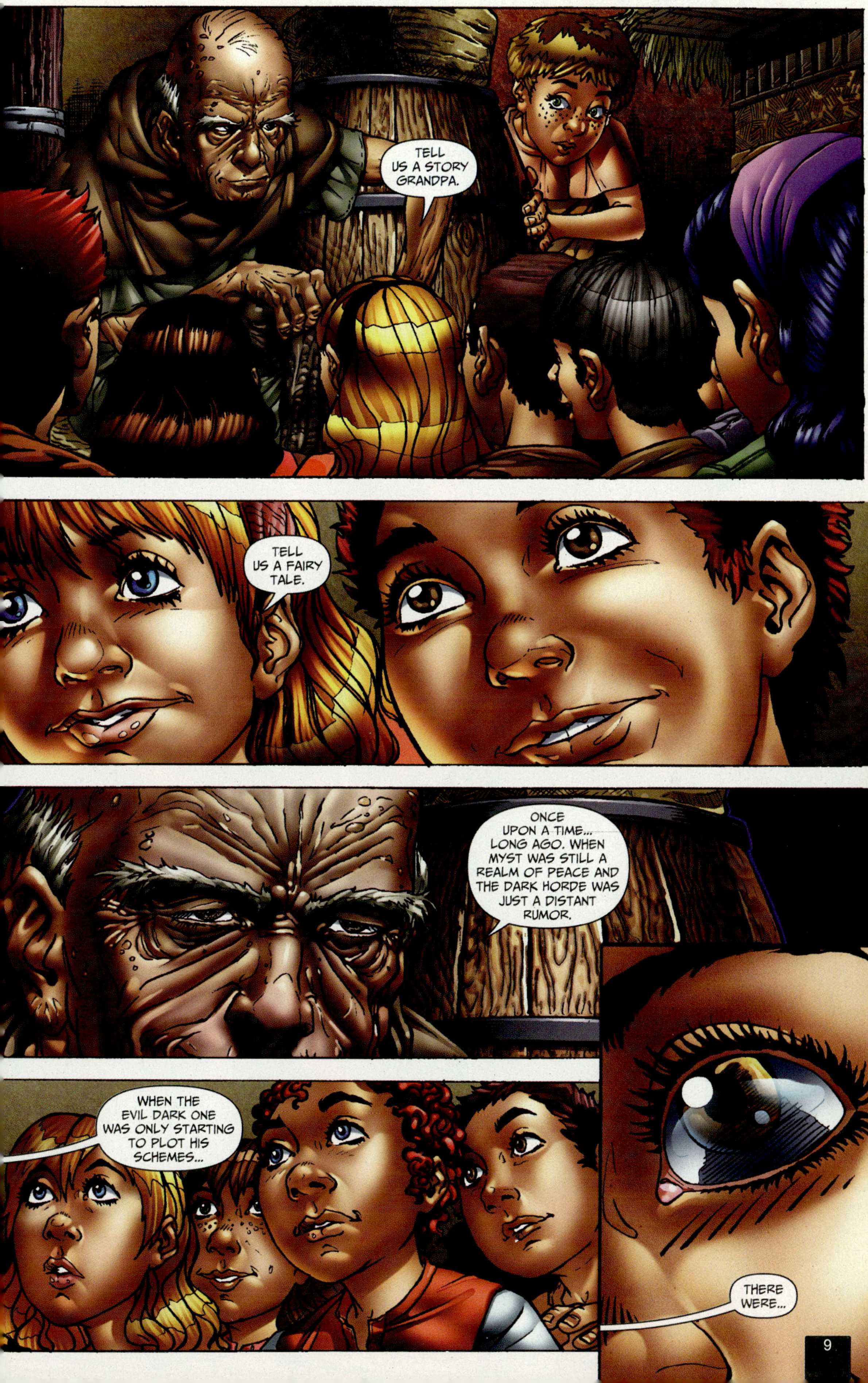
TELL US A STORY GRANDPA.
TELL US A FAIRY TALE.
ONCE UPON A TIME... LONG AGO. WHEN MYST WAS STILL A REALM OF PEACE AND THE DARK HORDE WAS JUST A DISTANT RUMOR.
WHEN THE EVIL DARK ONE WAS ONLY STARTING TO PLOT HIS SCHEMES...
THERE WERE...

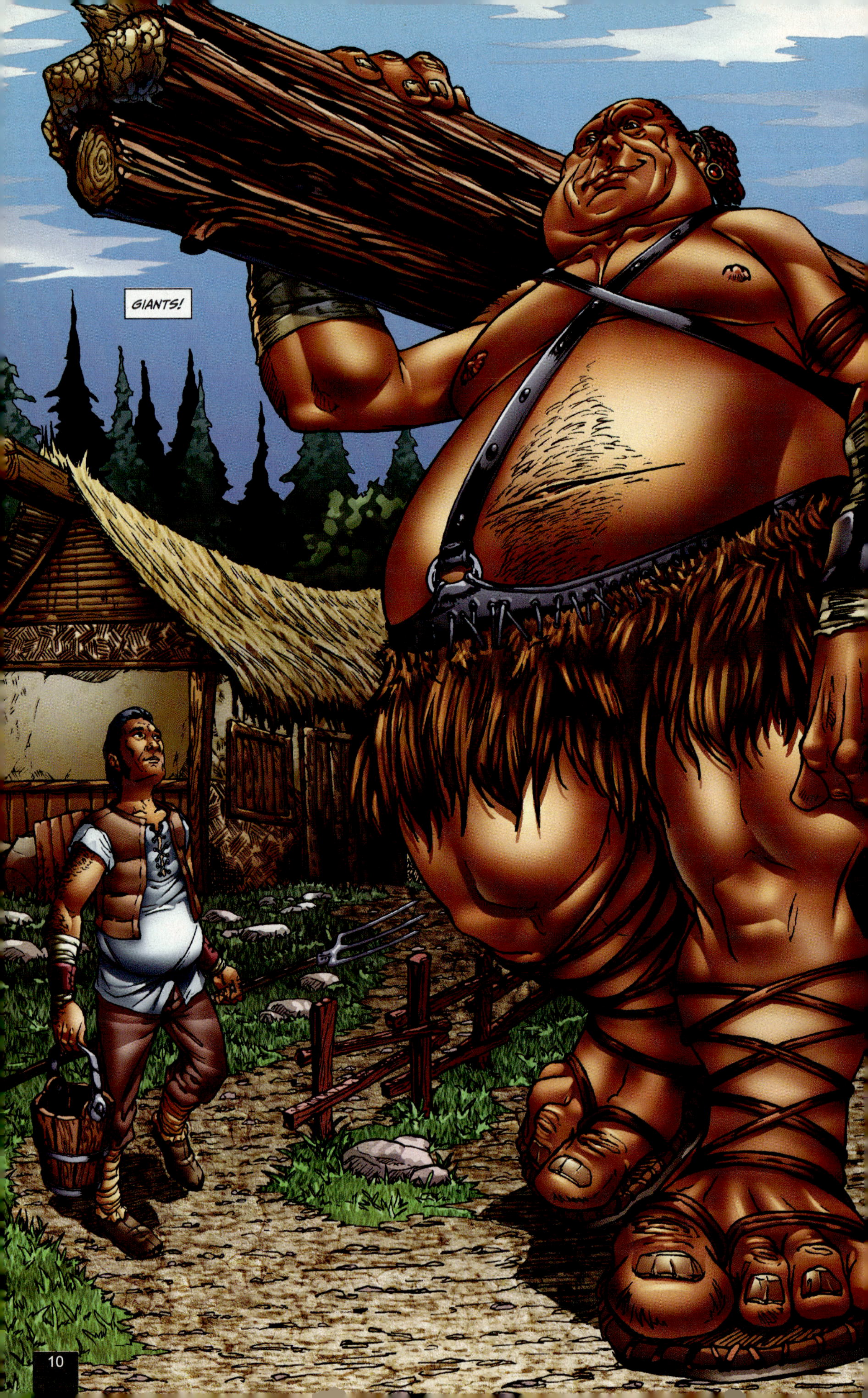
GIANTS!

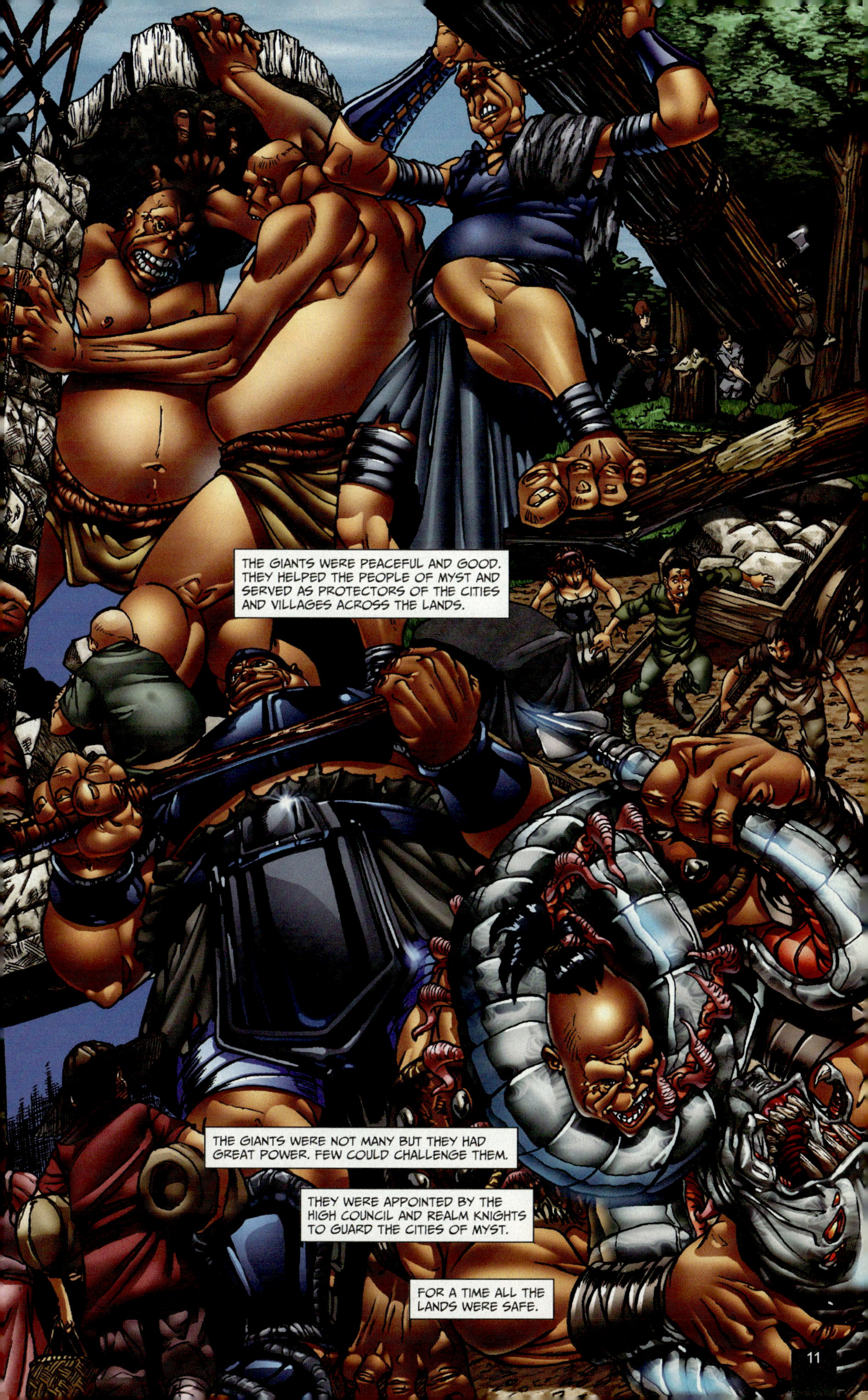
THE GIANTS WERE PEACEFUL AND GOOD. THEY HELPED THE PEOPLE OF MYST AND SERVED AS PROTECTORS OF THE CITIES AND VILLAGES ACROSS THE LANDS.
THE GIANTS WERE NOT MANY BUT THEY HAD GREAT POWER. FEW COULD CHALLENGE THEM.
THEY WERE APPOINTED BY THE HIGH COUNCIL AND REALM KNIGHTS TO GUARD THE CITIES OF MYST.
FOR A TIME ALL THE LANDS WERE SAFE.

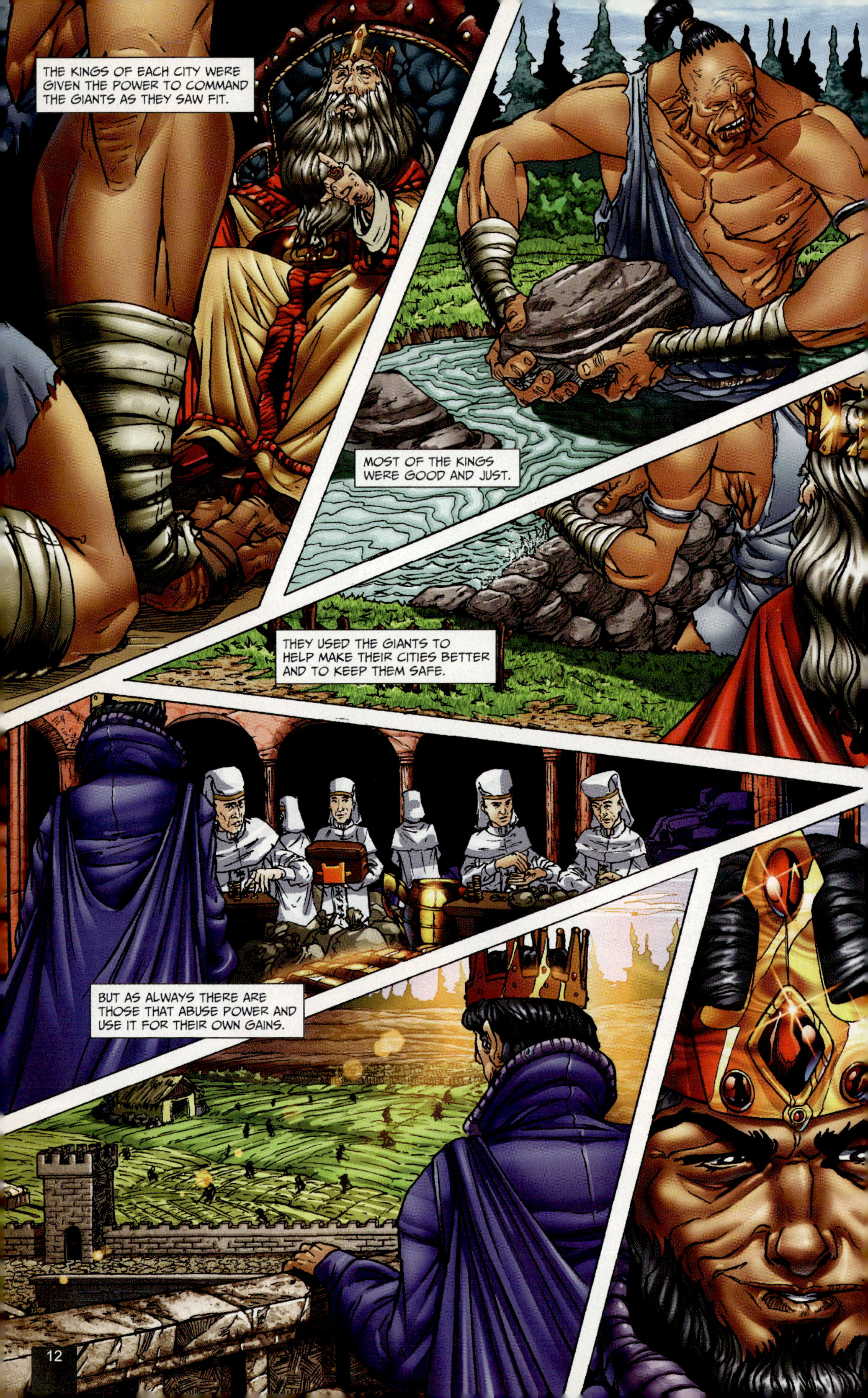
THE KINGS OF EACH CITY WERE GIVEN THE POWER TO COMMAND THE GIANTS AS THEY SAW FIT.
MOST OF THE KINGS WERE GOOD AND JUST.
THEY USED THE GIANTS TO HELP MAKE THEIR CITIES BETTER AND TO KEEP THEM SAFE.
BUT AS ALWAYS THERE ARE THOSE THAT ABUSE POWER AND USE IT FOR THEIR OWN GAINS.

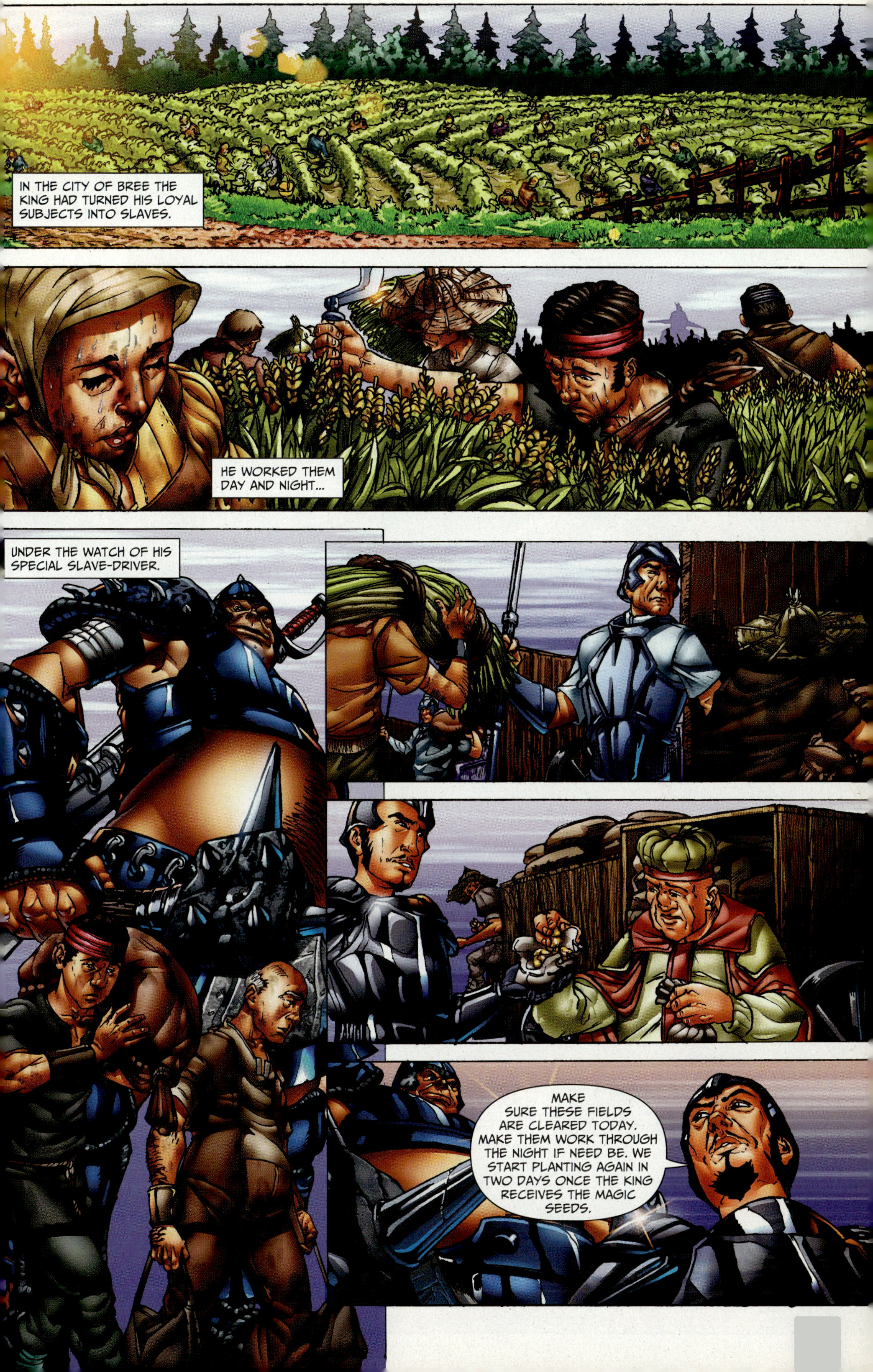
IN THE CITY OF BREE THE KING HAD TURNED HIS LOYAL SUBJECTS INTO SLAVES.
HE WORKED THEM DAY AND NIGHT...
UNDER THE WATCH OF HIS SPECIAL SLAVE-DRIVER.
MAKE SURE THESE FIELDS ARE CLEARED TODAY. MAKE THEM WORK THROUGH THE NIGHT IF NEED BE. WE START PLANTING AGAIN IN TWO DAYS ONCE THE KING RECEIVES THE MAGIC SEEDS.

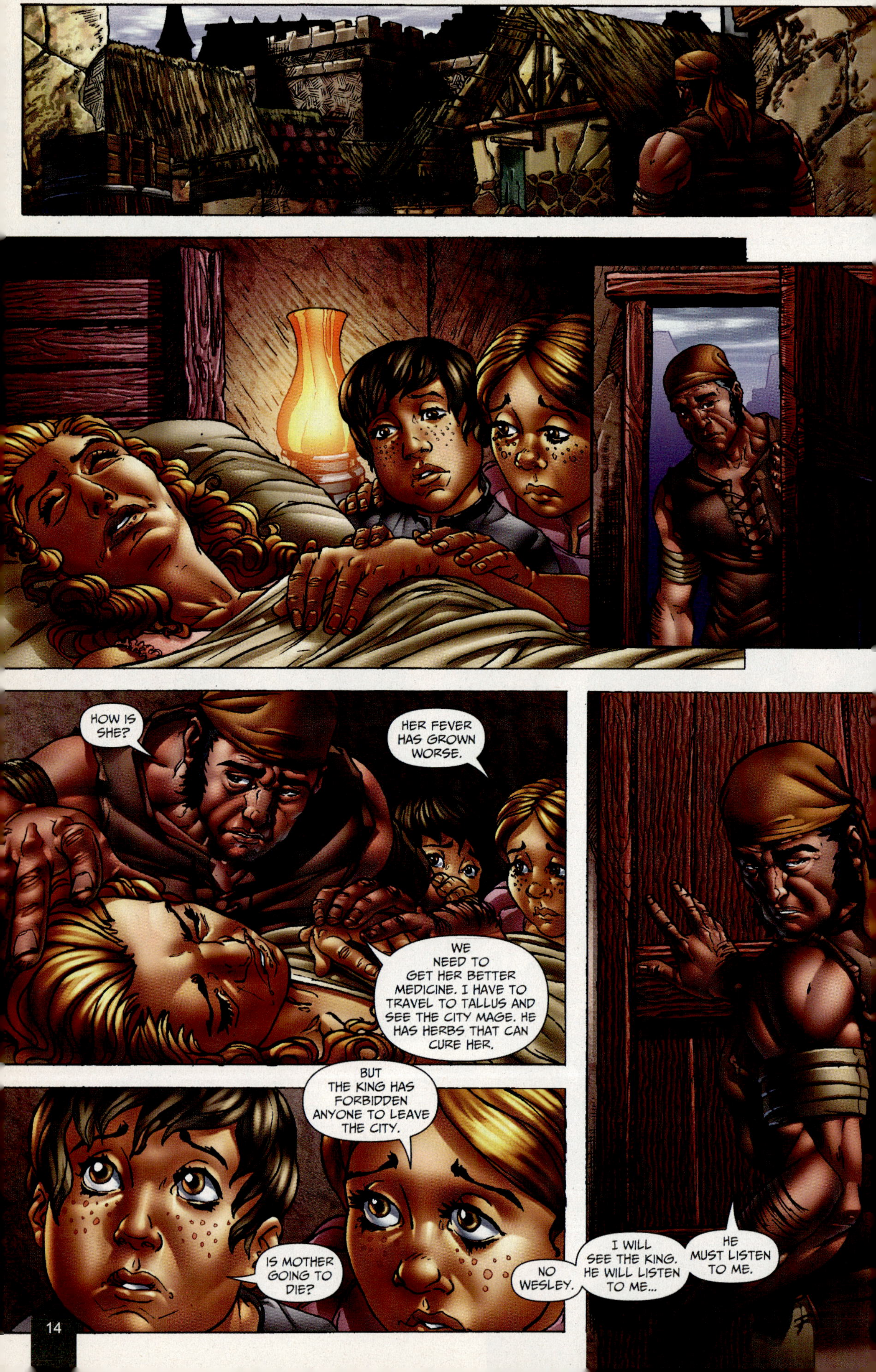
HOW IS SHE?
HER FEVER HAS GROWN WORSE.
WE NEED TO GET HER BETTER MEDICINE. I HAVE TO TRAVEL TO TALLUS AND SEE THE CITY MAGE. HE HAS HERBS THAT CAN CURE HER.
BUT THE KING HAS FORBIDDEN ANYONE TO LEAVE THE CITY.
IS MOTHER GOING TO DIE?
NO WESLEY.
I WILL SEE THE KING. HE WILL LISTEN TO ME...
HE MUST LISTEN TO ME.

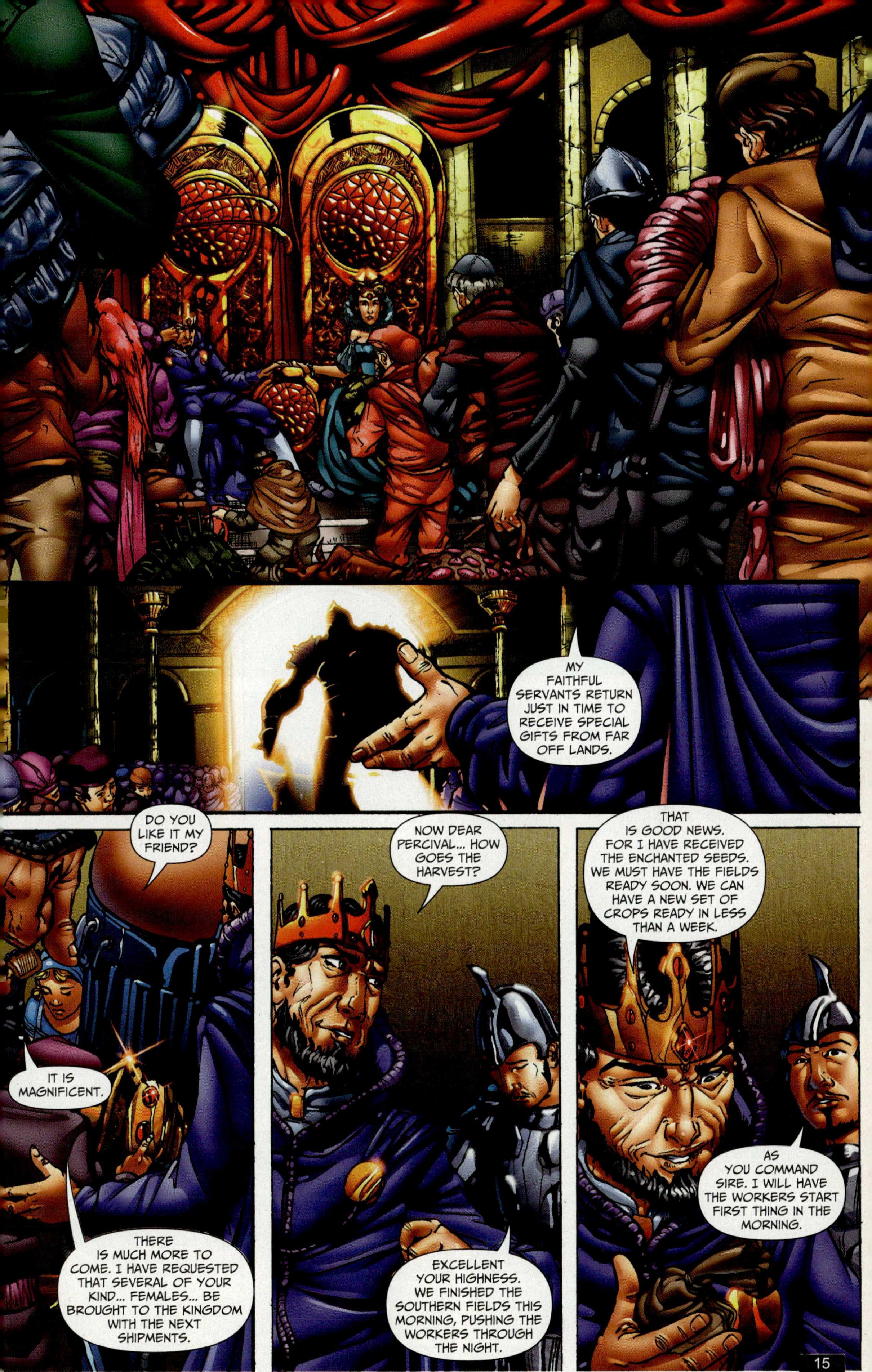
MY FAITHFUL SERVANTS RETURN JUST IN TIME TO RECEIVE SPECIAL GIFTS FROM FAR OFF LANDS.
DO YOU LIKE IT MY FRIEND?
IT IS MAGNIFICENT.
THERE IS MUCH MORE TO COME. I HAVE REQUESTED THAT SEVERAL OF YOUR KIND... FEMALES... BE BROUGHT TO THE KINGDOM WITH THE NEXT SHIPMENTS.
NOW DEAR PERCIVAL... HOW GOES THE HARVEST?
EXCELLENT YOUR HIGHNESS. WE FINISHED THE SOUTHERN FIELDS THIS MORNING, PUSHING THE WORKERS THROUGH THE NIGHT.
THAT IS GOOD NEWS. FOR I HAVE RECEIVED THE ENCHANTED SEEDS. WE MUST HAVE THE FIELDS READY SOON. WE CAN HAVE A NEW SET OF CROPS READY IN LESS THAN A WEEK.
AS YOU COMMAND SIRE. I WILL HAVE THE WORKERS START FIRST THING IN THE MORNING.

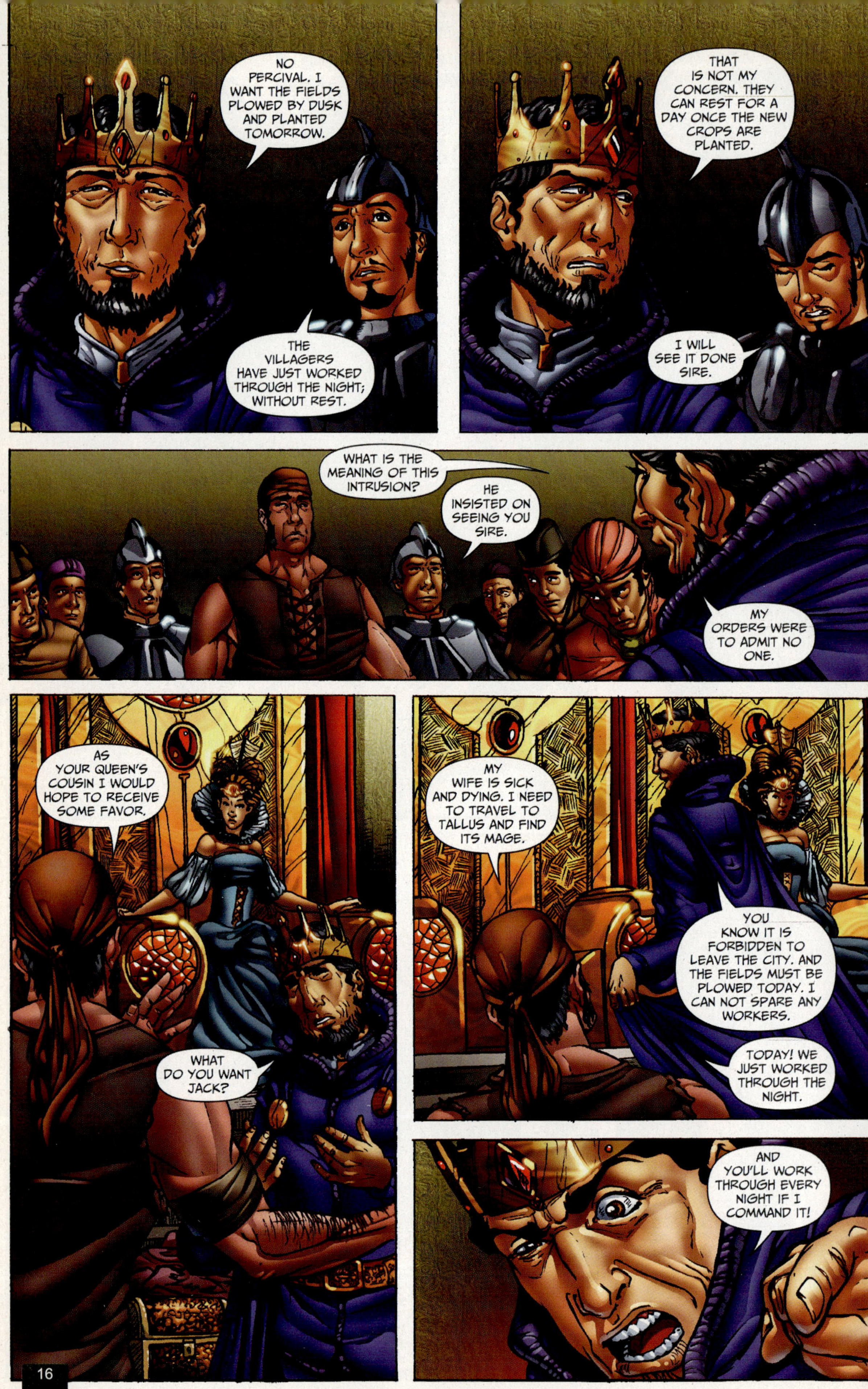
NO PERCIVAL. I WANT THE FIELDS PLOWED BY DUSK AND PLANTED TOMORROW.
THE VILLAGERS HAVE JUST WORKED THROUGH THE NIGHT; WITHOUT REST.
THAT IS NOT MY CONCERN. THEY CAN REST FOR A DAY ONCE THE NEW CROPS ARE PLANTED.
I WILL SEE IT DONE SIRE.
WHAT IS THE MEANING OF THIS INTRUSION?
HE INSISTED ON SEEING YOU SIRE.
MY ORDERS WERE TO ADMIT NO ONE.
AS YOUR QUEEN'S COUSIN I WOULD HOPE TO RECEIVE SOME FAVOR.
WHAT DO YOU WANT JACK?
MY WIFE IS SICK AND DYING. I NEED TO TRAVEL TO TALLUS AND FIND ITS MAGE.
YOU KNOW IT IS FORBIDDEN TO LEAVE THE CITY. AND THE FIELDS MUST BE PLOWED TODAY. I CAN NOT SPARE ANY WORKERS.
TODAY! WE JUST WORKED THROUGH THE NIGHT.
AND YOU'LL WORK THROUGH EVERY NIGHT IF I COMMAND IT!

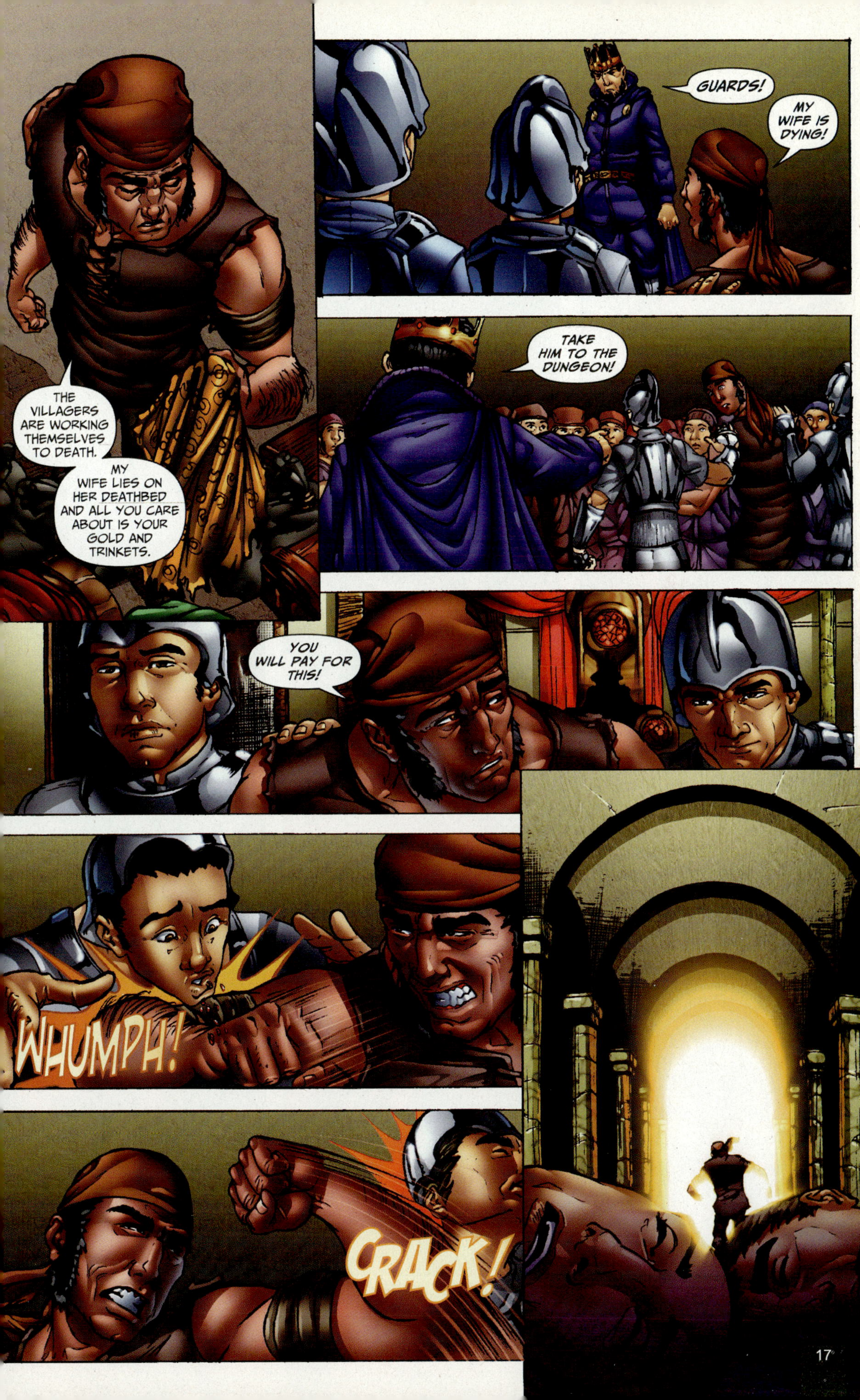
THE VILLAGERS ARE WORKING THEMSELVES TO DEATH.
MY WIFE LIES ON HER DEATHBED AND ALL YOU CARE ABOUT IS YOUR GOLD AND TRINKETS.
GUARDS!
MY WIFE IS DYING!
TAKE HIM TO THE DUNGEON!
YOU WILL PAY FOR THIS!
WHUMPH!
CRACK!

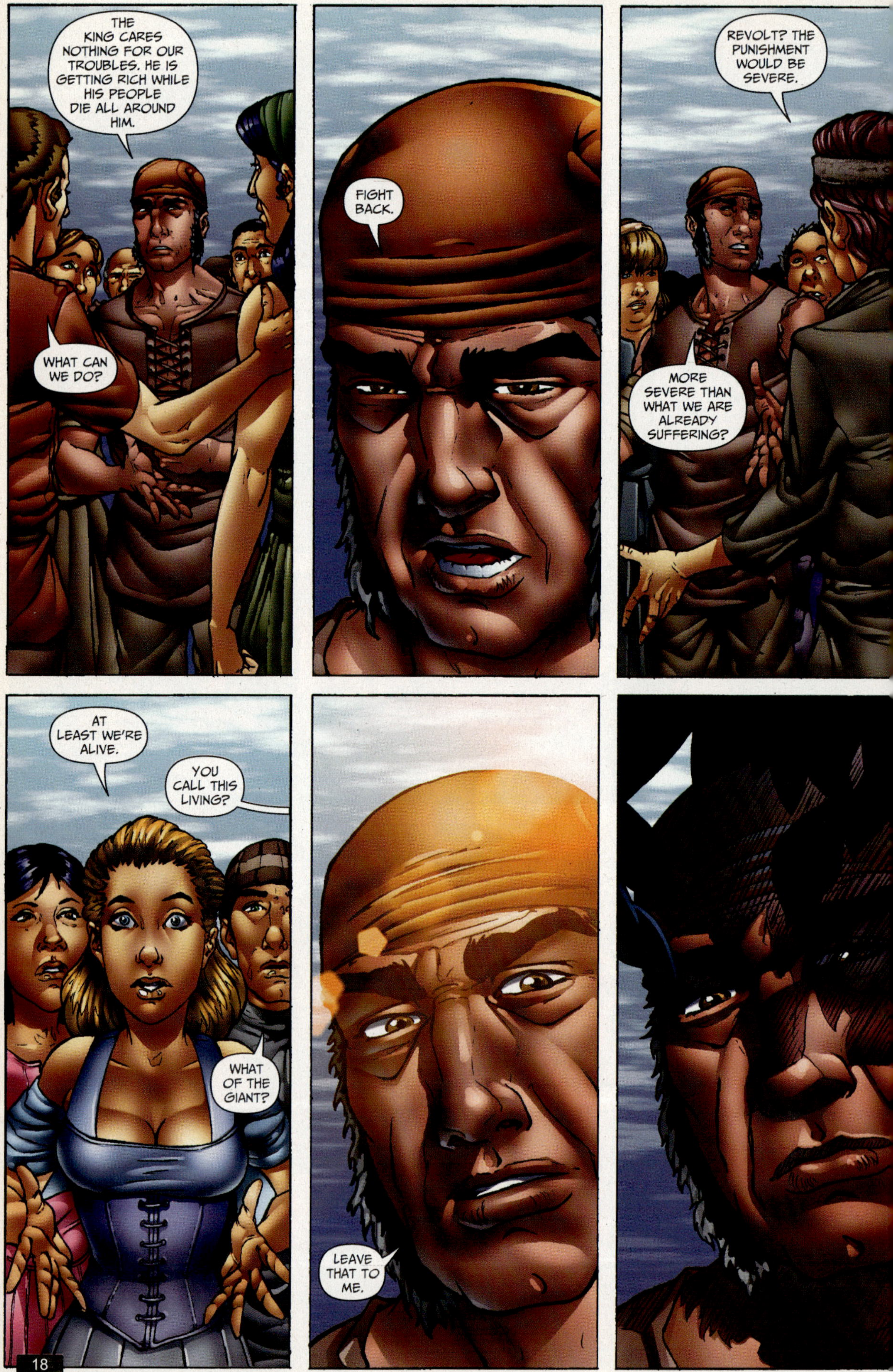

THE KING CARES NOTHING FOR OUR TROUBLES. HE IS GETTING RICH WHILE HIS PEOPLE DIE ALL AROUND HIM.
WHAT CAN WE DO?
FIGHT BACK.
REVOLT? THE PUNISHMENT WOULD BE SEVERE.
MORE SEVERE THAN WHAT WE ARE ALREADY SUFFERING?
AT LEAST WE'RE ALIVE.
YOU CALL THIS LIVING?
WHAT OF THE GIANT?
LEAVE THAT TO ME.

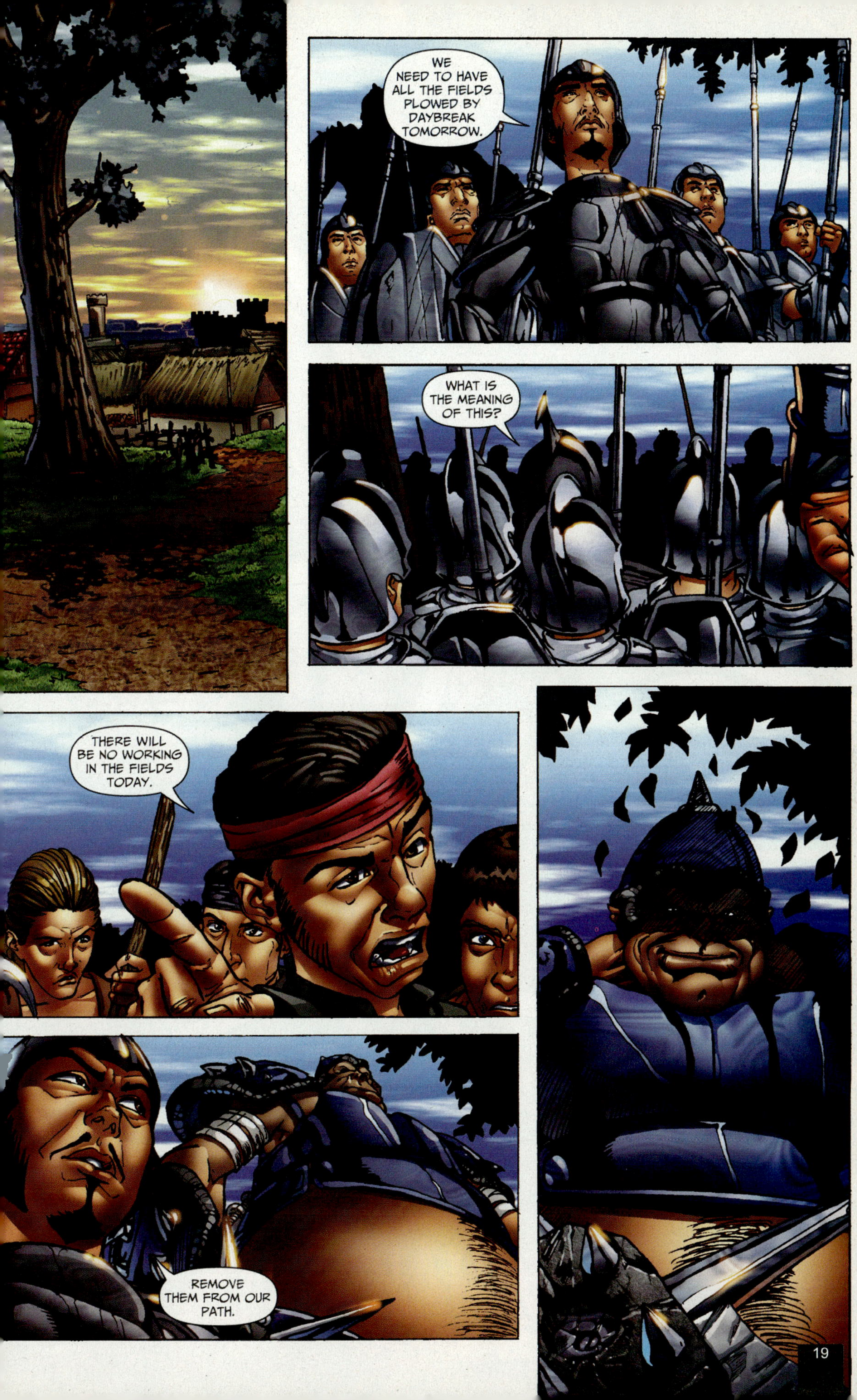
WE NEED TO HAVE ALL THE FIELDS PLOWED BY DAYBREAK TOMORROW.
WHAT IS THE MEANING OF THIS?
THERE WILL BE NO WORKING IN THE FIELDS TODAY.
REMOVE THEM FROM OUR PATH.

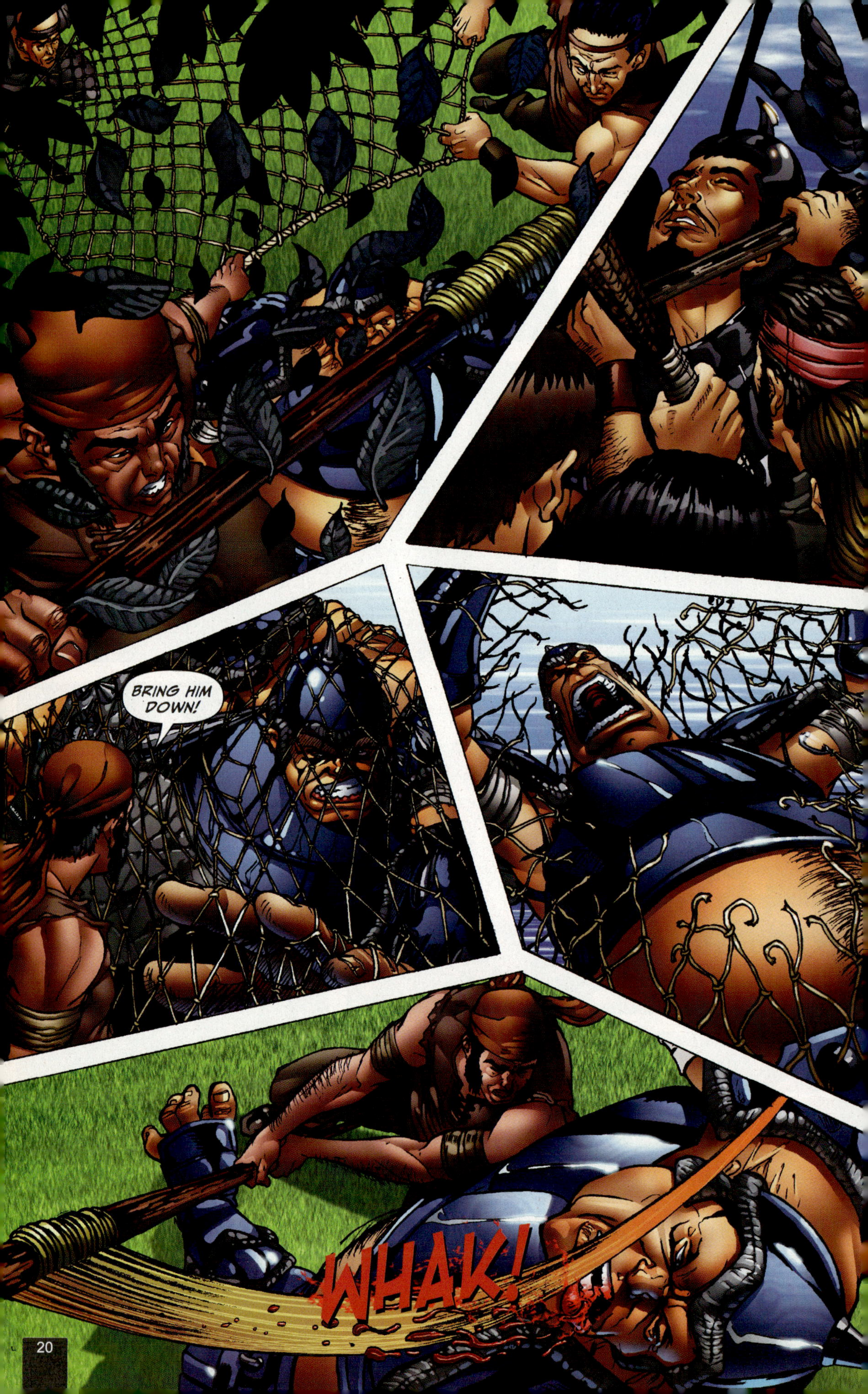
BRING HIM DOWN!
WHAK!

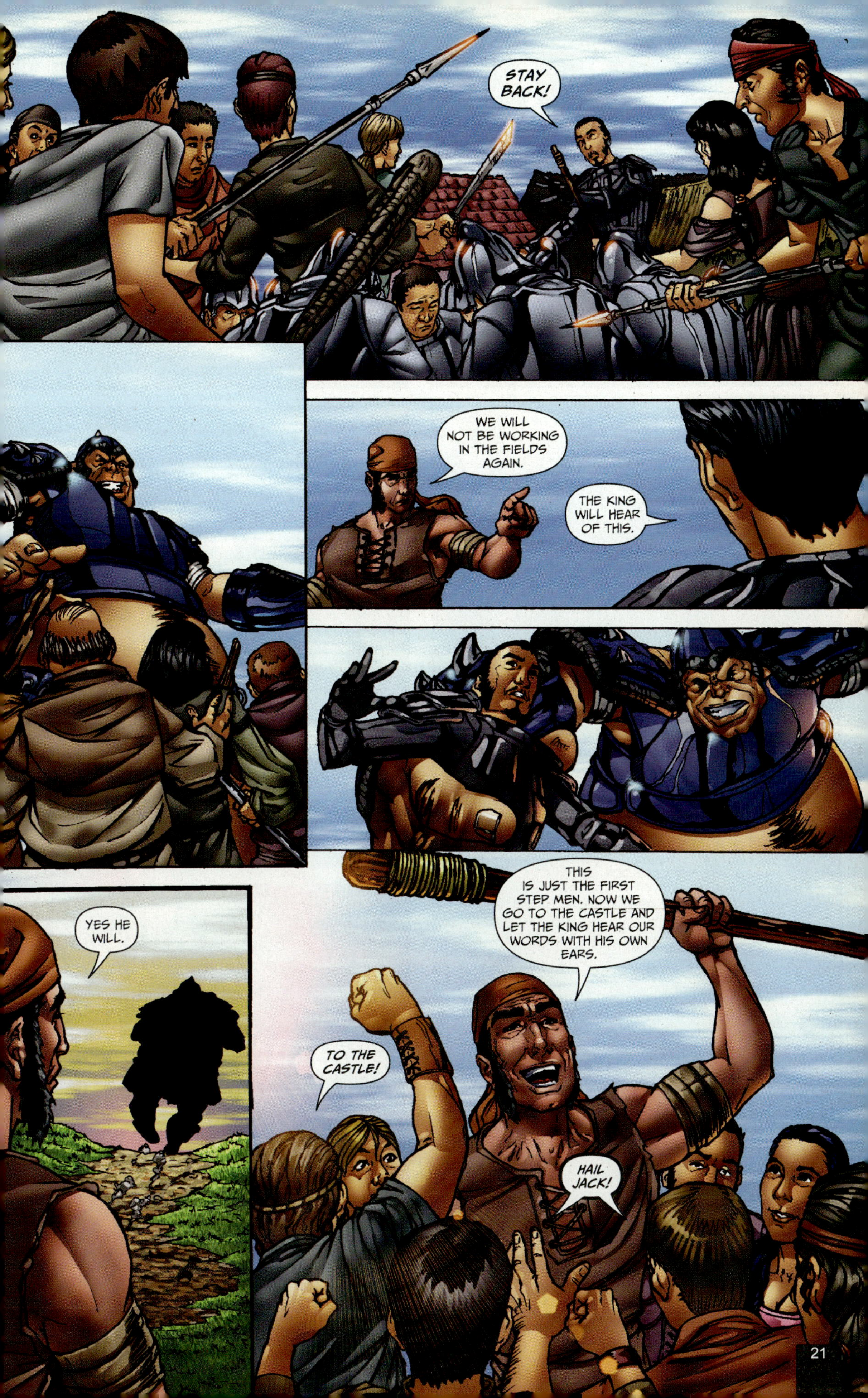
STAY BACK!
WE WILL NOT BE WORKING IN THE FIELDS AGAIN.
THE KING WILL HEAR OF THIS.
YES HE WILL.
THIS IS JUST THE FIRST STEP MEN. NOW WE GO TO THE CASTLE AND LET THE KING HEAR OUR WORDS WITH HIS OWN EARS.
TO THE CASTLE!
HAIL JACK!

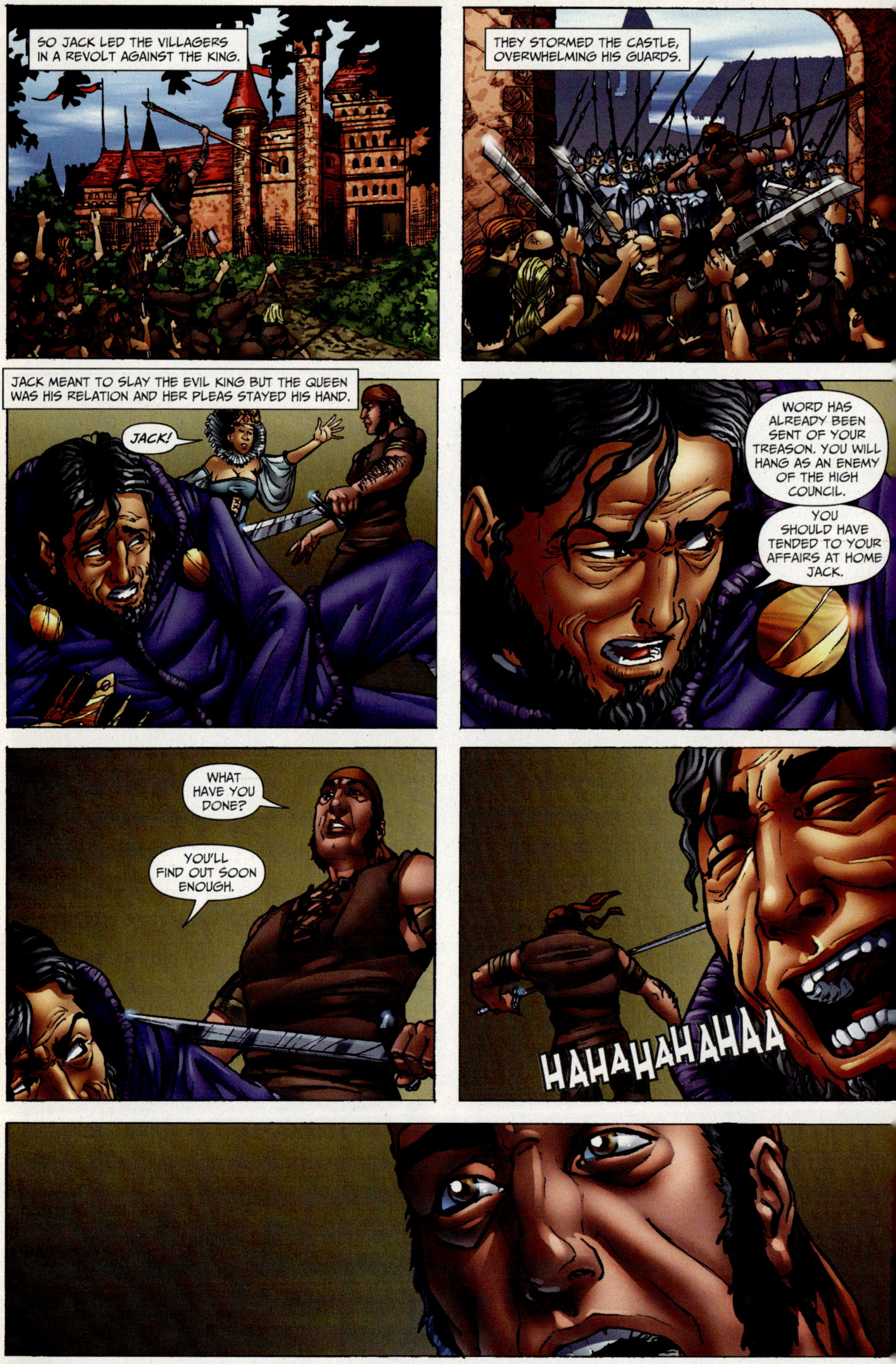

SO JACK LED THE VILLAGERS IN A REVOLT AGAINST THE KING.
THEY STORMED THE CASTLE, OVERWHELMING HIS GUARDS.
JACK MEANT TO SLAY THE EVIL KING BUT THE QUEEN WAS HIS RELATION AND HER PLEAS STAYED HIS HAND.
JACK!
WORD HAS ALREADY BEEN SENT OF YOUR TREASON. YOU WILL HANG AS AN ENEMY OF THE HIGH COUNCIL.
YOU SHOULD HAVE TENDED TO YOUR AFFAIRS AT HOME JACK.
WHAT HAVE YOU DONE?
YOU'LL FIND OUT SOON ENOUGH.
HAHAHAHAHAA

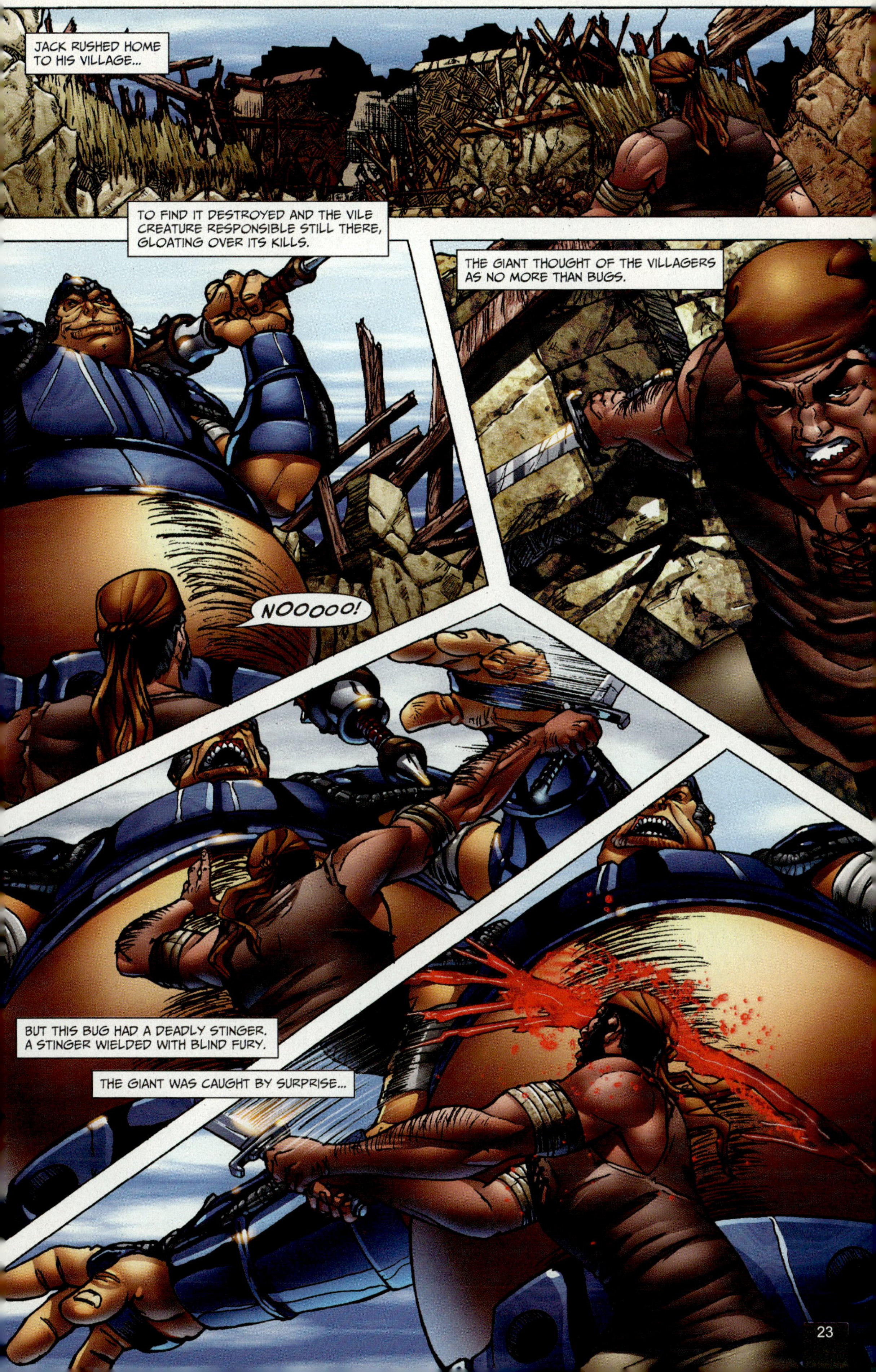
JACK RUSHED HOME TO HIS VILLAGE...
TO FIND IT DESTROYED AND THE VILE CREATURE RESPONSIBLE STILL THERE, GLOATING OVER ITS KILLS.
THE GIANT THOUGHT OF THE VILLAGERS AS NO MORE THAN BUGS.
NOOOOO!
BUT THIS BUG HAD A DEADLY STINGER. A STINGER WIELDED WITH BLIND FURY.
THE GIANT WAS CAUGHT BY SURPRISE...

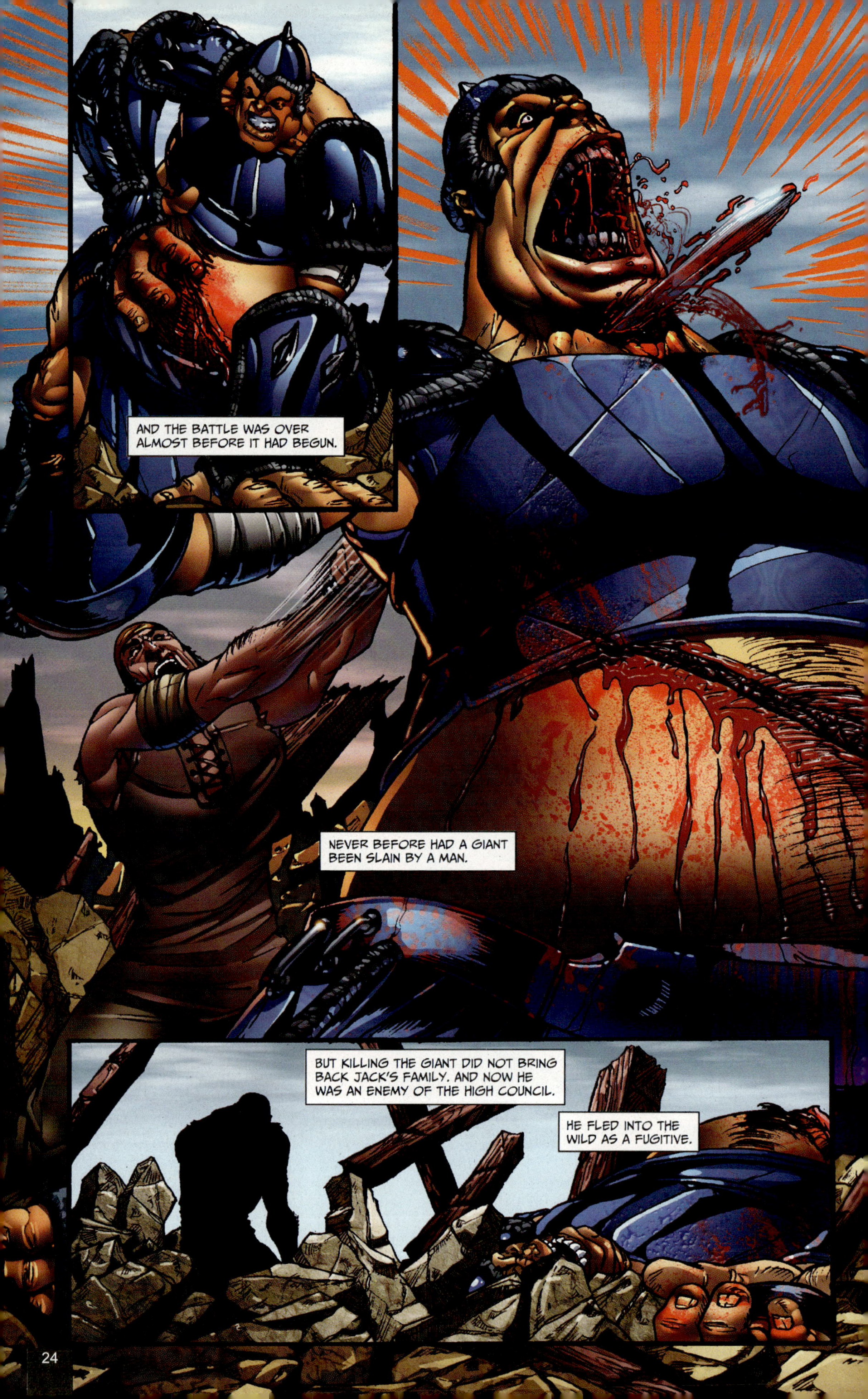
AND THE BATTLE WAS OVER ALMOST BEFORE IT HAD BEGUN.
NEVER BEFORE HAD A GIANT BEEN SLAIN BY A MAN.
BUT KILLING THE GIANT DID NOT BRING BACK JACK'S FAMILY. AND NOW HE WAS AN ENEMY OF THE HIGH COUNCIL.
HE FLED INTO THE WILD AS A FUGITIVE.

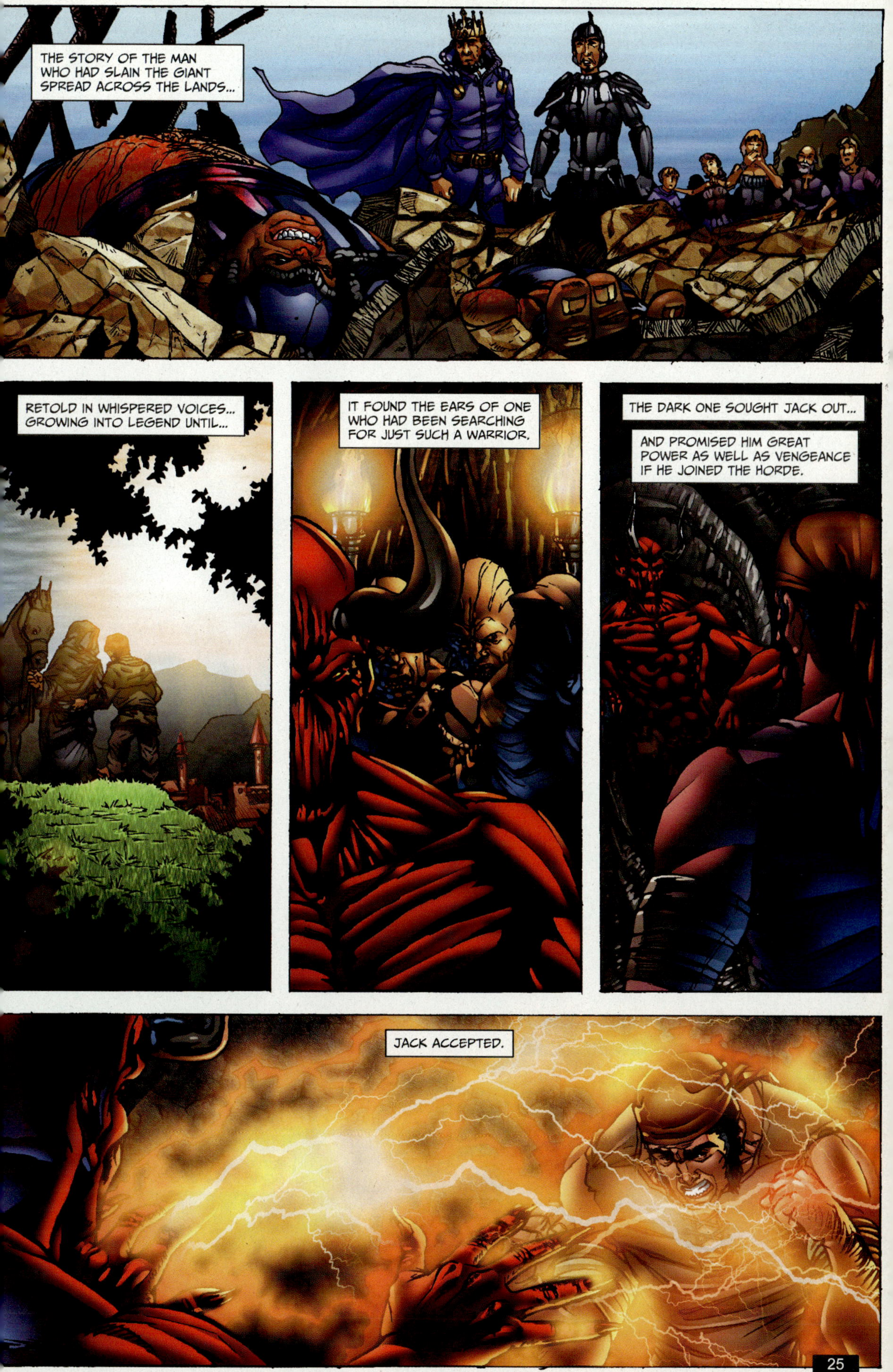
THE STORY OF THE MAN WHO HAD SLAIN THE GIANT SPREAD ACROSS THE LANDS...
RETOLD IN WHISPERED VOICES... GROWING INTO LEGEND UNTIL...
IT FOUND THE EARS OF ONE WHO HAD BEEN SEARCHING FOR JUST SUCH A WARRIOR.
THE DARK ONE SOUGHT JACK OUT...
AND PROMISED HIM GREAT POWER AS WELL AS VENGEANCE IF HE JOINED THE HORDE.
JACK ACCEPTED.

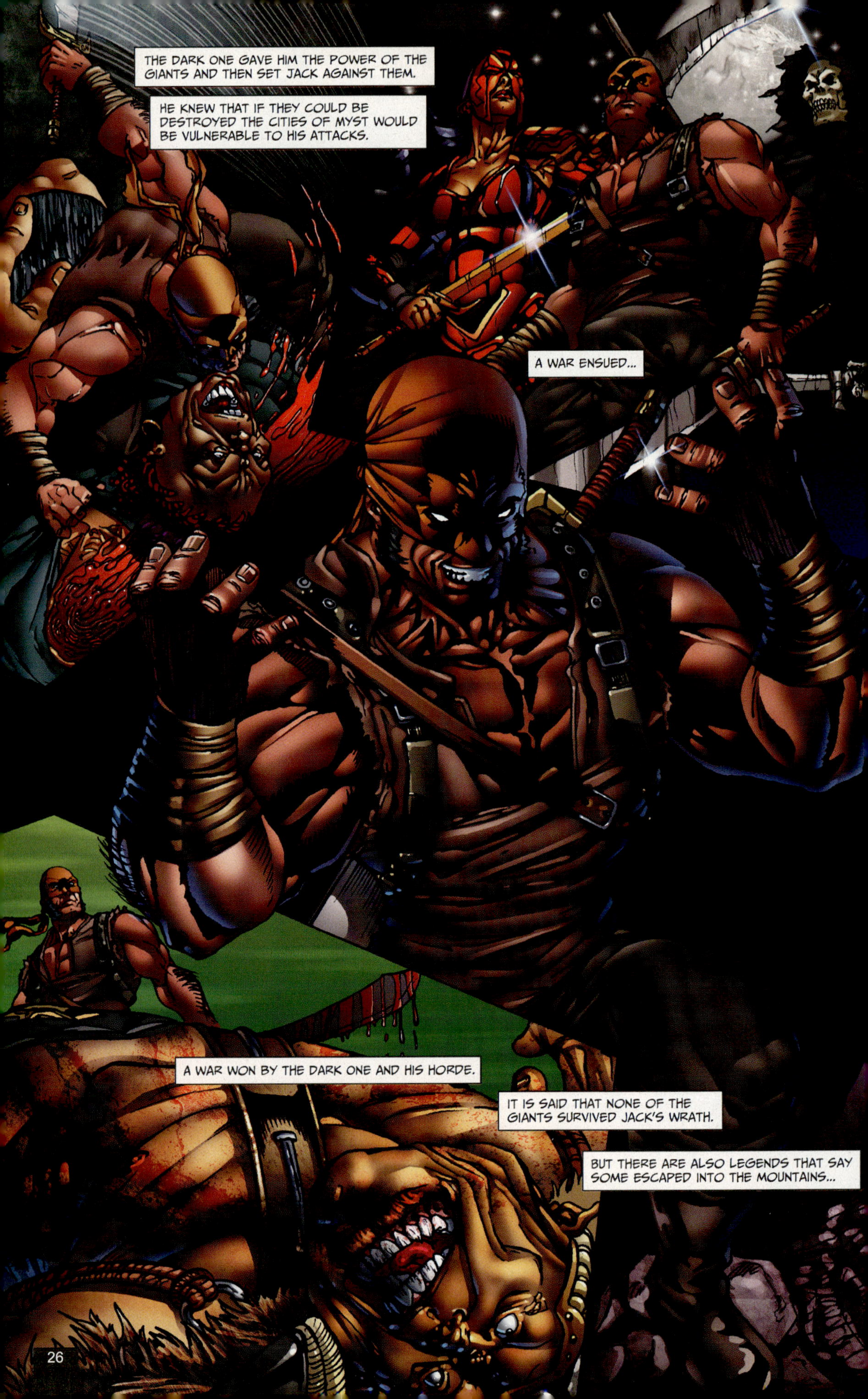
THE DARK ONE GAVE HIM THE POWER OF THE GIANTS AND THEN SET JACK AGAINST THEM.
HE KNEW THAT IF THEY COULD BE DESTROYED THE CITIES OF MYST WOULD BE VULNERABLE TO HIS ATTACKS.
A WAR ENSUED...
A WAR WON BY THE DARK ONE AND HIS HORDE.
IT IS SAID THAT NONE OF THE GIANTS SURVIVED JACK'S WRATH.
BUT THERE ARE ALSO LEGENDS THAT SAY SOME ESCAPED INTO THE MOUNTAINS...

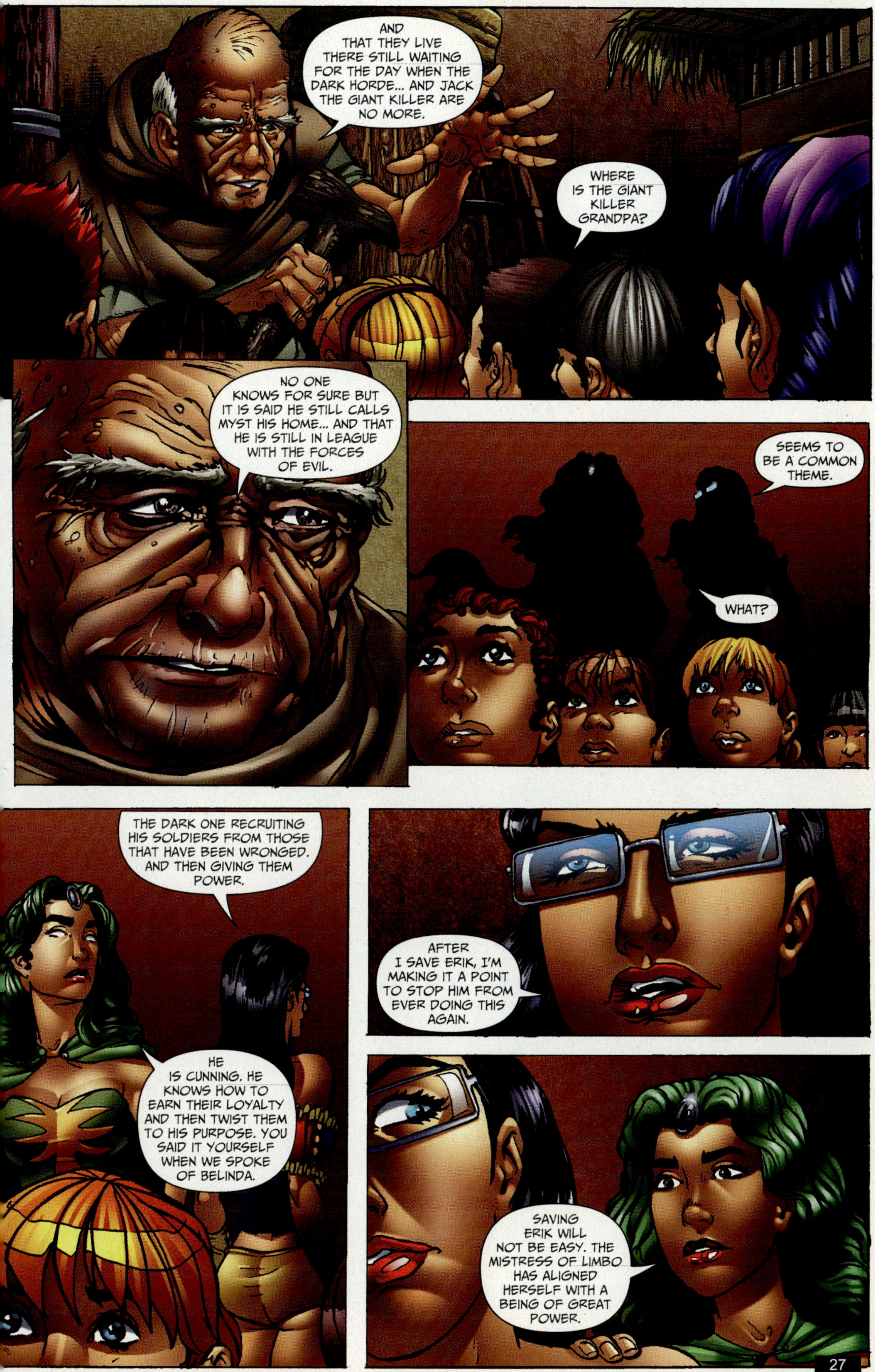
AND THAT THEY LIVE THERE STILL WAITING FOR THE DAY WHEN THE DARK HORDE... AND JACK THE GIANT KILLER ARE NO MORE.
WHERE IS THE GIANT KILLER GRANDPA?
NO ONE KNOWS FOR SURE BUT IT IS SAID HE STILL CALLS MYST HIS HOME... AND THAT HE IS STILL IN LEAGUE WITH THE FORCES OF EVIL.
SEEMS TO BE A COMMON THEME.
WHAT?
THE DARK ONE RECRUITING HIS SOLDIERS FROM THOSE THAT HAVE BEEN WRONGED. AND THEN GIVING THEM POWER.
HE IS CUNNING. HE KNOWS HOW TO EARN THEIR LOYALTY AND THEN TWIST THEM TO HIS PURPOSE. YOU SAID IT YOURSELF WHEN WE SPOKE OF BELINDA.
AFTER I SAVE ERIK, I'M MAKING IT A POINT TO STOP HIM FROM EVER DOING THIS AGAIN.
SAVING ERIK WILL NOT BE EASY. THE MISTRESS OF LIMBO HAS ALIGNED HERSELF WITH A BEING OF GREAT POWER.

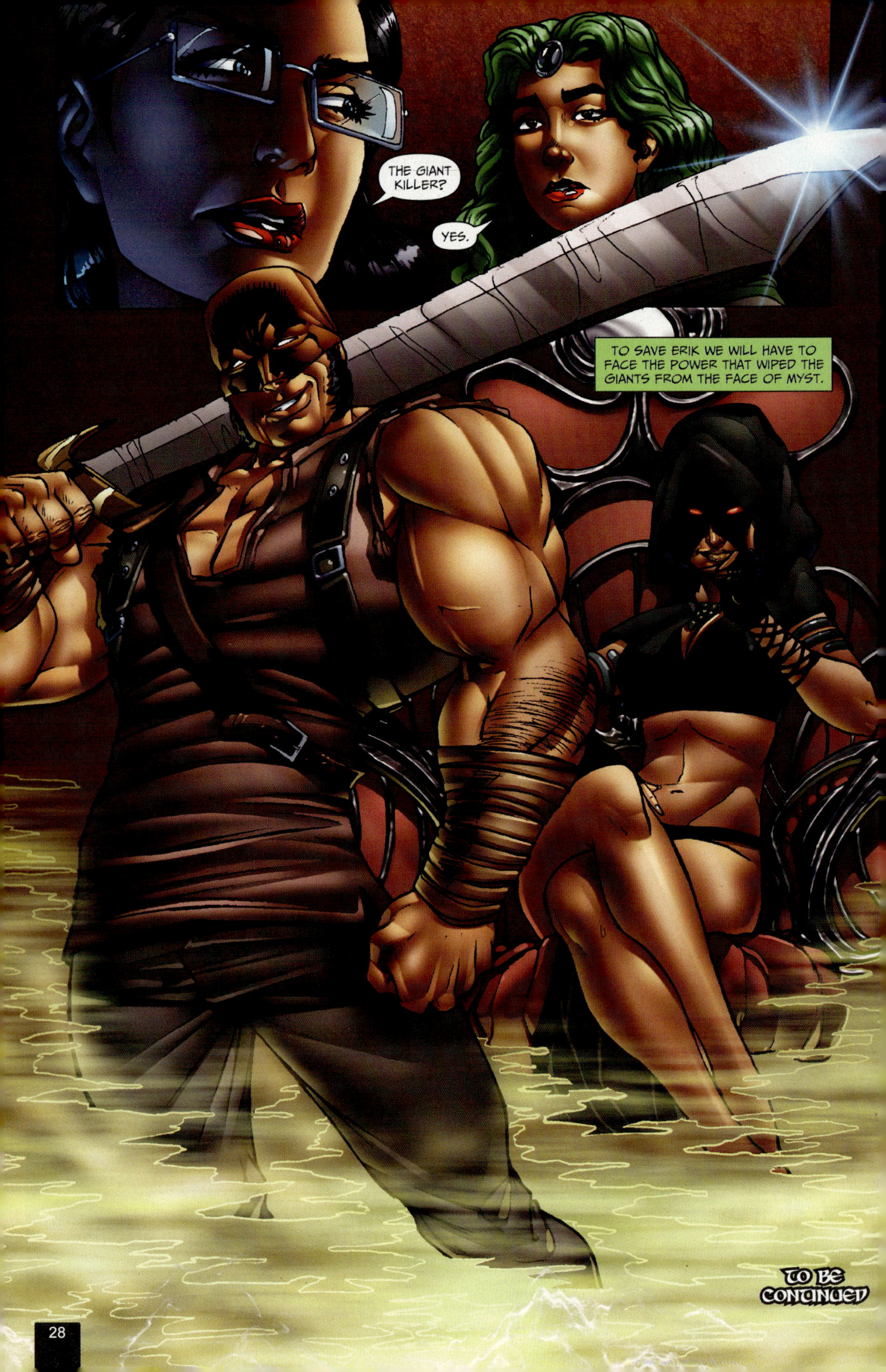
THE GIANT KILLER?
YES.
TO SAVE ERIK WE WILL HAVE TO FACE THE POWER THAT WIPED THE GIANTS FROM THE FACE OF MYST.
TO BE CONTINUED

Grimm Fairy Tales
Volume 11

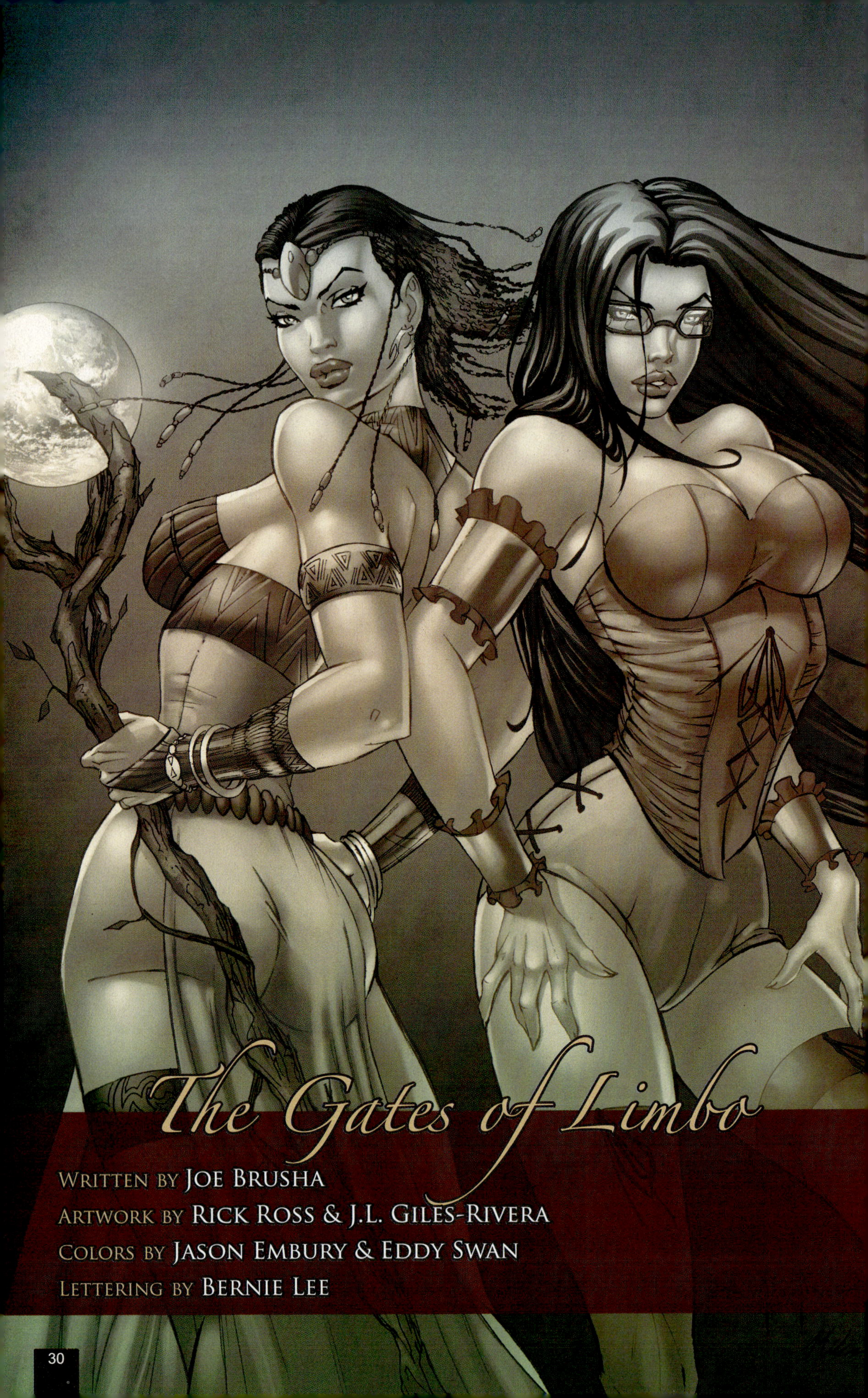

The Gates of Limbo

Written by Joe Brusha
Artwork by Rick Ross & J.L. Giles-Rivera
Colors by Jason Embury & Eddy Swan
Lettering by Bernie Lee

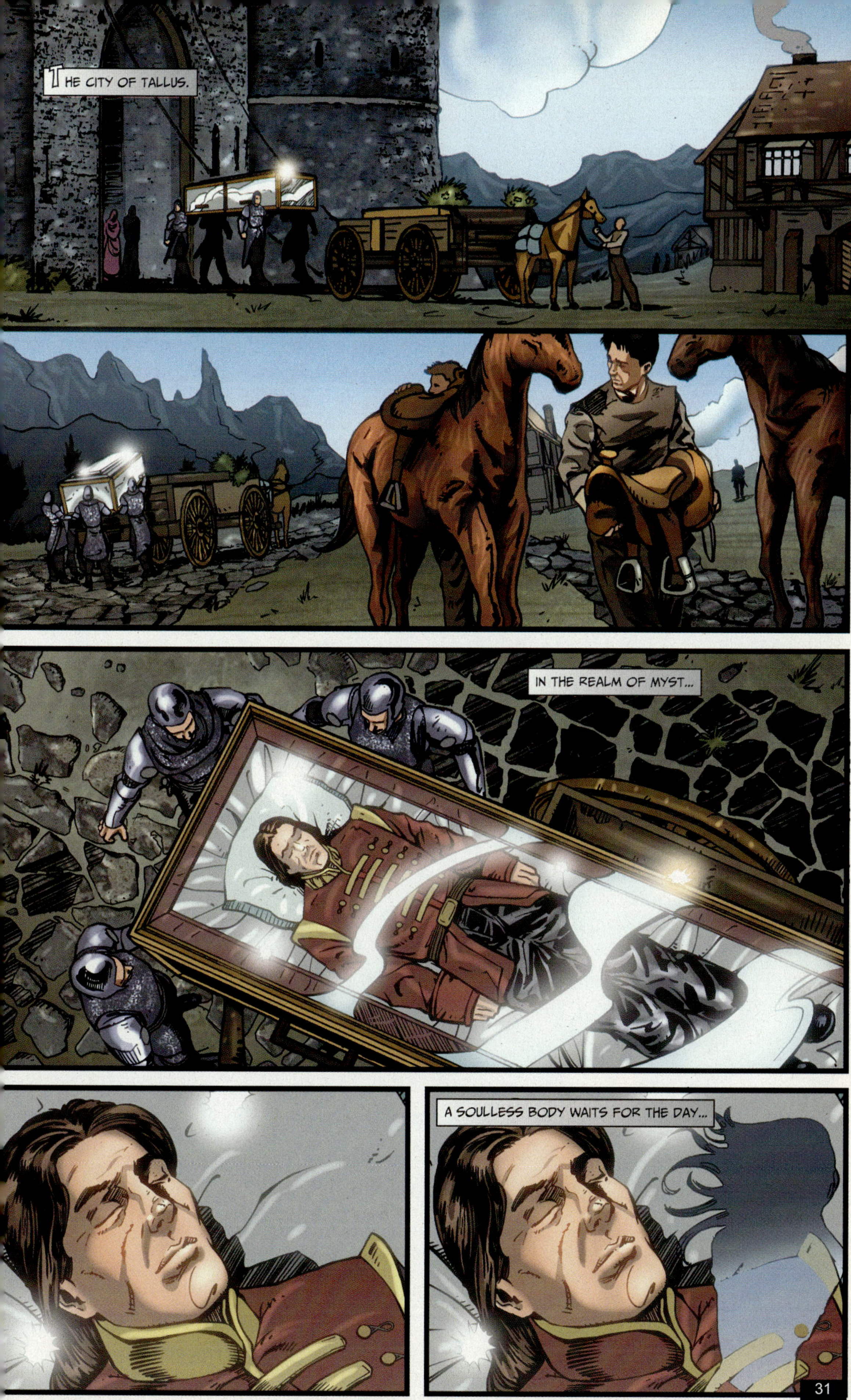
THE CITY OF TALLUS.
IN THE REALM OF MYST...
A SOULLESS BODY WAITS FOR THE DAY...

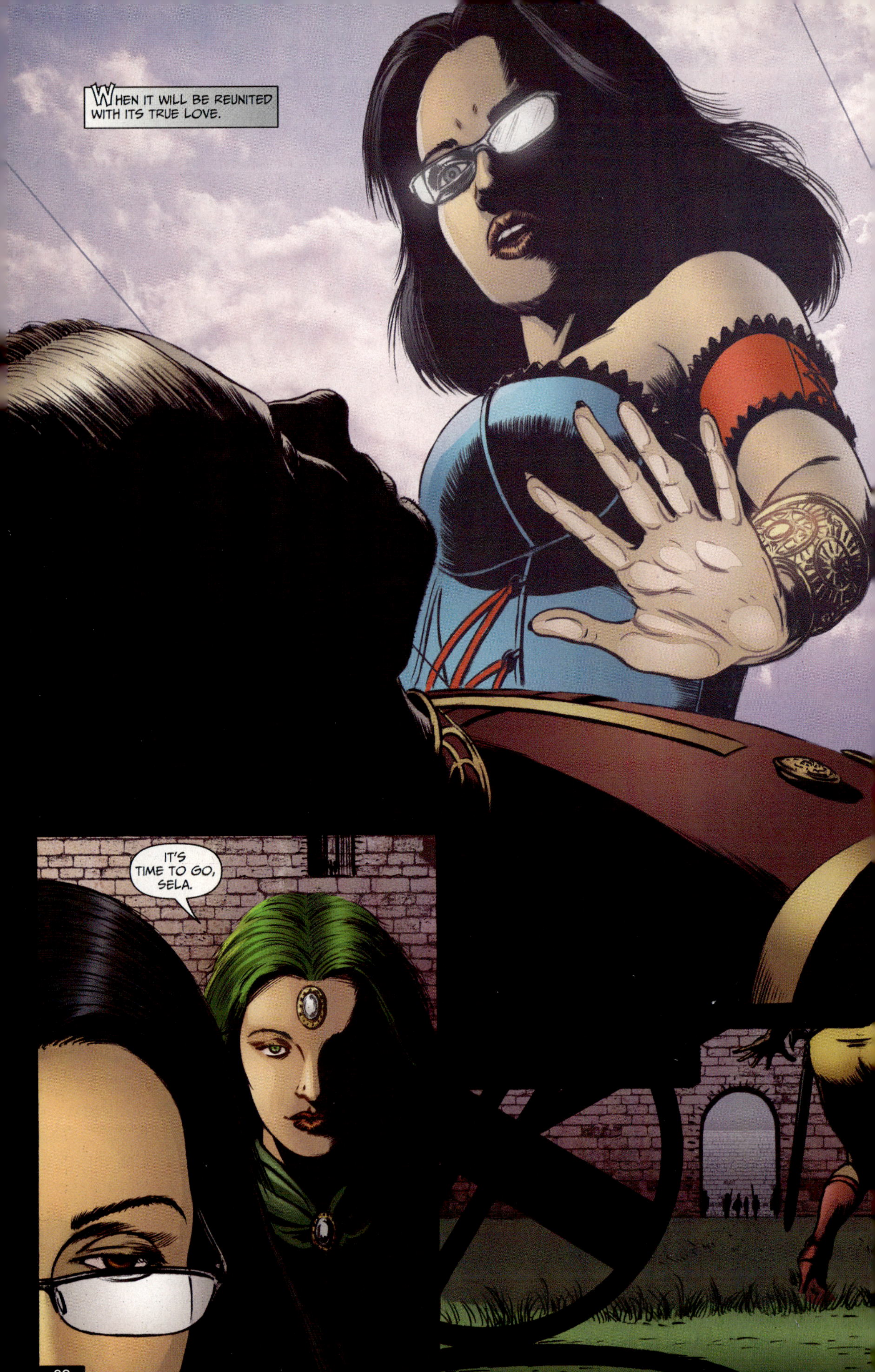
WHEN IT WILL BE REUNITED WITH ITS TRUE LOVE.
IT'S TIME TO GO, SELA.

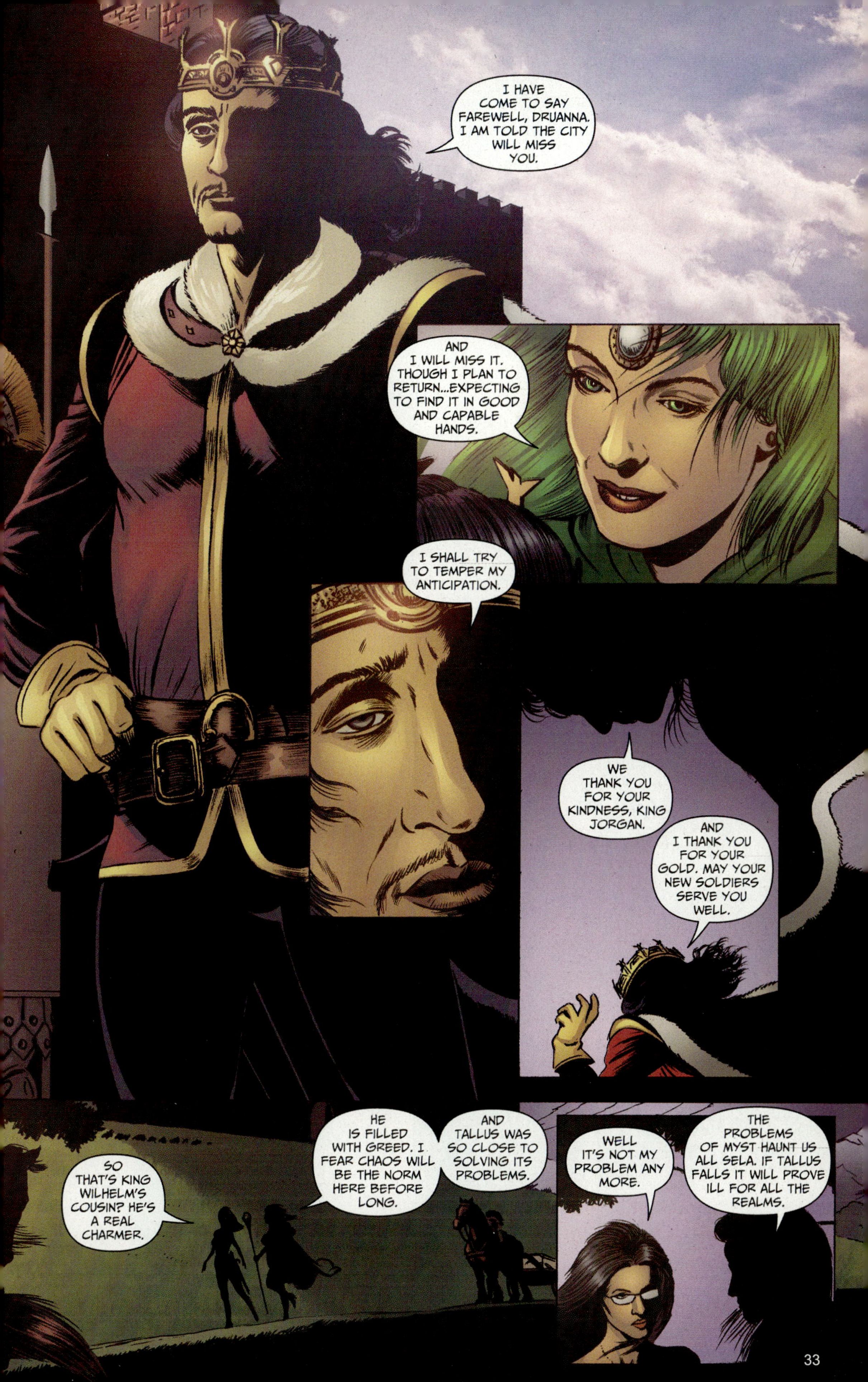
I HAVE COME TO SAY FAREWELL, DRUANNA. I AM TOLD THE CITY WILL MISS YOU.
AND I WILL MISS IT. THOUGH I PLAN TO RETURN...EXPECTING TO FIND IT IN GOOD AND CAPABLE HANDS.
I SHALL TRY TO TEMPER MY ANTICIPATION.
WE THANK YOU FOR YOUR KINDNESS, KING JORGAN.
AND I THANK YOU FOR YOUR GOLD. MAY YOUR NEW SOLDIERS SERVE YOU WELL.
SO THAT'S KING WILHELM'S COUSIN? HE'S A REAL CHARMER.
HE IS FILLED WITH GREED. I FEAR CHAOS WILL BE THE NORM HERE BEFORE LONG.
AND TALLUS WAS SO CLOSE TO SOLVING ITS PROBLEMS.
WELL IT'S NOT MY PROBLEM ANY MORE.
THE PROBLEMS OF MYST HAUNT US ALL SELA. IF TALLUS FALLS IT WILL PROVE ILL FOR ALL THE REALMS.

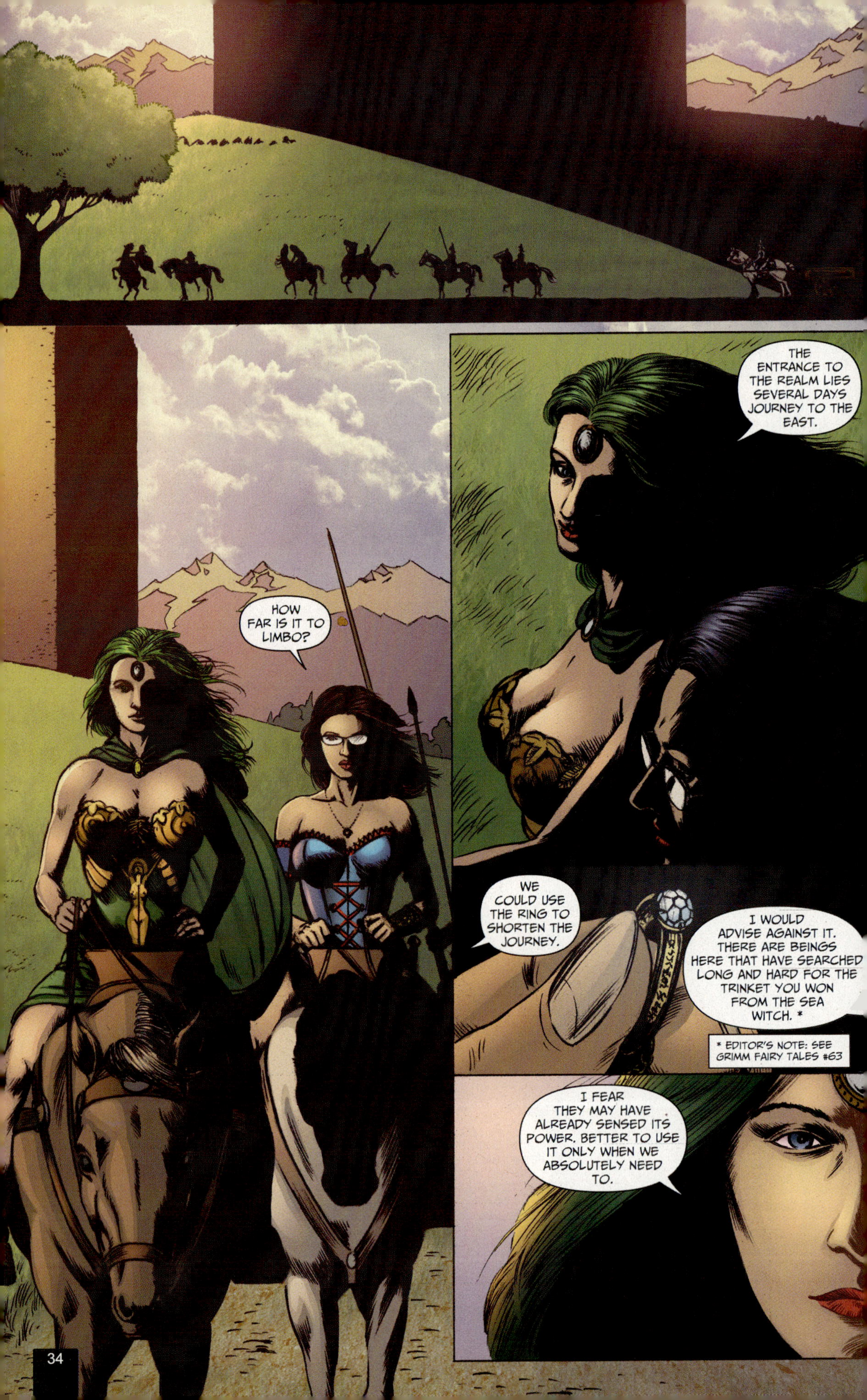
HOW FAR IS IT TO LIMBO?
THE ENTRANCE TO THE REALM LIES SEVERAL DAYS JOURNEY TO THE EAST.
WE COULD USE THE RING TO SHORTEN THE JOURNEY.
I WOULD ADVISE AGAINST IT. THERE ARE BEINGS HERE THAT HAVE SEARCHED LONG AND HARD FOR THE TRINKET YOU WON FROM THE SEA WITCH. *
* EDITOR'S NOTE: SEE GRIMM FAIRY TALES #63
I FEAR THEY MAY HAVE ALREADY SENSED ITS POWER. BETTER TO USE IT ONLY WHEN WE ABSOLUTELY NEED TO.
34

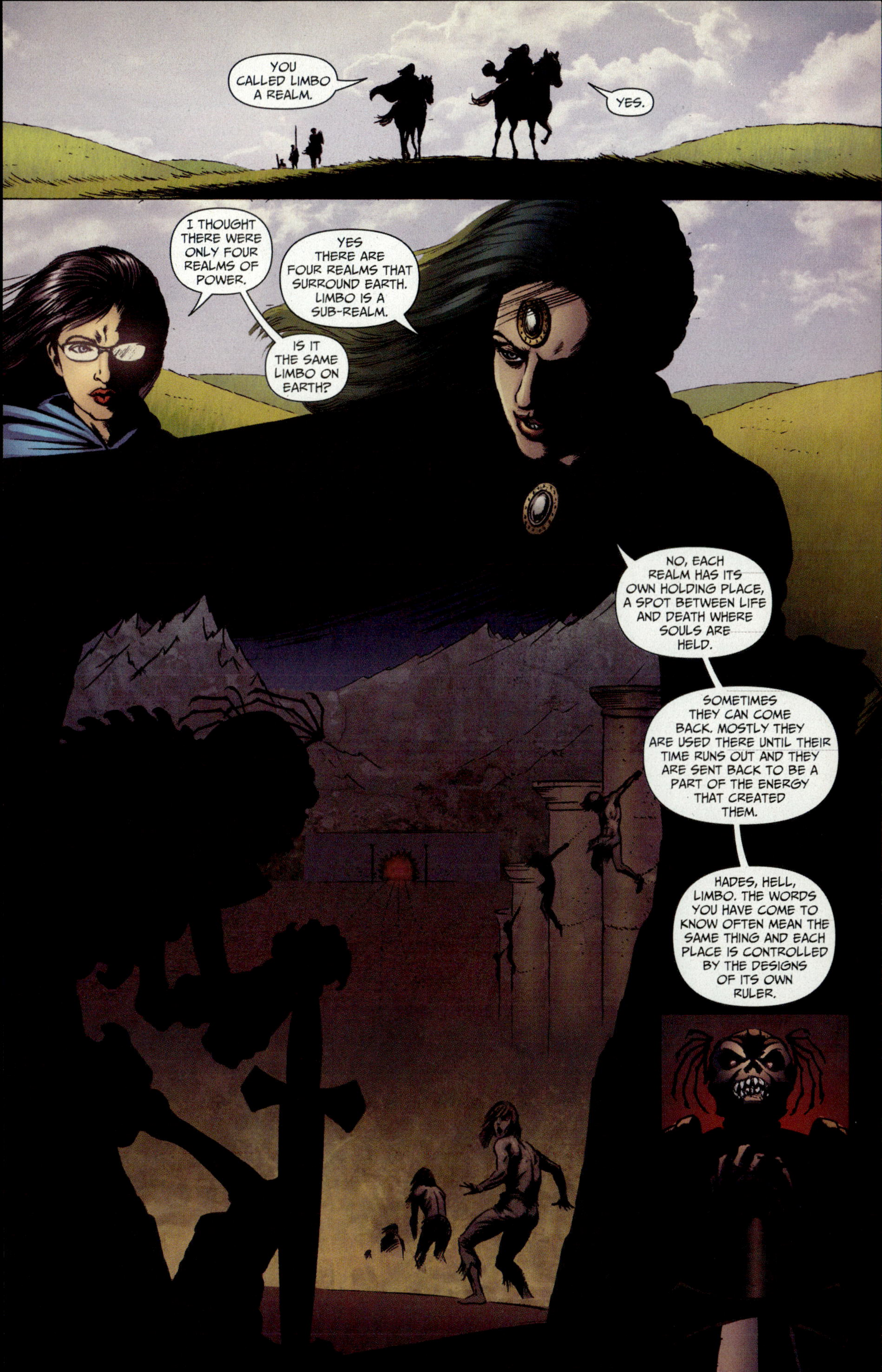
YOU CALLED LIMBO A REALM.
YES.
I THOUGHT THERE WERE ONLY FOUR REALMS OF POWER.
YES THERE ARE FOUR REALMS THAT SURROUND EARTH. LIMBO IS A SUB-REALM.
IS IT THE SAME LIMBO ON EARTH?
NO, EACH REALM HAS ITS OWN HOLDING PLACE, A SPOT BETWEEN LIFE AND DEATH WHERE SOULS ARE HELD.
SOMETIMES THEY CAN COME BACK. MOSTLY THEY ARE USED THERE UNTIL THEIR TIME RUNS OUT AND THEY ARE SENT BACK TO BE A PART OF THE ENERGY THAT CREATED THEM.
HADES, HELL, LIMBO. THE WORDS YOU HAVE COME TO KNOW OFTEN MEAN THE SAME THING AND EACH PLACE IS CONTROLLED BY THE DESIGNS OF ITS OWN RULER.

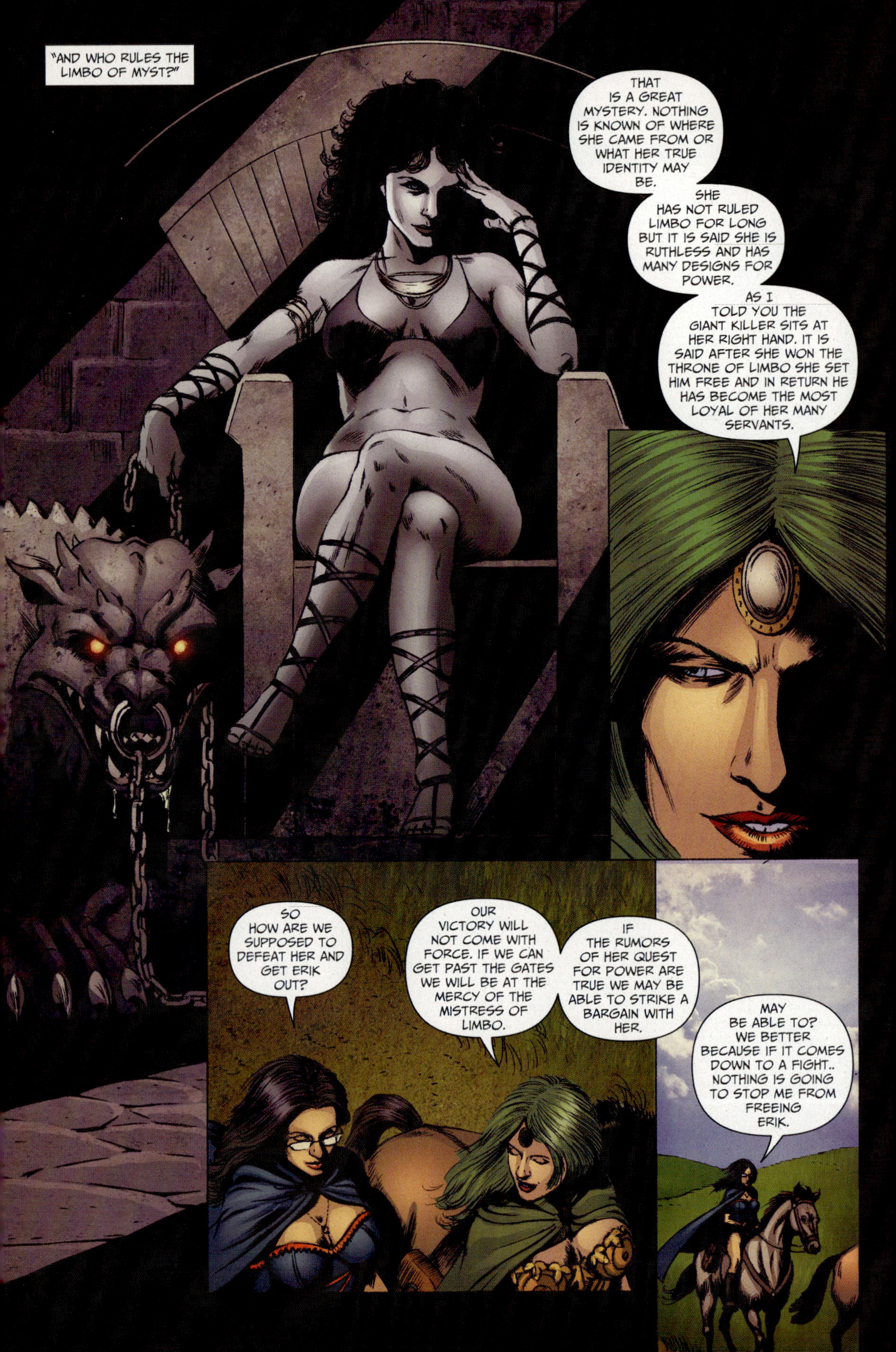
"AND WHO RULES THE LIMBO OF MYST?"
THAT IS A GREAT MYSTERY. NOTHING IS KNOWN OF WHERE SHE CAME FROM OR WHAT HER TRUE IDENTITY MAY BE.
SHE HAS NOT RULED LIMBO FOR LONG BUT IT IS SAID SHE IS RUTHLESS AND HAS MANY DESIGNS FOR POWER.
AS I TOLD YOU THE GIANT KILLER SITS AT HER RIGHT HAND. IT IS SAID AFTER SHE WON THE THRONE OF LIMBO SHE SET HIM FREE AND IN RETURN HE HAS BECOME THE MOST LOYAL OF HER MANY SERVANTS.
SO HOW ARE WE SUPPOSED TO DEFEAT HER AND GET ERIK OUT?
OUR VICTORY WILL NOT COME WITH FORCE. IF WE CAN GET PAST THE GATES WE WILL BE AT THE MERCY OF THE MISTRESS OF LIMBO.
IF THE RUMORS OF HER QUEST FOR POWER ARE TRUE WE MAY BE ABLE TO STRIKE A BARGAIN WITH HER.
MAY BE ABLE TO? WE BETTER BECAUSE IF IT COMES DOWN TO A FIGHT.. NOTHING IS GOING TO STOP ME FROM FREEING ERIK.

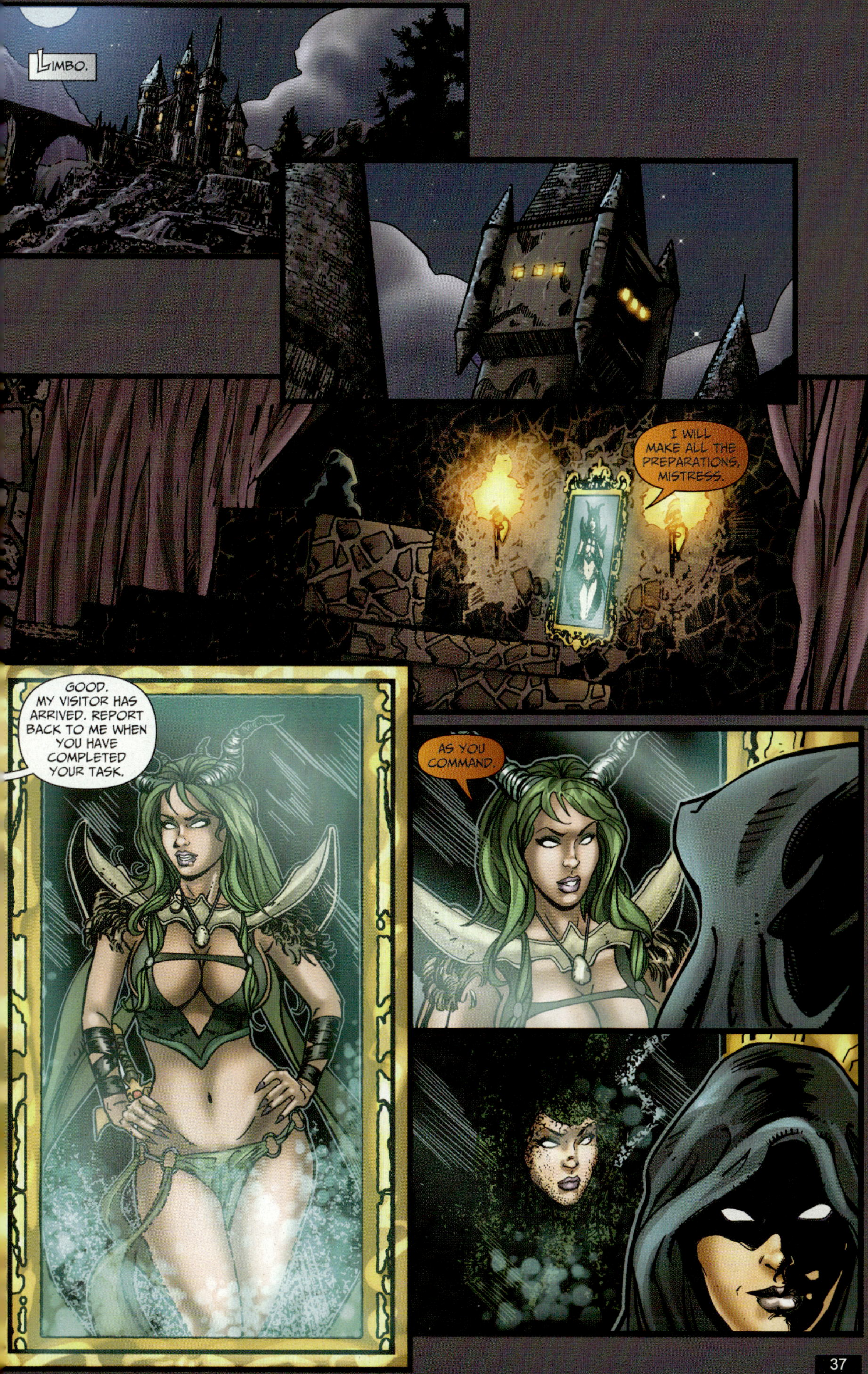
LIMBO.
I WILL MAKE ALL THE PREPARATIONS, MISTRESS.
GOOD. MY VISITOR HAS ARRIVED. REPORT BACK TO ME WHEN YOU HAVE COMPLETED YOUR TASK.
AS YOU COMMAND.

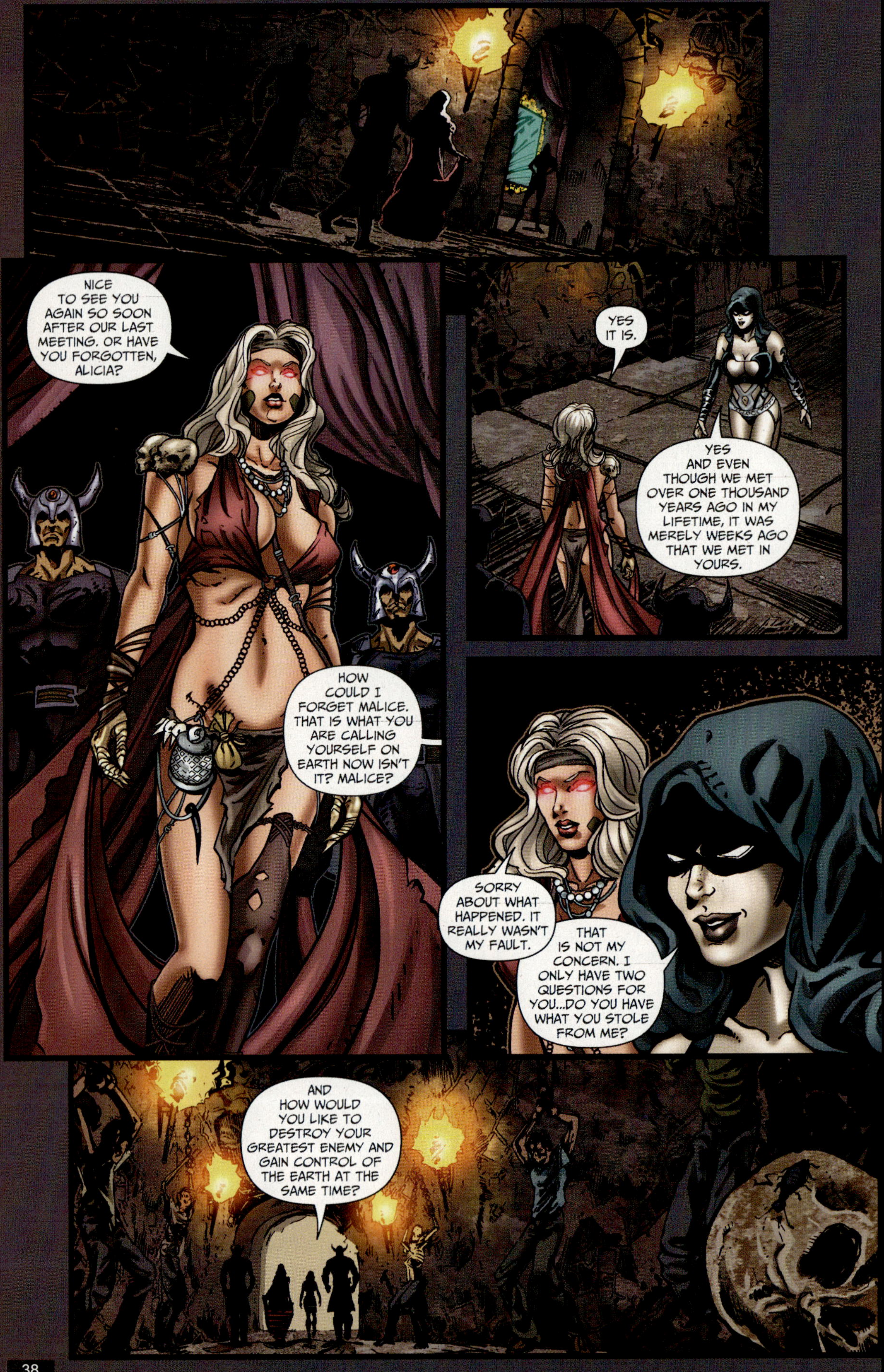
NICE TO SEE YOU AGAIN SO SOON AFTER OUR LAST MEETING. OR HAVE YOU FORGOTTEN, ALICIA?
HOW COULD I FORGET MALICE. THAT IS WHAT YOU ARE CALLING YOURSELF ON EARTH NOW ISN'T IT? MALICE?
YES IT IS.
YES AND EVEN THOUGH WE MET OVER ONE THOUSAND YEARS AGO IN MY LIFETIME, IT WAS MERELY WEEKS AGO THAT WE MET IN YOURS.
SORRY ABOUT WHAT HAPPENED. IT REALLY WASN'T MY FAULT.
THAT IS NOT MY CONCERN. I ONLY HAVE TWO QUESTIONS FOR YOU...DO YOU HAVE WHAT YOU STOLE FROM ME?
AND HOW WOULD YOU LIKE TO DESTROY YOUR GREATEST ENEMY AND GAIN CONTROL OF THE EARTH AT THE SAME TIME?

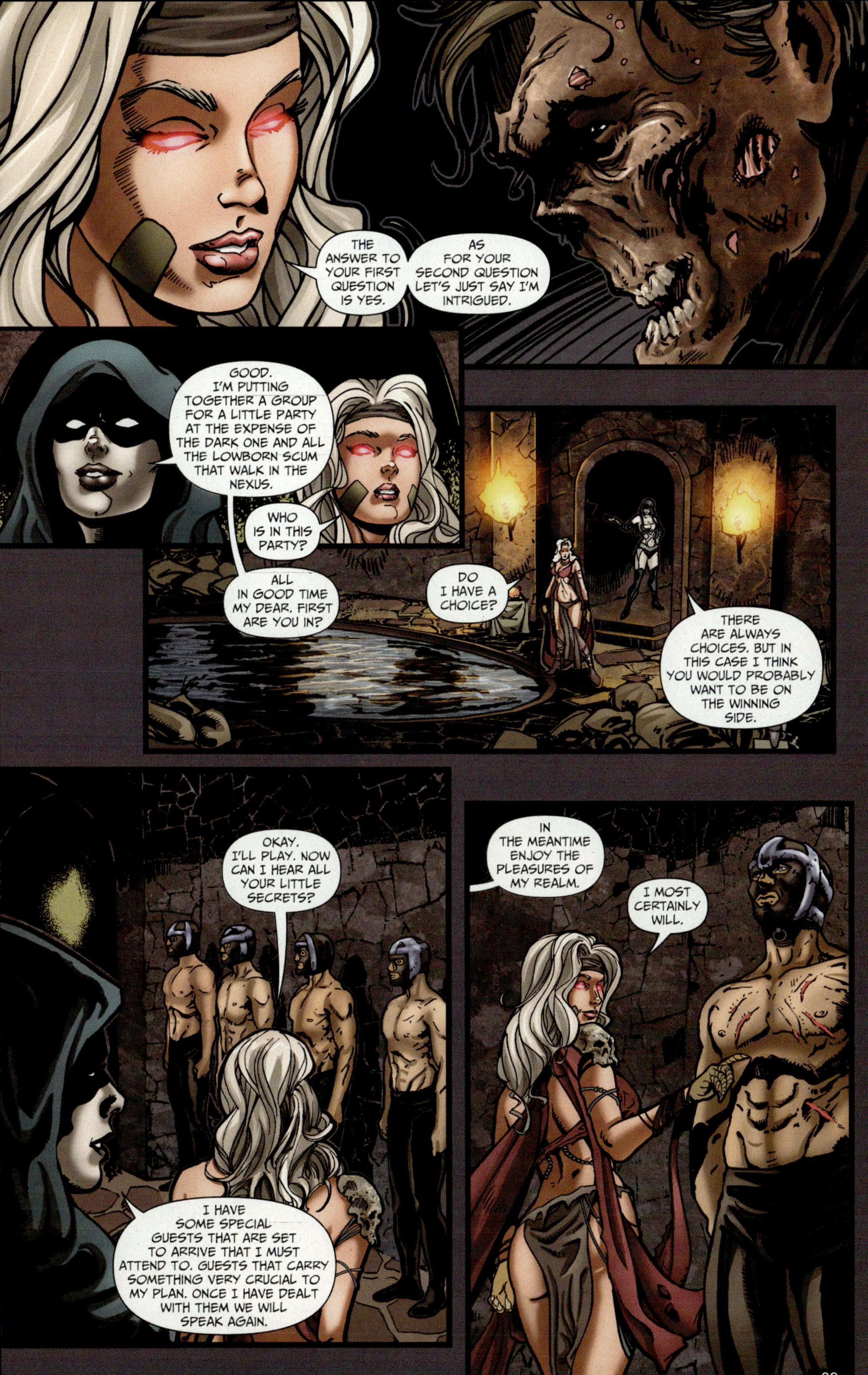
THE ANSWER TO YOUR FIRST QUESTION IS YES.
AS FOR YOUR SECOND QUESTION LET'S JUST SAY I'M INTRIGUED.
GOOD. I'M PUTTING TOGETHER A GROUP FOR A LITTLE PARTY AT THE EXPENSE OF THE DARK ONE AND ALL THE LOWBORN SCUM THAT WALK IN THE NEXUS.
WHO IS IN THIS PARTY?
ALL IN GOOD TIME MY DEAR. FIRST ARE YOU IN?
DO I HAVE A CHOICE?
THERE ARE ALWAYS CHOICES. BUT IN THIS CASE I THINK YOU WOULD PROBABLY WANT TO BE ON THE WINNING SIDE.
OKAY. I'LL PLAY. NOW CAN I HEAR ALL YOUR LITTLE SECRETS?
I HAVE SOME SPECIAL GUESTS THAT ARE SET TO ARRIVE THAT I MUST ATTEND TO. GUESTS THAT CARRY SOMETHING VERY CRUCIAL TO MY PLAN. ONCE I HAVE DEALT WITH THEM WE WILL SPEAK AGAIN.
IN THE MEANTIME ENJOY THE PLEASURES OF MY REALM.
I MOST CERTAINLY WILL.

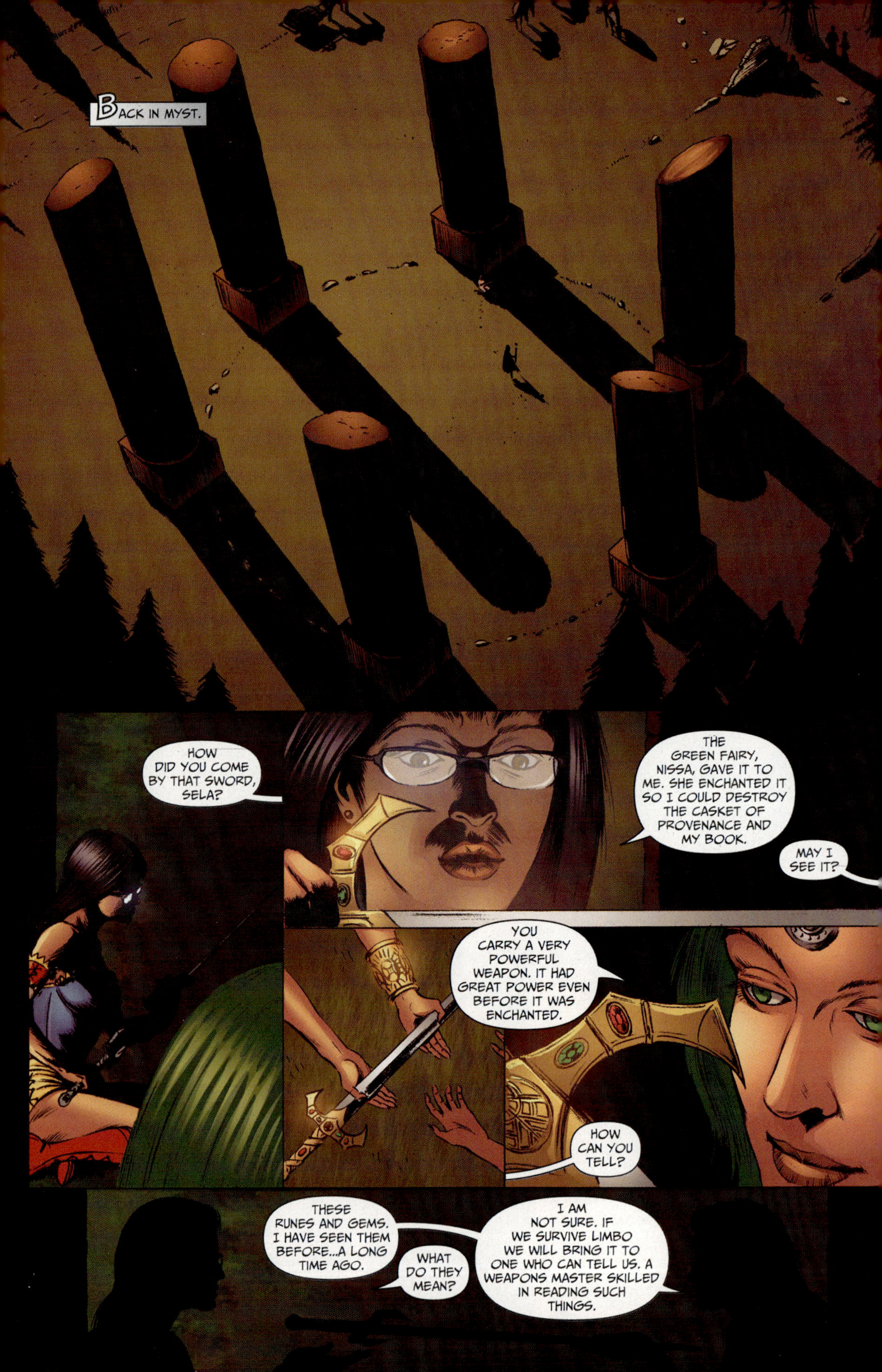
BACK IN MYST.
HOW DID YOU COME BY THAT SWORD, SELA?
THE GREEN FAIRY, NISSA, GAVE IT TO ME. SHE ENCHANTED IT SO I COULD DESTROY THE CASKET OF PROVENANCE AND MY BOOK.
MAY I SEE IT?
YOU CARRY A VERY POWERFUL WEAPON. IT HAD GREAT POWER EVEN BEFORE IT WAS ENCHANTED.
HOW CAN YOU TELL?
THESE RUNES AND GEMS. I HAVE SEEN THEM BEFORE...A LONG TIME AGO.
WHAT DO THEY MEAN?
I AM NOT SURE. IF WE SURVIVE LIMBO WE WILL BRING IT TO ONE WHO CAN TELL US. A WEAPONS MASTER SKILLED IN READING SUCH THINGS.

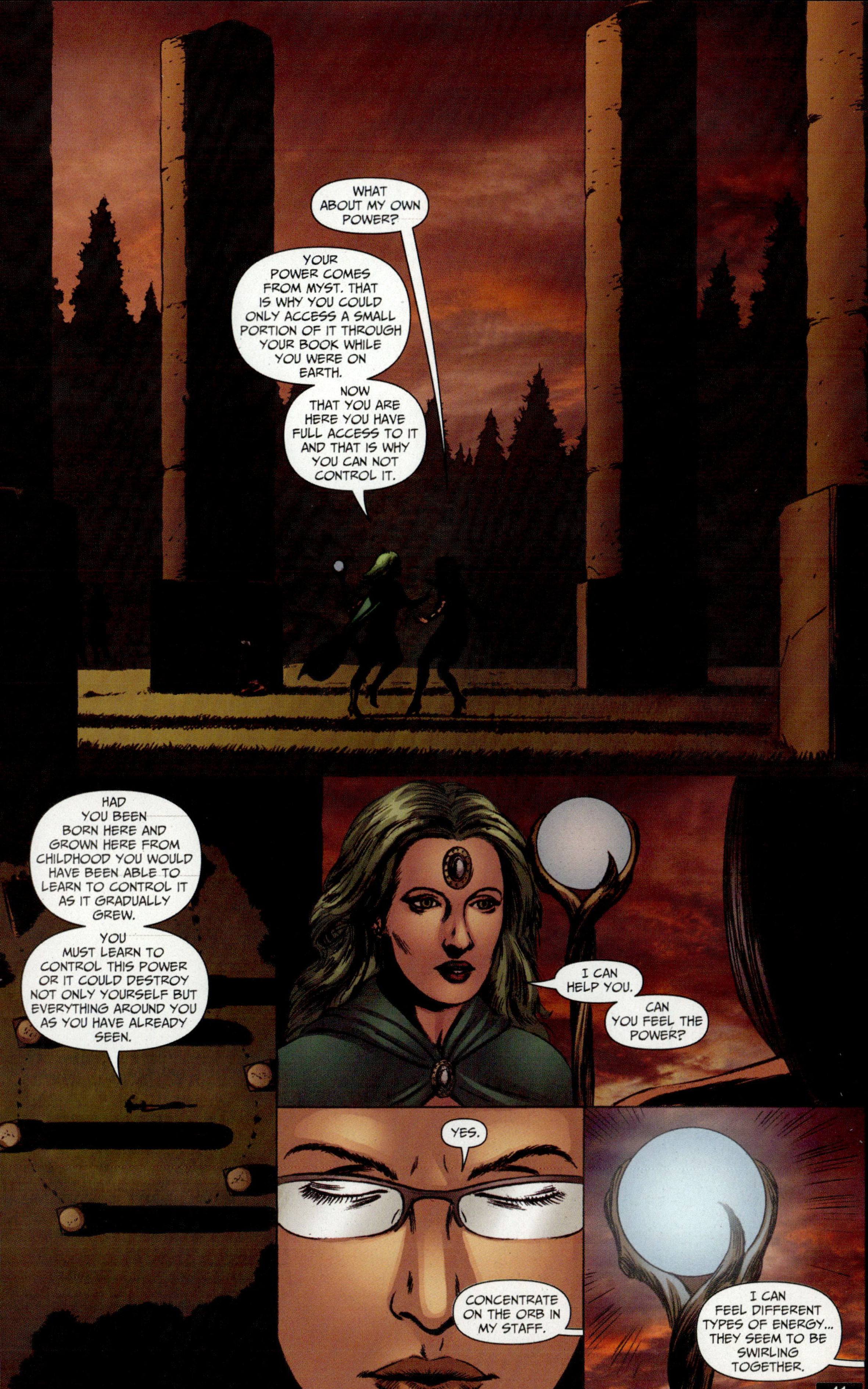
WHAT ABOUT MY OWN POWER?
YOUR POWER COMES FROM MYST. THAT IS WHY YOU COULD ONLY ACCESS A SMALL PORTION OF IT THROUGH YOUR BOOK WHILE YOU WERE ON EARTH.
NOW THAT YOU ARE HERE YOU HAVE FULL ACCESS TO IT AND THAT IS WHY YOU CAN NOT CONTROL IT.
HAD YOU BEEN BORN HERE AND GROWN HERE FROM CHILDHOOD YOU WOULD HAVE BEEN ABLE TO LEARN TO CONTROL IT AS IT GRADUALLY GREW.
YOU MUST LEARN TO CONTROL THIS POWER OR IT COULD DESTROY NOT ONLY YOURSELF BUT EVERYTHING AROUND YOU AS YOU HAVE ALREADY SEEN.
I CAN HELP YOU.
CAN YOU FEEL THE POWER?
YES.
CONCENTRATE ON THE ORB IN MY STAFF.
I CAN FEEL DIFFERENT TYPES OF ENERGY... THEY SEEM TO BE SWIRLING TOGETHER.

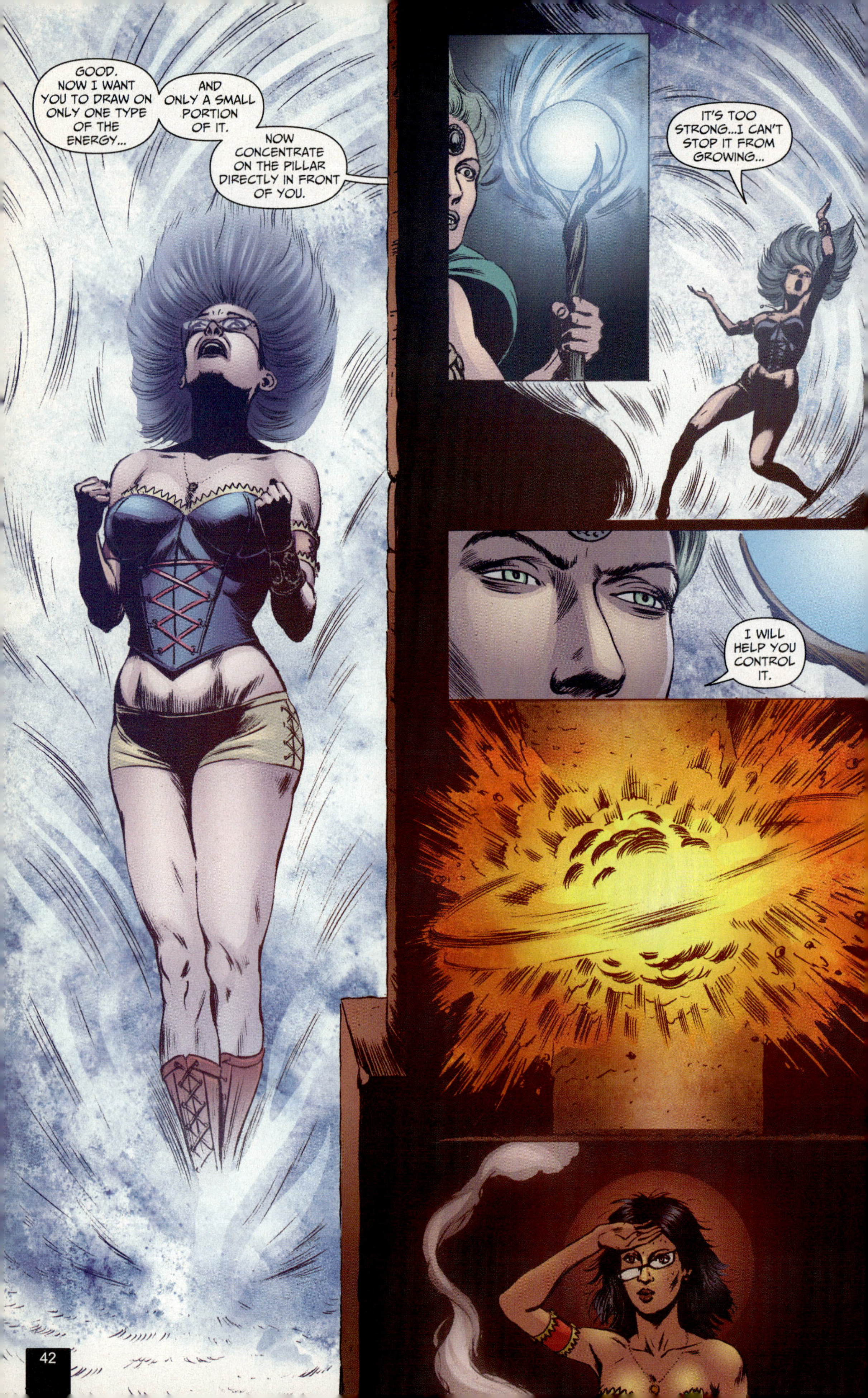
GOOD. NOW I WANT YOU TO DRAW ON ONLY ONE TYPE OF THE ENERGY...
AND ONLY A SMALL PORTION OF IT.
NOW CONCENTRATE ON THE PILLAR DIRECTLY IN FRONT OF YOU.
IT'S TOO STRONG...I CAN'T STOP IT FROM GROWING...
I WILL HELP YOU CONTROL IT.

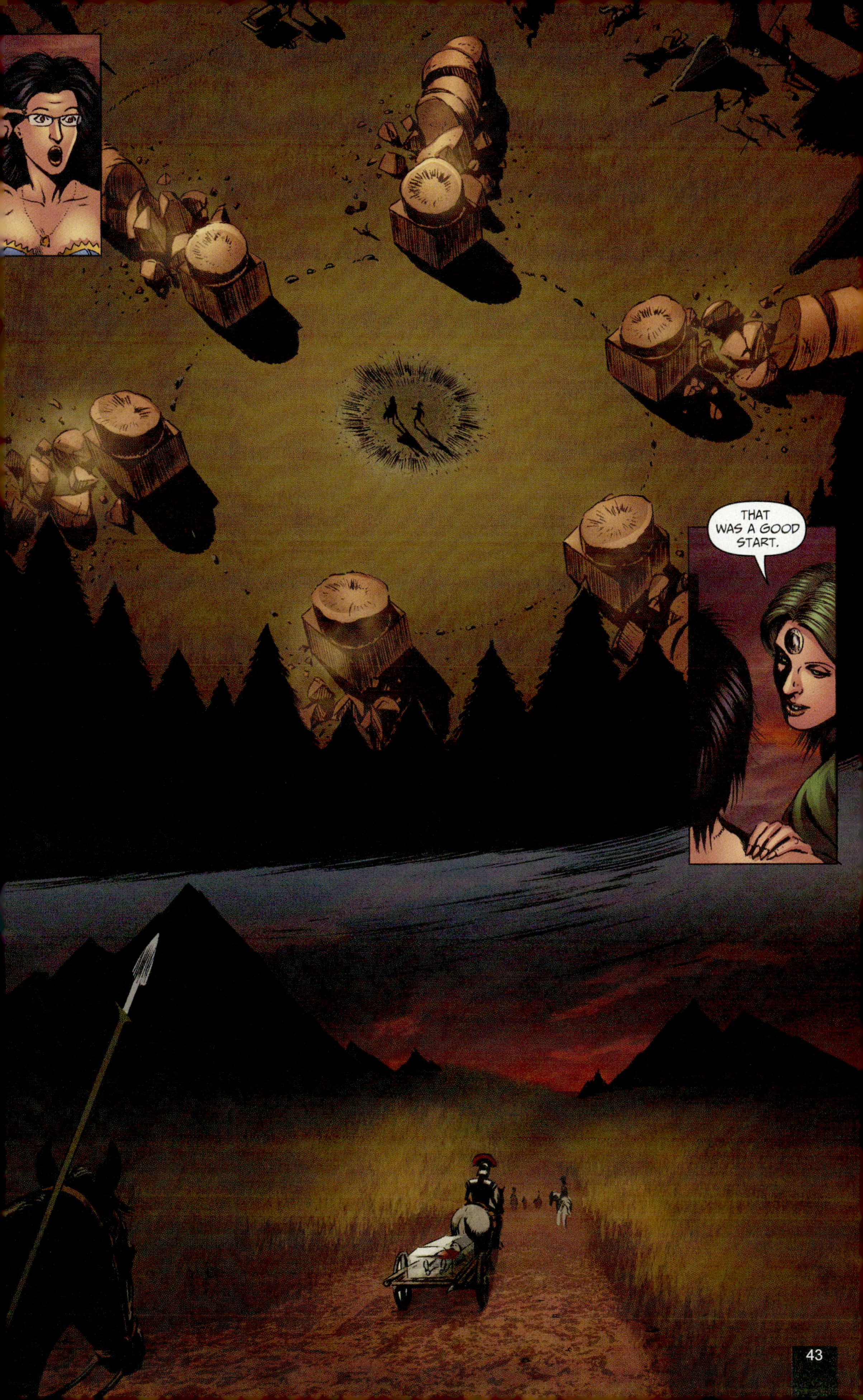
THAT WAS A GOOD START.

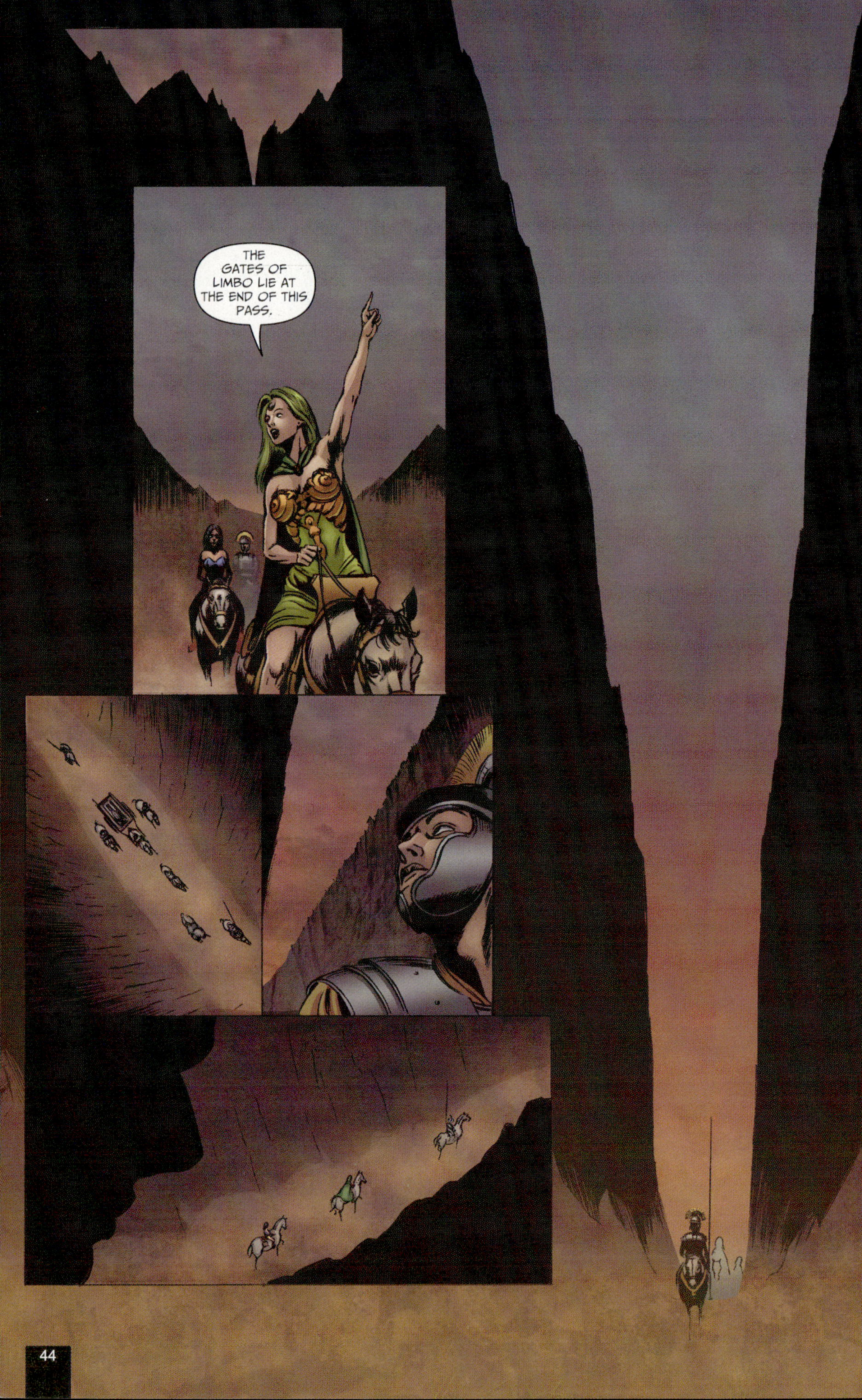
THE GATES OF LIMBO LIE AT THE END OF THIS PASS.

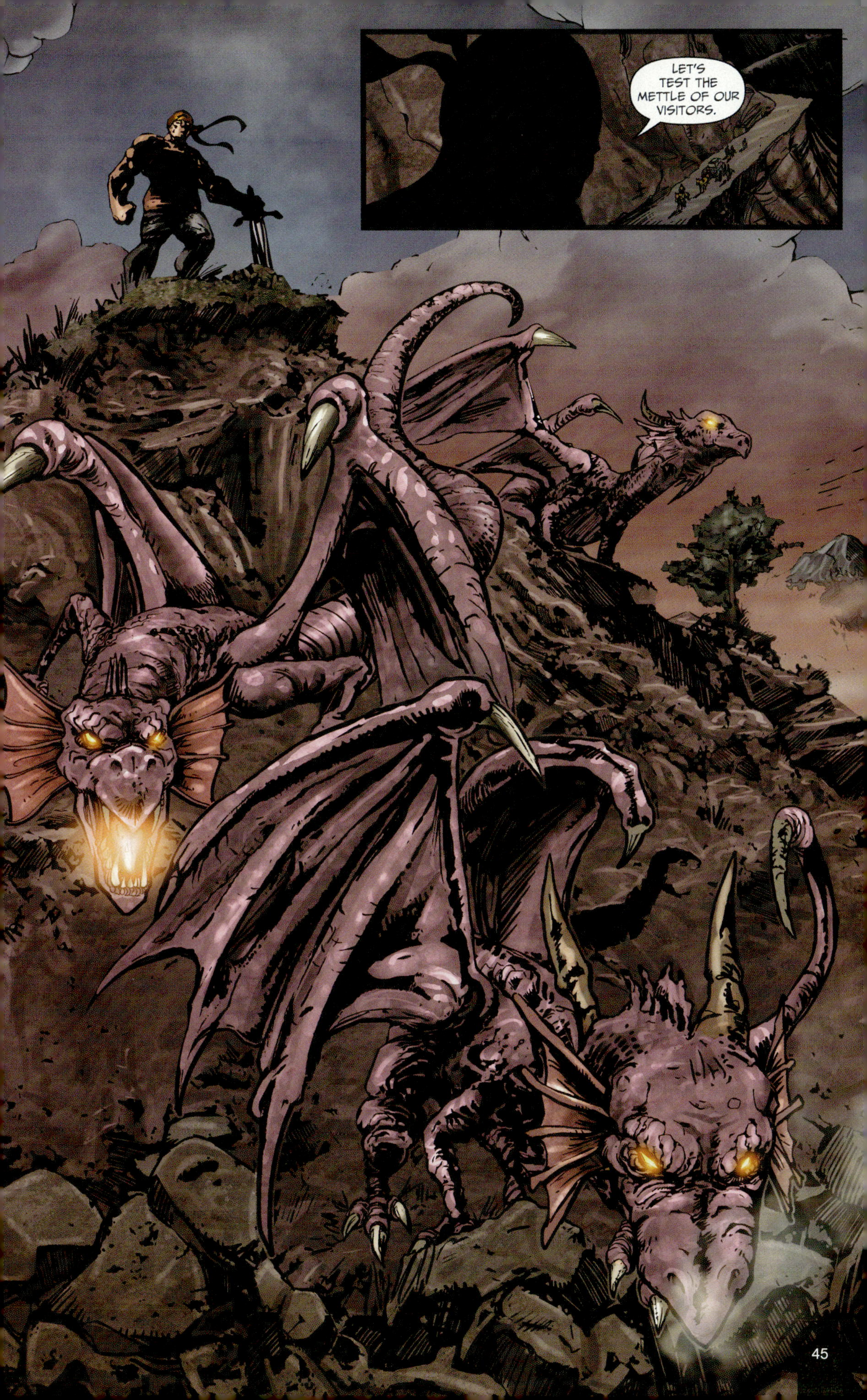
LET'S TEST THE METTLE OF OUR VISITORS.

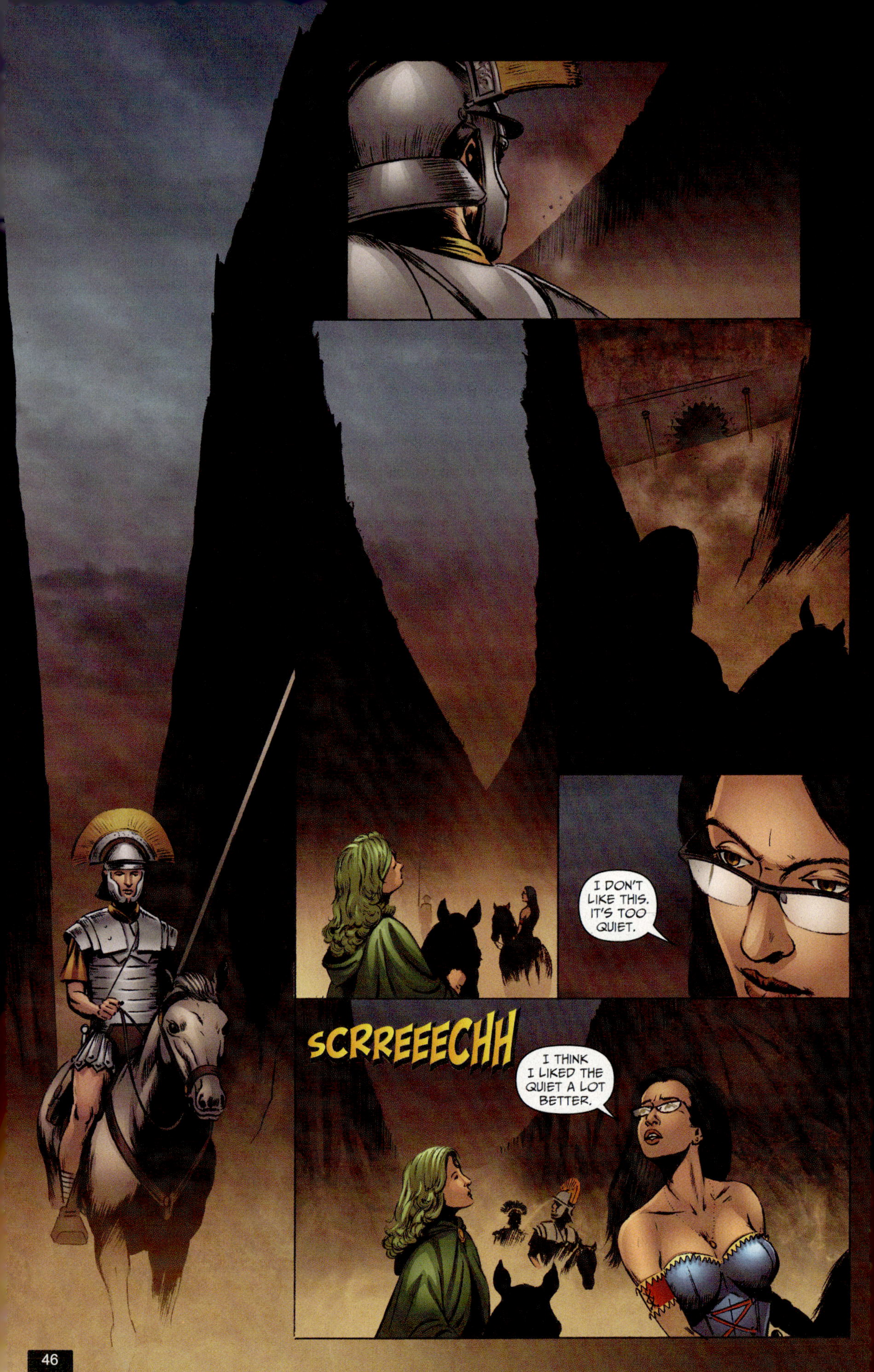
I DON'T LIKE THIS. IT'S TOO QUIET.
SCRREEECHH
I THINK I LIKED THE QUIET A LOT BETTER.

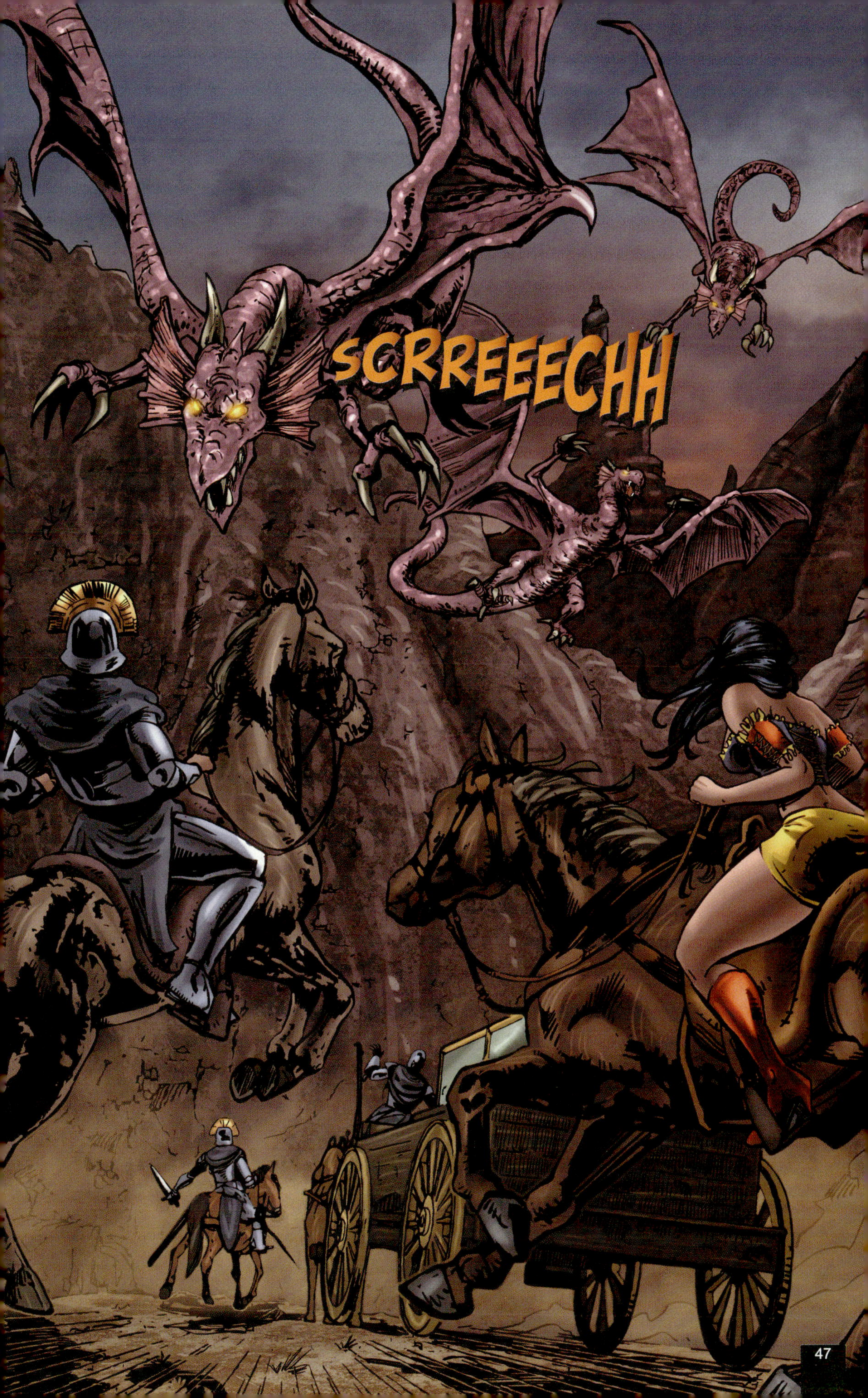
SCRREEECHH

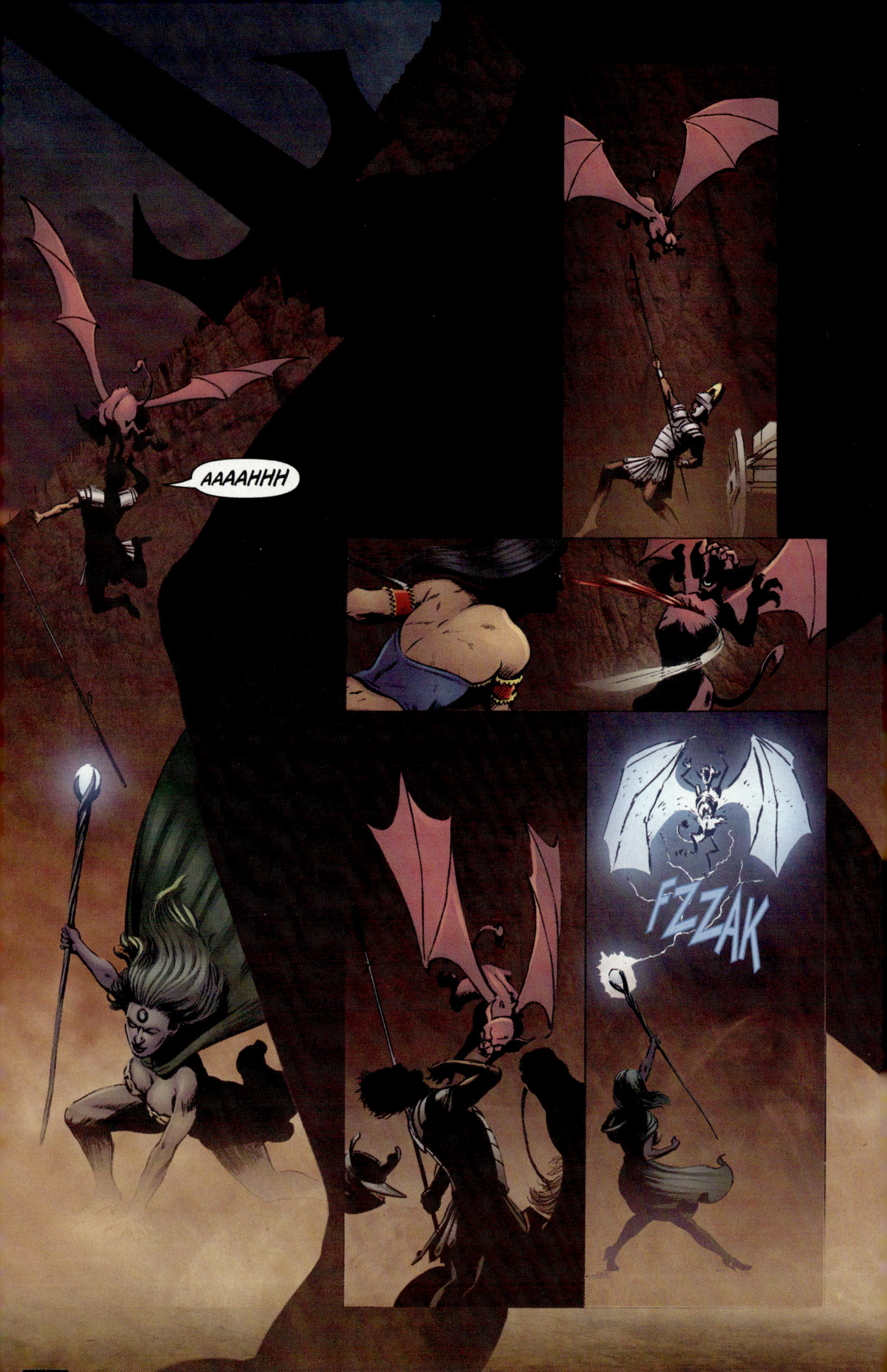
AAAAHHH
FZZAK

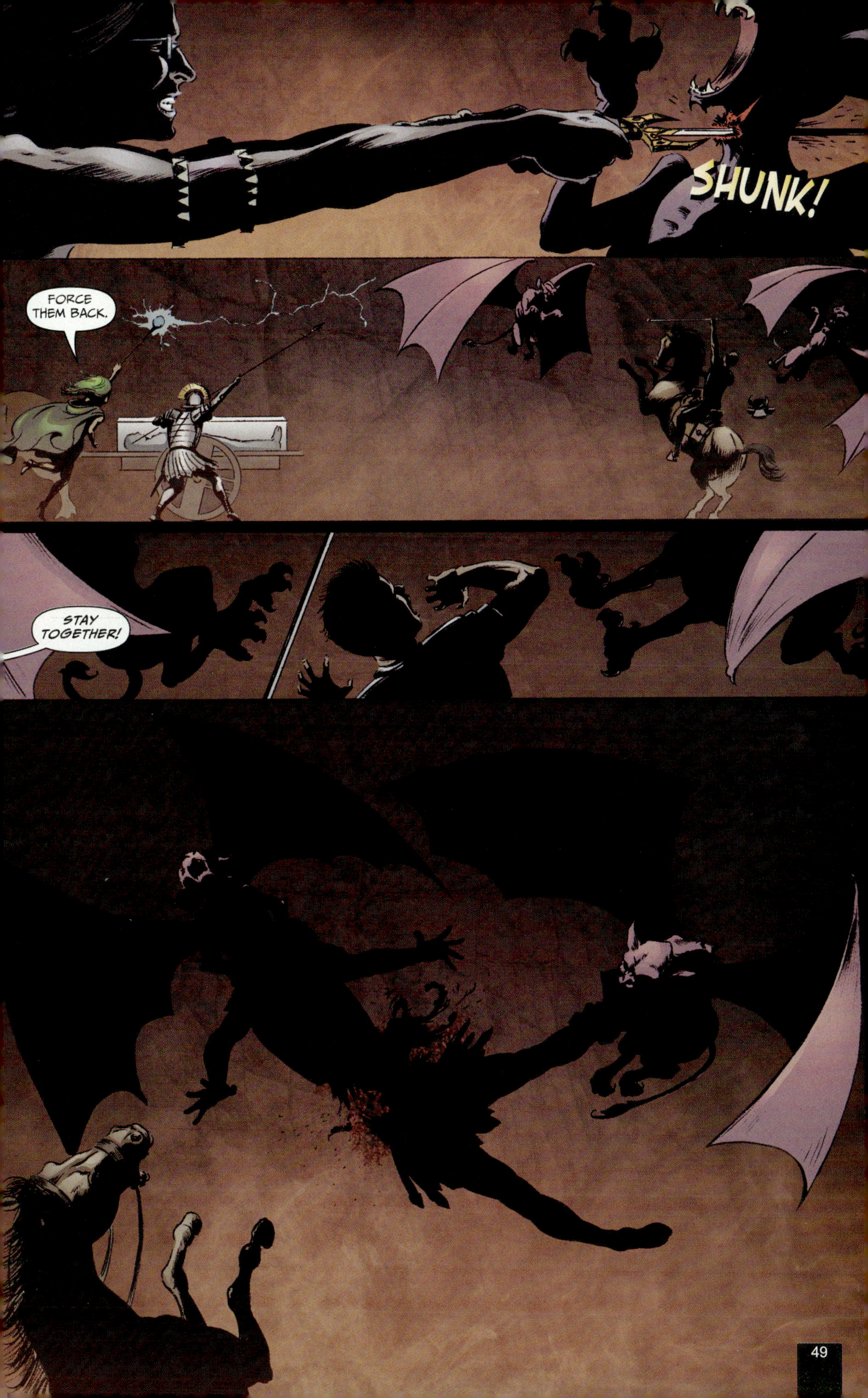
SHUNK!
FORCE THEM BACK.
STAY TOGETHER!

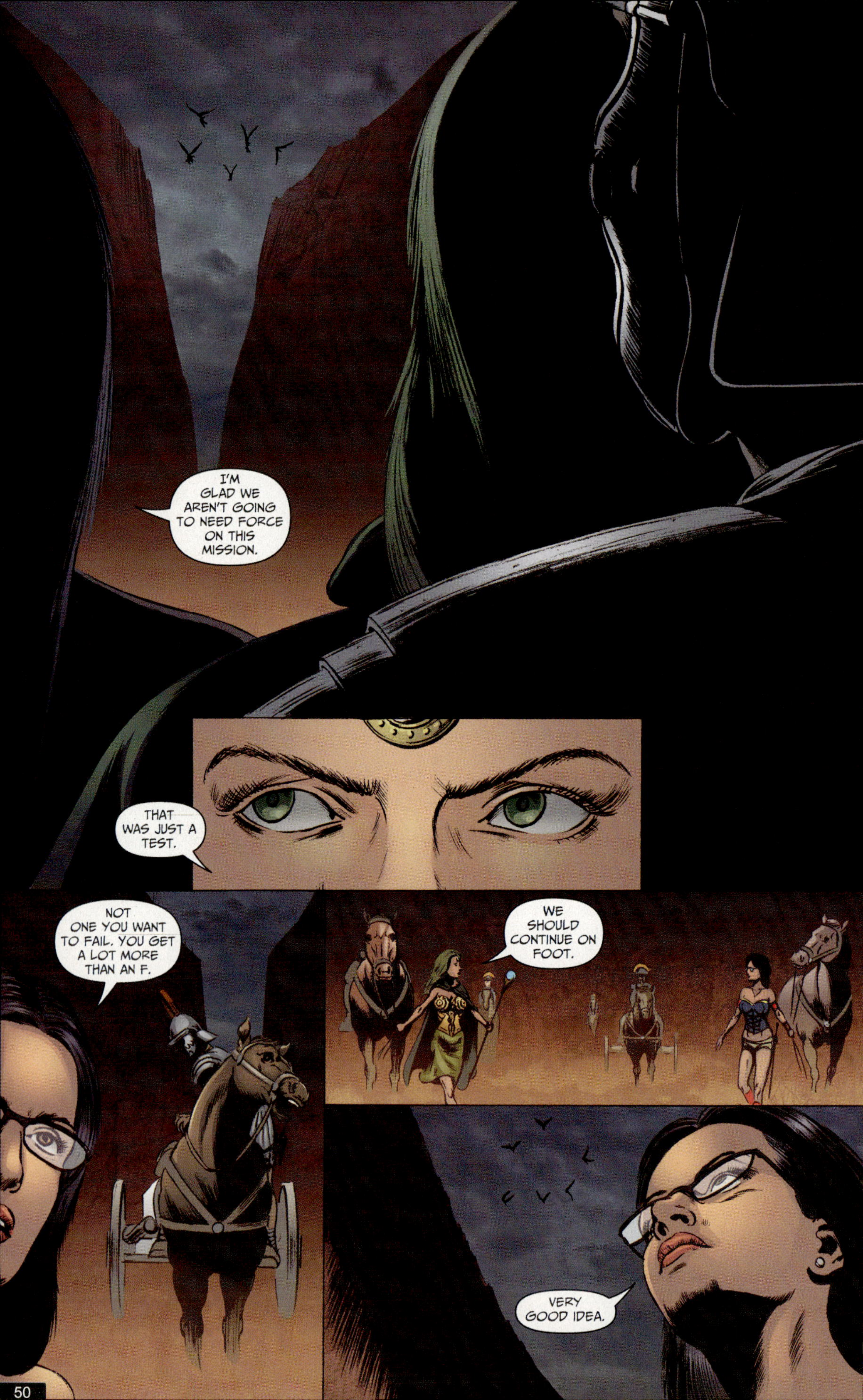
I'M GLAD WE AREN'T GOING TO NEED FORCE ON THIS MISSION.
THAT WAS JUST A TEST.
NOT ONE YOU WANT TO FAIL. YOU GET A LOT MORE THAN AN F.
WE SHOULD CONTINUE ON FOOT.
VERY GOOD IDEA.

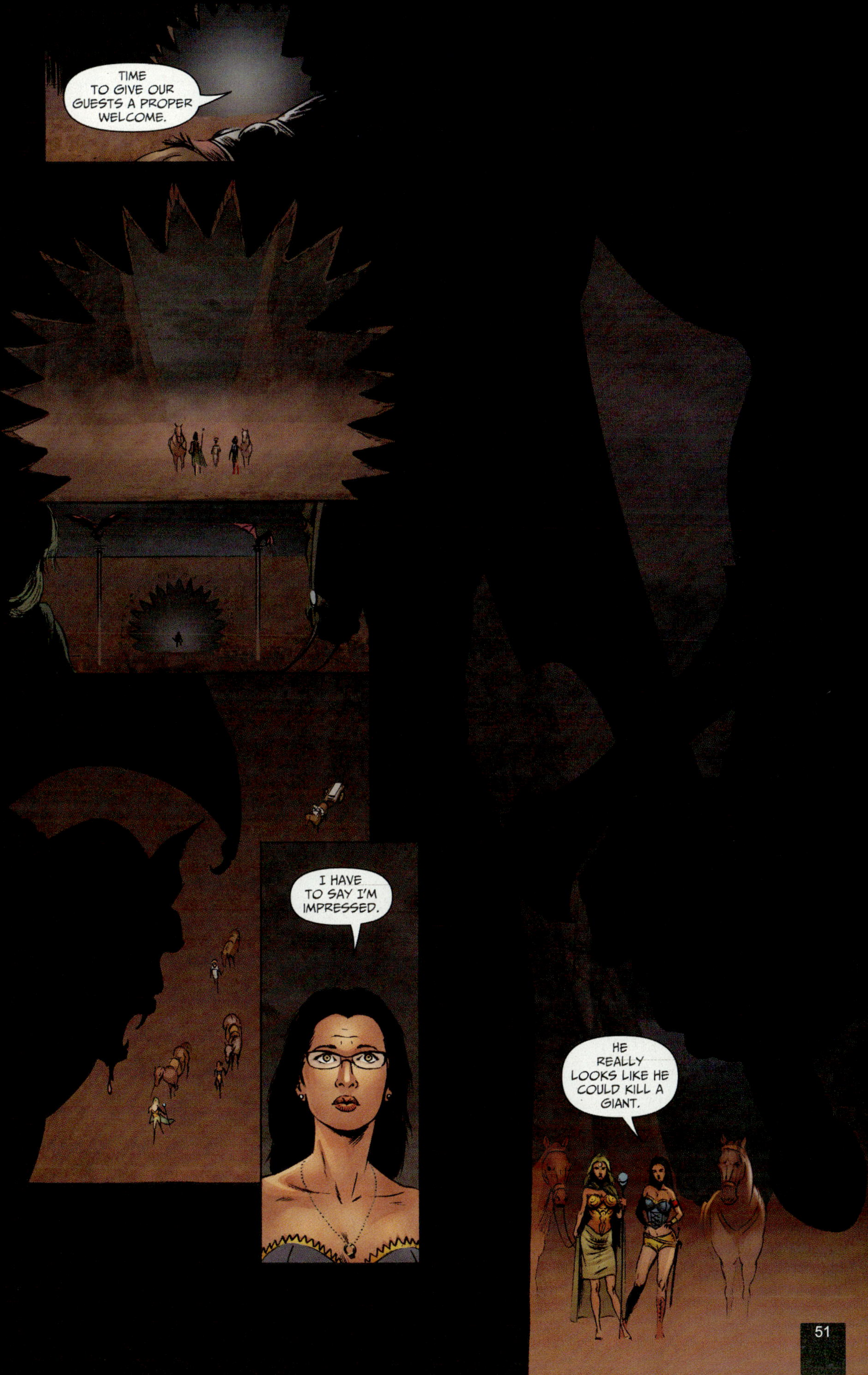
TIME TO GIVE OUR GUESTS A PROPER WELCOME.
I HAVE TO SAY I'M IMPRESSED.
HE REALLY LOOKS LIKE HE COULD KILL A GIANT.

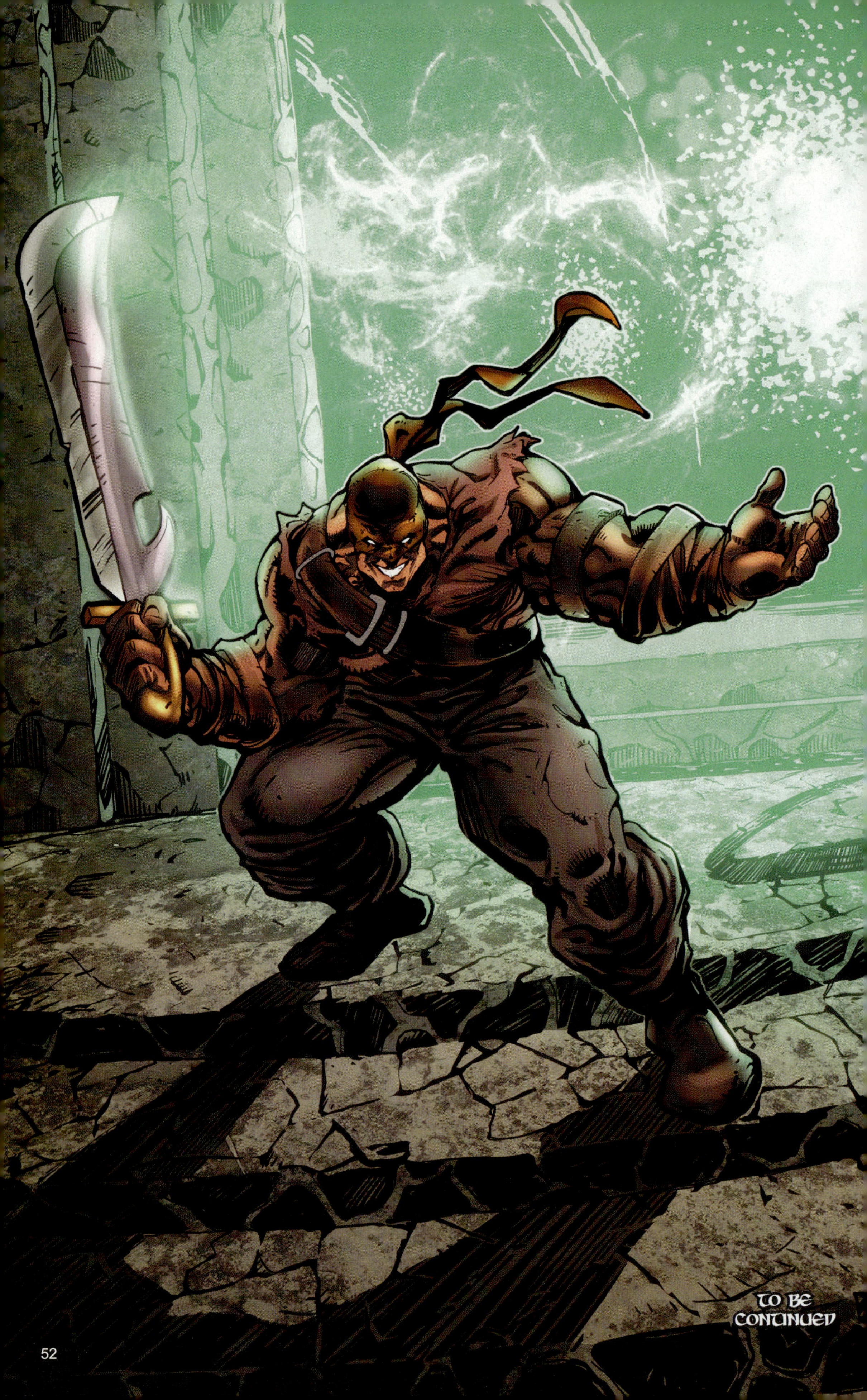
TO BE CONTINUED

Grimm Fairy Tales
Volume 11

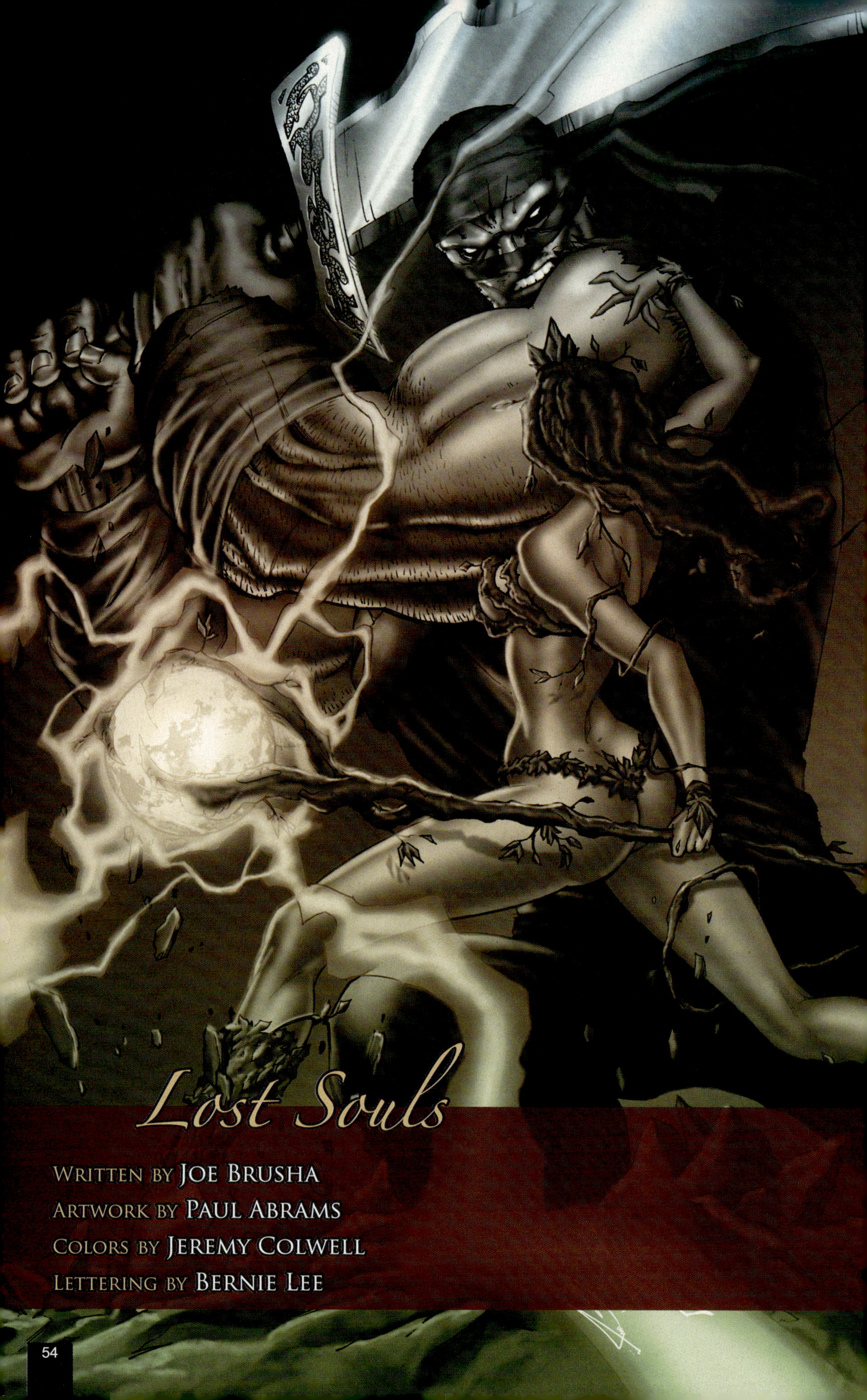

Lost Souls

Written by Joe Brusha
Artwork by Paul Abrams
Colors by Jeremy Colwell
Lettering by Bernie Lee

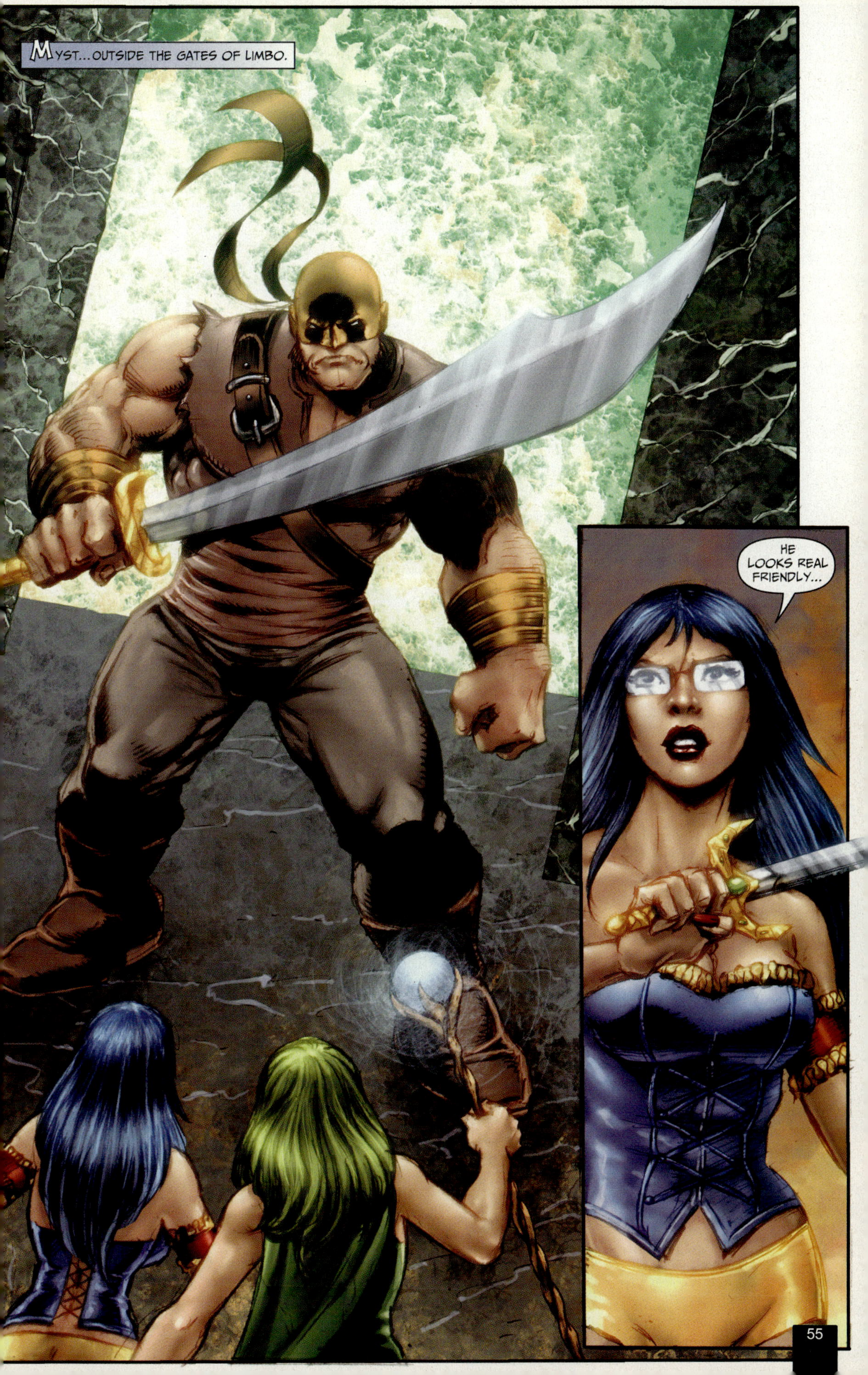
MYST...OUTSIDE THE GATES OF LIMBO.
HE LOOKS REAL FRIENDLY...

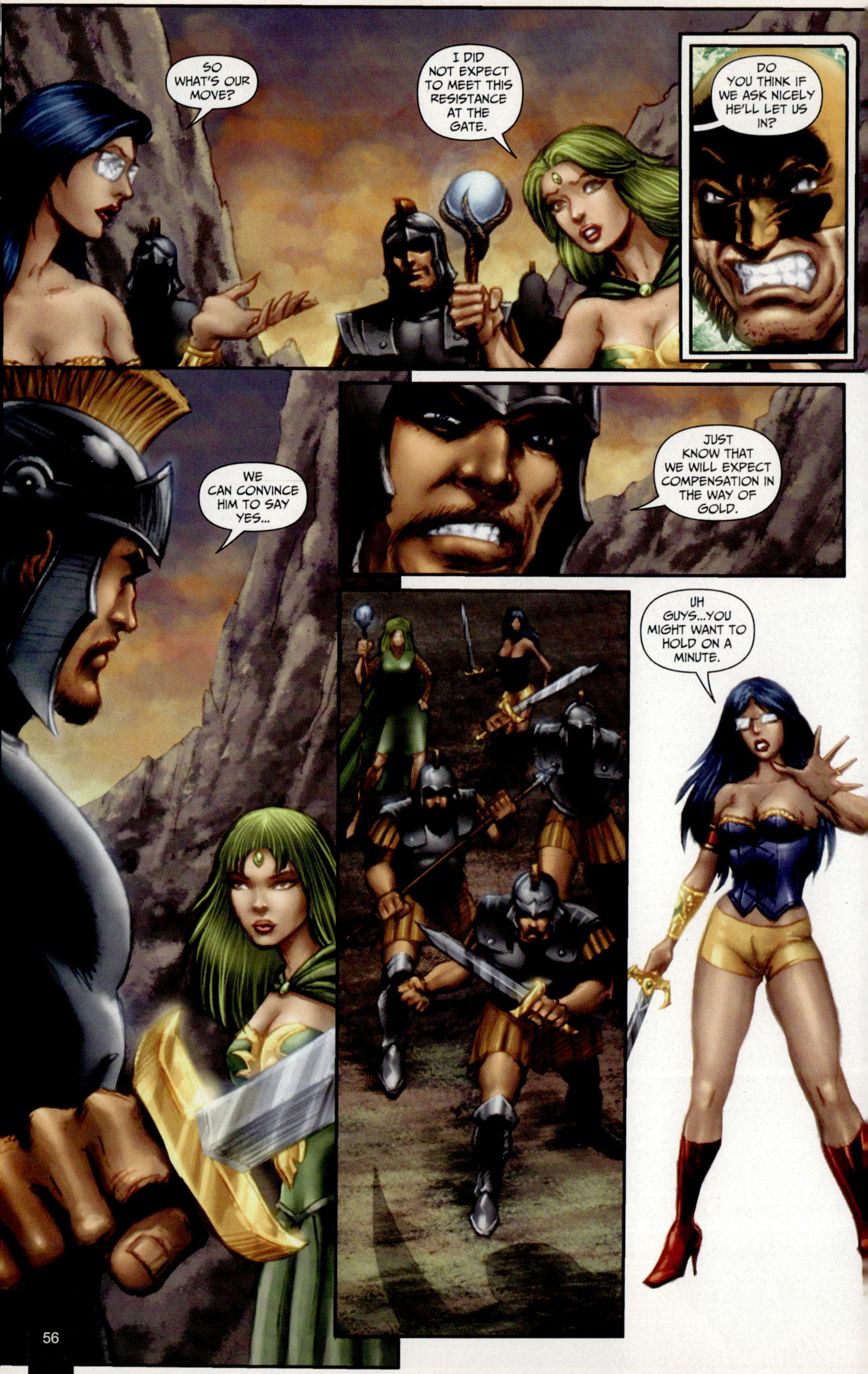
SO WHAT'S OUR MOVE?
I DID NOT EXPECT TO MEET THIS RESISTANCE AT THE GATE.
DO YOU THINK IF WE ASK NICELY HE'LL LET US IN?
WE CAN CONVINCE HIM TO SAY YES...
JUST KNOW THAT WE WILL EXPECT COMPENSATION IN THE WAY OF GOLD.
UH GUYS...YOU MIGHT WANT TO HOLD ON A MINUTE.

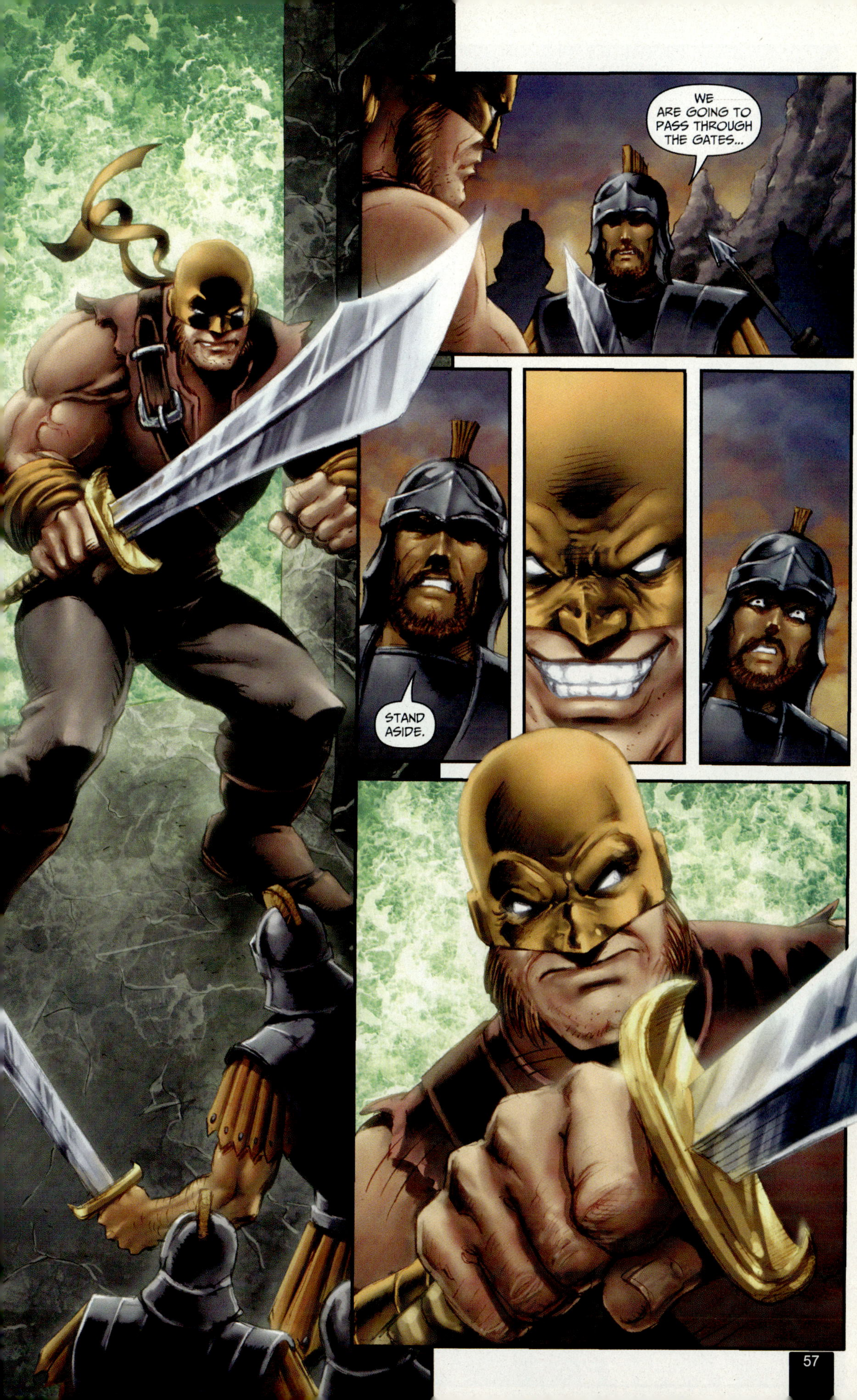
WE ARE GOING TO PASS THROUGH THE GATES...
STAND ASIDE.

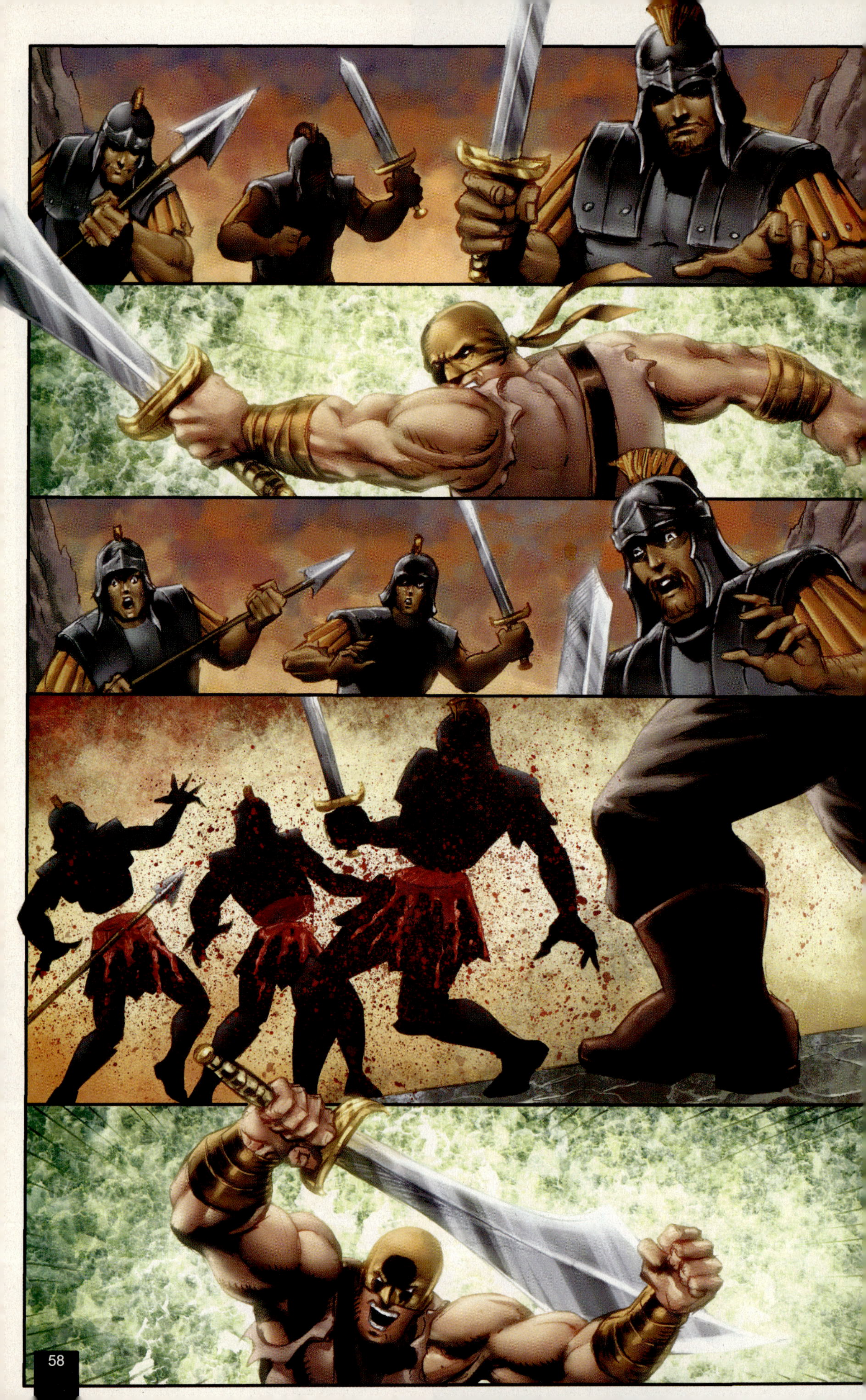

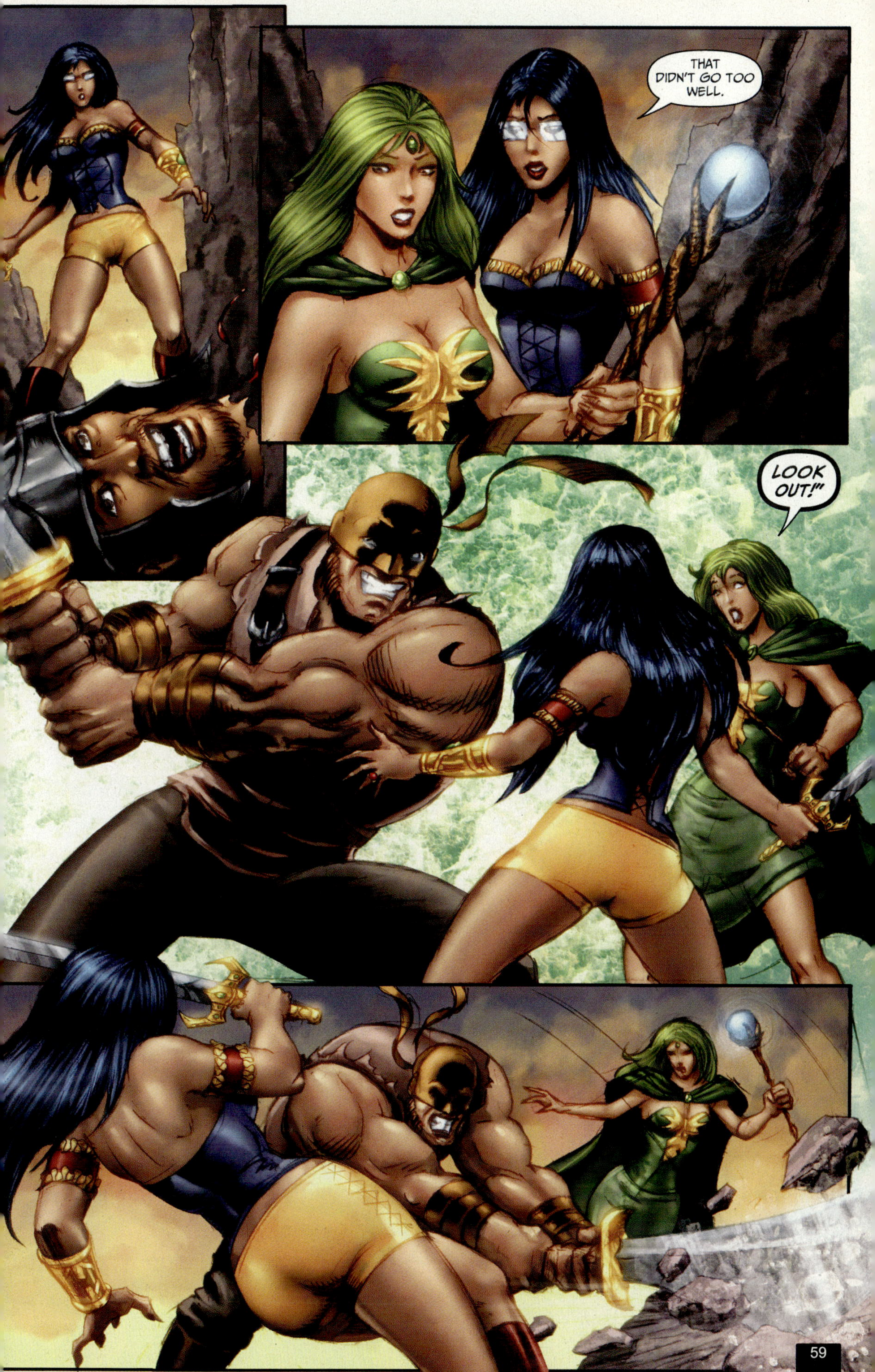
THAT DIDN'T GO TOO WELL.
LOOK OUT!"

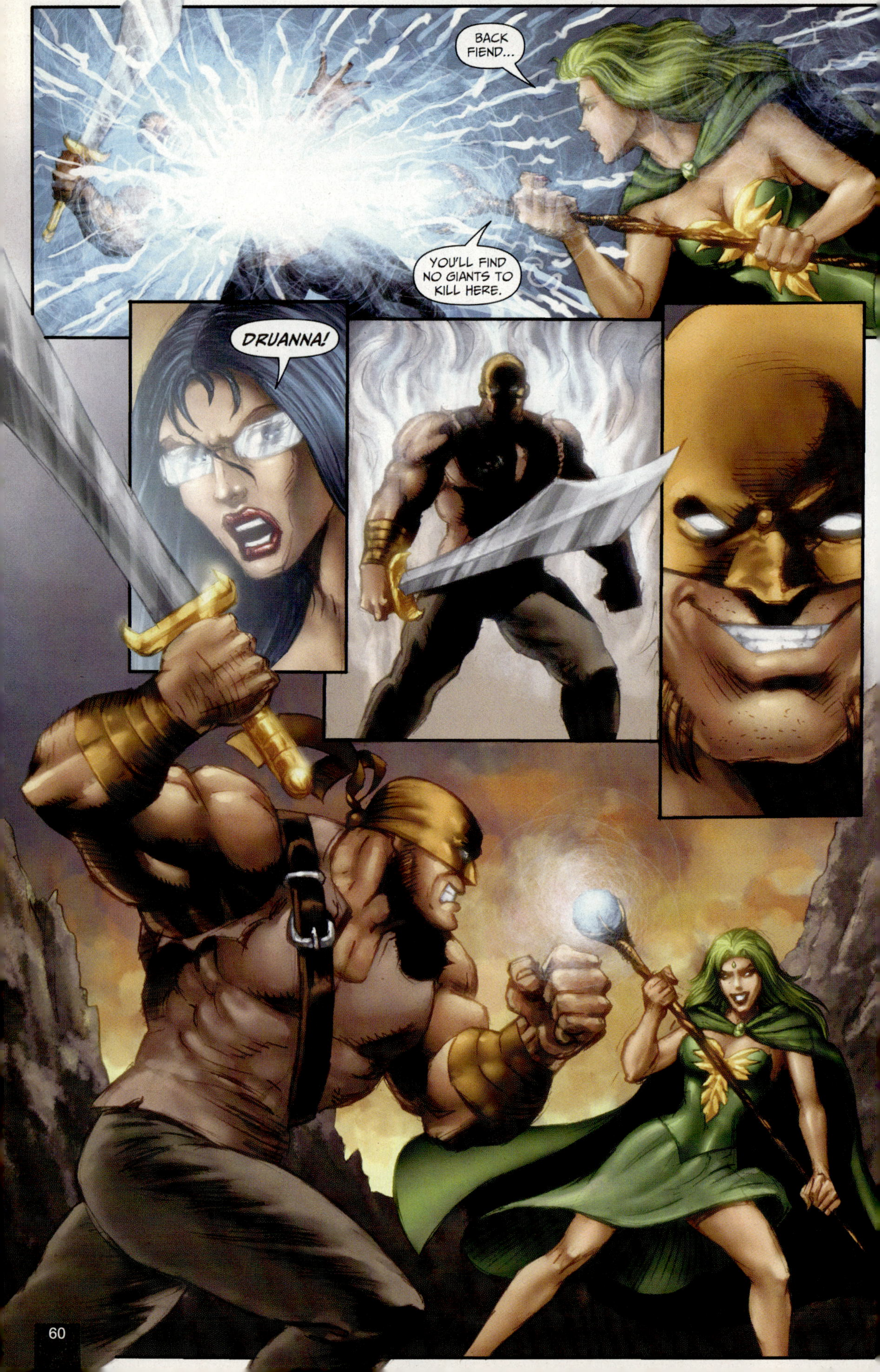
BACK FIEND...
YOU'LL FIND NO GIANTS TO KILL HERE.
DRUANNA!

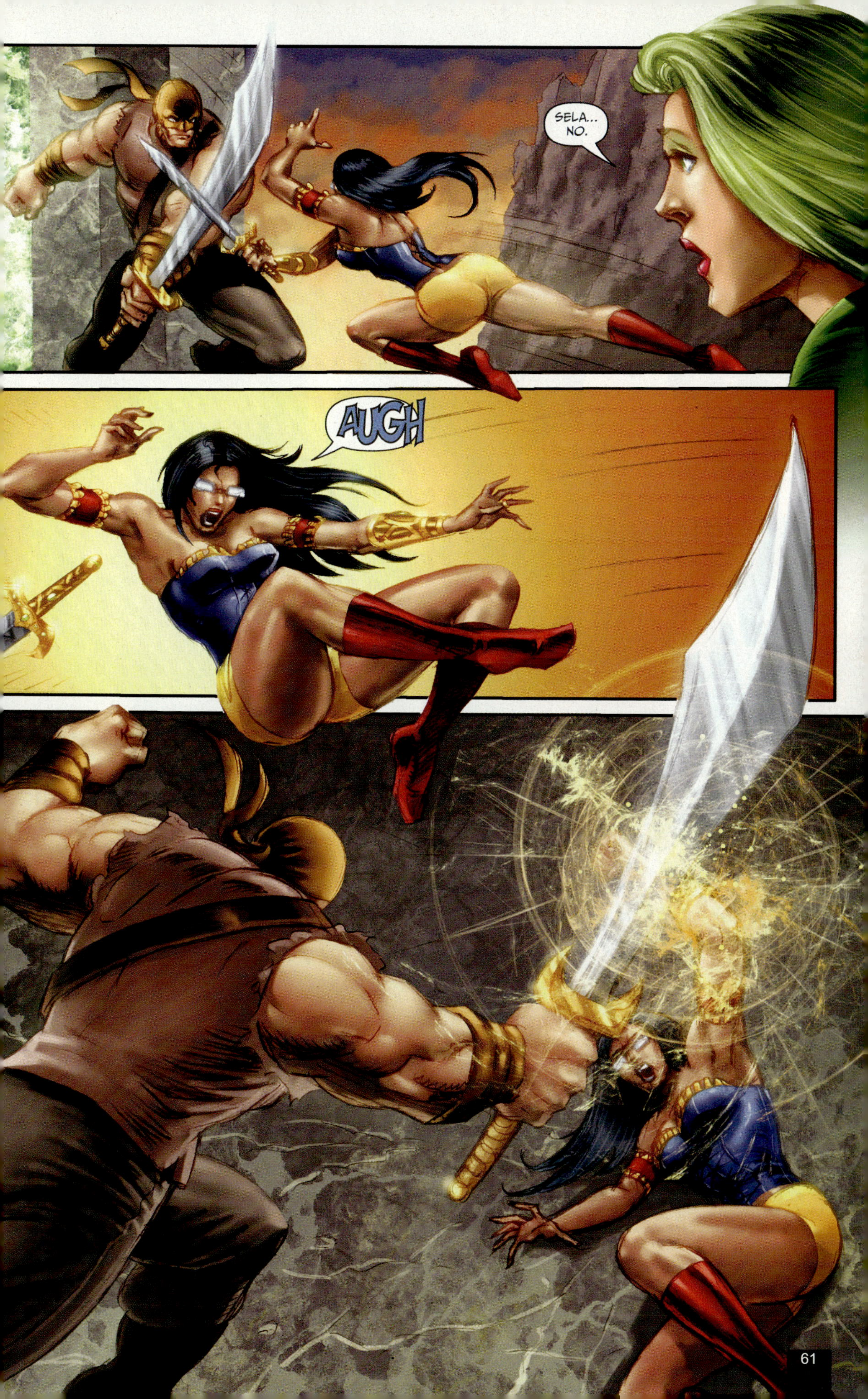
SELA...
NO.
AUGH

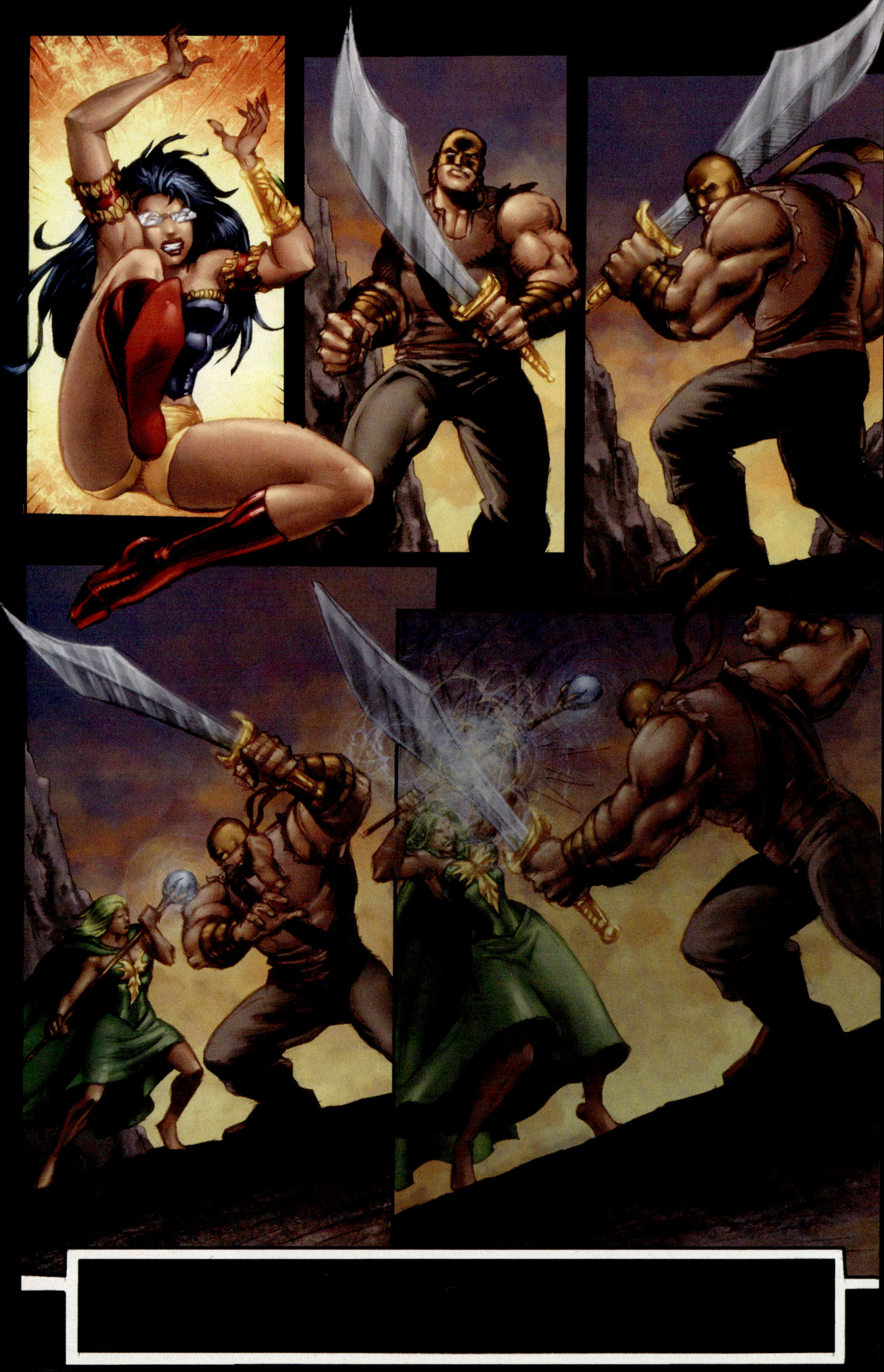

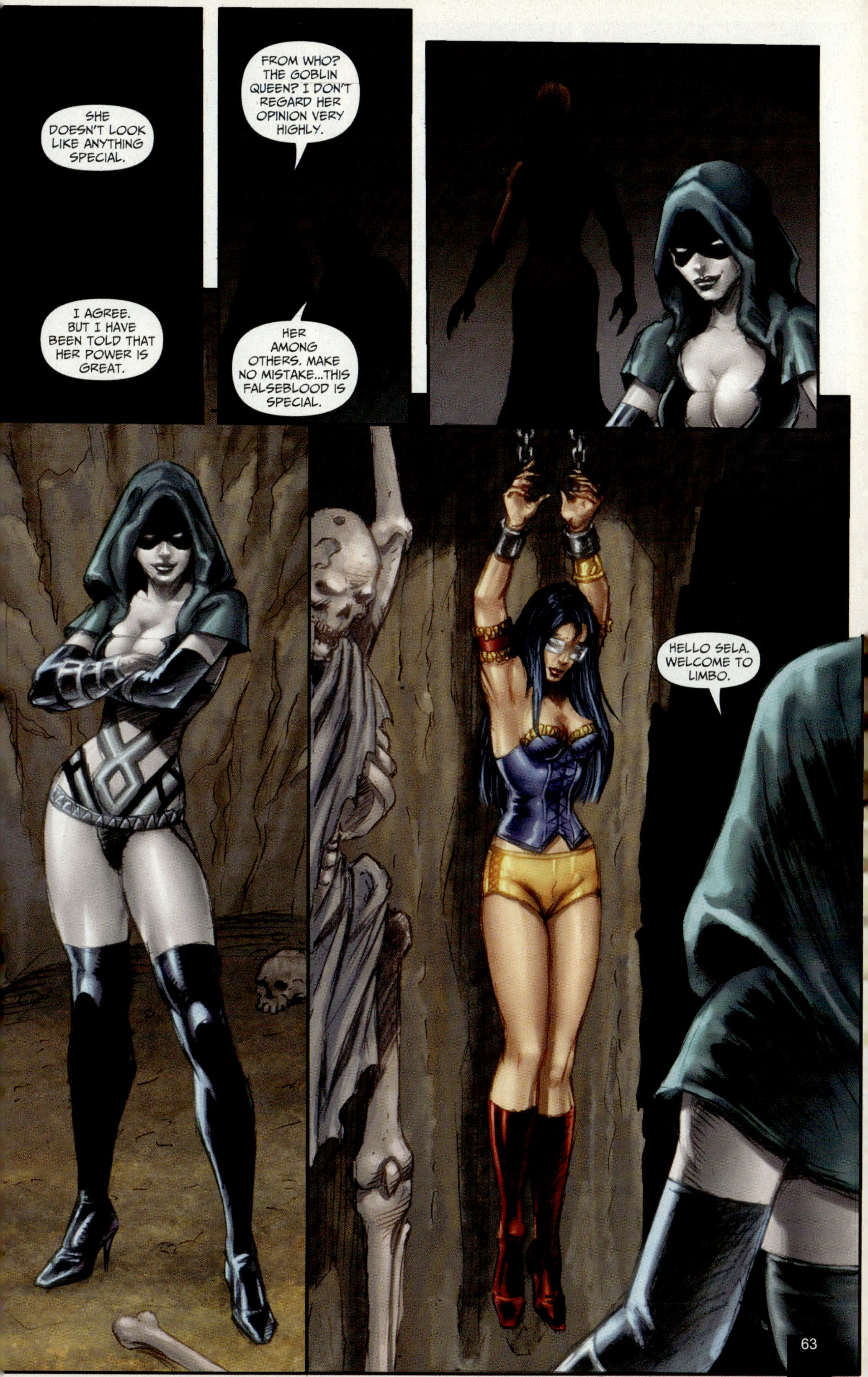
SHE DOESN'T LOOK LIKE ANYTHING SPECIAL.
FROM WHO? THE GOBLIN QUEEN? I DON'T REGARD HER OPINION VERY HIGHLY.
I AGREE. BUT I HAVE BEEN TOLD THAT HER POWER IS GREAT.
HER AMONG OTHERS. MAKE NO MISTAKE...THIS FALSEBLOOD IS SPECIAL.
HELLO SELA. WELCOME TO LIMBO.

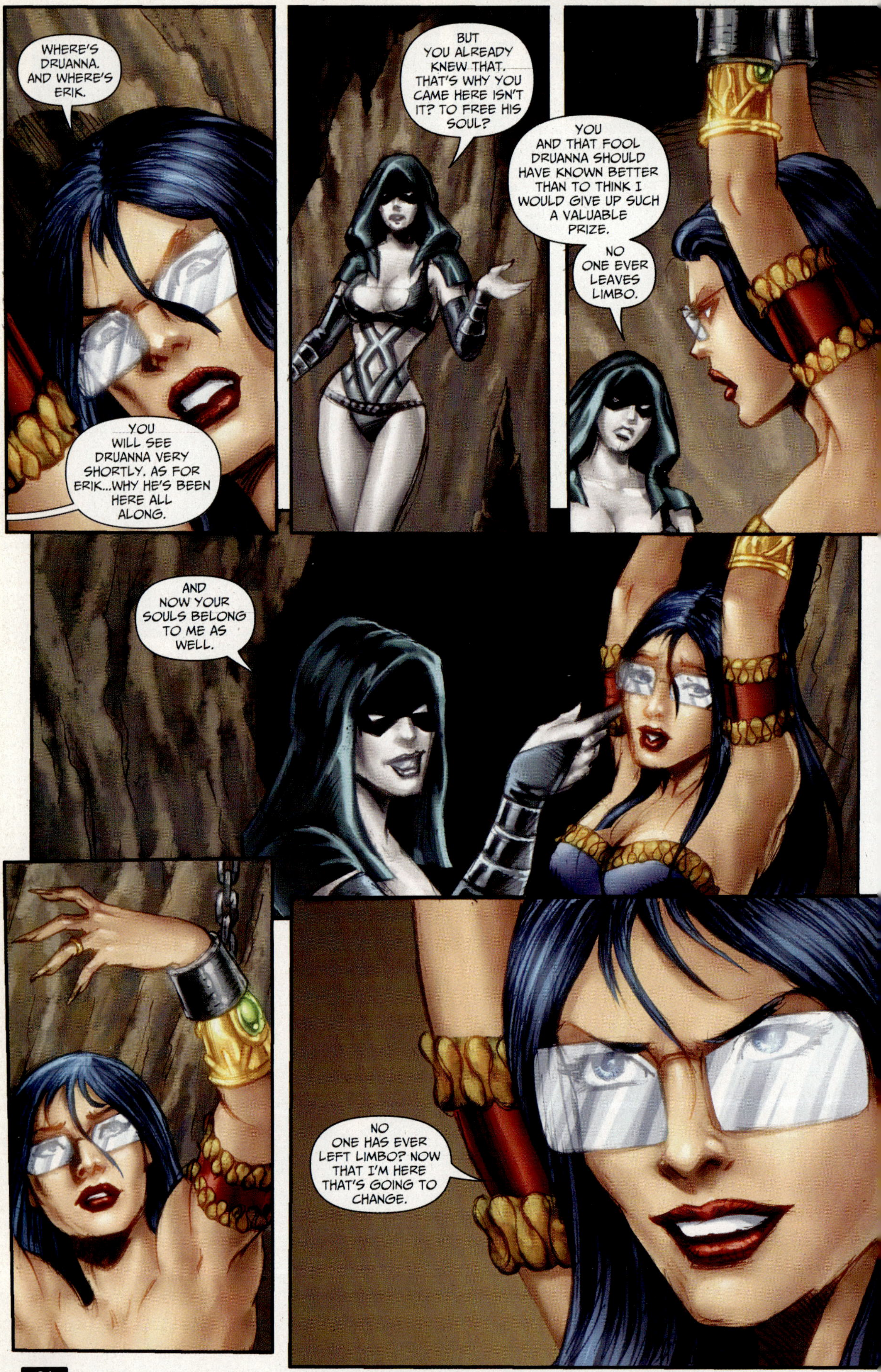
WHERE'S DRUANNA. AND WHERE'S ERIK.
YOU WILL SEE DRUANNA VERY SHORTLY. AS FOR ERIK...WHY HE'S BEEN HERE ALL ALONG.
BUT YOU ALREADY KNEW THAT. THAT'S WHY YOU CAME HERE ISN'T IT? TO FREE HIS SOUL?
YOU AND THAT FOOL DRUANNA SHOULD HAVE KNOWN BETTER THAN TO THINK I WOULD GIVE UP SUCH A VALUABLE PRIZE.
NO ONE EVER LEAVES LIMBO.
AND NOW YOUR SOULS BELONG TO ME AS WELL.
NO ONE HAS EVER LEFT LIMBO? NOW THAT I'M HERE THAT'S GOING TO CHANGE.

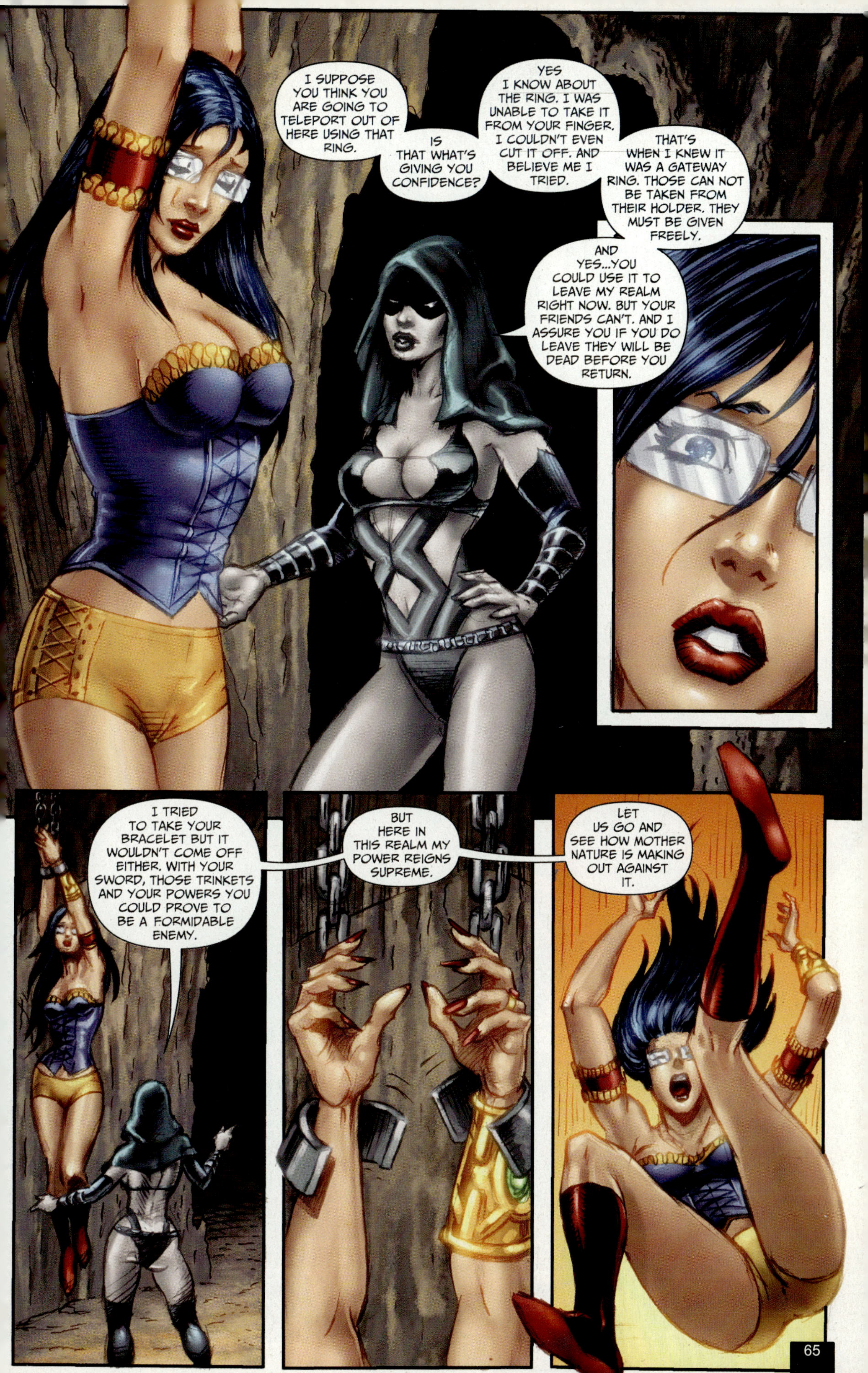
I SUPPOSE YOU THINK YOU ARE GOING TO TELEPORT OUT OF HERE USING THAT RING.
IS THAT WHAT'S GIVING YOU CONFIDENCE?
YES I KNOW ABOUT THE RING. I WAS UNABLE TO TAKE IT FROM YOUR FINGER. I COULDN'T EVEN CUT IT OFF. AND BELIEVE ME I TRIED.
THAT'S WHEN I KNEW IT WAS A GATEWAY RING. THOSE CAN NOT BE TAKEN FROM THEIR HOLDER. THEY MUST BE GIVEN FREELY.
AND YES...YOU COULD USE IT TO LEAVE MY REALM RIGHT NOW. BUT YOUR FRIENDS CAN'T. AND I ASSURE YOU IF YOU DO LEAVE THEY WILL BE DEAD BEFORE YOU RETURN.
I TRIED TO TAKE YOUR BRACELET BUT IT WOULDN'T COME OFF EITHER. WITH YOUR SWORD, THOSE TRINKETS AND YOUR POWERS YOU COULD PROVE TO BE A FORMIDABLE ENEMY.
BUT HERE IN THIS REALM MY POWER REIGNS SUPREME.
LET US GO AND SEE HOW MOTHER NATURE IS MAKING OUT AGAINST IT.

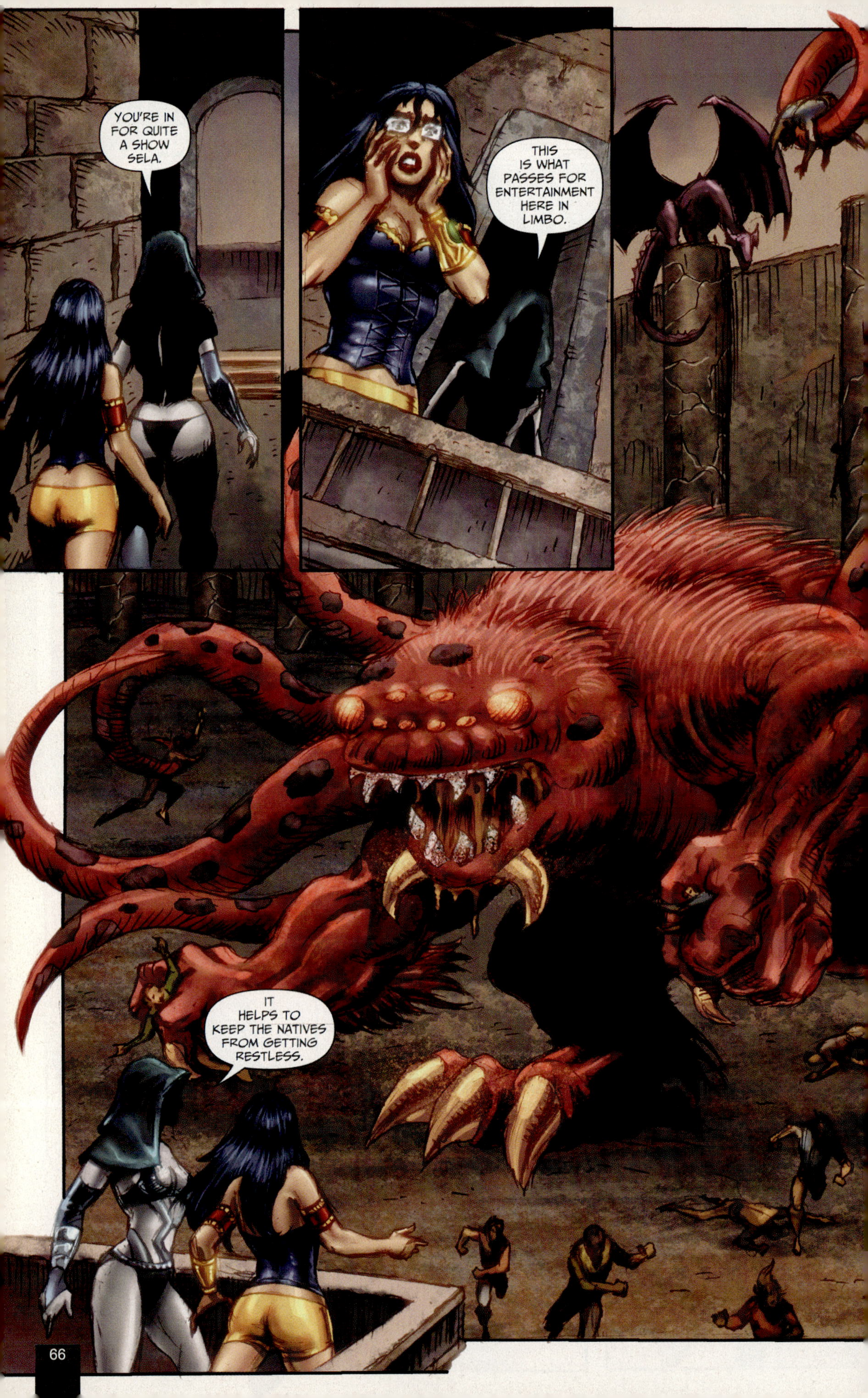
YOU'RE IN FOR QUITE A SHOW SELA.
THIS IS WHAT PASSES FOR ENTERTAINMENT HERE IN LIMBO.
IT HELPS TO KEEP THE NATIVES FROM GETTING RESTLESS.

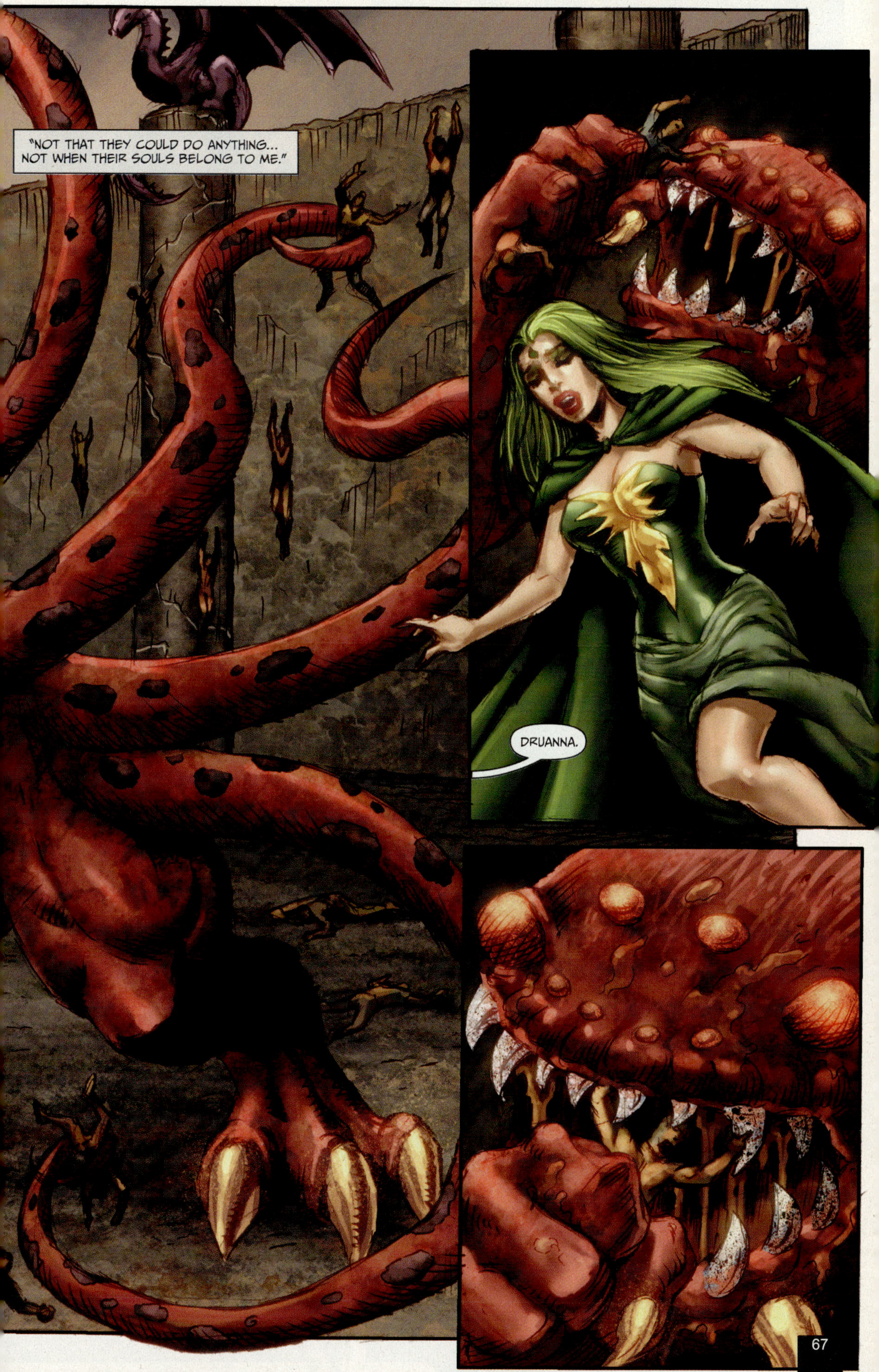
"NOT THAT THEY COULD DO ANYTHING... NOT WHEN THEIR SOULS BELONG TO ME."
DRUANNA.

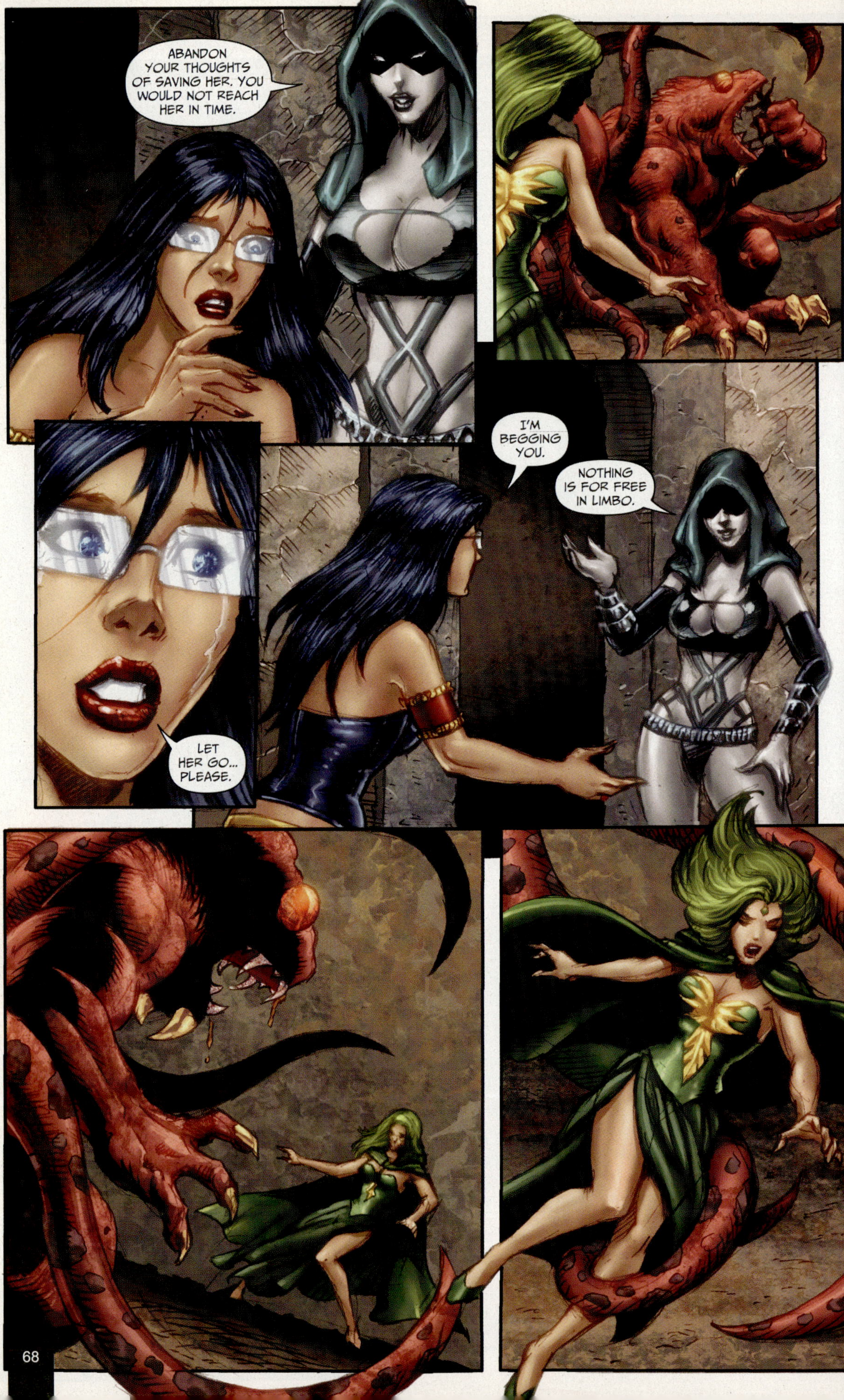
ABANDON YOUR THOUGHTS OF SAVING HER. YOU WOULD NOT REACH HER IN TIME.
LET HER GO... PLEASE.
I'M BEGGING YOU.
NOTHING IS FOR FREE IN LIMBO.

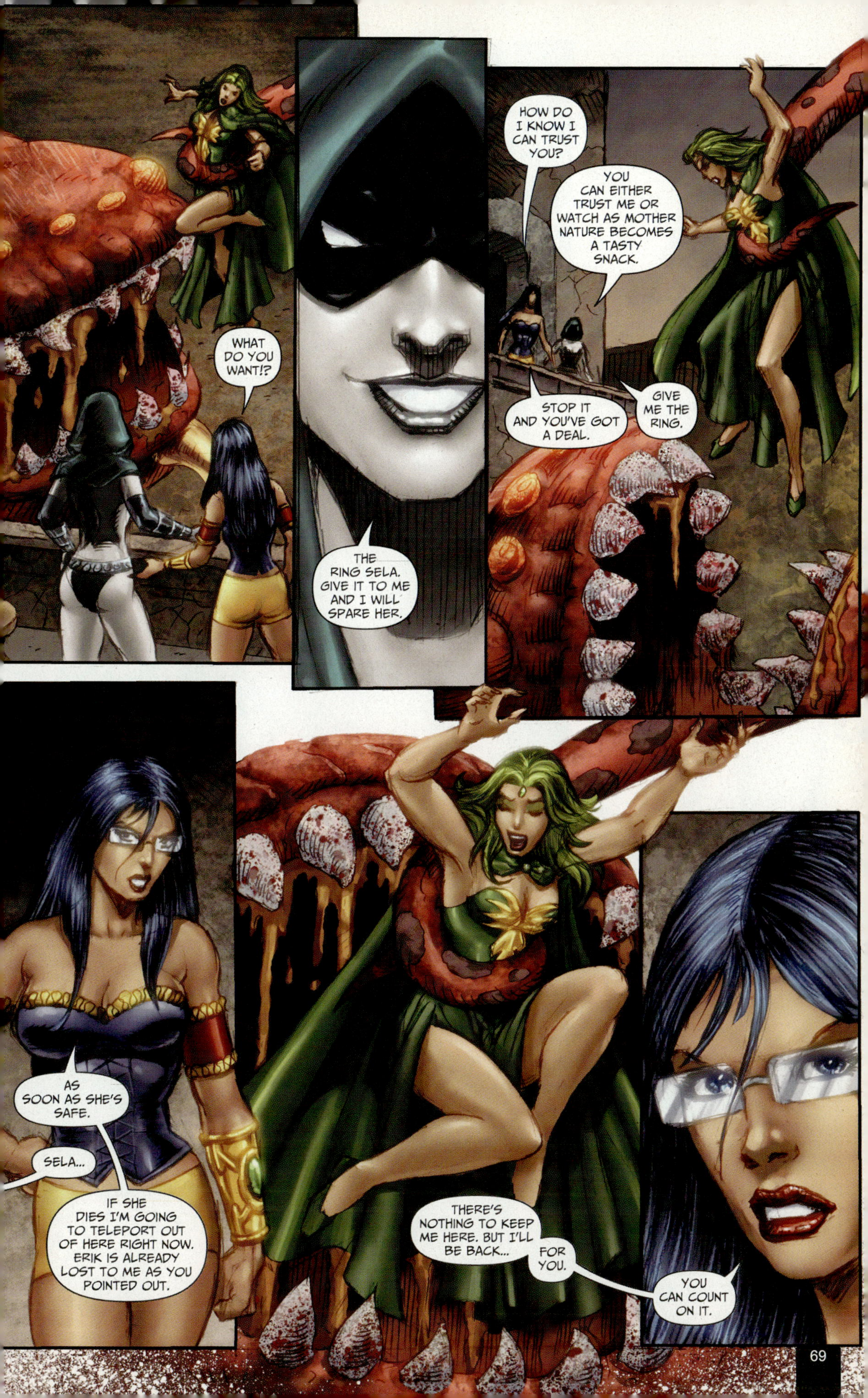
WHAT DO YOU WANT!?
THE RING SELA. GIVE IT TO ME AND I WILL SPARE HER.
HOW DO I KNOW I CAN TRUST YOU?
YOU CAN EITHER TRUST ME OR WATCH AS MOTHER NATURE BECOMES A TASTY SNACK.
GIVE ME THE RING.
STOP IT AND YOU'VE GOT A DEAL.
AS SOON AS SHE'S SAFE.
SELA...
IF SHE DIES I'M GOING TO TELEPORT OUT OF HERE RIGHT NOW. ERIK IS ALREADY LOST TO ME AS YOU POINTED OUT.
THERE'S NOTHING TO KEEP ME HERE. BUT I'LL BE BACK...
FOR YOU.
YOU CAN COUNT ON IT.

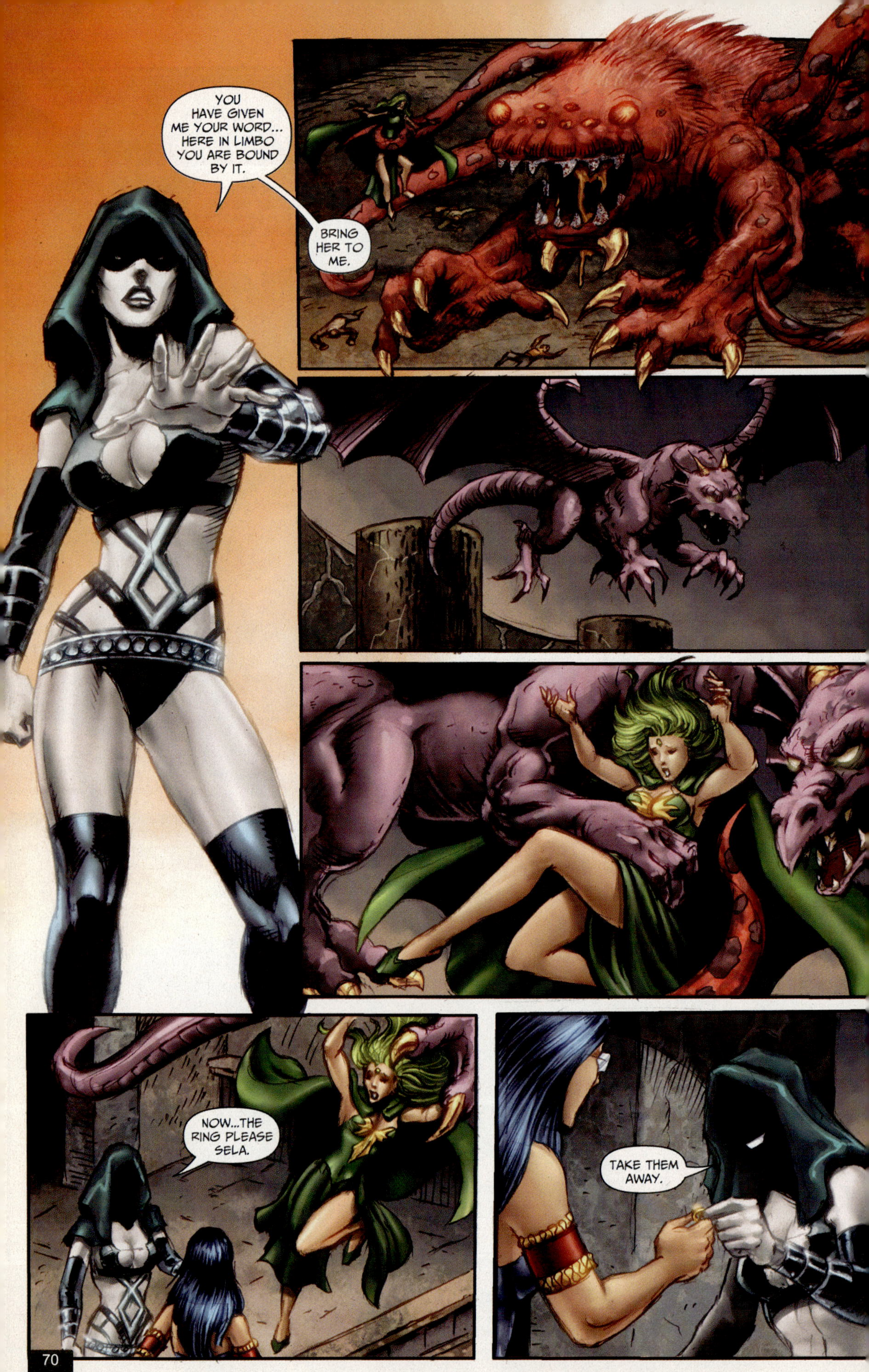
YOU HAVE GIVEN ME YOUR WORD... HERE IN LIMBO YOU ARE BOUND BY IT.
BRING HER TO ME.
NOW...THE RING PLEASE SELA.
TAKE THEM AWAY.

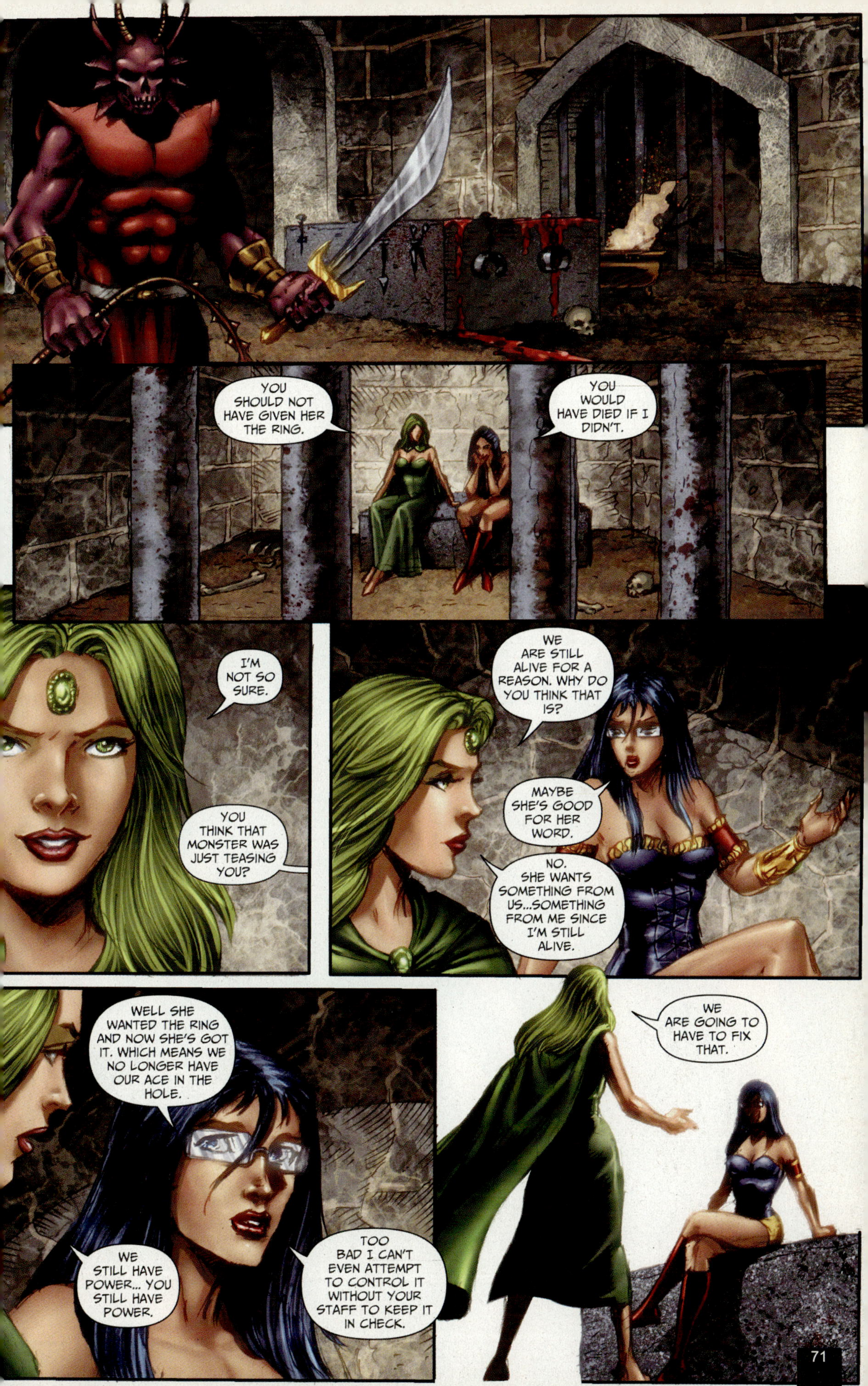
YOU SHOULD NOT HAVE GIVEN HER THE RING.
YOU WOULD HAVE DIED IF I DIDN'T.
I'M NOT SO SURE.
YOU THINK THAT MONSTER WAS JUST TEASING YOU?
WE ARE STILL ALIVE FOR A REASON. WHY DO YOU THINK THAT IS?
MAYBE SHE'S GOOD FOR HER WORD.
NO. SHE WANTS SOMETHING FROM US...SOMETHING FROM ME SINCE I'M STILL ALIVE.
WELL SHE WANTED THE RING AND NOW SHE'S GOT IT. WHICH MEANS WE NO LONGER HAVE OUR ACE IN THE HOLE.
WE STILL HAVE POWER... YOU STILL HAVE POWER.
TOO BAD I CAN'T EVEN ATTEMPT TO CONTROL IT WITHOUT YOUR STAFF TO KEEP IT IN CHECK.
WE ARE GOING TO HAVE TO FIX THAT.

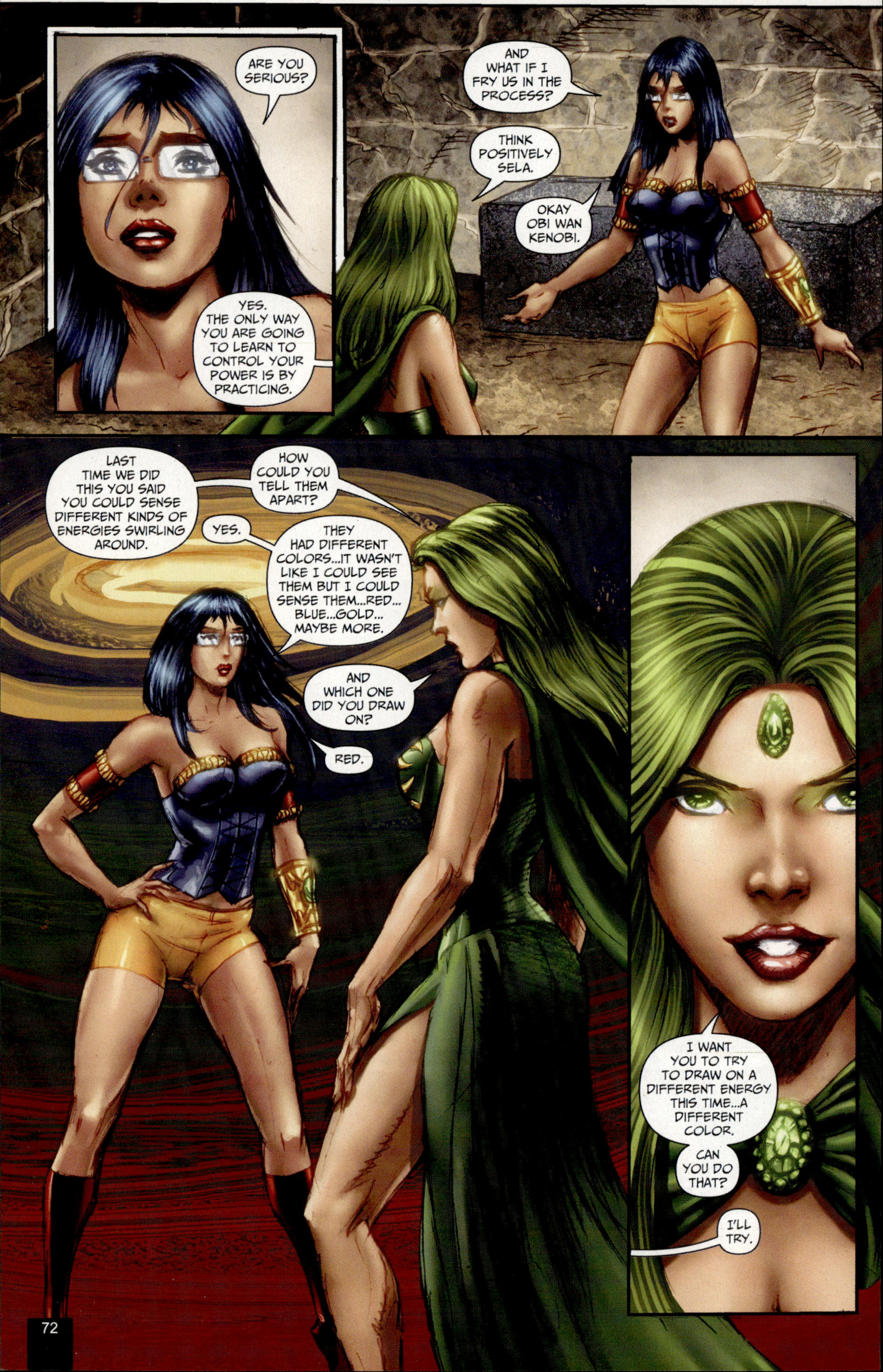
ARE YOU SERIOUS?
YES. THE ONLY WAY YOU ARE GOING TO LEARN TO CONTROL YOUR POWER IS BY PRACTICING.
AND WHAT IF I FRY US IN THE PROCESS?
THINK POSITIVELY SELA.
OKAY OBI WAN KENOBI.
LAST TIME WE DID THIS YOU SAID YOU COULD SENSE DIFFERENT KINDS OF ENERGIES SWIRLING AROUND.
YES.
HOW COULD YOU TELL THEM APART?
THEY HAD DIFFERENT COLORS...IT WASN'T LIKE I COULD SEE THEM BUT I COULD SENSE THEM...RED... BLUE...GOLD... MAYBE MORE.
AND WHICH ONE DID YOU DRAW ON?
RED.
I WANT YOU TO TRY TO DRAW ON A DIFFERENT ENERGY THIS TIME...A DIFFERENT COLOR.
CAN YOU DO THAT?
I'LL TRY.

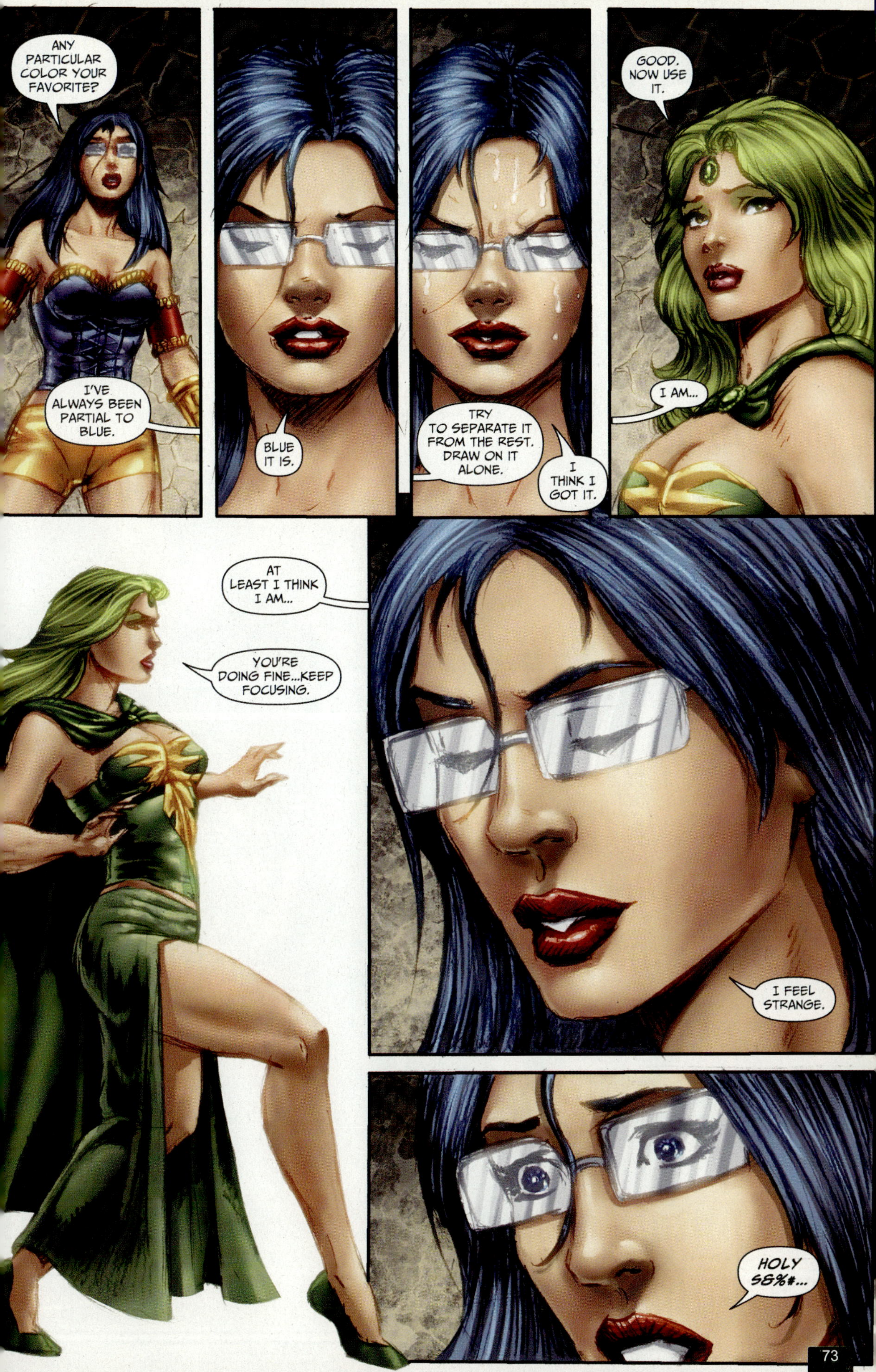
ANY PARTICULAR COLOR YOUR FAVORITE?
I'VE ALWAYS BEEN PARTIAL TO BLUE.
BLUE IT IS.
TRY TO SEPARATE IT FROM THE REST. DRAW ON IT ALONE.
I THINK I GOT IT.
GOOD. NOW USE IT.
I AM...
AT LEAST I THINK I AM...
YOU'RE DOING FINE...KEEP FOCUSING.
I FEEL STRANGE.
HOLY $&%#...

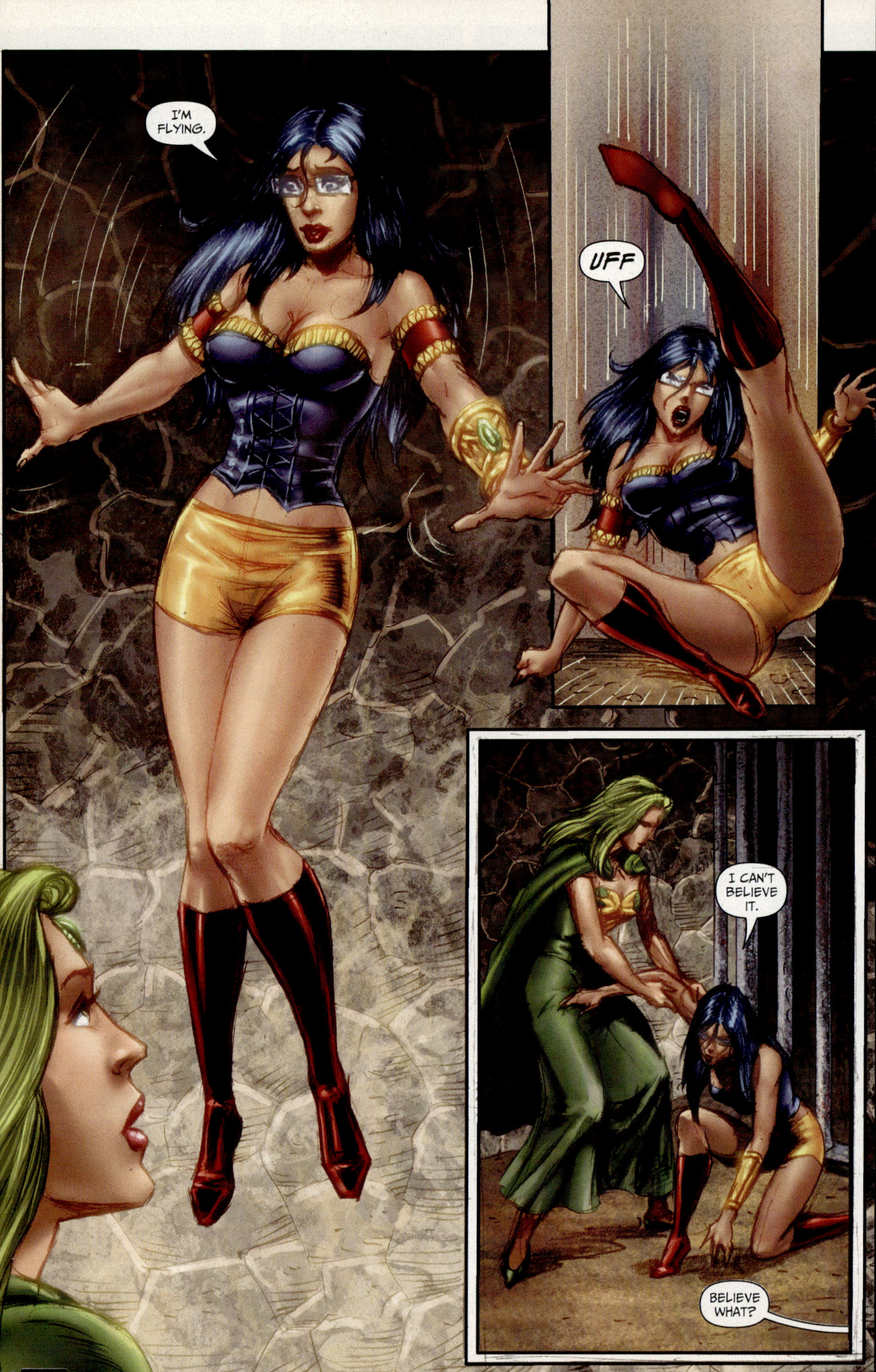
I'M FLYING.
UFF
I CAN'T BELIEVE IT.
BELIEVE WHAT?

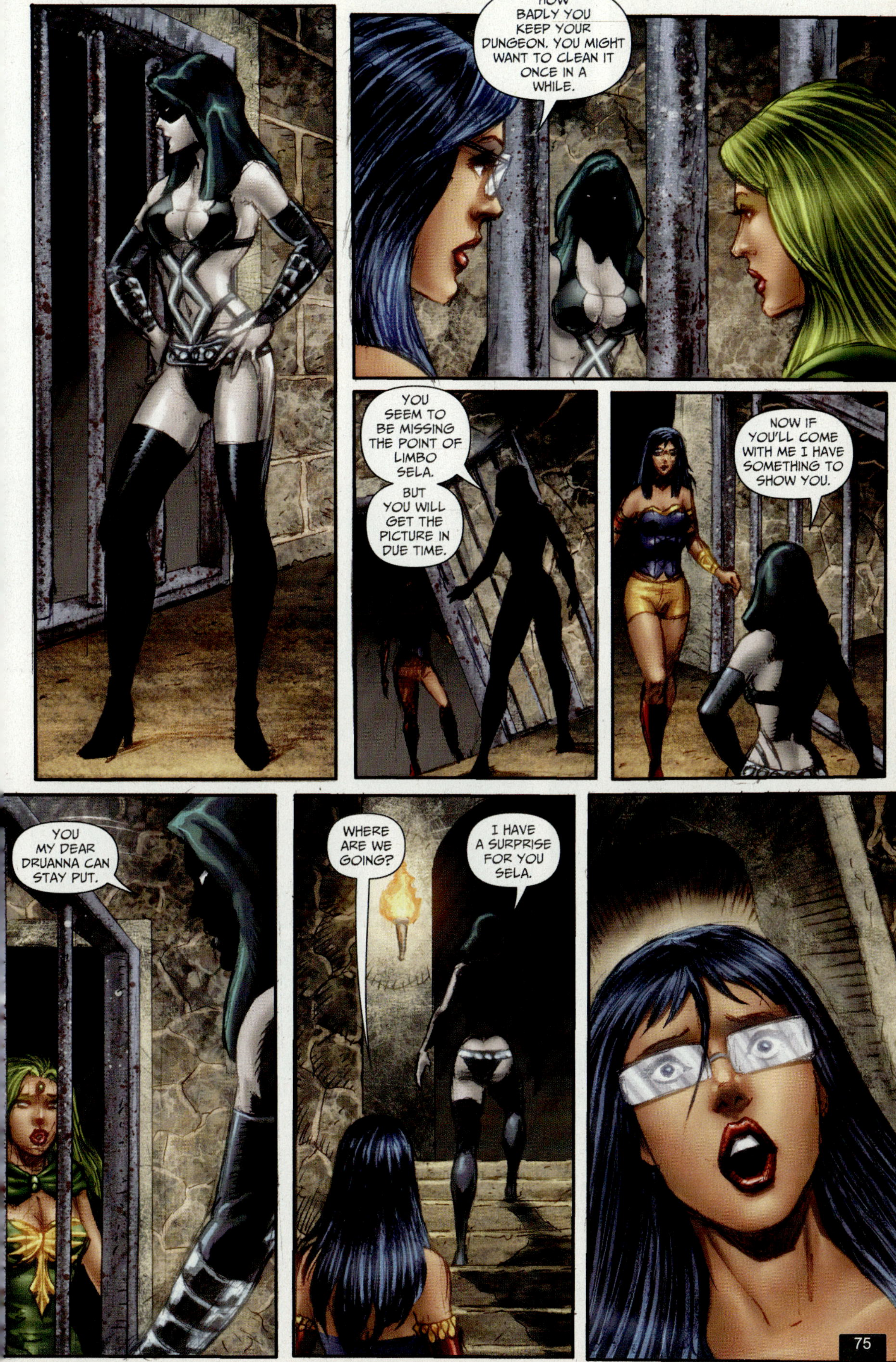
HOW BADLY YOU KEEP YOUR DUNGEON. YOU MIGHT WANT TO CLEAN IT ONCE IN A WHILE.
YOU SEEM TO BE MISSING THE POINT OF LIMBO SELA.
BUT YOU WILL GET THE PICTURE IN DUE TIME.
NOW IF YOU'LL COME WITH ME I HAVE SOMETHING TO SHOW YOU.
YOU MY DEAR DRUANNA CAN STAY PUT.
WHERE ARE WE GOING?
I HAVE A SURPRISE FOR YOU SELA.

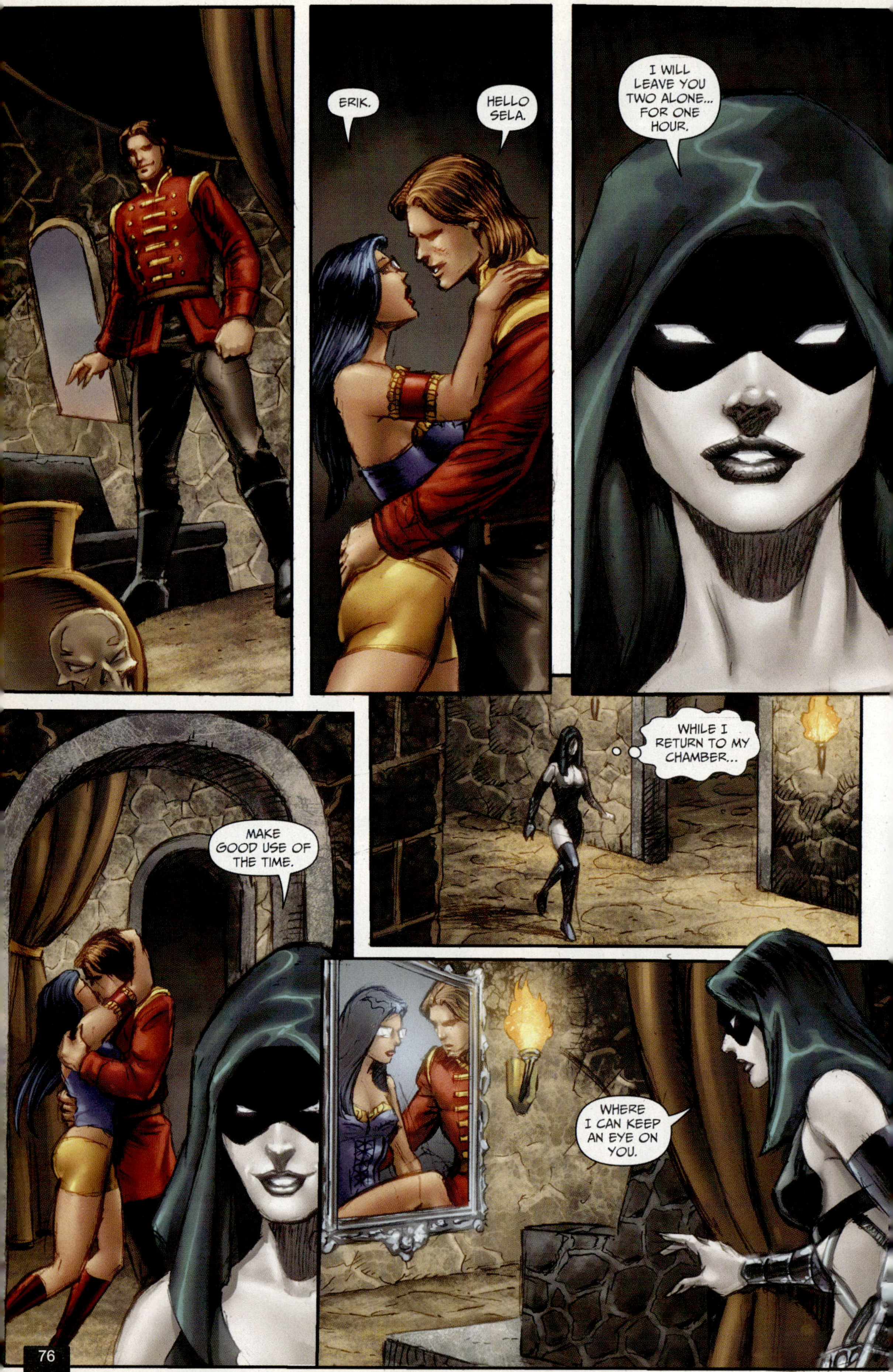
ERIK.
HELLO SELA.
I WILL LEAVE YOU TWO ALONE... FOR ONE HOUR.
MAKE GOOD USE OF THE TIME.
WHILE I RETURN TO MY CHAMBER...
WHERE I CAN KEEP AN EYE ON YOU.

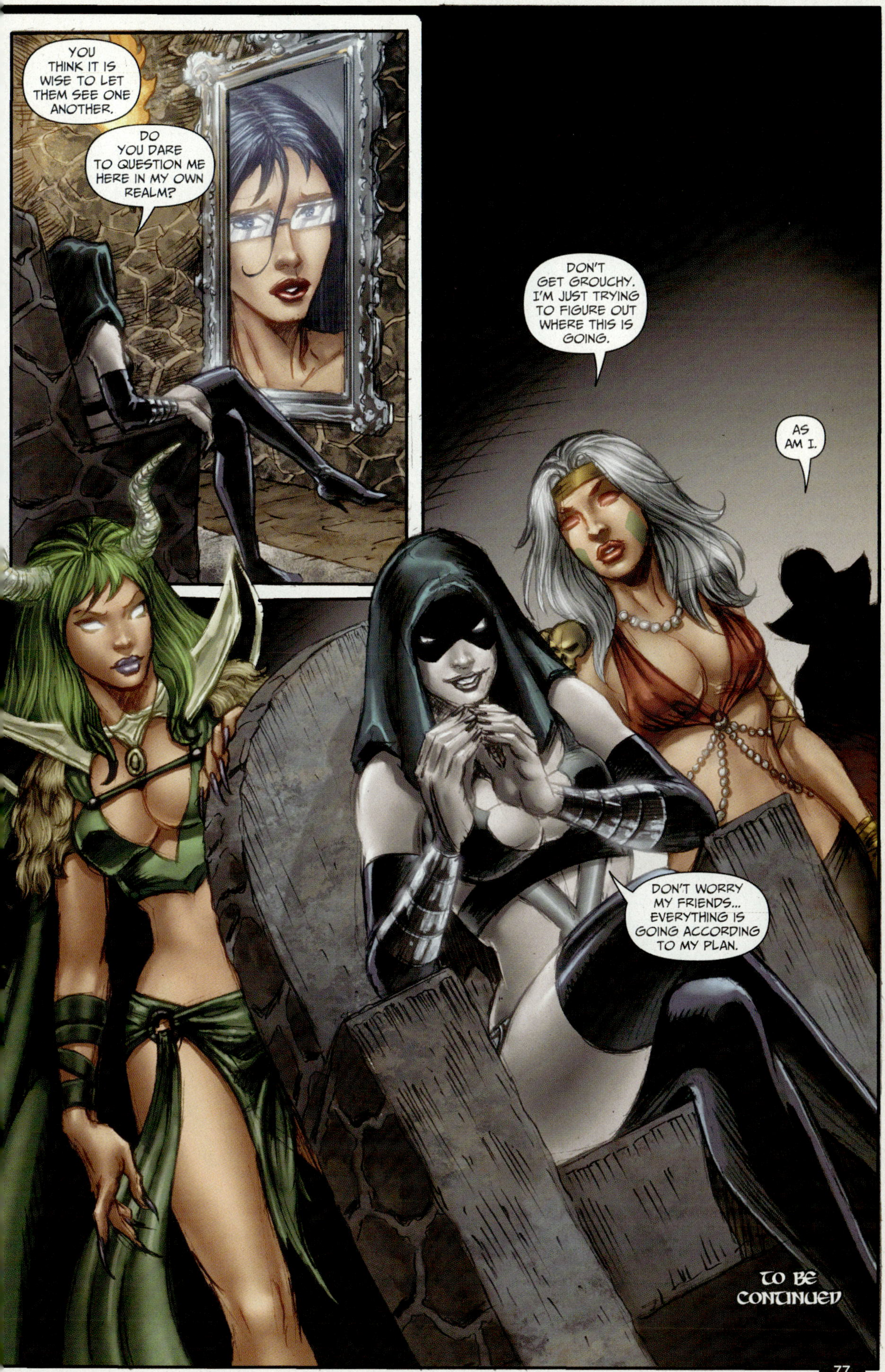
YOU THINK IT IS WISE TO LET THEM SEE ONE ANOTHER.
DO YOU DARE TO QUESTION ME HERE IN MY OWN REALM?
DON'T GET GROUCHY. I'M JUST TRYING TO FIGURE OUT WHERE THIS IS GOING.
AS AM I.
DON'T WORRY MY FRIENDS... EVERYTHING IS GOING ACCORDING TO MY PLAN.
TO BE CONTINUED

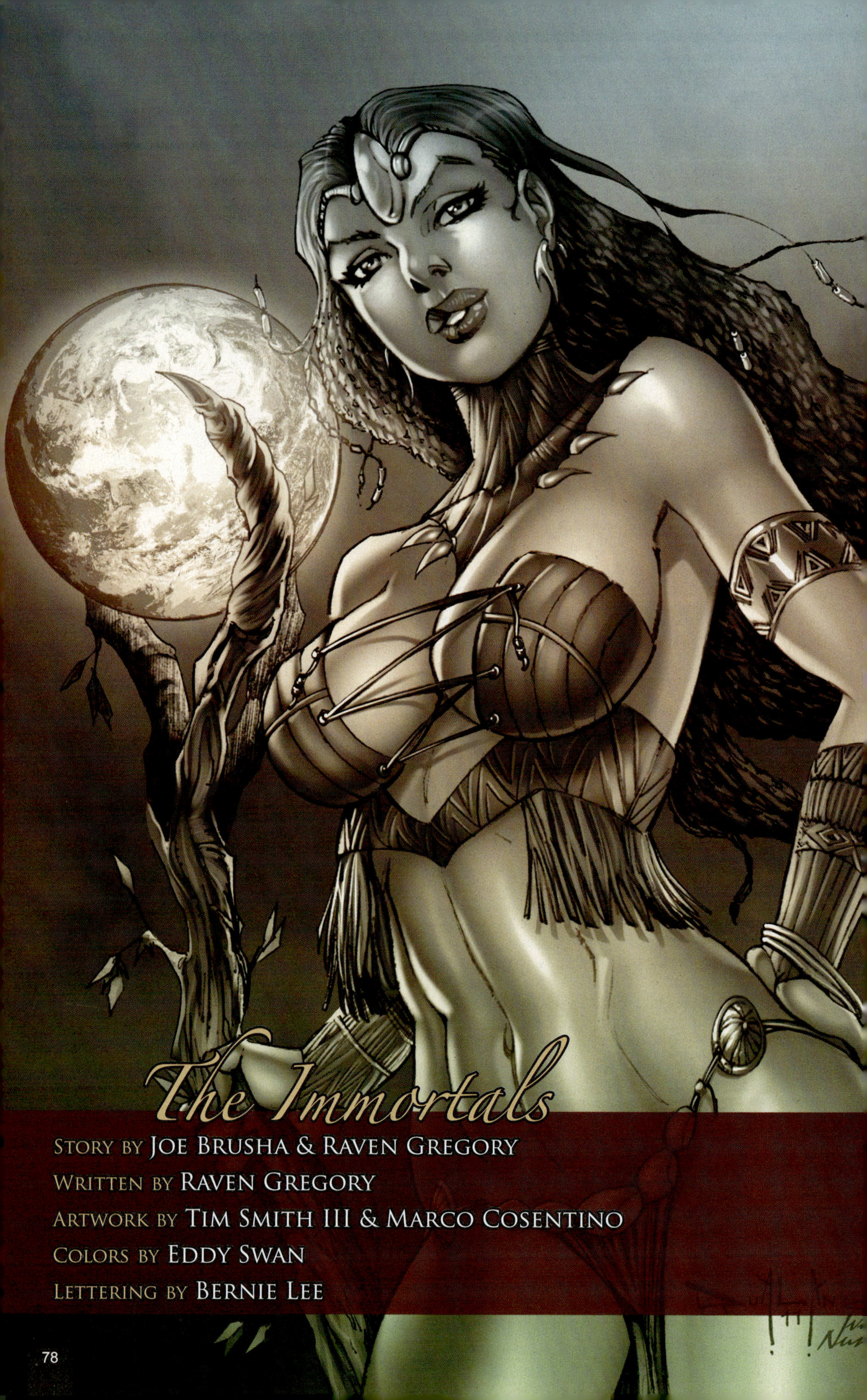

The Immortals

Story by Joe Brusha & Raven Gregory
Written by Raven Gregory
Artwork by Tim Smith III & Marco Cosentino
Colors by Eddy Swan
Lettering by Bernie Lee

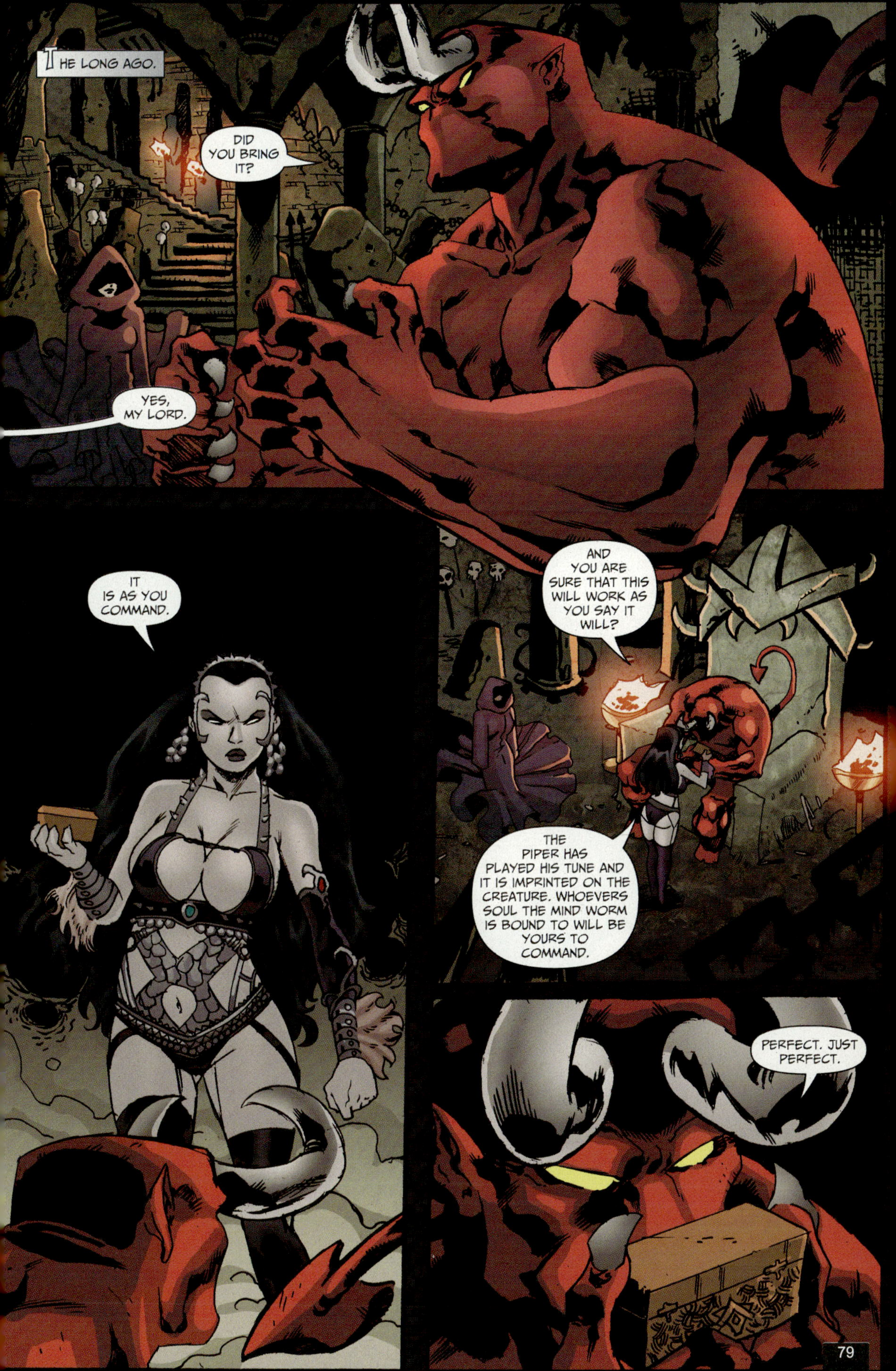
THE LONG AGO.
DID YOU BRING IT?
YES, MY LORD.
IT IS AS YOU COMMAND.
AND YOU ARE SURE THAT THIS WILL WORK AS YOU SAY IT WILL?
THE PIPER HAS PLAYED HIS TUNE AND IT IS IMPRINTED ON THE CREATURE. WHOEVERS SOUL THE MIND WORM IS BOUND TO WILL BE YOURS TO COMMAND.
PERFECT. JUST PERFECT.

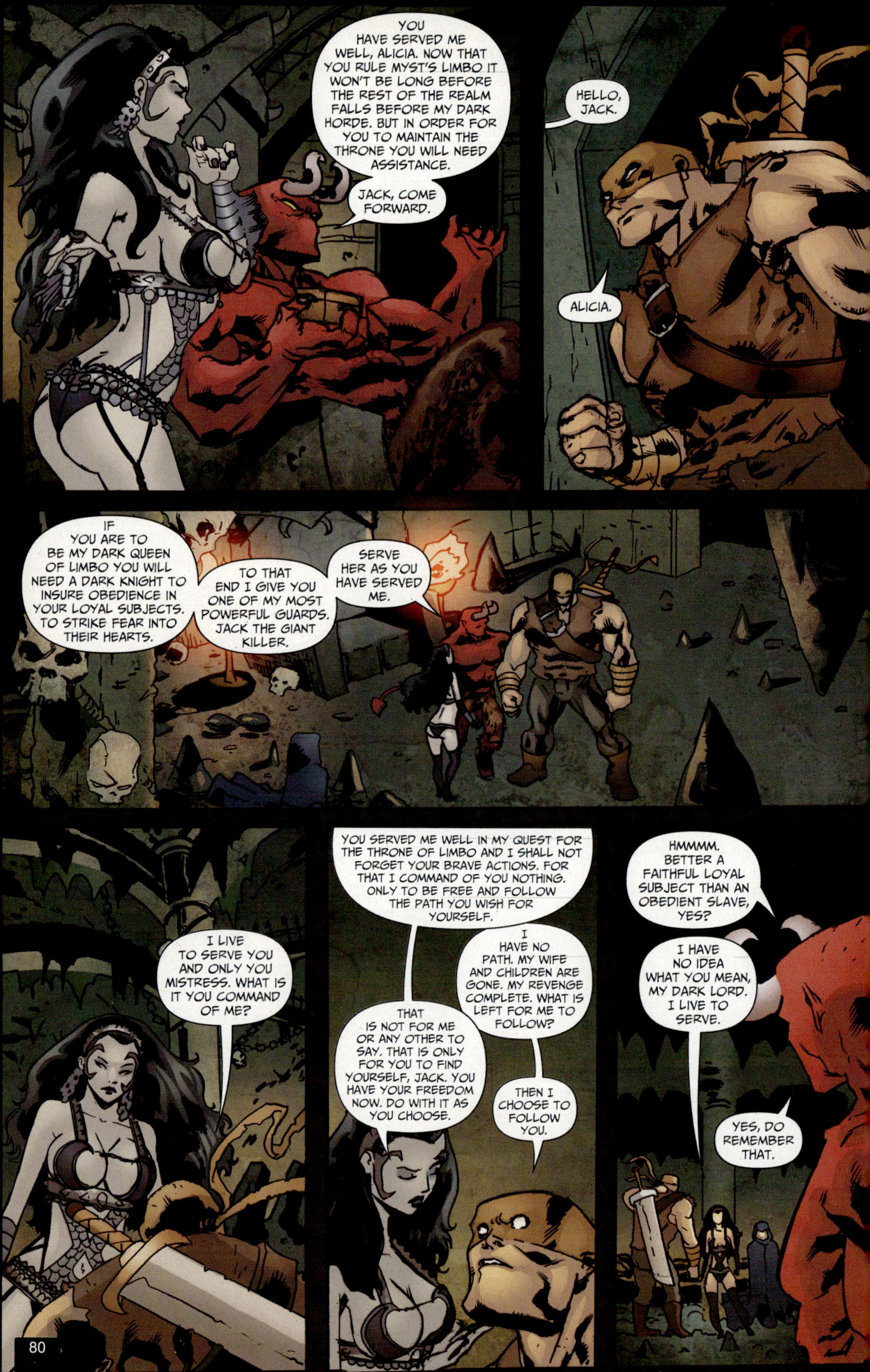
YOU HAVE SERVED ME WELL, ALICIA. NOW THAT YOU RULE MYST'S LIMBO IT WON'T BE LONG BEFORE THE REST OF THE REALM FALLS BEFORE MY DARK HORDE. BUT IN ORDER FOR YOU TO MAINTAIN THE THRONE YOU WILL NEED ASSISTANCE.
JACK, COME FORWARD.
HELLO, JACK.
ALICIA.
IF YOU ARE TO BE MY DARK QUEEN OF LIMBO YOU WILL NEED A DARK KNIGHT TO INSURE OBEDIENCE IN YOUR LOYAL SUBJECTS. TO STRIKE FEAR INTO THEIR HEARTS.
TO THAT END I GIVE YOU ONE OF MY MOST POWERFUL GUARDS. JACK THE GIANT KILLER.
SERVE HER AS YOU HAVE SERVED ME.
I LIVE TO SERVE YOU AND ONLY YOU MISTRESS. WHAT IS IT YOU COMMAND OF ME?
YOU SERVED ME WELL IN MY QUEST FOR THE THRONE OF LIMBO AND I SHALL NOT FORGET YOUR BRAVE ACTIONS. FOR THAT I COMMAND OF YOU NOTHING. ONLY TO BE FREE AND FOLLOW THE PATH YOU WISH FOR YOURSELF.
I HAVE NO PATH. MY WIFE AND CHILDREN ARE GONE. MY REVENGE COMPLETE. WHAT IS LEFT FOR ME TO FOLLOW?
THAT IS NOT FOR ME OR ANY OTHER TO SAY. THAT IS ONLY FOR YOU TO FIND YOURSELF, JACK. YOU HAVE YOUR FREEDOM NOW. DO WITH IT AS YOU CHOOSE.
THEN I CHOOSE TO FOLLOW YOU.
HMMMM. BETTER A FAITHFUL LOYAL SUBJECT THAN AN OBEDIENT SLAVE, YES?
I HAVE NO IDEA WHAT YOU MEAN, MY DARK LORD. I LIVE TO SERVE.
YES, DO REMEMBER THAT.

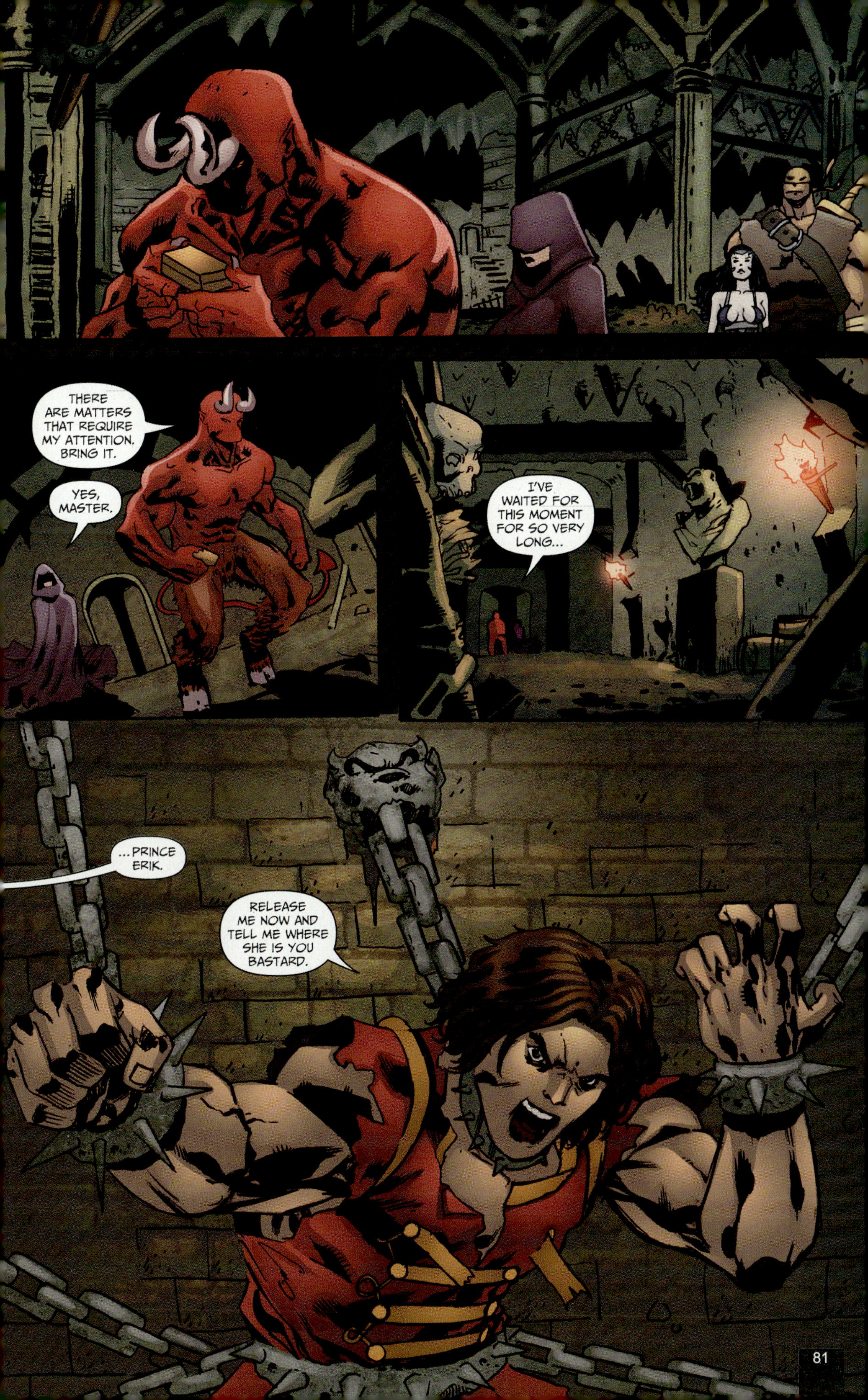
THERE ARE MATTERS THAT REQUIRE MY ATTENTION. BRING IT.
YES, MASTER.
I'VE WAITED FOR THIS MOMENT FOR SO VERY LONG...
...PRINCE ERIK.
RELEASE ME NOW AND TELL ME WHERE SHE IS YOU BASTARD.

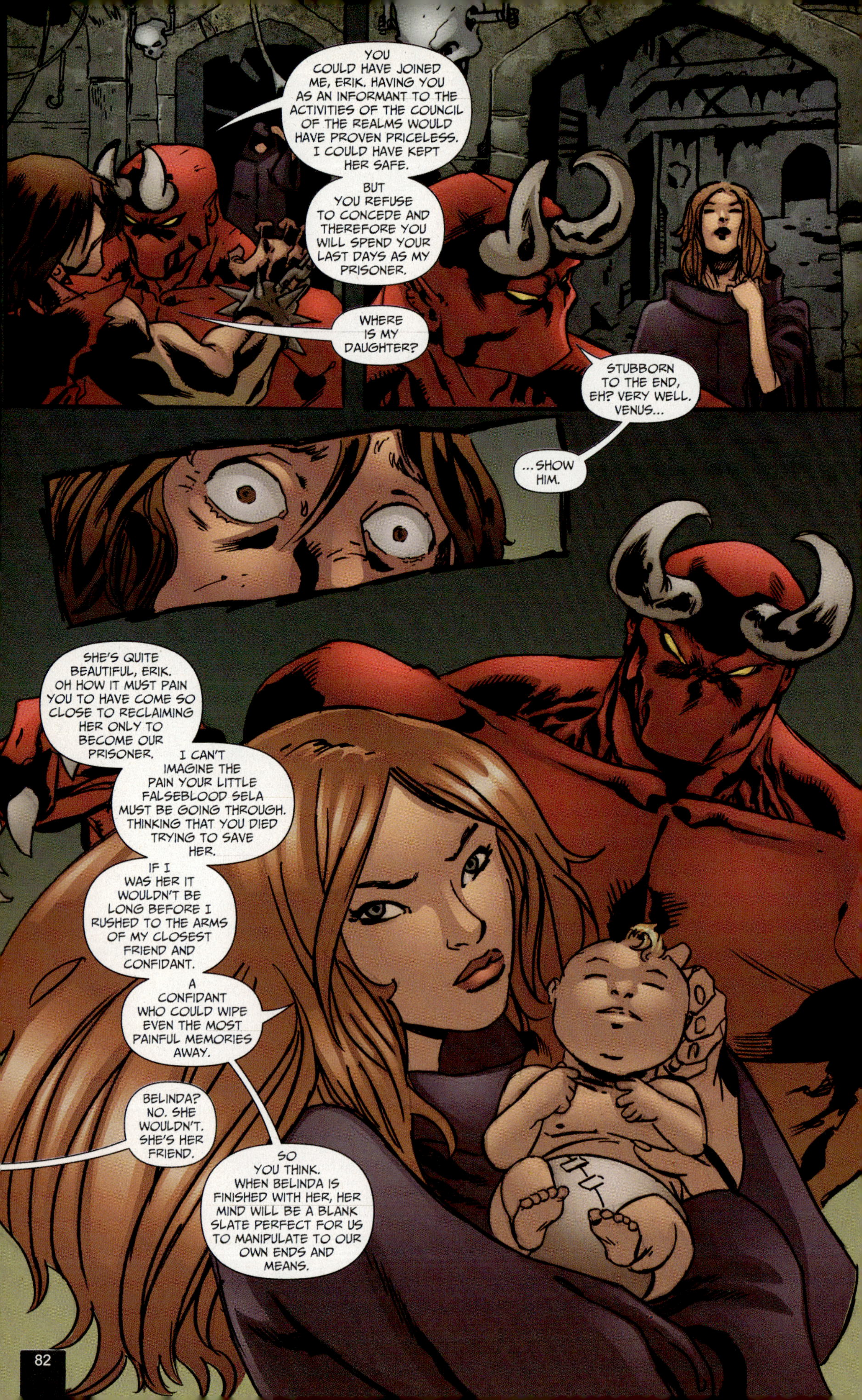
YOU COULD HAVE JOINED ME, ERIK. HAVING YOU AS AN INFORMANT TO THE ACTIVITIES OF THE COUNCIL OF THE REALMS WOULD HAVE PROVEN PRICELESS. I COULD HAVE KEPT HER SAFE.
BUT YOU REFUSE TO CONCEDE AND THEREFORE YOU WILL SPEND YOUR LAST DAYS AS MY PRISONER.
WHERE IS MY DAUGHTER?
STUBBORN TO THE END, EH? VERY WELL. VENUS...
...SHOW HIM.
SHE'S QUITE BEAUTIFUL, ERIK. OH HOW IT MUST PAIN YOU TO HAVE COME SO CLOSE TO RECLAIMING HER ONLY TO BECOME OUR PRISONER.
I CAN'T IMAGINE THE PAIN YOUR LITTLE FALSEBLOOD SELA MUST BE GOING THROUGH. THINKING THAT YOU DIED TRYING TO SAVE HER.
IF I WAS HER IT WOULDN'T BE LONG BEFORE I RUSHED TO THE ARMS OF MY CLOSEST FRIEND AND CONFIDANT.
A CONFIDANT WHO COULD WIPE EVEN THE MOST PAINFUL MEMORIES AWAY.
BELINDA? NO. SHE WOULDN'T. SHE'S HER FRIEND.
SO YOU THINK. WHEN BELINDA IS FINISHED WITH HER, HER MIND WILL BE A BLANK SLATE PERFECT FOR US TO MANIPULATE TO OUR OWN ENDS AND MEANS.

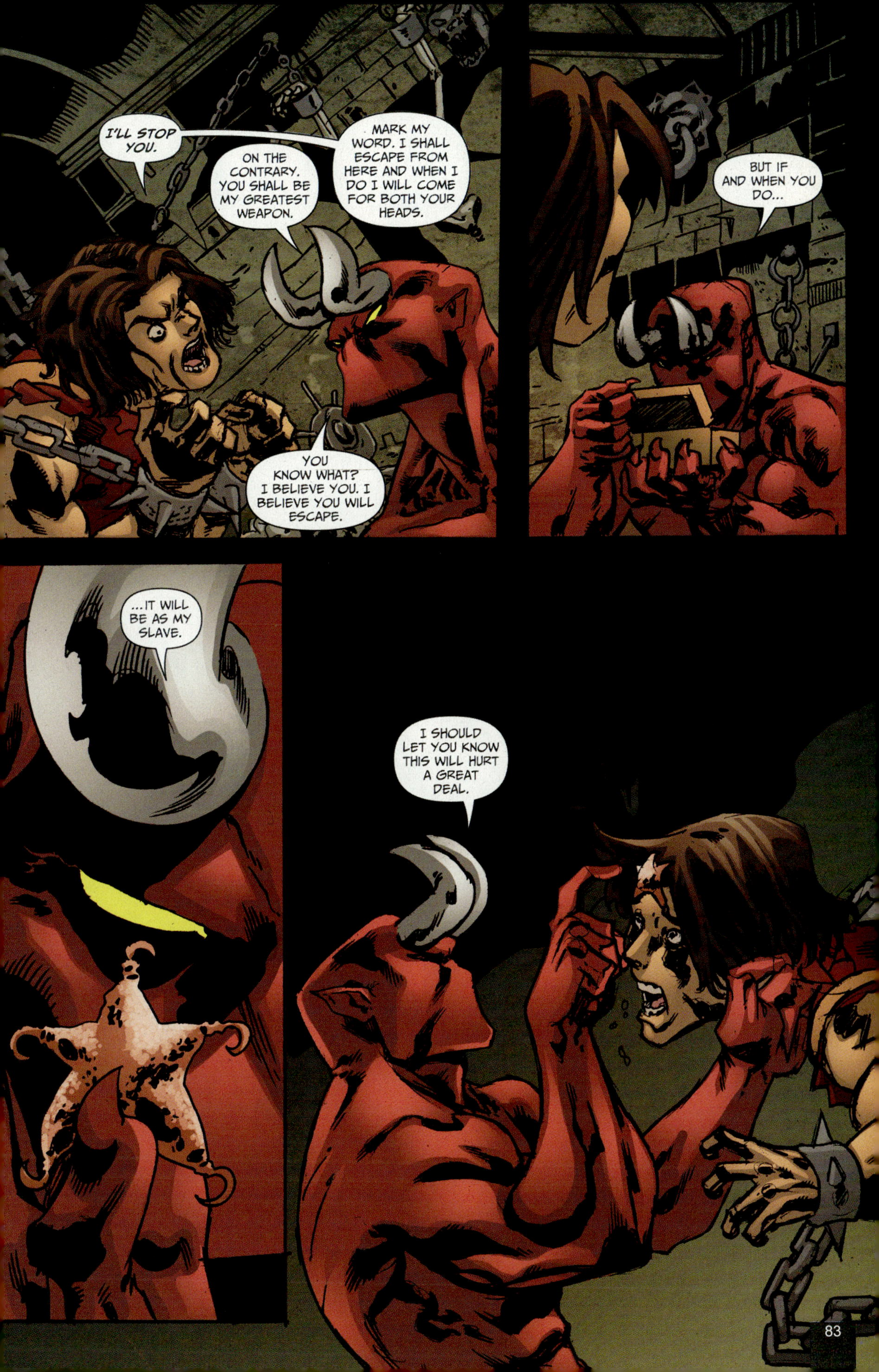
I'LL STOP YOU.
ON THE CONTRARY. YOU SHALL BE MY GREATEST WEAPON.
MARK MY WORD. I SHALL ESCAPE FROM HERE AND WHEN I DO I WILL COME FOR BOTH YOUR HEADS.
YOU KNOW WHAT? I BELIEVE YOU. I BELIEVE YOU WILL ESCAPE.
BUT IF AND WHEN YOU DO...
...IT WILL BE AS MY SLAVE.
I SHOULD LET YOU KNOW THIS WILL HURT A GREAT DEAL.

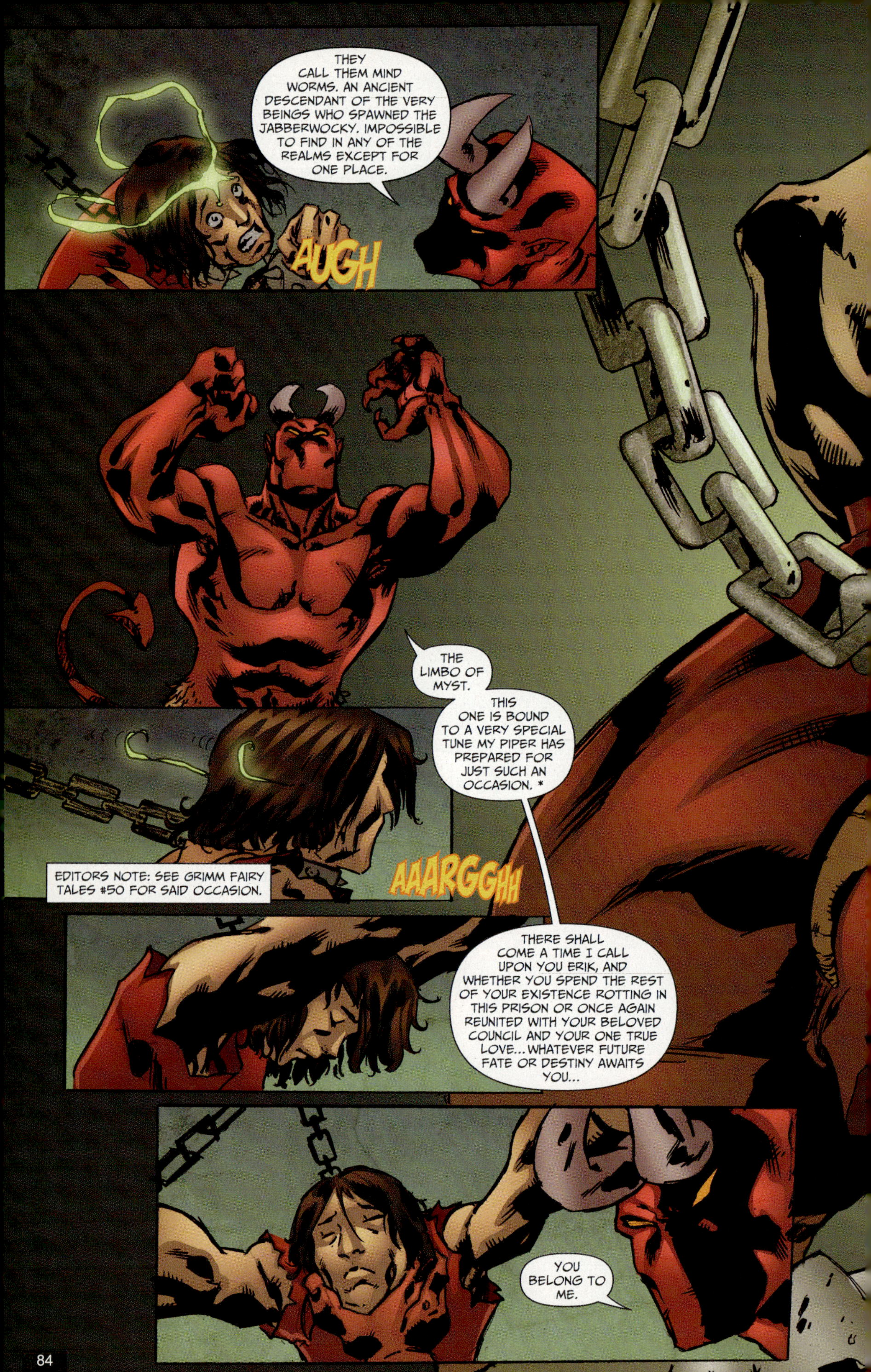
THEY CALL THEM MIND WORMS. AN ANCIENT DESCENDANT OF THE VERY BEINGS WHO SPAWNED THE JABBERWOCKY. IMPOSSIBLE TO FIND IN ANY OF THE REALMS EXCEPT FOR ONE PLACE.
AUGH
THE LIMBO OF MYST.
THIS ONE IS BOUND TO A VERY SPECIAL TUNE MY PIPER HAS PREPARED FOR JUST SUCH AN OCCASION. *
AAARGGHH
EDITORS NOTE: SEE GRIMM FAIRY TALES #50 FOR SAID OCCASION.
THERE SHALL COME A TIME I CALL UPON YOU ERIK, AND WHETHER YOU SPEND THE REST OF YOUR EXISTENCE ROTTING IN THIS PRISON OR ONCE AGAIN REUNITED WITH YOUR BELOVED COUNCIL AND YOUR ONE TRUE LOVE...WHATEVER FUTURE FATE OR DESTINY AWAITS YOU...
YOU BELONG TO ME.

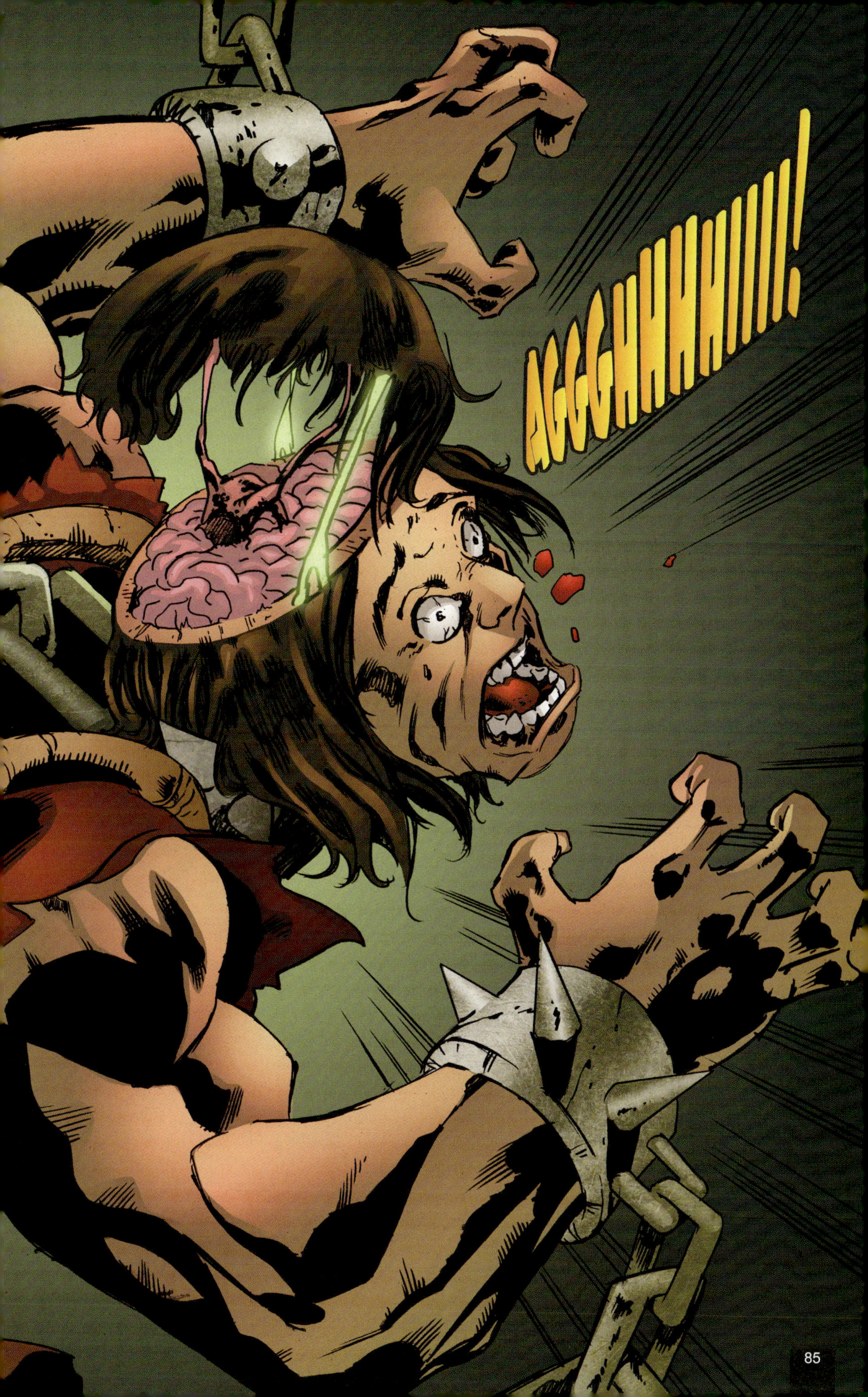
AGGGHHHHIIII!

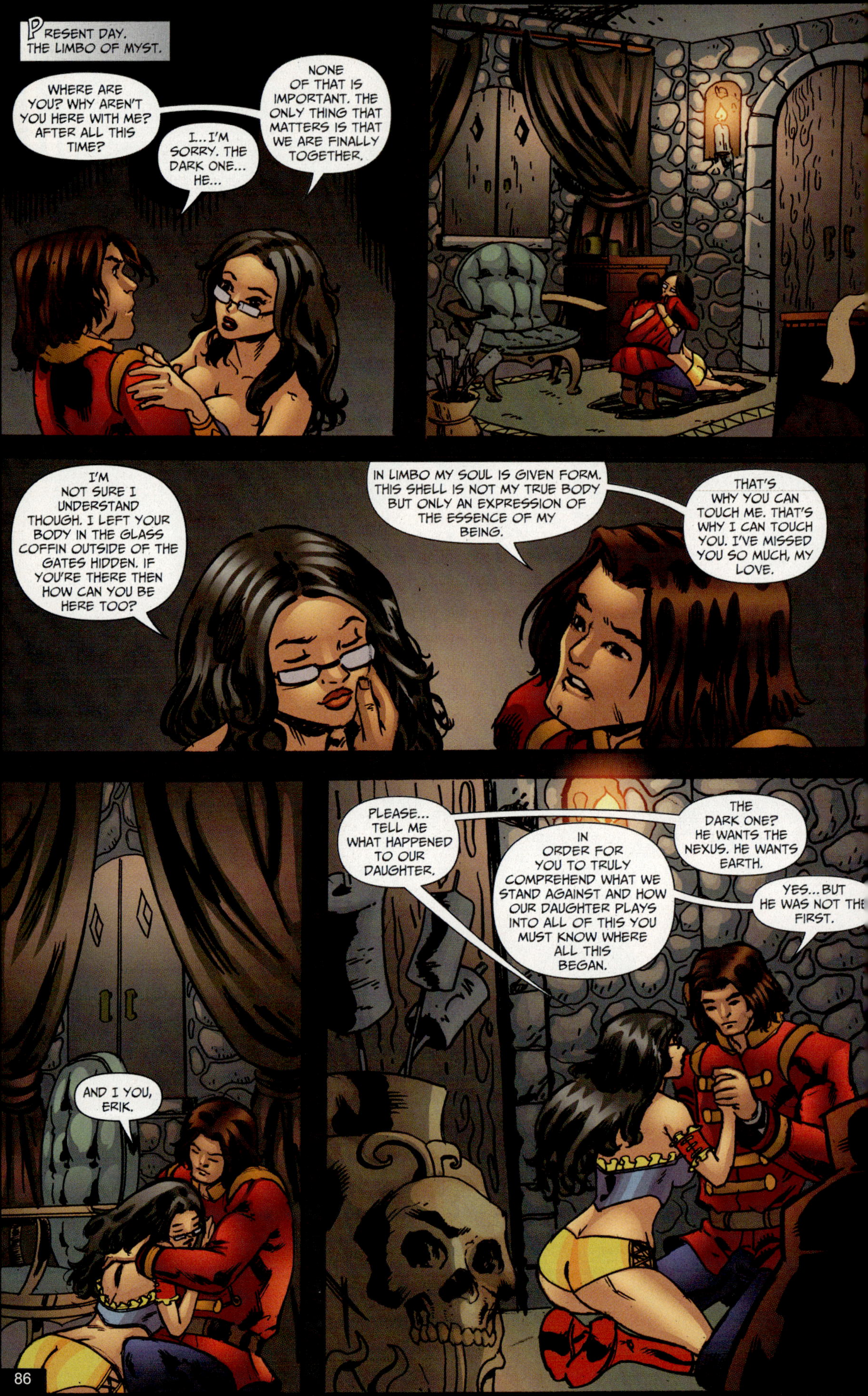
PRESENT DAY. THE LIMBO OF MYST.
WHERE ARE YOU? WHY AREN'T YOU HERE WITH ME? AFTER ALL THIS TIME?
I...I'M SORRY. THE DARK ONE... HE...
NONE OF THAT IS IMPORTANT. THE ONLY THING THAT MATTERS IS THAT WE ARE FINALLY TOGETHER.
I'M NOT SURE I UNDERSTAND THOUGH. I LEFT YOUR BODY IN THE GLASS COFFIN OUTSIDE OF THE GATES HIDDEN. IF YOU'RE THERE THEN HOW CAN YOU BE HERE TOO?
IN LIMBO MY SOUL IS GIVEN FORM. THIS SHELL IS NOT MY TRUE BODY BUT ONLY AN EXPRESSION OF THE ESSENCE OF MY BEING.
THAT'S WHY YOU CAN TOUCH ME. THAT'S WHY I CAN TOUCH YOU. I'VE MISSED YOU SO MUCH, MY LOVE.
AND I YOU, ERIK.
PLEASE... TELL ME WHAT HAPPENED TO OUR DAUGHTER.
THE DARK ONE? HE WANTS THE NEXUS. HE WANTS EARTH.
IN ORDER FOR YOU TO TRULY COMPREHEND WHAT WE STAND AGAINST AND HOW OUR DAUGHTER PLAYS INTO ALL OF THIS YOU MUST KNOW WHERE ALL THIS BEGAN.
YES...BUT HE WAS NOT THE FIRST.

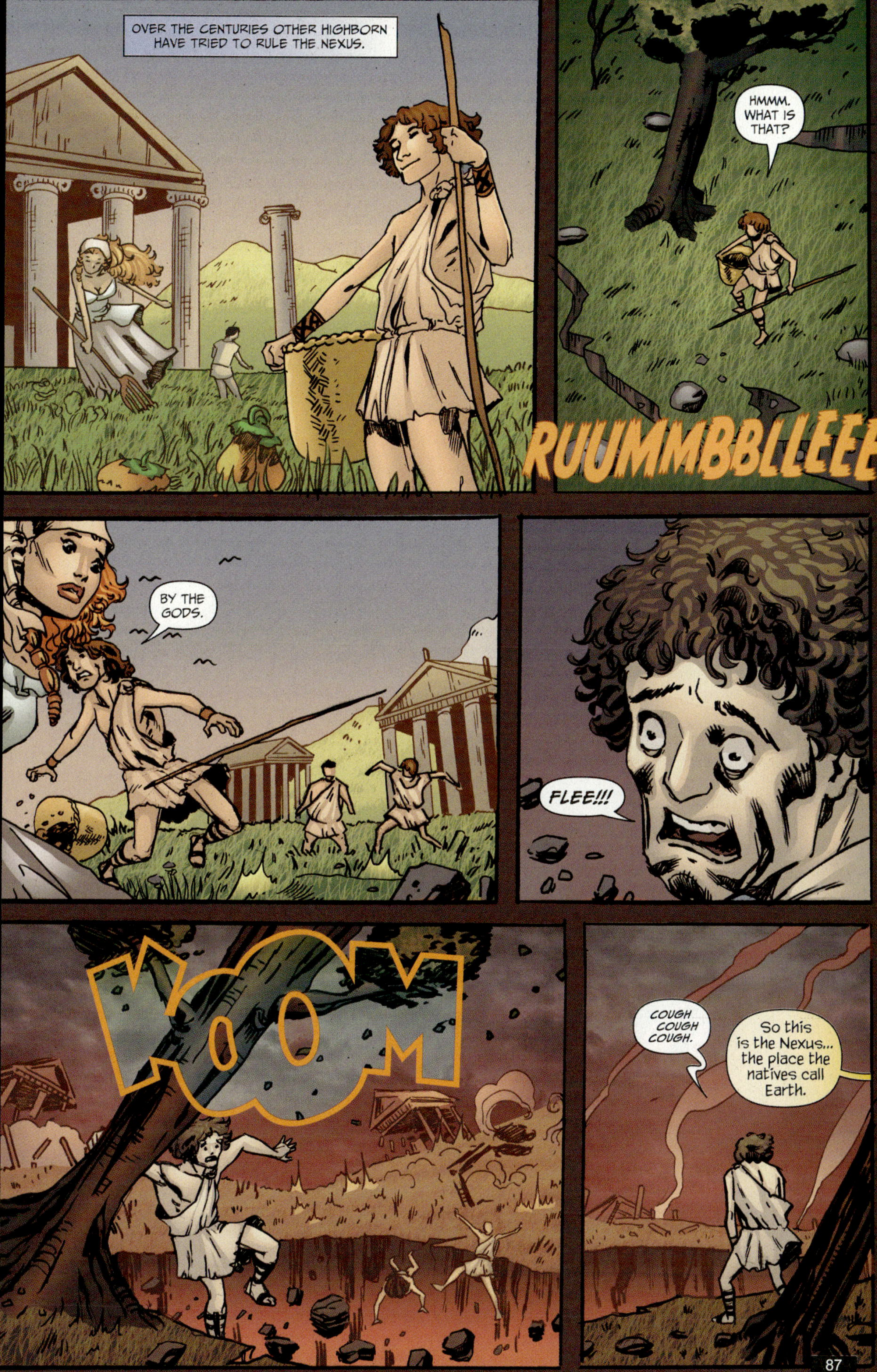
OVER THE CENTURIES OTHER HIGHBORN HAVE TRIED TO RULE THE NEXUS.
HMMM. WHAT IS THAT?
RUUMMBBLLEEE
BY THE GODS.
FLEE!!!
KOOM
COUGH COUGH COUGH.
So this is the Nexus... the place the natives call Earth.

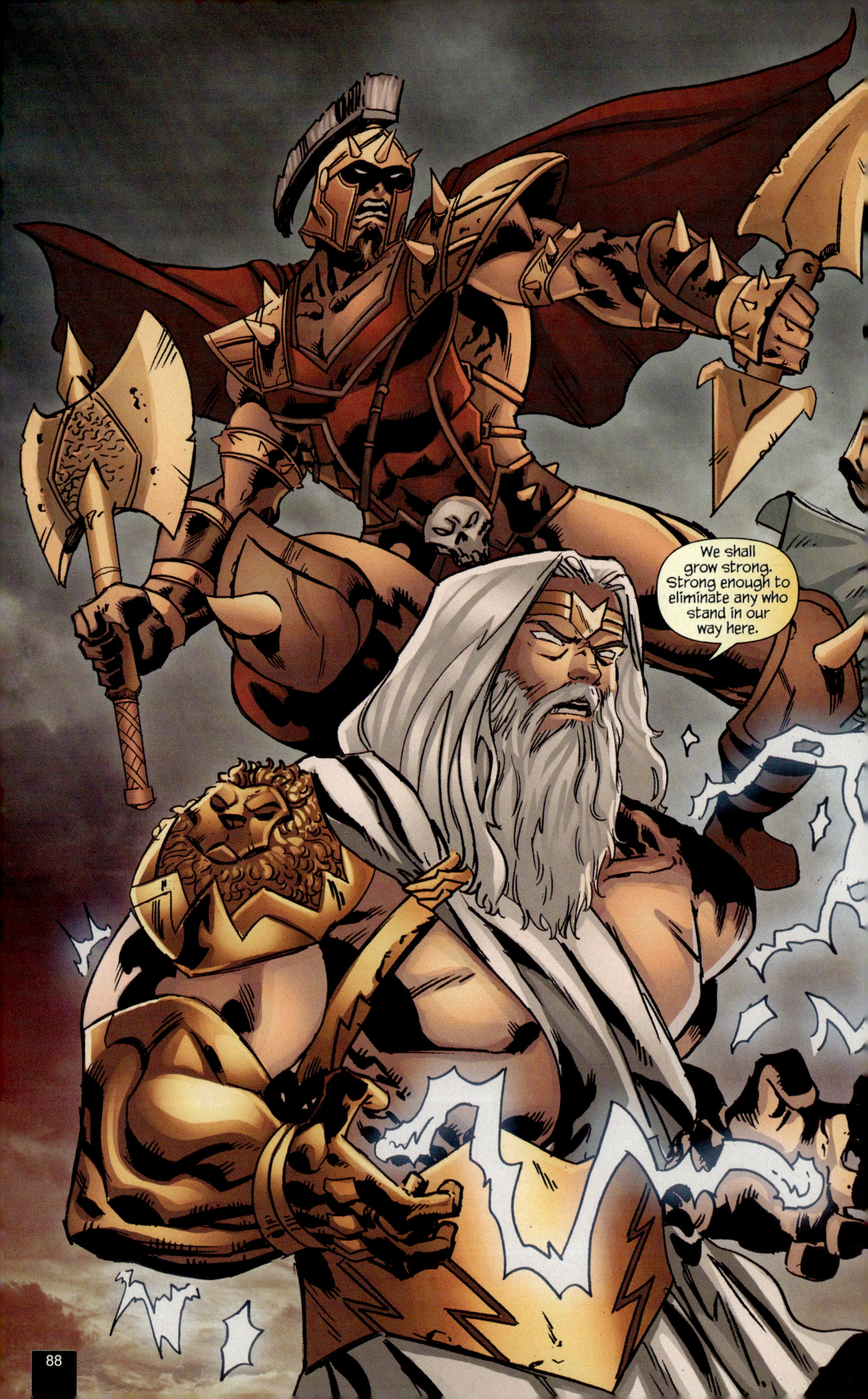
We shall grow strong. Strong enough to eliminate any who stand in our way here.

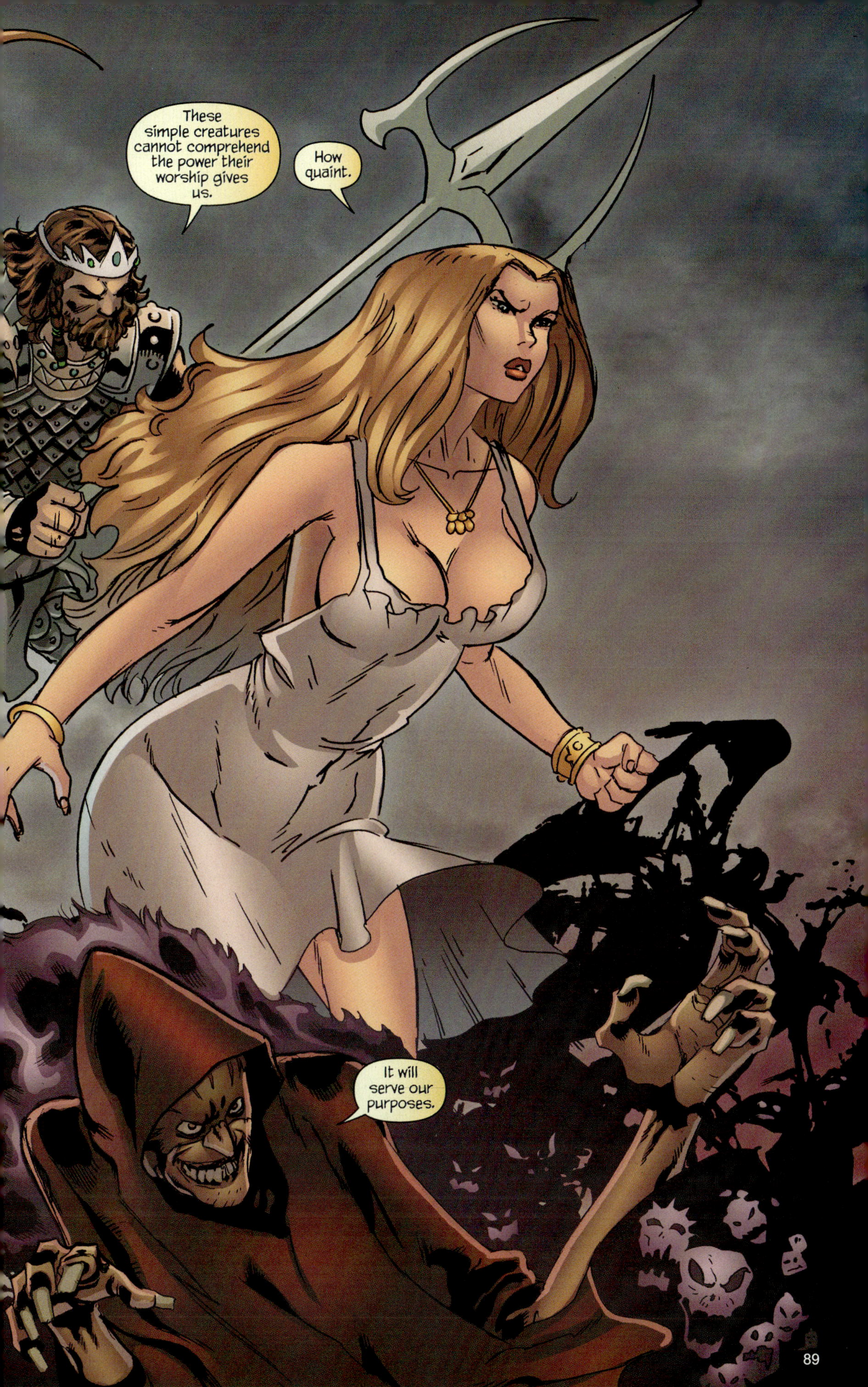

These simple creatures cannot comprehend the power their worship gives us.
How quaint.
It will serve our purposes.

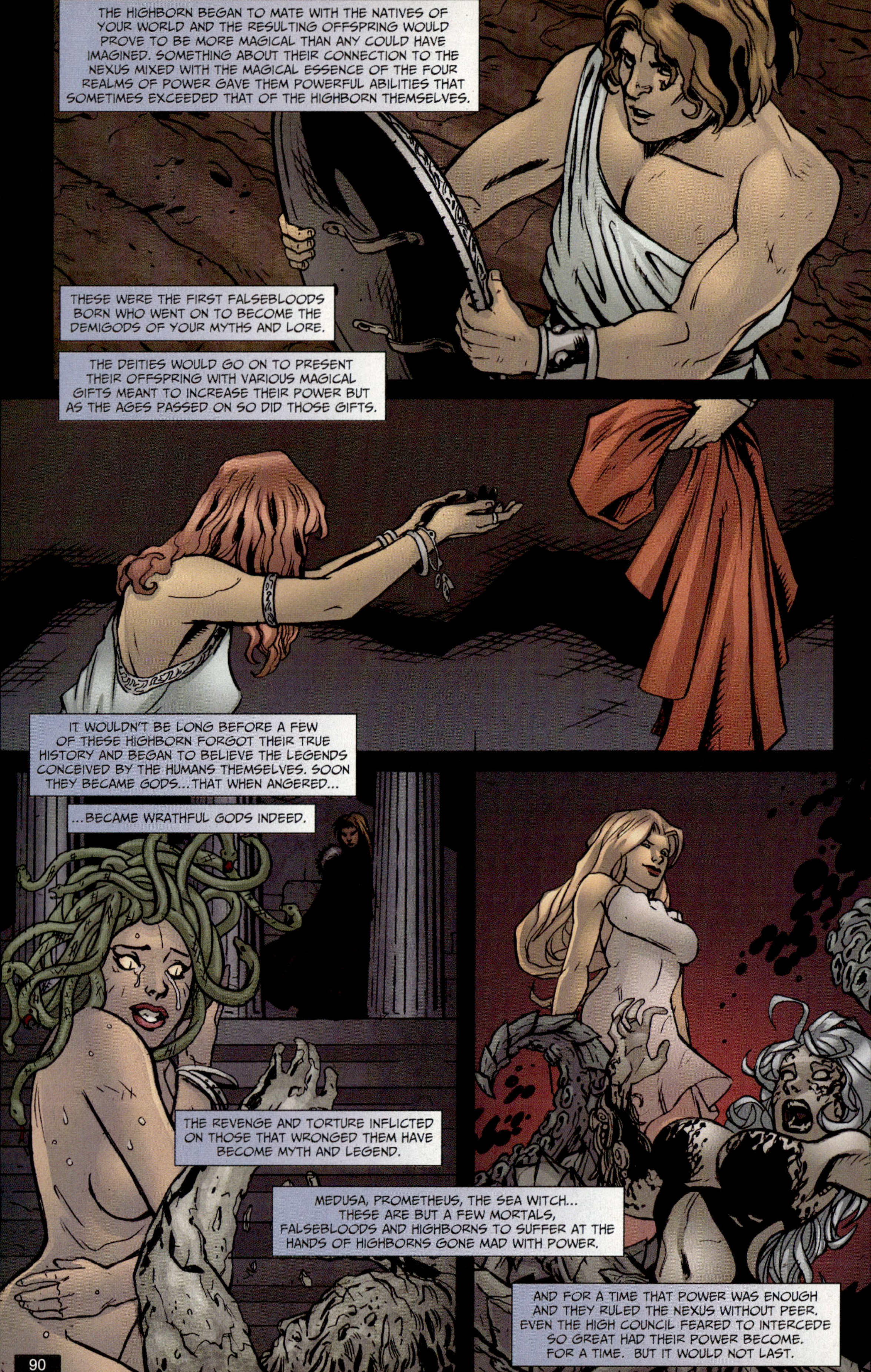
THE HIGHBORN BEGAN TO MATE WITH THE NATIVES OF YOUR WORLD AND THE RESULTING OFFSPRING WOULD PROVE TO BE MORE MAGICAL THAN ANY COULD HAVE IMAGINED. SOMETHING ABOUT THEIR CONNECTION TO THE NEXUS MIXED WITH THE MAGICAL ESSENCE OF THE FOUR REALMS OF POWER GAVE THEM POWERFUL ABILITIES THAT SOMETIMES EXCEEDED THAT OF THE HIGHBORN THEMSELVES.
THESE WERE THE FIRST FALSEBLOODS BORN WHO WENT ON TO BECOME THE DEMIGODS OF YOUR MYTHS AND LORE.
THE DEITIES WOULD GO ON TO PRESENT THEIR OFFSPRING WITH VARIOUS MAGICAL GIFTS MEANT TO INCREASE THEIR POWER BUT AS THE AGES PASSED ON SO DID THOSE GIFTS.
IT WOULDN'T BE LONG BEFORE A FEW OF THESE HIGHBORN FORGOT THEIR TRUE HISTORY AND BEGAN TO BELIEVE THE LEGENDS CONCEIVED BY THE HUMANS THEMSELVES. SOON THEY BECAME GODS...THAT WHEN ANGERED...
...BECAME WRATHFUL GODS INDEED.
THE REVENGE AND TORTURE INFLICTED ON THOSE THAT WRONGED THEM HAVE BECOME MYTH AND LEGEND.
MEDUSA, PROMETHEUS, THE SEA WITCH... THESE ARE BUT A FEW MORTALS, FALSEBLOODS AND HIGHBORNS TO SUFFER AT THE HANDS OF HIGHBORNS GONE MAD WITH POWER.
AND FOR A TIME THAT POWER WAS ENOUGH AND THEY RULED THE NEXUS WITHOUT PEER. EVEN THE HIGH COUNCIL FEARED TO INTERCEDE SO GREAT HAD THEIR POWER BECOME. FOR A TIME. BUT IT WOULD NOT LAST.

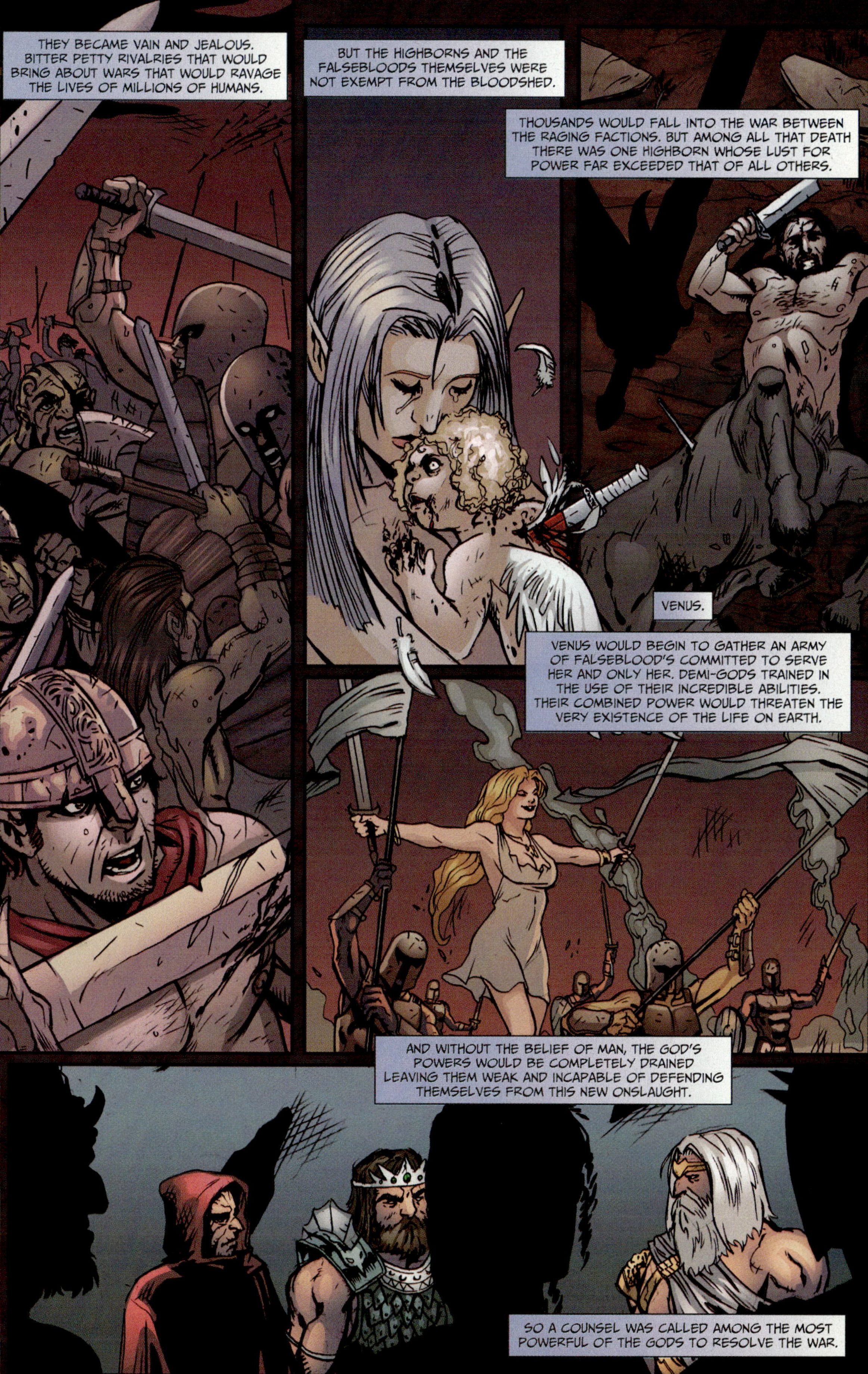
THEY BECAME VAIN AND JEALOUS. BITTER PETTY RIVALRIES THAT WOULD BRING ABOUT WARS THAT WOULD RAVAGE THE LIVES OF MILLIONS OF HUMANS.
BUT THE HIGHBORNS AND THE FALSEBLOODS THEMSELVES WERE NOT EXEMPT FROM THE BLOODSHED.
THOUSANDS WOULD FALL INTO THE WAR BETWEEN THE RAGING FACTIONS. BUT AMONG ALL THAT DEATH THERE WAS ONE HIGHBORN WHOSE LUST FOR POWER FAR EXCEEDED THAT OF ALL OTHERS.
VENUS.
VENUS WOULD BEGIN TO GATHER AN ARMY OF FALSEBLOOD'S COMMITTED TO SERVE HER AND ONLY HER. DEMI-GODS TRAINED IN THE USE OF THEIR INCREDIBLE ABILITIES. THEIR COMBINED POWER WOULD THREATEN THE VERY EXISTENCE OF THE LIFE ON EARTH.
AND WITHOUT THE BELIEF OF MAN, THE GOD'S POWERS WOULD BE COMPLETELY DRAINED LEAVING THEM WEAK AND INCAPABLE OF DEFENDING THEMSELVES FROM THIS NEW ONSLAUGHT.
SO A COUNSEL WAS CALLED AMONG THE MOST POWERFUL OF THE GODS TO RESOLVE THE WAR.

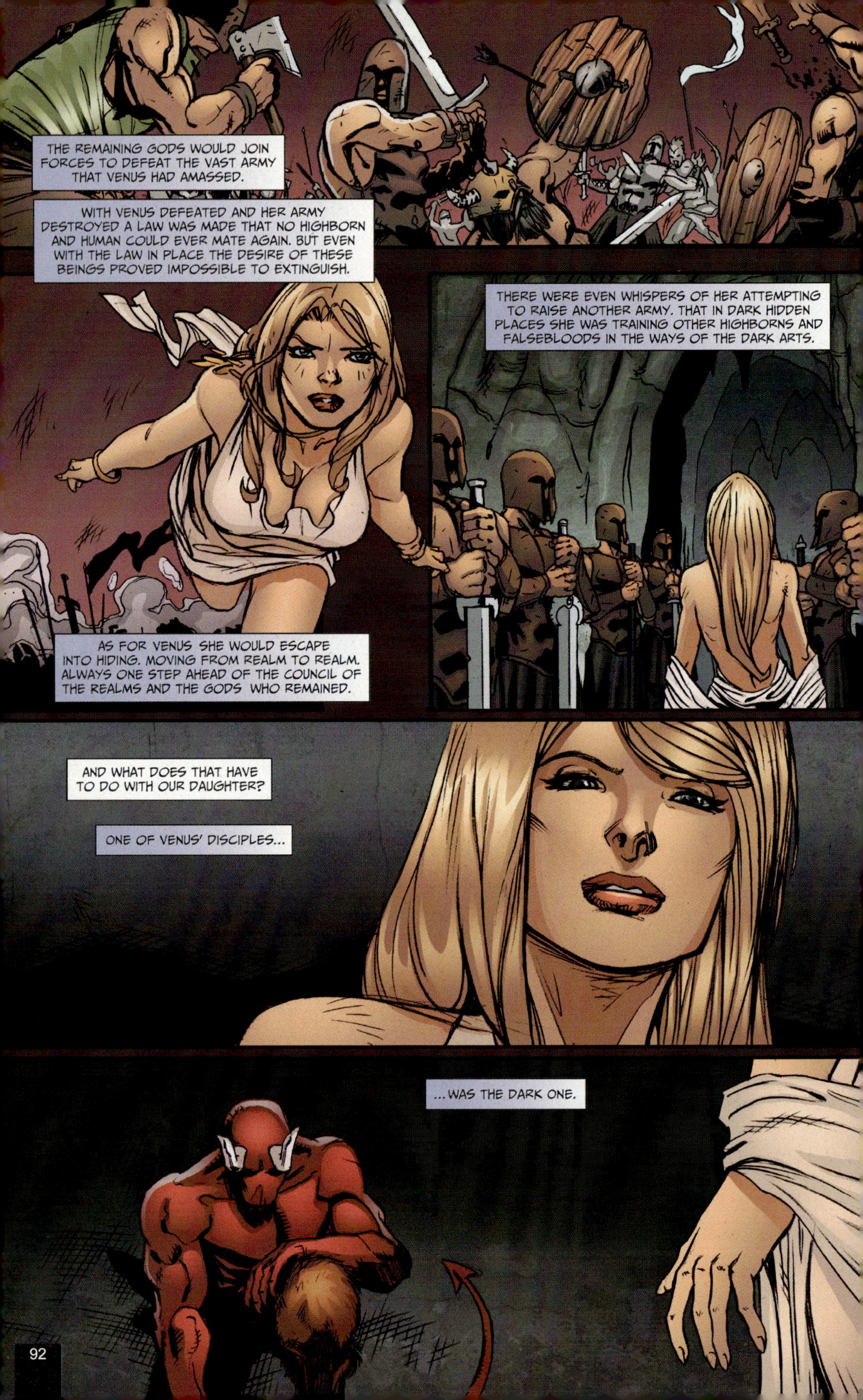
THE REMAINING GODS WOULD JOIN FORCES TO DEFEAT THE VAST ARMY THAT VENUS HAD AMASSED.
WITH VENUS DEFEATED AND HER ARMY DESTROYED A LAW WAS MADE THAT NO HIGHBORN AND HUMAN COULD EVER MATE AGAIN. BUT EVEN WITH THE LAW IN PLACE THE DESIRE OF THESE BEINGS PROVED IMPOSSIBLE TO EXTINGUISH.
AS FOR VENUS SHE WOULD ESCAPE INTO HIDING. MOVING FROM REALM TO REALM. ALWAYS ONE STEP AHEAD OF THE COUNCIL OF THE REALMS AND THE GODS WHO REMAINED.
THERE WERE EVEN WHISPERS OF HER ATTEMPTING TO RAISE ANOTHER ARMY. THAT IN DARK HIDDEN PLACES SHE WAS TRAINING OTHER HIGHBORNS AND FALSEBLOODS IN THE WAYS OF THE DARK ARTS.
AND WHAT DOES THAT HAVE TO DO WITH OUR DAUGHTER?
ONE OF VENUS' DISCIPLES...
...WAS THE DARK ONE.

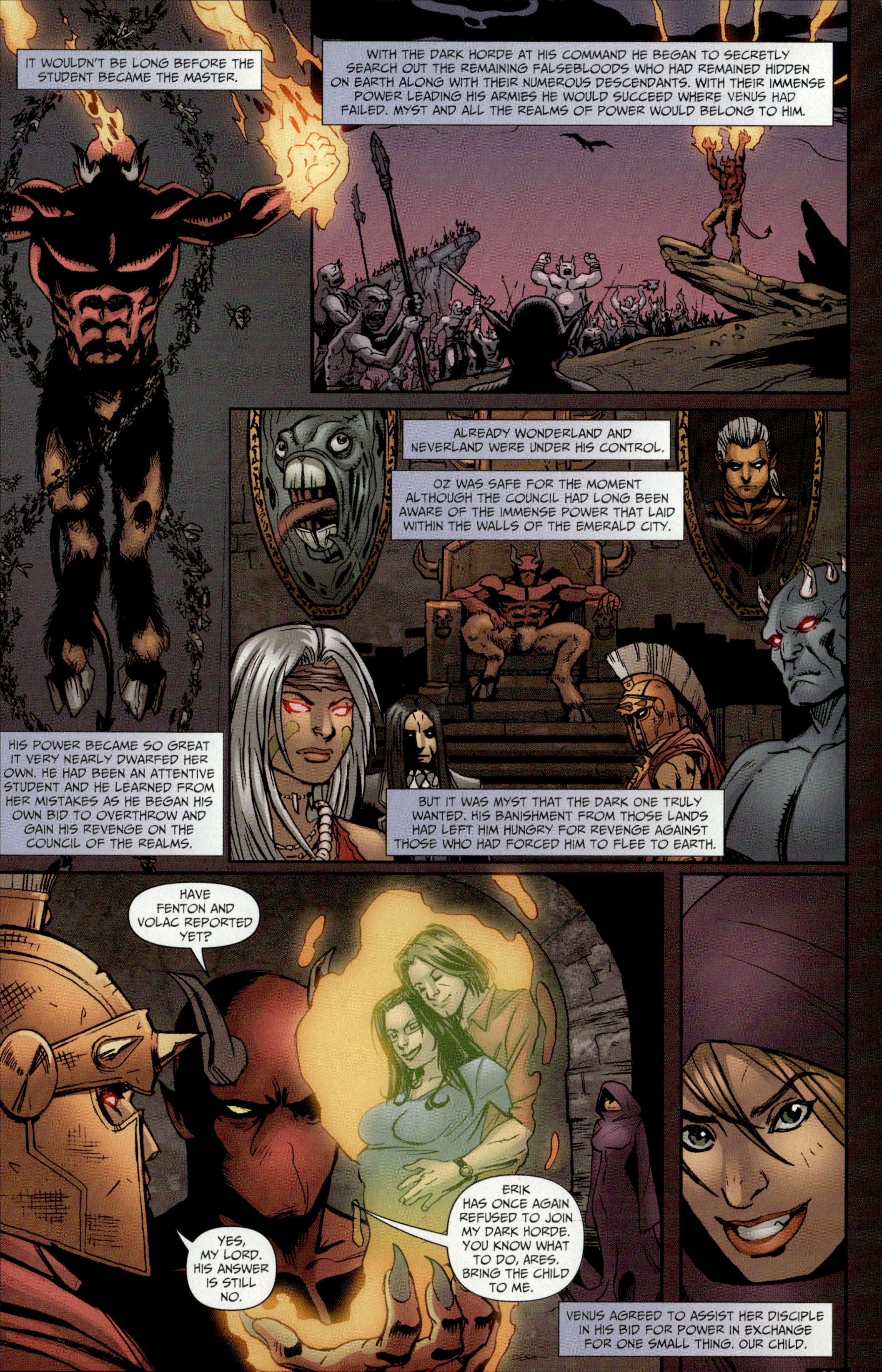

IT WOULDN'T BE LONG BEFORE THE STUDENT BECAME THE MASTER.
WITH THE DARK HORDE AT HIS COMMAND HE BEGAN TO SECRETLY SEARCH OUT THE REMAINING FALSEBLOODS WHO HAD REMAINED HIDDEN ON EARTH ALONG WITH THEIR NUMEROUS DESCENDANTS. WITH THEIR IMMENSE POWER LEADING HIS ARMIES HE WOULD SUCCEED WHERE VENUS HAD FAILED. MYST AND ALL THE REALMS OF POWER WOULD BELONG TO HIM.
ALREADY WONDERLAND AND NEVERLAND WERE UNDER HIS CONTROL.
OZ WAS SAFE FOR THE MOMENT ALTHOUGH THE COUNCIL HAD LONG BEEN AWARE OF THE IMMENSE POWER THAT LAID WITHIN THE WALLS OF THE EMERALD CITY.
HIS POWER BECAME SO GREAT IT VERY NEARLY DWARFED HER OWN. HE HAD BEEN AN ATTENTIVE STUDENT AND HE LEARNED FROM HER MISTAKES AS HE BEGAN HIS OWN BID TO OVERTHROW AND GAIN HIS REVENGE ON THE COUNCIL OF THE REALMS.
BUT IT WAS MYST THAT THE DARK ONE TRULY WANTED. HIS BANISHMENT FROM THOSE LANDS HAD LEFT HIM HUNGRY FOR REVENGE AGAINST THOSE WHO HAD FORCED HIM TO FLEE TO EARTH.
HAVE FENTON AND VOLAC REPORTED YET?
YES, MY LORD. HIS ANSWER IS STILL NO.
ERIK HAS ONCE AGAIN REFUSED TO JOIN MY DARK HORDE. YOU KNOW WHAT TO DO, ARES. BRING THE CHILD TO ME.
VENUS AGREED TO ASSIST HER DISCIPLE IN HIS BID FOR POWER IN EXCHANGE FOR ONE SMALL THING. OUR CHILD.

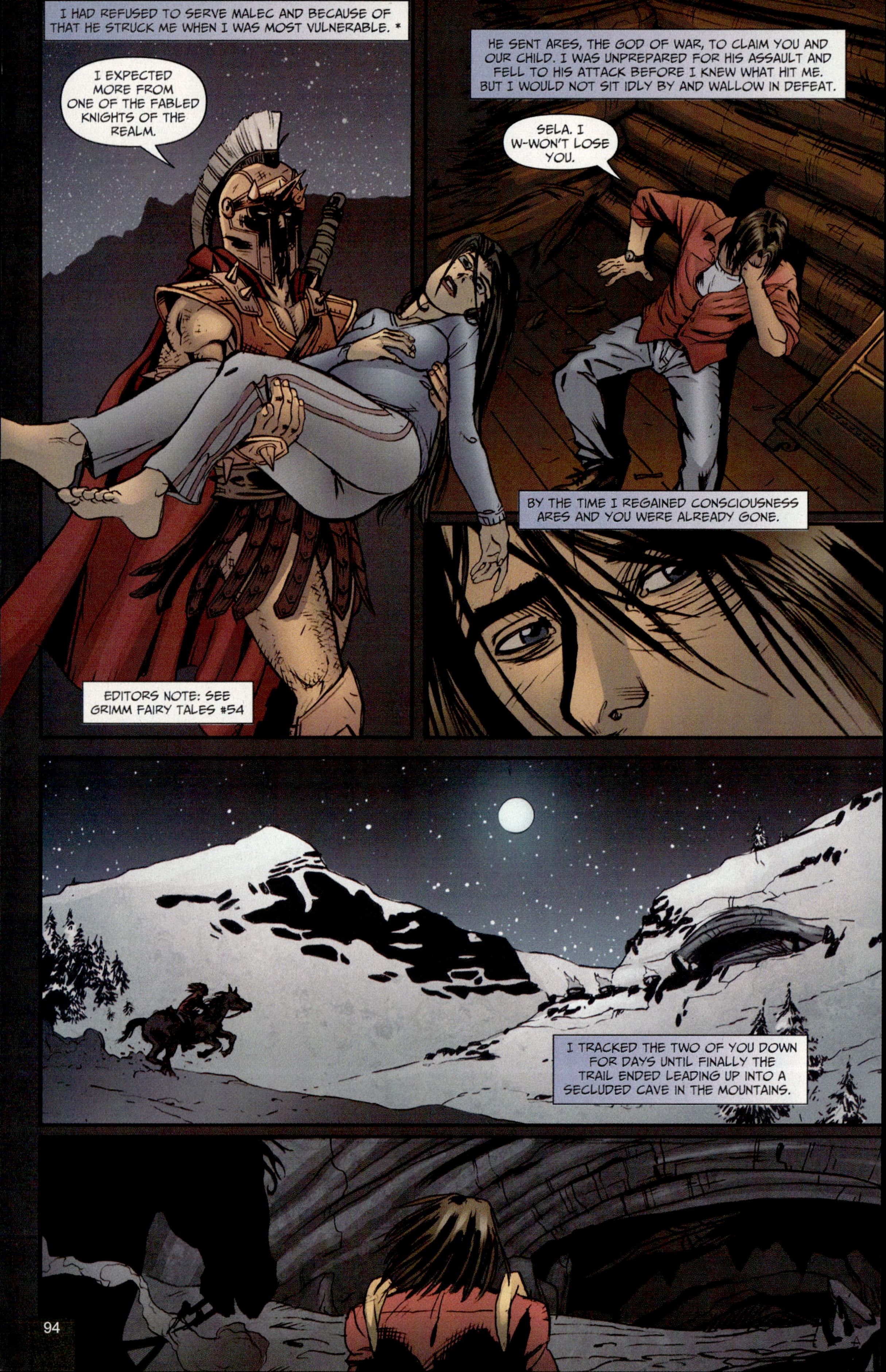
I HAD REFUSED TO SERVE MALEC AND BECAUSE OF THAT HE STRUCK ME WHEN I WAS MOST VULNERABLE. *
I EXPECTED MORE FROM ONE OF THE FABLED KNIGHTS OF THE REALM.
EDITORS NOTE: SEE GRIMM FAIRY TALES #54
HE SENT ARES, THE GOD OF WAR, TO CLAIM YOU AND OUR CHILD. I WAS UNPREPARED FOR HIS ASSAULT AND FELL TO HIS ATTACK BEFORE I KNEW WHAT HIT ME. BUT I WOULD NOT SIT IDLY BY AND WALLOW IN DEFEAT.
SELA. I W-WON'T LOSE YOU.
BY THE TIME I REGAINED CONSCIOUSNESS ARES AND YOU WERE ALREADY GONE.
I TRACKED THE TWO OF YOU DOWN FOR DAYS UNTIL FINALLY THE TRAIL ENDED LEADING UP INTO A SECLUDED CAVE IN THE MOUNTAINS.

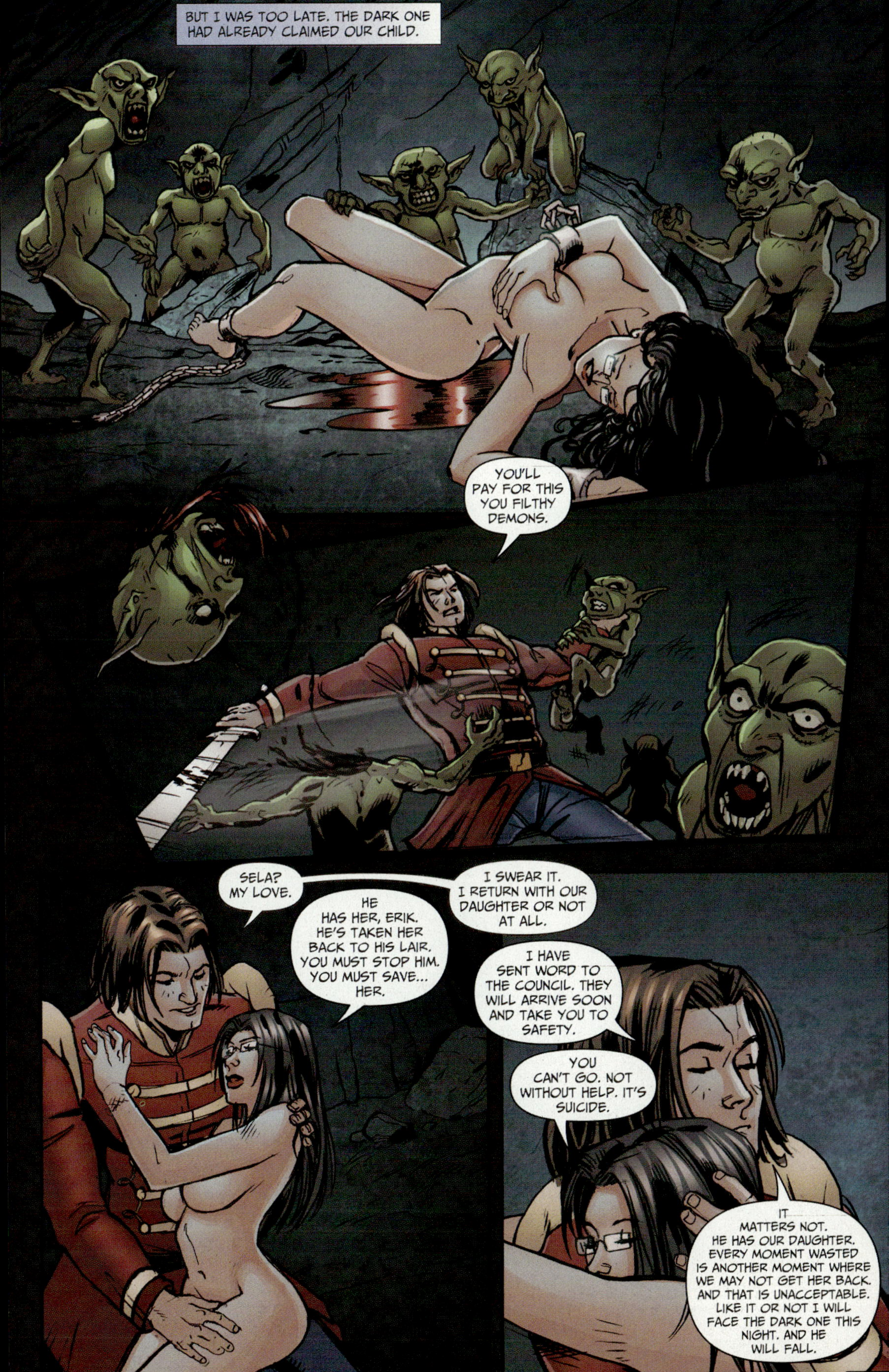
BUT I WAS TOO LATE. THE DARK ONE HAD ALREADY CLAIMED OUR CHILD.
YOU'LL PAY FOR THIS YOU FILTHY DEMONS.
SELA? MY LOVE.
HE HAS HER, ERIK. HE'S TAKEN HER BACK TO HIS LAIR. YOU MUST STOP HIM. YOU MUST SAVE... HER.
I SWEAR IT. I RETURN WITH OUR DAUGHTER OR NOT AT ALL.
I HAVE SENT WORD TO THE COUNCIL. THEY WILL ARRIVE SOON AND TAKE YOU TO SAFETY.
YOU CAN'T GO. NOT WITHOUT HELP. IT'S SUICIDE.
IT MATTERS NOT. HE HAS OUR DAUGHTER. EVERY MOMENT WASTED IS ANOTHER MOMENT WHERE WE MAY NOT GET HER BACK. AND THAT IS UNACCEPTABLE. LIKE IT OR NOT I WILL FACE THE DARK ONE THIS NIGHT. AND HE WILL FALL.

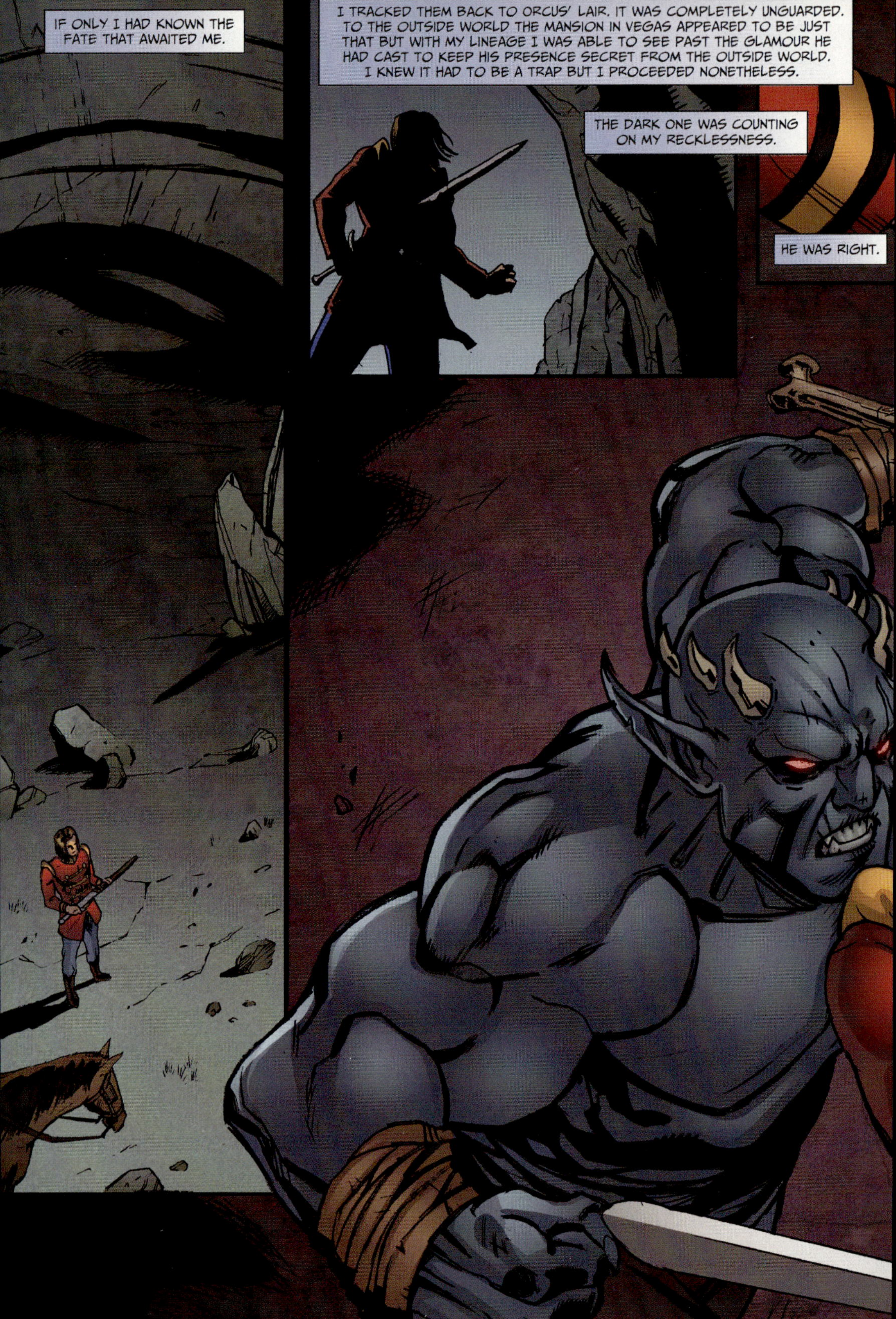
IF ONLY I HAD KNOWN THE FATE THAT AWAITED ME.
I TRACKED THEM BACK TO ORCUS' LAIR. IT WAS COMPLETELY UNGUARDED. TO THE OUTSIDE WORLD THE MANSION IN VEGAS APPEARED TO BE JUST THAT BUT WITH MY LINEAGE I WAS ABLE TO SEE PAST THE GLAMOUR HE HAD CAST TO KEEP HIS PRESENCE SECRET FROM THE OUTSIDE WORLD. I KNEW IT HAD TO BE A TRAP BUT I PROCEEDED NONETHELESS.
THE DARK ONE WAS COUNTING ON MY RECKLESSNESS.
HE WAS RIGHT.

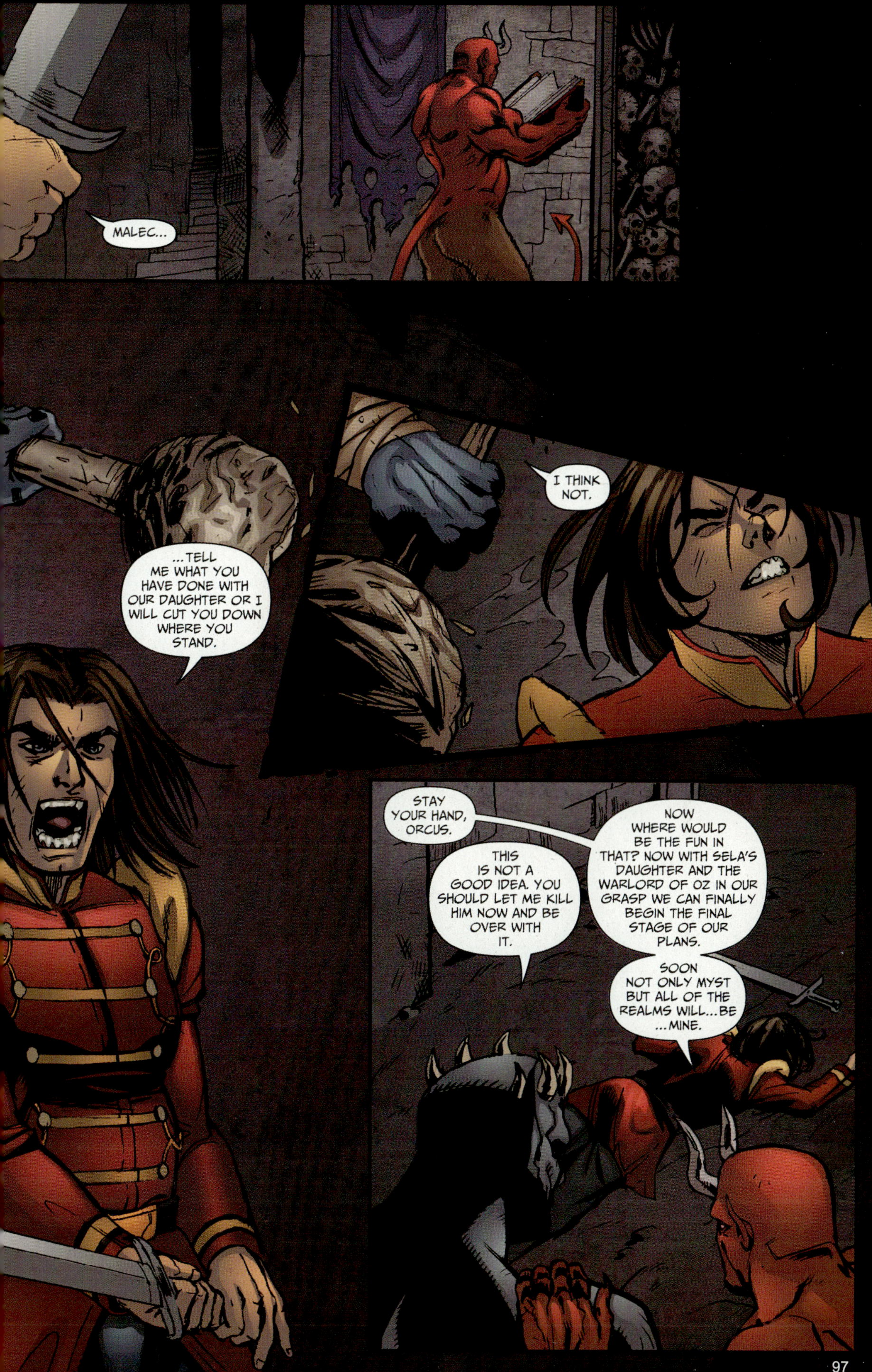
MALEC...
...TELL ME WHAT YOU HAVE DONE WITH OUR DAUGHTER OR I WILL CUT YOU DOWN WHERE YOU STAND.
I THINK NOT.
STAY YOUR HAND, ORCUS.
THIS IS NOT A GOOD IDEA. YOU SHOULD LET ME KILL HIM NOW AND BE OVER WITH IT.
NOW WHERE WOULD BE THE FUN IN THAT? NOW WITH SELA'S DAUGHTER AND THE WARLORD OF OZ IN OUR GRASP WE CAN FINALLY BEGIN THE FINAL STAGE OF OUR PLANS.
SOON NOT ONLY MYST BUT ALL OF THE REALMS WILL...BE ...MINE.

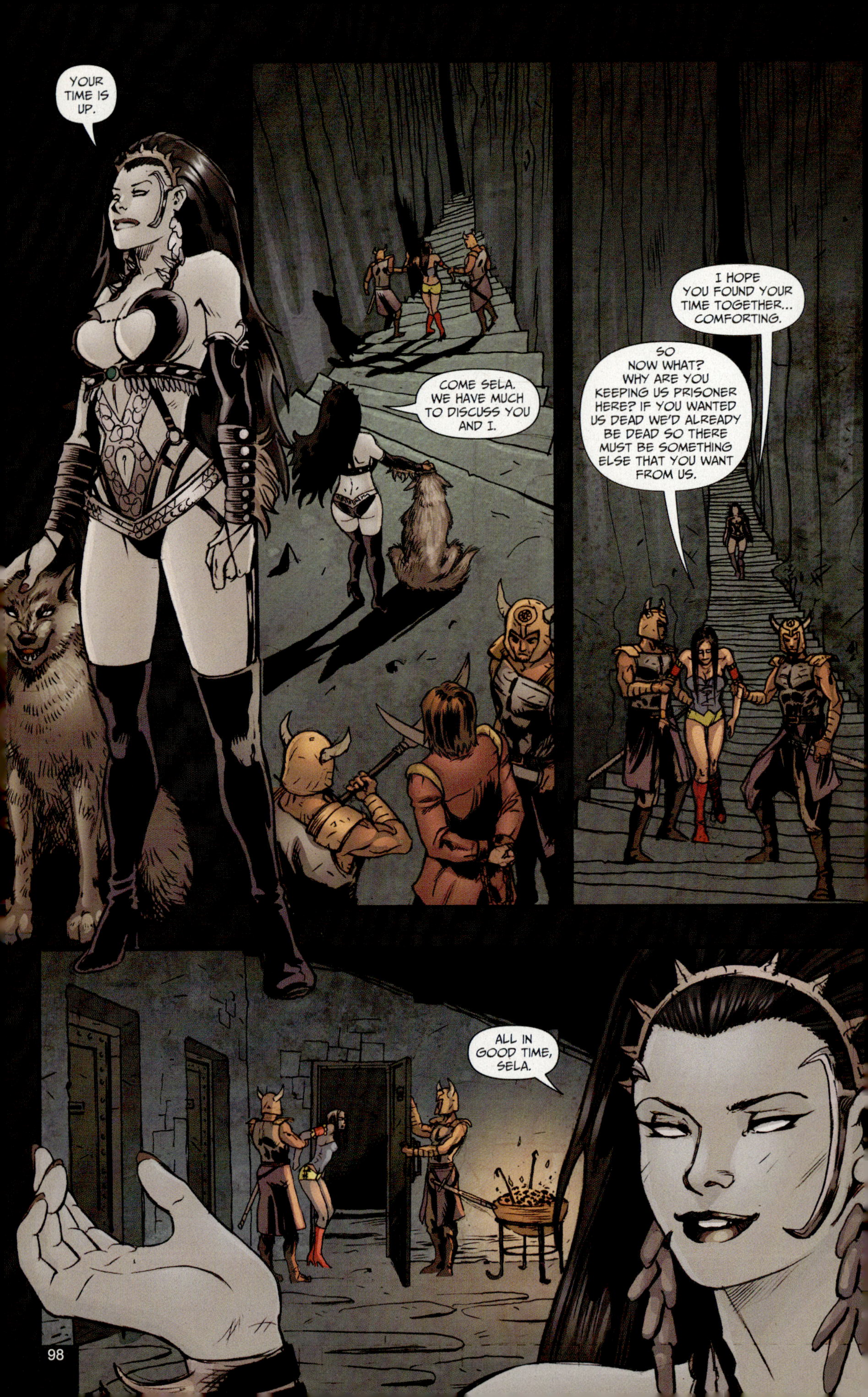
YOUR TIME IS UP.
COME SELA. WE HAVE MUCH TO DISCUSS YOU AND I.
I HOPE YOU FOUND YOUR TIME TOGETHER... COMFORTING.
SO NOW WHAT? WHY ARE YOU KEEPING US PRISONER HERE? IF YOU WANTED US DEAD WE'D ALREADY BE DEAD SO THERE MUST BE SOMETHING ELSE THAT YOU WANT FROM US.
ALL IN GOOD TIME, SELA.

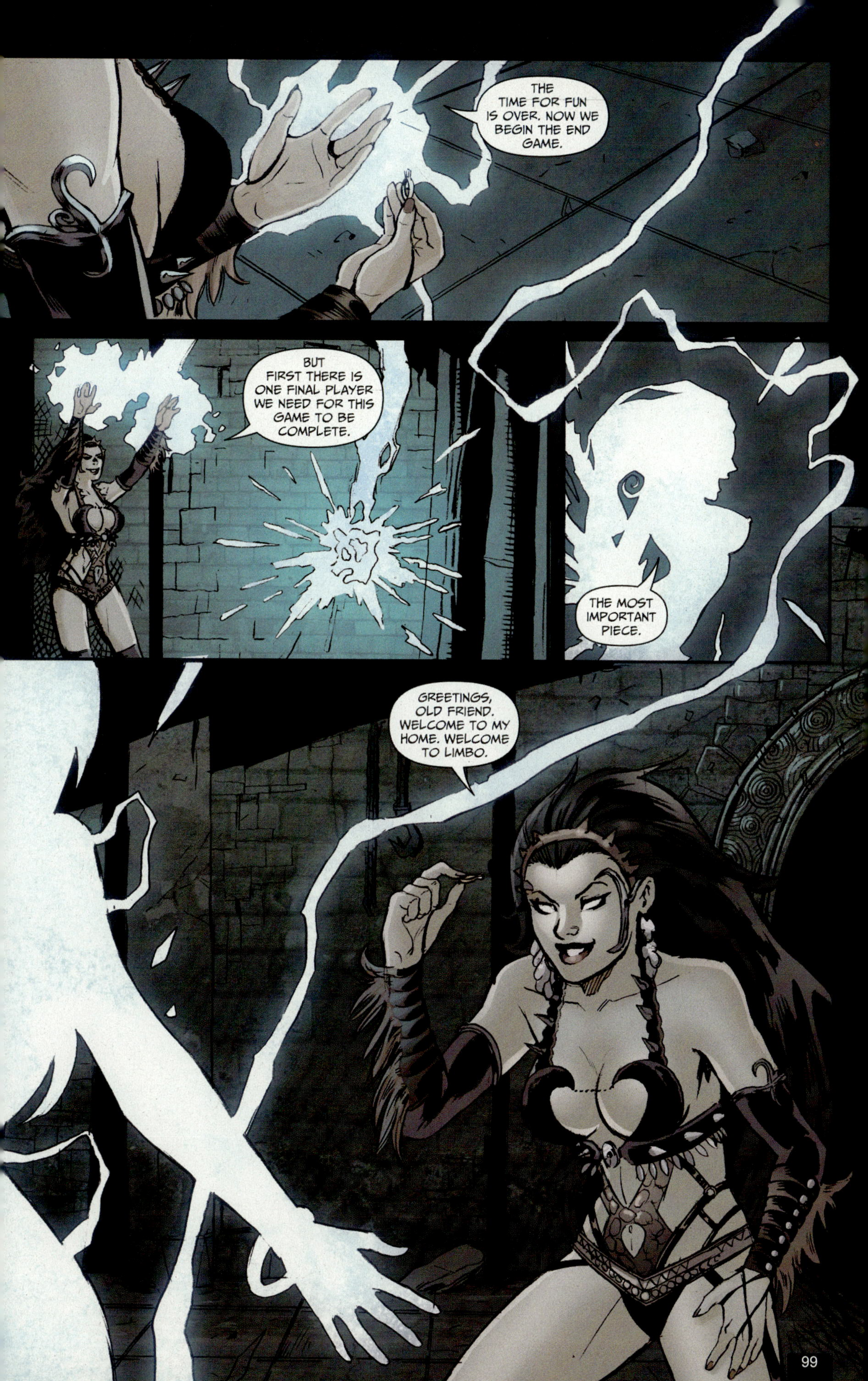
THE TIME FOR FUN IS OVER. NOW WE BEGIN THE END GAME.
BUT FIRST THERE IS ONE FINAL PLAYER WE NEED FOR THIS GAME TO BE COMPLETE.
THE MOST IMPORTANT PIECE.
GREETINGS, OLD FRIEND. WELCOME TO MY HOME. WELCOME TO LIMBO.

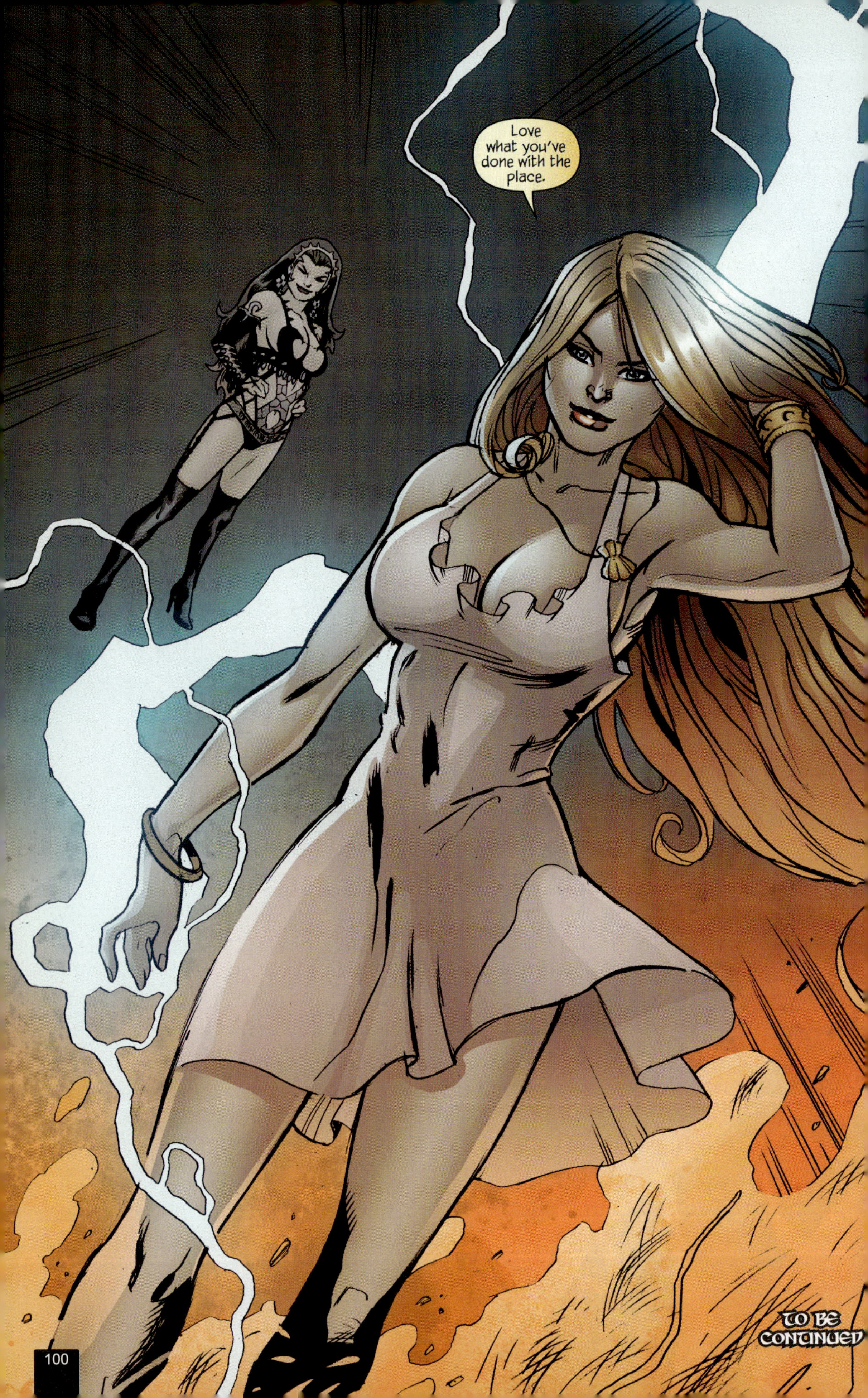
Love what you've done with the place.
TO BE CONTINUED

Grimm Fairy Tales
Volume 11

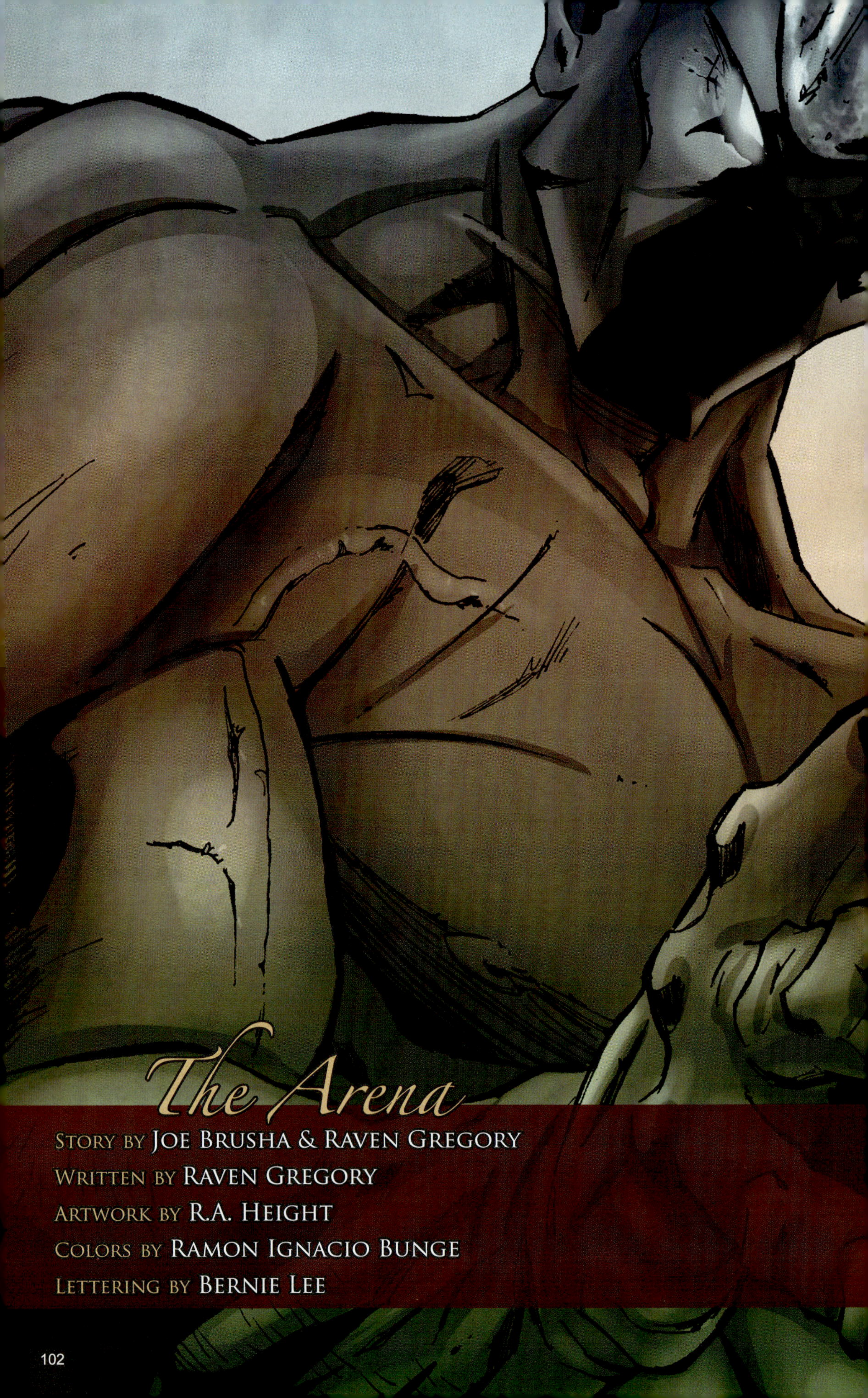

The Arena

Story by Joe Brusha & Raven Gregory
Written by Raven Gregory
Artwork by R.A. Height
Colors by Ramon Ignacio Bunge
Lettering by Bernie Lee

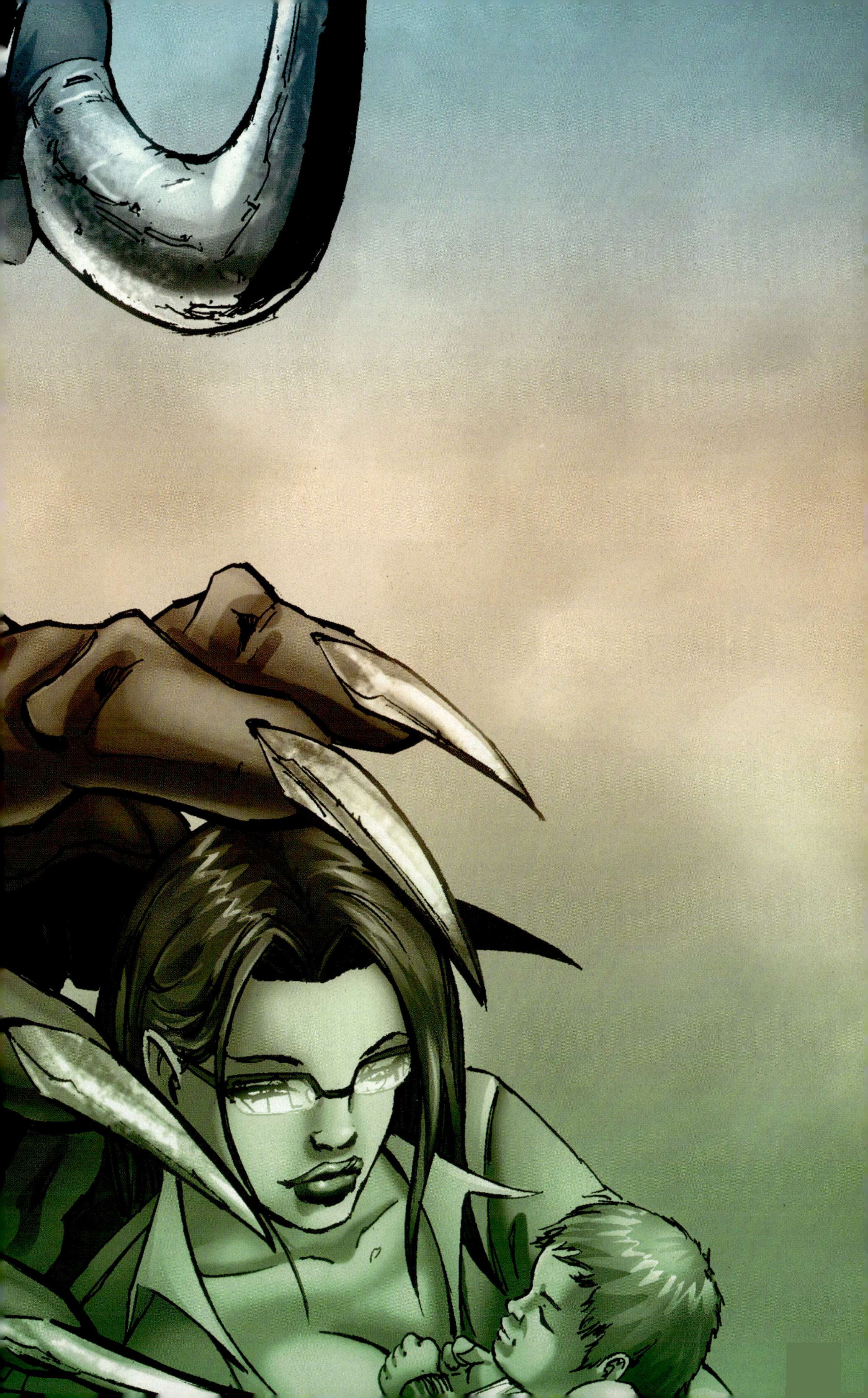

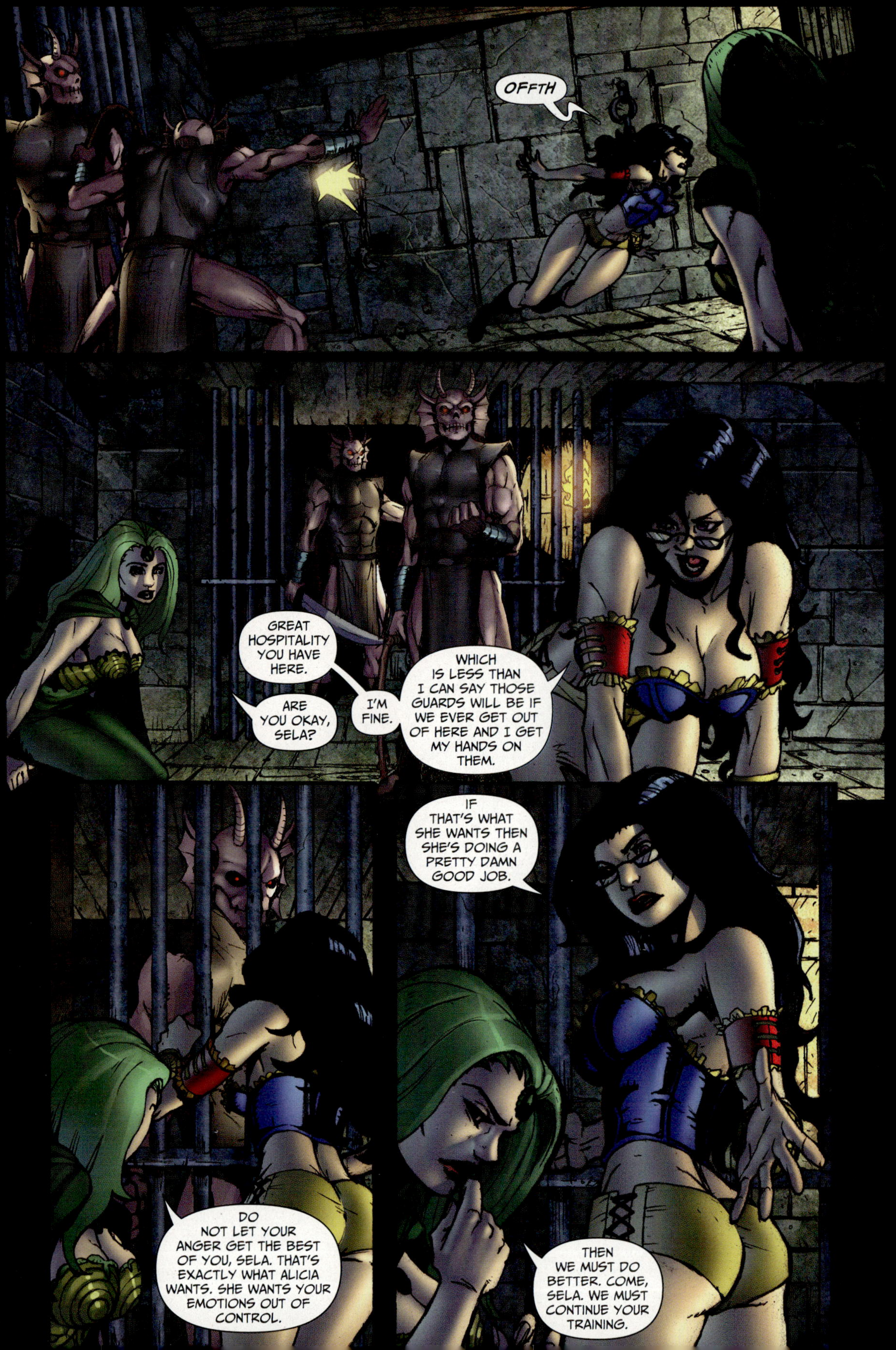
OFFTH
GREAT HOSPITALITY YOU HAVE HERE.
ARE YOU OKAY, SELA?
I'M FINE.
WHICH IS LESS THAN I CAN SAY THOSE GUARDS WILL BE IF WE EVER GET OUT OF HERE AND I GET MY HANDS ON THEM.
DO NOT LET YOUR ANGER GET THE BEST OF YOU, SELA. THAT'S EXACTLY WHAT ALICIA WANTS. SHE WANTS YOUR EMOTIONS OUT OF CONTROL.
IF THAT'S WHAT SHE WANTS THEN SHE'S DOING A PRETTY DAMN GOOD JOB.
THEN WE MUST DO BETTER. COME, SELA. WE MUST CONTINUE YOUR TRAINING.

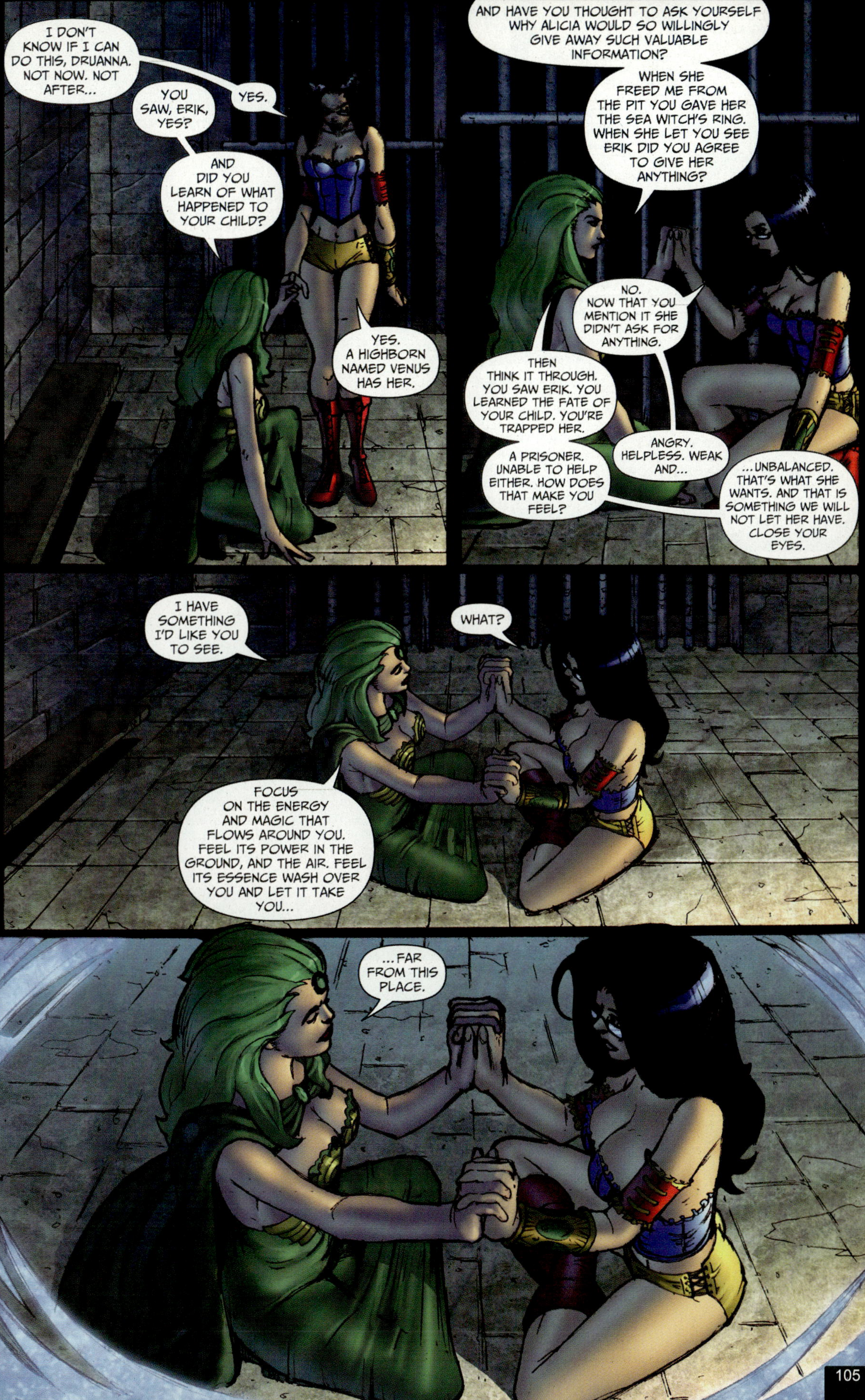
I DON'T KNOW IF I CAN DO THIS, DRUANNA. NOT NOW. NOT AFTER...
YES.
YOU SAW, ERIK, YES?
AND DID YOU LEARN OF WHAT HAPPENED TO YOUR CHILD?
YES. A HIGHBORN NAMED VENUS HAS HER.
AND HAVE YOU THOUGHT TO ASK YOURSELF WHY ALICIA WOULD SO WILLINGLY GIVE AWAY SUCH VALUABLE INFORMATION?
WHEN SHE FREED ME FROM THE PIT YOU GAVE HER THE SEA WITCH'S RING. WHEN SHE LET YOU SEE ERIK DID YOU AGREE TO GIVE HER ANYTHING?
NO. NOW THAT YOU MENTION IT SHE DIDN'T ASK FOR ANYTHING.
THEN THINK IT THROUGH. YOU SAW ERIK. YOU LEARNED THE FATE OF YOUR CHILD. YOU'RE TRAPPED HER.
A PRISONER. UNABLE TO HELP EITHER. HOW DOES THAT MAKE YOU FEEL?
ANGRY. HELPLESS. WEAK AND...
...UNBALANCED. THAT'S WHAT SHE WANTS. AND THAT IS SOMETHING WE WILL NOT LET HER HAVE. CLOSE YOUR EYES.
I HAVE SOMETHING I'D LIKE YOU TO SEE.
WHAT?
FOCUS ON THE ENERGY AND MAGIC THAT FLOWS AROUND YOU. FEEL ITS POWER IN THE GROUND, AND THE AIR. FEEL ITS ESSENCE WASH OVER YOU AND LET IT TAKE YOU...
...FAR FROM THIS PLACE.

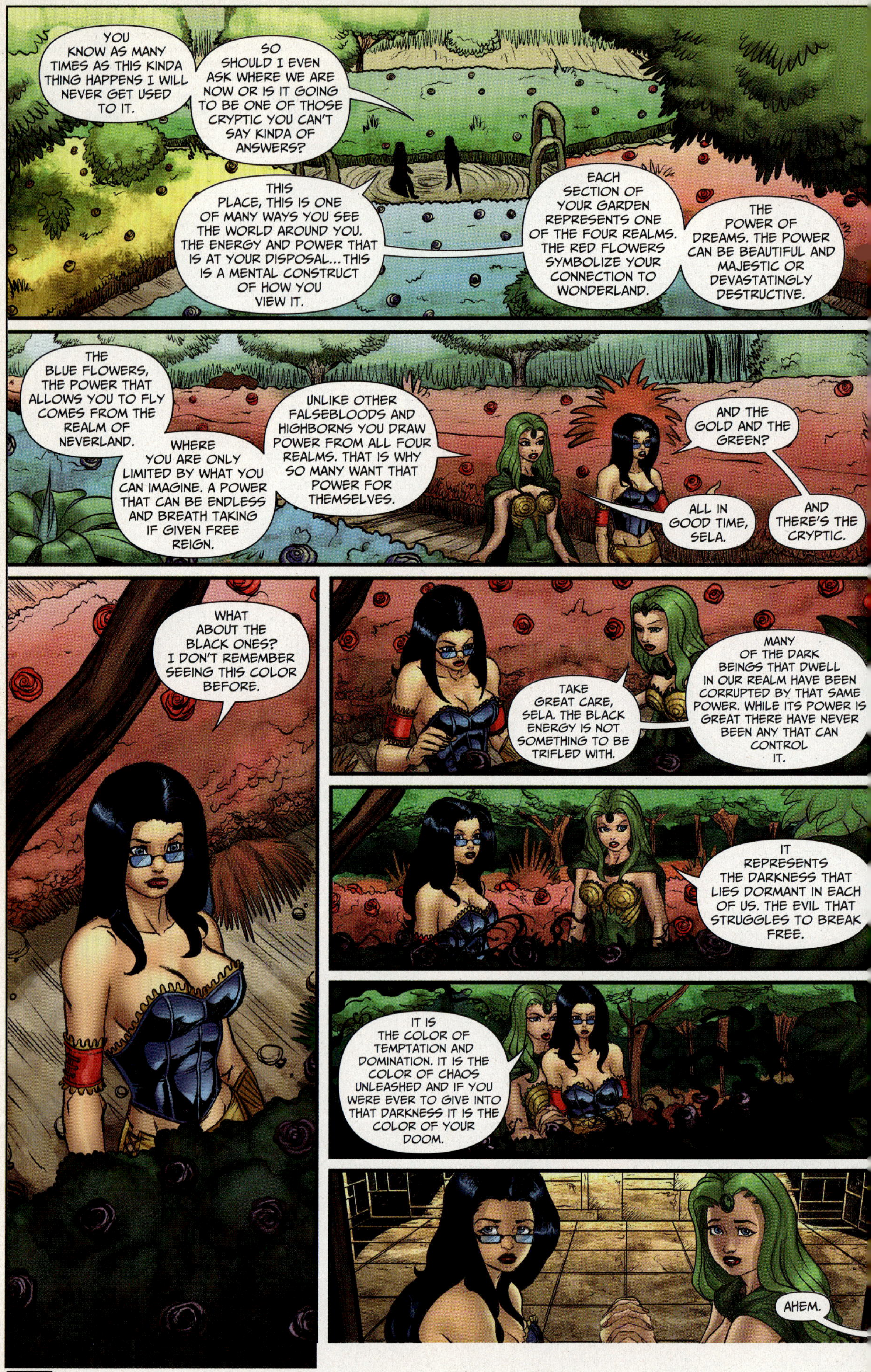
YOU KNOW AS MANY TIMES AS THIS KINDA THING HAPPENS I WILL NEVER GET USED TO IT.
SO SHOULD I EVEN ASK WHERE WE ARE NOW OR IS IT GOING TO BE ONE OF THOSE CRYPTIC YOU CAN'T SAY KINDA OF ANSWERS?
THIS PLACE, THIS IS ONE OF MANY WAYS YOU SEE THE WORLD AROUND YOU. THE ENERGY AND POWER THAT IS AT YOUR DISPOSAL... THIS IS A MENTAL CONSTRUCT OF HOW YOU VIEW IT.
EACH SECTION OF YOUR GARDEN REPRESENTS ONE OF THE FOUR REALMS. THE RED FLOWERS SYMBOLIZE YOUR CONNECTION TO WONDERLAND.
THE POWER OF DREAMS. THE POWER CAN BE BEAUTIFUL AND MAJESTIC OR DEVASTATINGLY DESTRUCTIVE.
THE BLUE FLOWERS, THE POWER THAT ALLOWS YOU TO FLY COMES FROM THE REALM OF NEVERLAND.
WHERE YOU ARE ONLY LIMITED BY WHAT YOU CAN IMAGINE. A POWER THAT CAN BE ENDLESS AND BREATH TAKING IF GIVEN FREE REIGN.
UNLIKE OTHER FALSEBLOODS AND HIGHBORNS YOU DRAW POWER FROM ALL FOUR REALMS. THAT IS WHY SO MANY WANT THAT POWER FOR THEMSELVES.
AND THE GOLD AND THE GREEN?
ALL IN GOOD TIME, SELA.
AND THERE'S THE CRYPTIC.
WHAT ABOUT THE BLACK ONES? I DON'T REMEMBER SEEING THIS COLOR BEFORE.
TAKE GREAT CARE, SELA. THE BLACK ENERGY IS NOT SOMETHING TO BE TRIFLED WITH.
MANY OF THE DARK BEINGS THAT DWELL IN OUR REALM HAVE BEEN CORRUPTED BY THAT SAME POWER. WHILE ITS POWER IS GREAT THERE HAVE NEVER BEEN ANY THAT CAN CONTROL IT.
IT REPRESENTS THE DARKNESS THAT LIES DORMANT IN EACH OF US. THE EVIL THAT STRUGGLES TO BREAK FREE.
IT IS THE COLOR OF TEMPTATION AND DOMINATION. IT IS THE COLOR OF CHAOS UNLEASHED AND IF YOU WERE EVER TO GIVE INTO THAT DARKNESS IT IS THE COLOR OF YOUR DOOM.
AHEM.

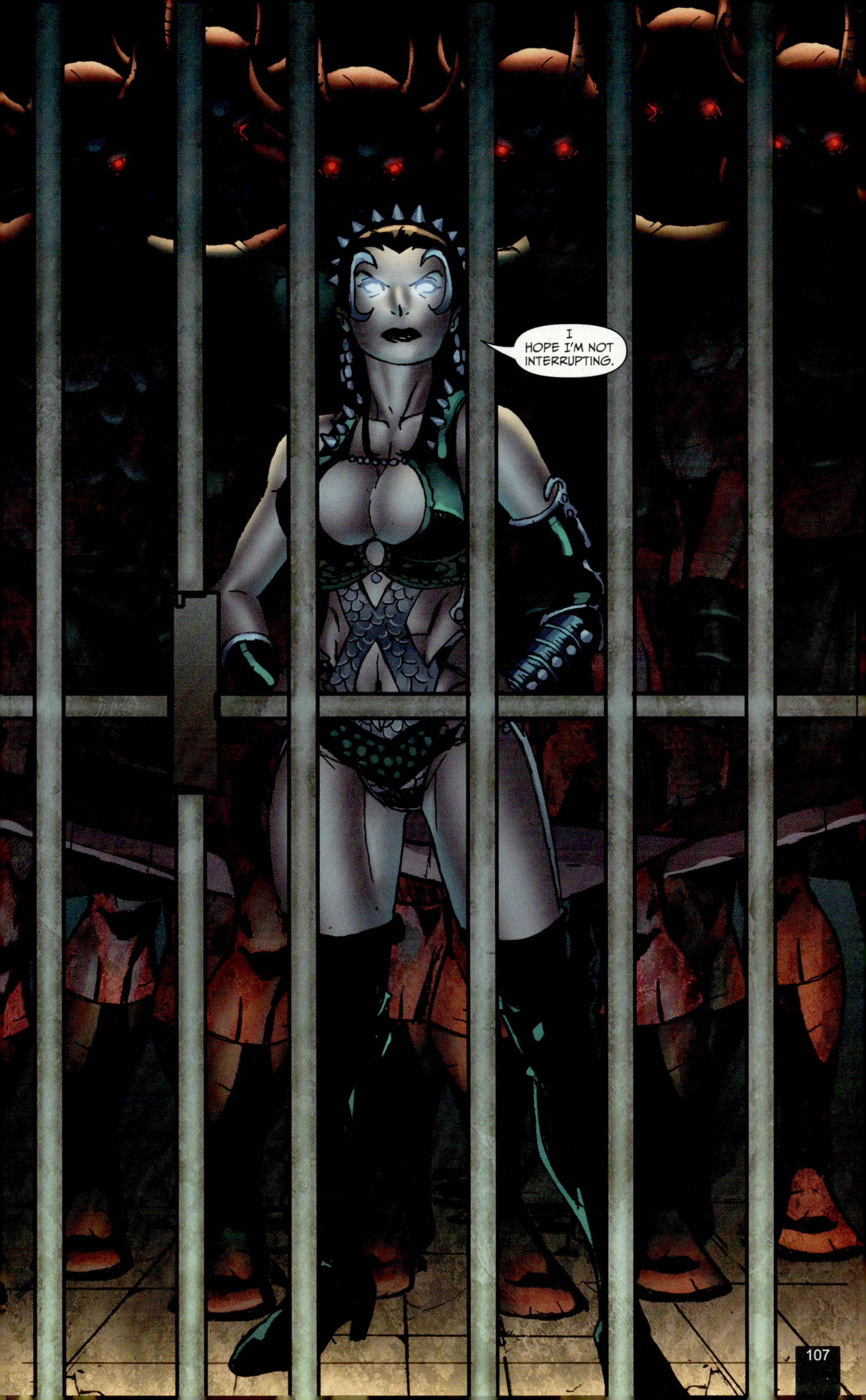
I HOPE I'M NOT INTERRUPTING.

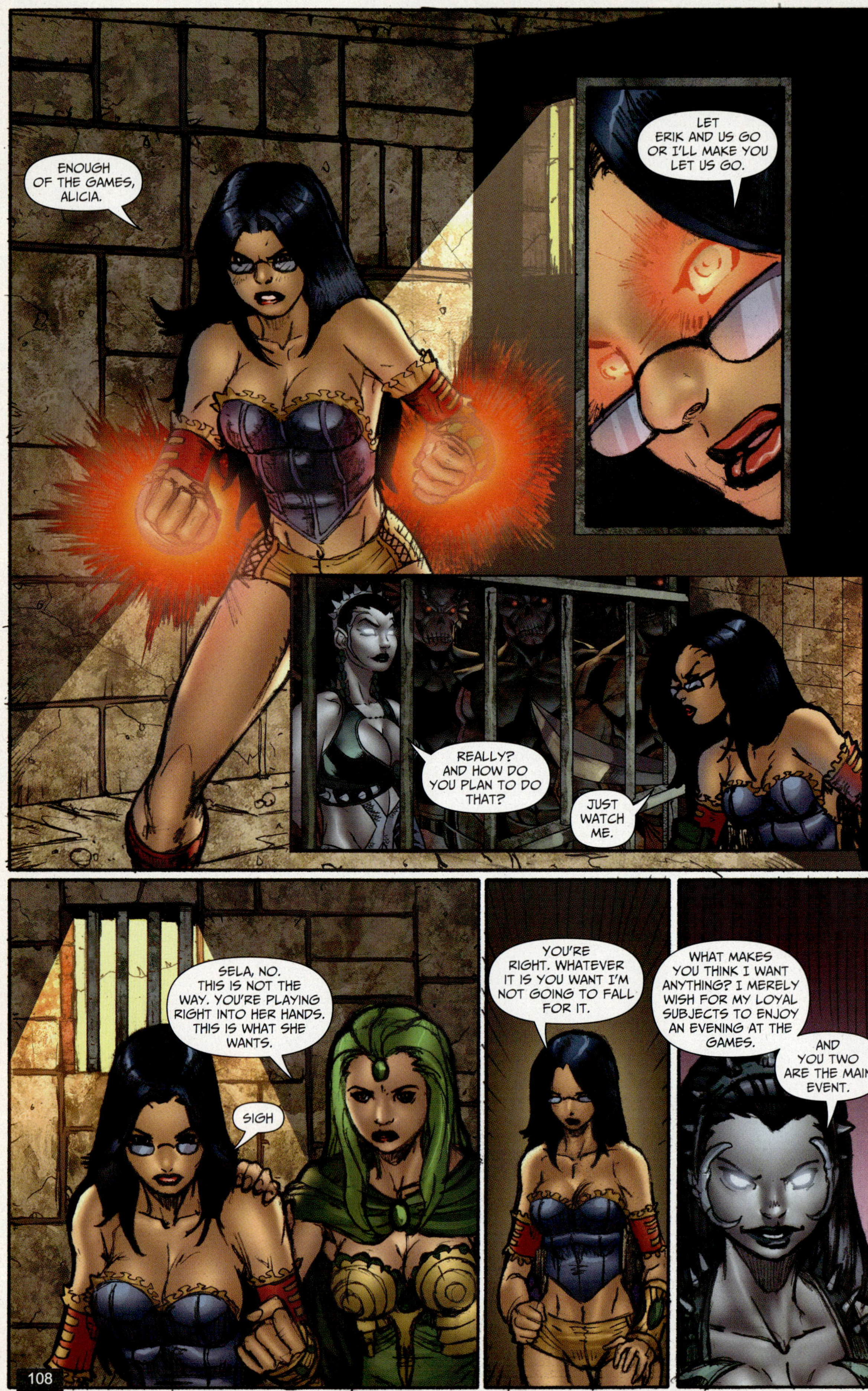
ENOUGH OF THE GAMES, ALICIA.
LET ERIK AND US GO OR I'LL MAKE YOU LET US GO.
REALLY? AND HOW DO YOU PLAN TO DO THAT?
JUST WATCH ME.
SELA, NO. THIS IS NOT THE WAY. YOU'RE PLAYING RIGHT INTO HER HANDS. THIS IS WHAT SHE WANTS.
SIGH
YOU'RE RIGHT. WHATEVER IT IS YOU WANT I'M NOT GOING TO FALL FOR IT.
WHAT MAKES YOU THINK I WANT ANYTHING? I MERELY WISH FOR MY LOYAL SUBJECTS TO ENJOY AN EVENING AT THE GAMES.
AND YOU TWO ARE THE MAIN EVENT.

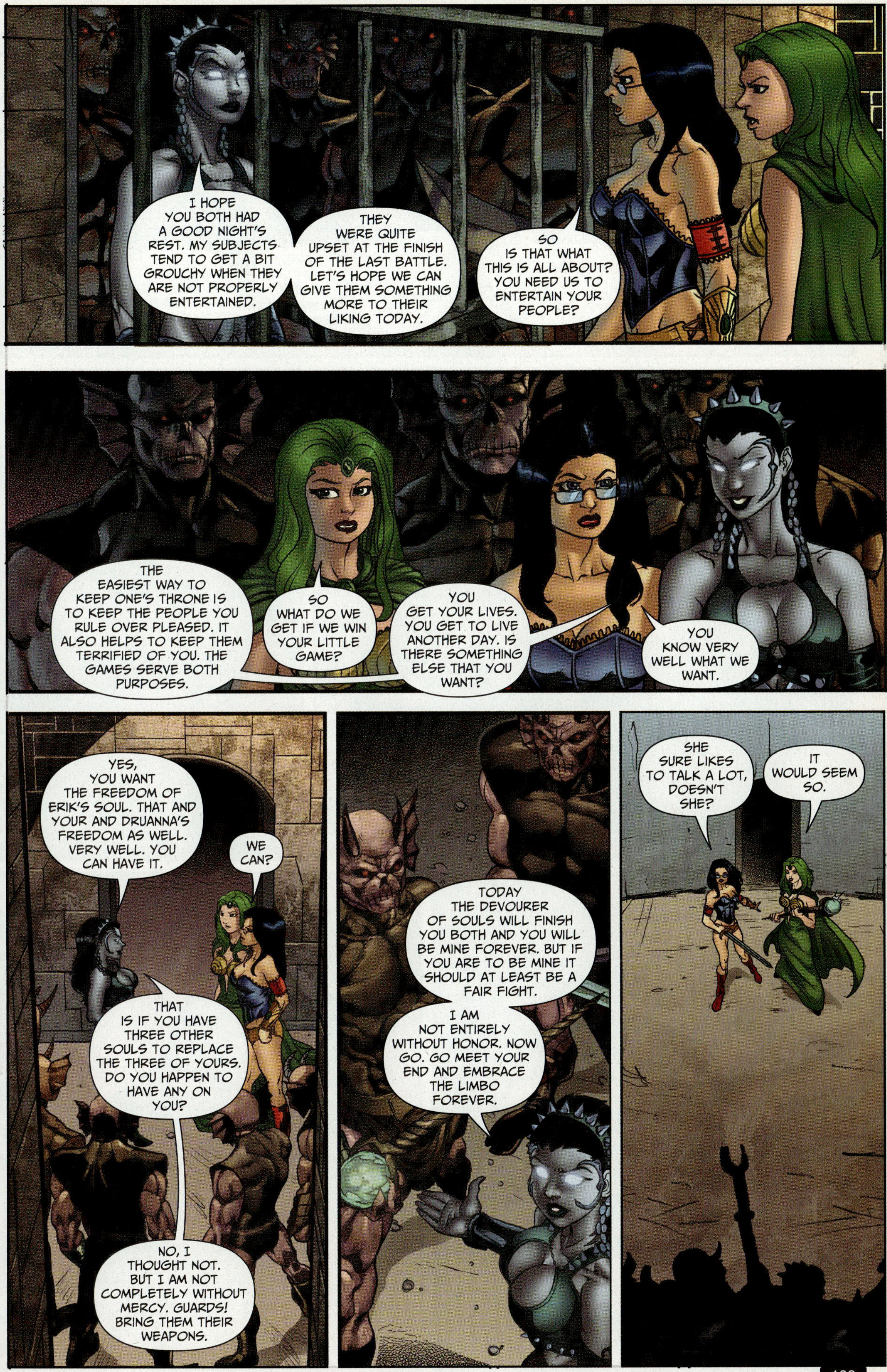
I HOPE YOU BOTH HAD A GOOD NIGHT'S REST. MY SUBJECTS TEND TO GET A BIT GROUCHY WHEN THEY ARE NOT PROPERLY ENTERTAINED.
THEY WERE QUITE UPSET AT THE FINISH OF THE LAST BATTLE. LET'S HOPE WE CAN GIVE THEM SOMETHING MORE TO THEIR LIKING TODAY.
SO IS THAT WHAT THIS IS ALL ABOUT? YOU NEED US TO ENTERTAIN YOUR PEOPLE?
THE EASIEST WAY TO KEEP ONE'S THRONE IS TO KEEP THE PEOPLE YOU RULE OVER PLEASED. IT ALSO HELPS TO KEEP THEM TERRIFIED OF YOU. THE GAMES SERVE BOTH PURPOSES.
SO WHAT DO WE GET IF WE WIN YOUR LITTLE GAME?
YOU GET YOUR LIVES. YOU GET TO LIVE ANOTHER DAY. IS THERE SOMETHING ELSE THAT YOU WANT?
YOU KNOW VERY WELL WHAT WE WANT.
YES, YOU WANT THE FREEDOM OF ERIK'S SOUL. THAT AND YOUR AND DRUANNA'S FREEDOM AS WELL. VERY WELL. YOU CAN HAVE IT.
WE CAN?
THAT IS IF YOU HAVE THREE OTHER SOULS TO REPLACE THE THREE OF YOURS. DO YOU HAPPEN TO HAVE ANY ON YOU?
NO, I THOUGHT NOT. BUT I AM NOT COMPLETELY WITHOUT MERCY. GUARDS! BRING THEM THEIR WEAPONS.
TODAY THE DEVOURER OF SOULS WILL FINISH YOU BOTH AND YOU WILL BE MINE FOREVER. BUT IF YOU ARE TO BE MINE IT SHOULD AT LEAST BE A FAIR FIGHT.
I AM NOT ENTIRELY WITHOUT HONOR. NOW GO. GO MEET YOUR END AND EMBRACE THE LIMBO FOREVER.
SHE SURE LIKES TO TALK A LOT, DOESN'T SHE?
IT WOULD SEEM SO.

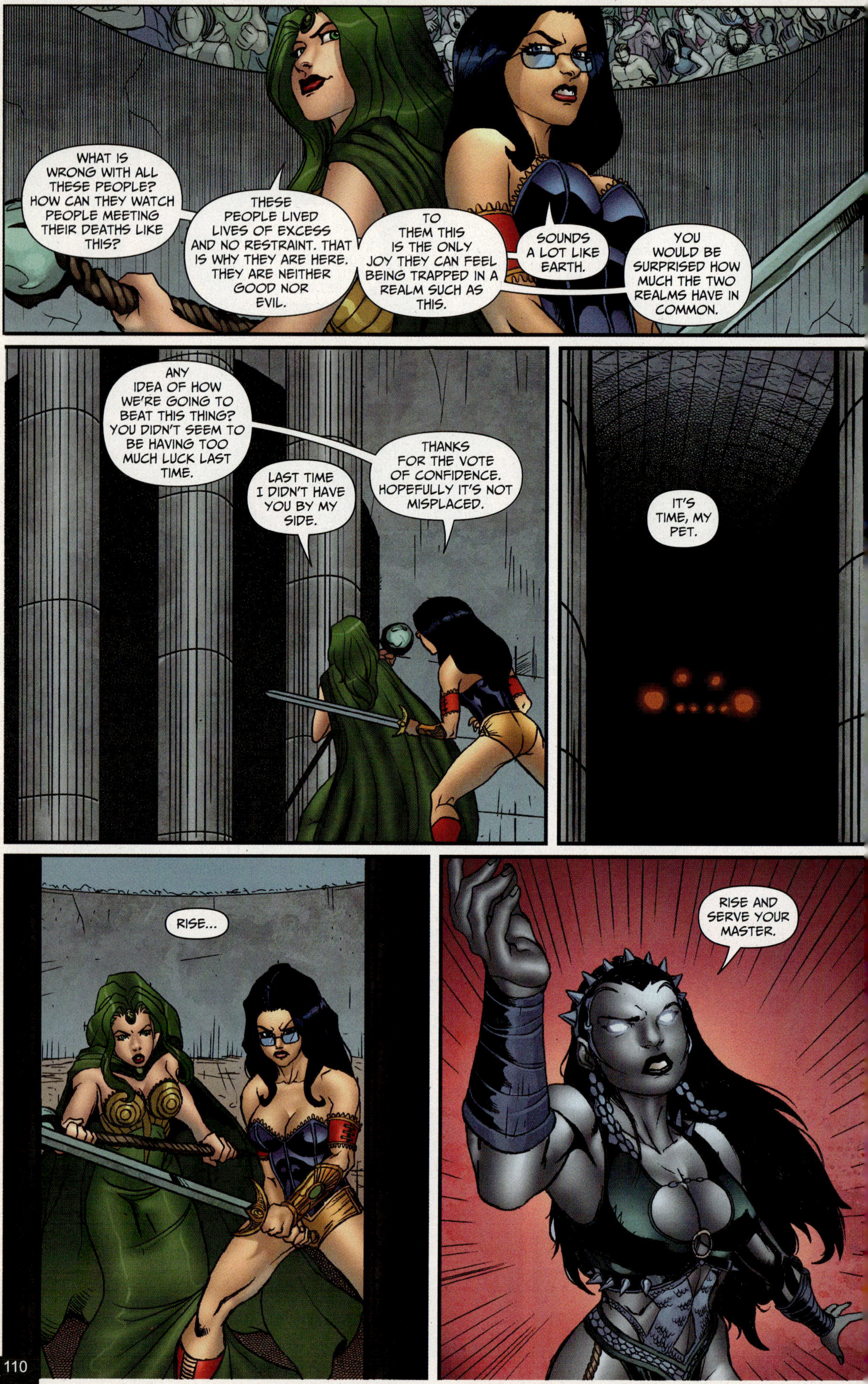
WHAT IS WRONG WITH ALL THESE PEOPLE? HOW CAN THEY WATCH PEOPLE MEETING THEIR DEATHS LIKE THIS?
THESE PEOPLE LIVED LIVES OF EXCESS AND NO RESTRAINT. THAT IS WHY THEY ARE HERE. THEY ARE NEITHER GOOD NOR EVIL.
TO THEM THIS IS THE ONLY JOY THEY CAN FEEL BEING TRAPPED IN A REALM SUCH AS THIS.
SOUNDS A LOT LIKE EARTH.
YOU WOULD BE SURPRISED HOW MUCH THE TWO REALMS HAVE IN COMMON.
ANY IDEA OF HOW WE'RE GOING TO BEAT THIS THING? YOU DIDN'T SEEM TO BE HAVING TOO MUCH LUCK LAST TIME.
LAST TIME I DIDN'T HAVE YOU BY MY SIDE.
THANKS FOR THE VOTE OF CONFIDENCE. HOPEFULLY IT'S NOT MISPLACED.
IT'S TIME, MY PET.
RISE...
RISE AND SERVE YOUR MASTER.

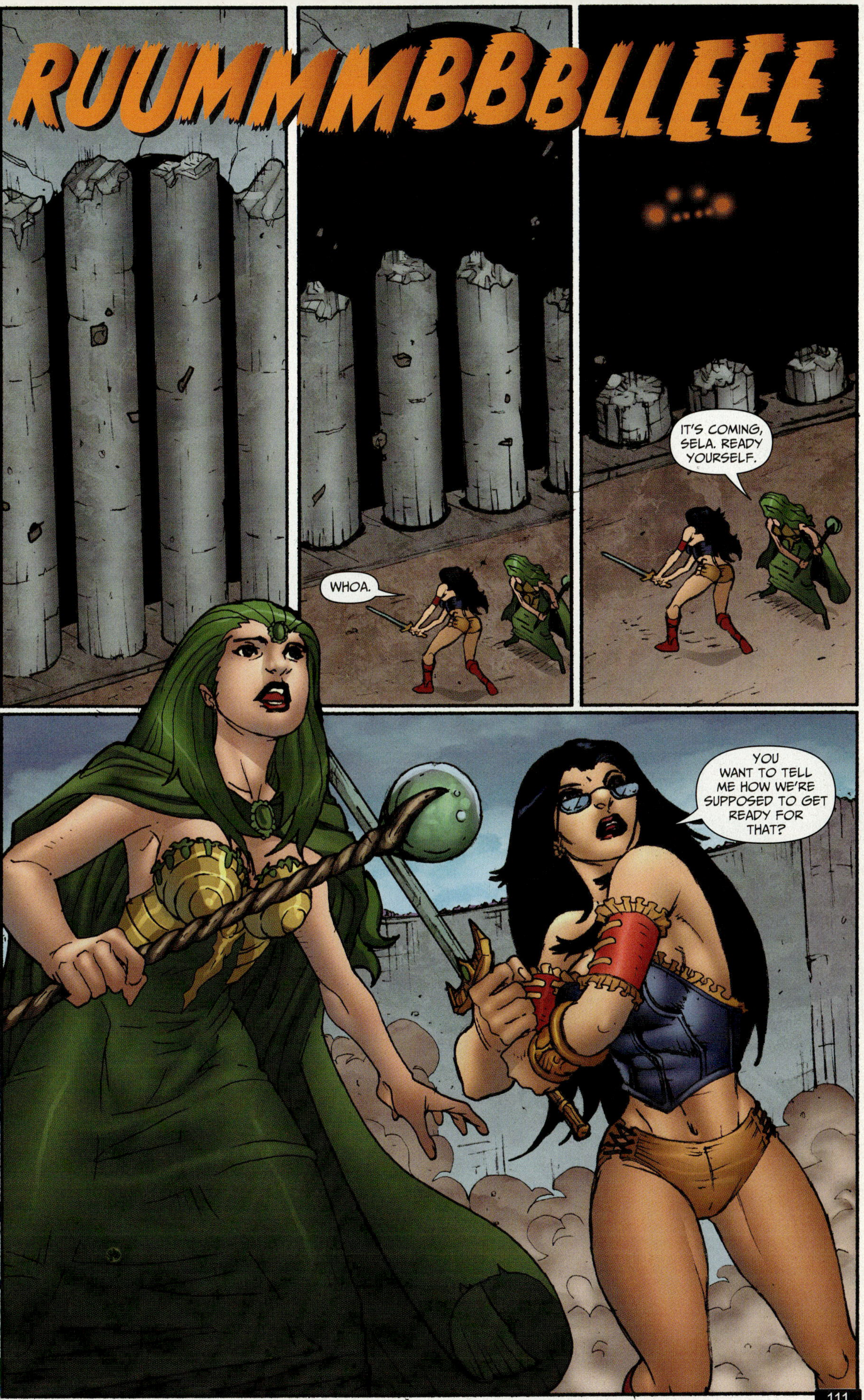
RUUMMMBBBLLEEE
WHOA.
IT'S COMING, SELA. READY YOURSELF.
YOU WANT TO TELL ME HOW WE'RE SUPPOSED TO GET READY FOR THAT?

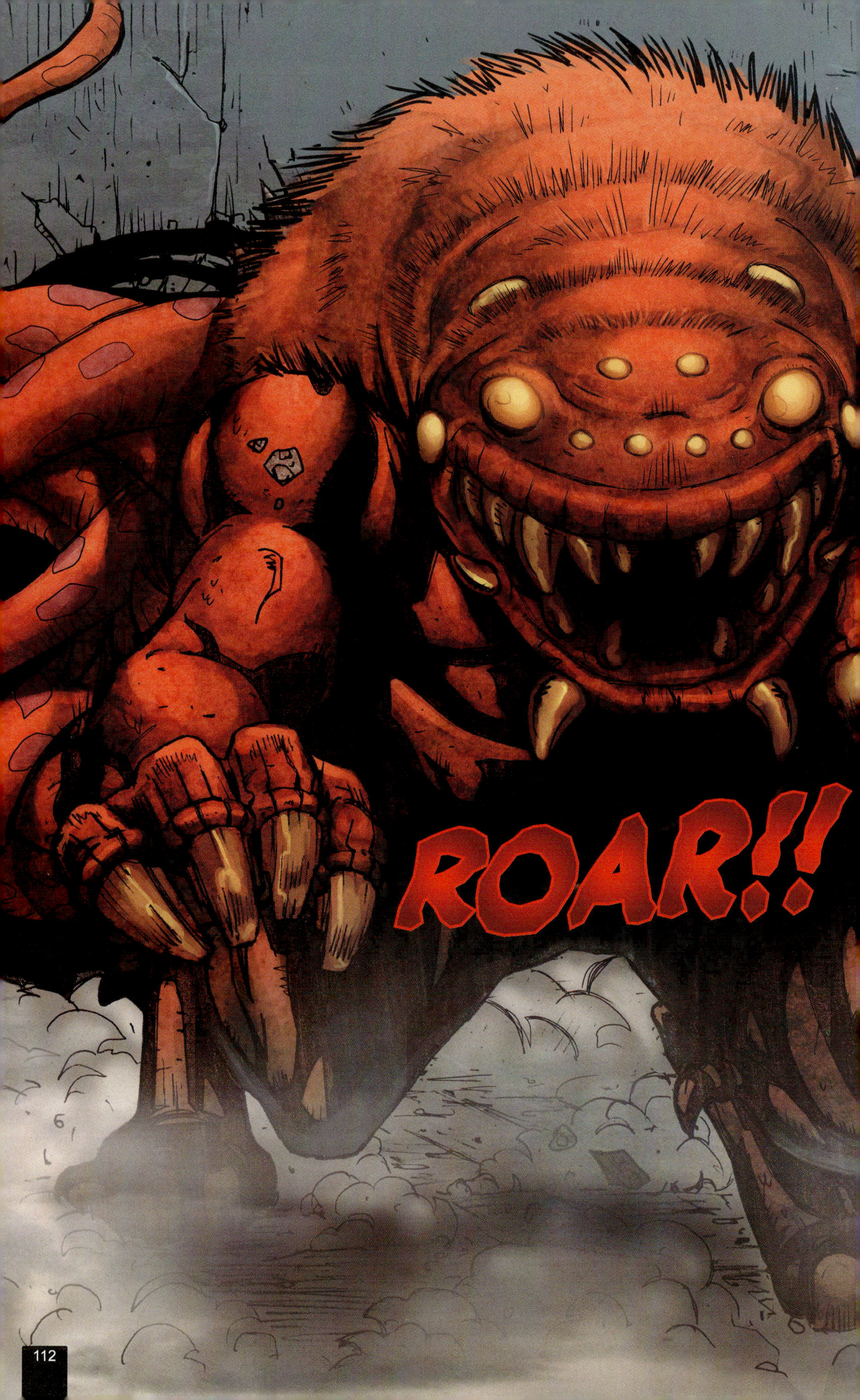
ROAR!!

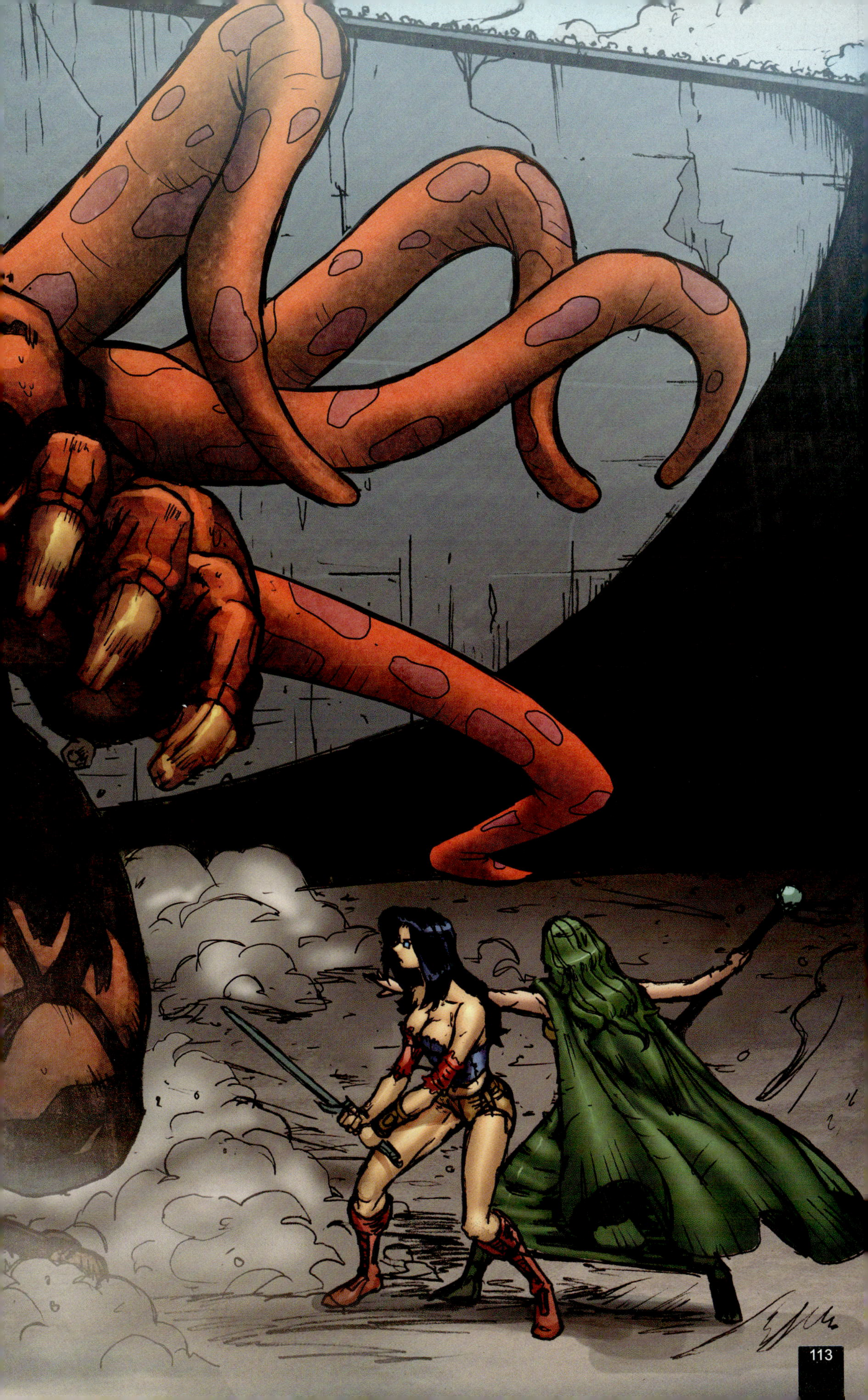

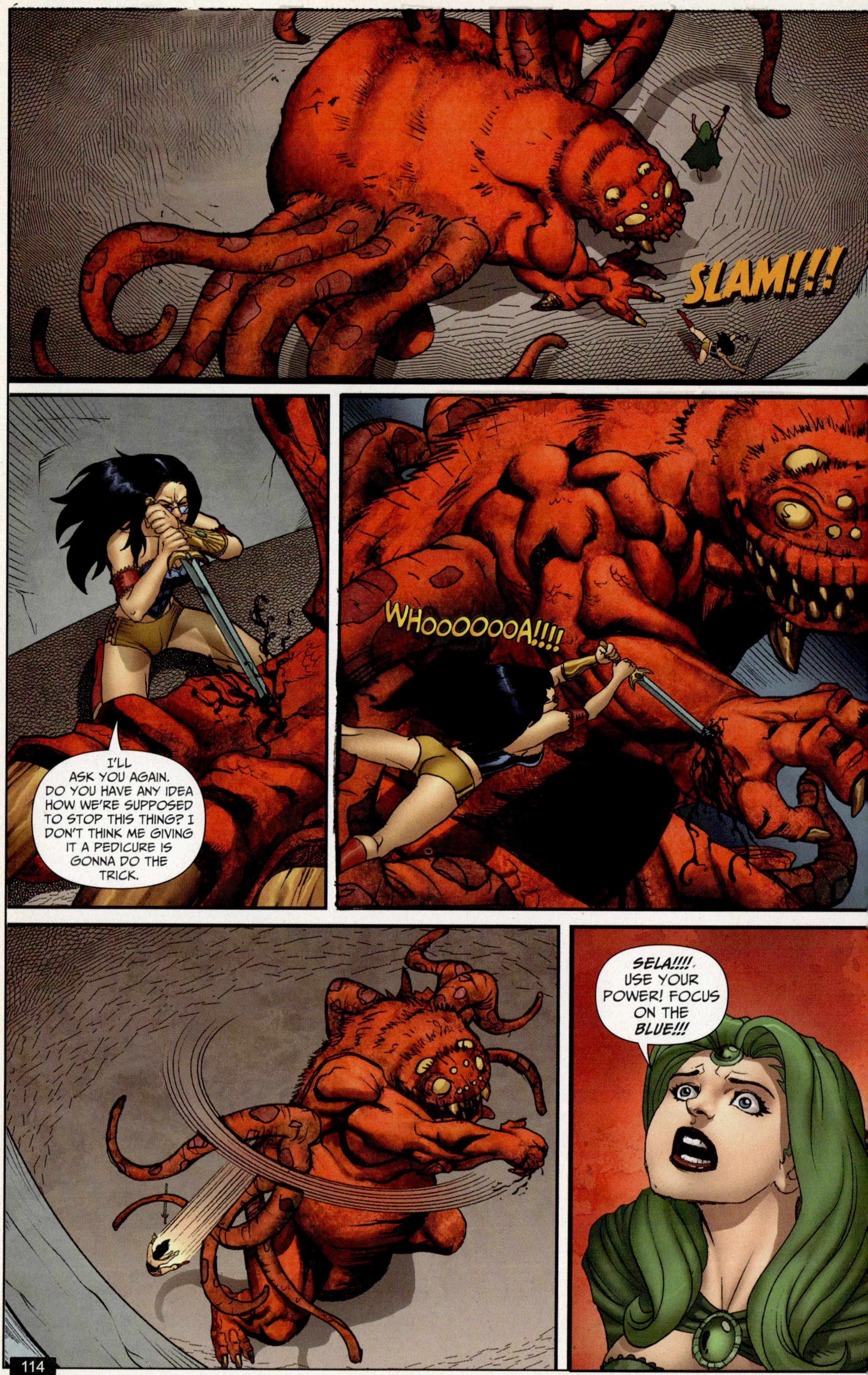
SLAM!!!
I'LL ASK YOU AGAIN. DO YOU HAVE ANY IDEA HOW WE'RE SUPPOSED TO STOP THIS THING? I DON'T THINK ME GIVING IT A PEDICURE IS GONNA DO THE TRICK.
WHOOOOOOA!!!!
SELA!!!! USE YOUR POWER! FOCUS ON THE BLUE!!!

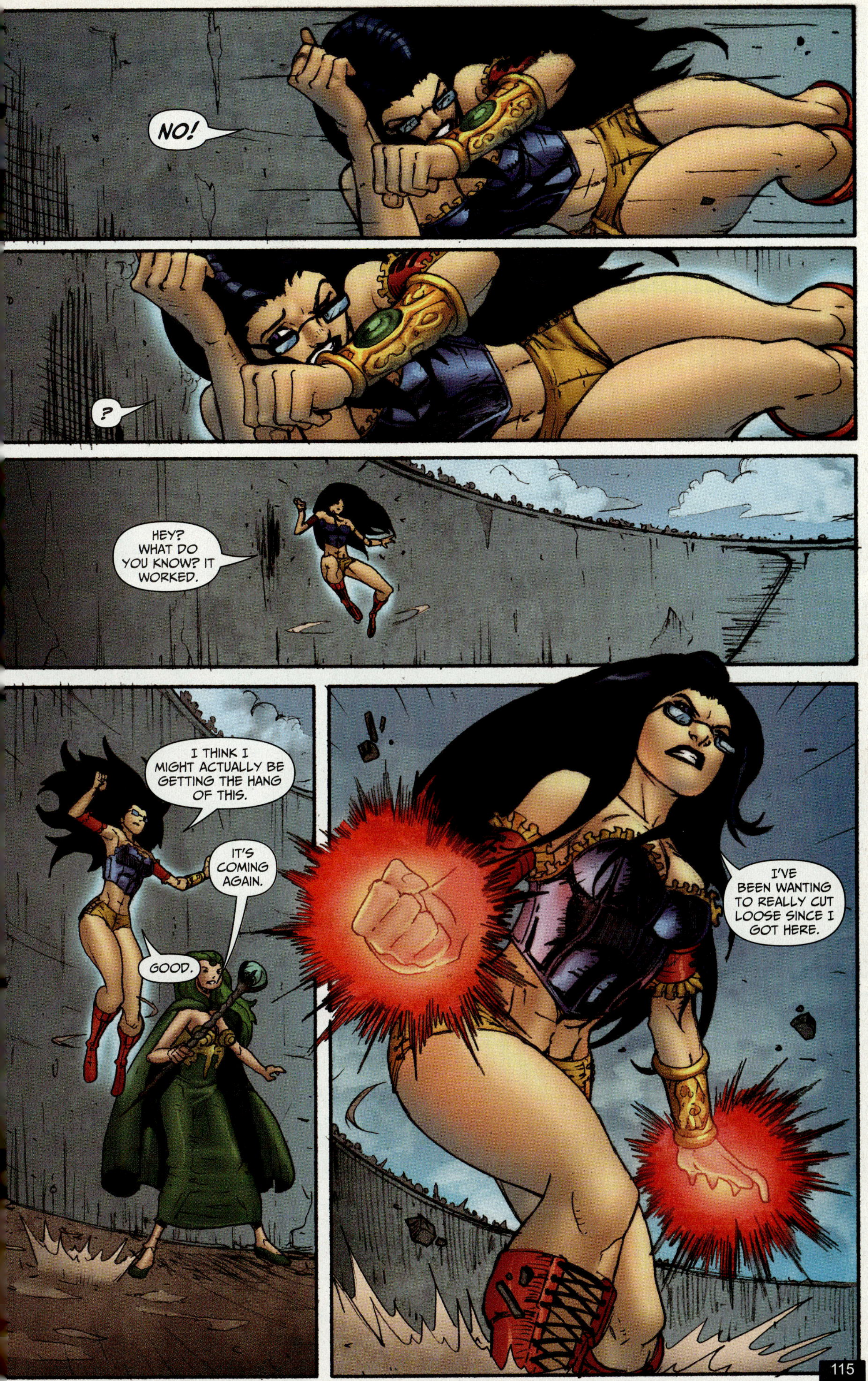
NO!
?
HEY? WHAT DO YOU KNOW? IT WORKED.
I THINK I MIGHT ACTUALLY BE GETTING THE HANG OF THIS.
IT'S COMING AGAIN.
GOOD.
I'VE BEEN WANTING TO REALLY CUT LOOSE SINCE I GOT HERE.

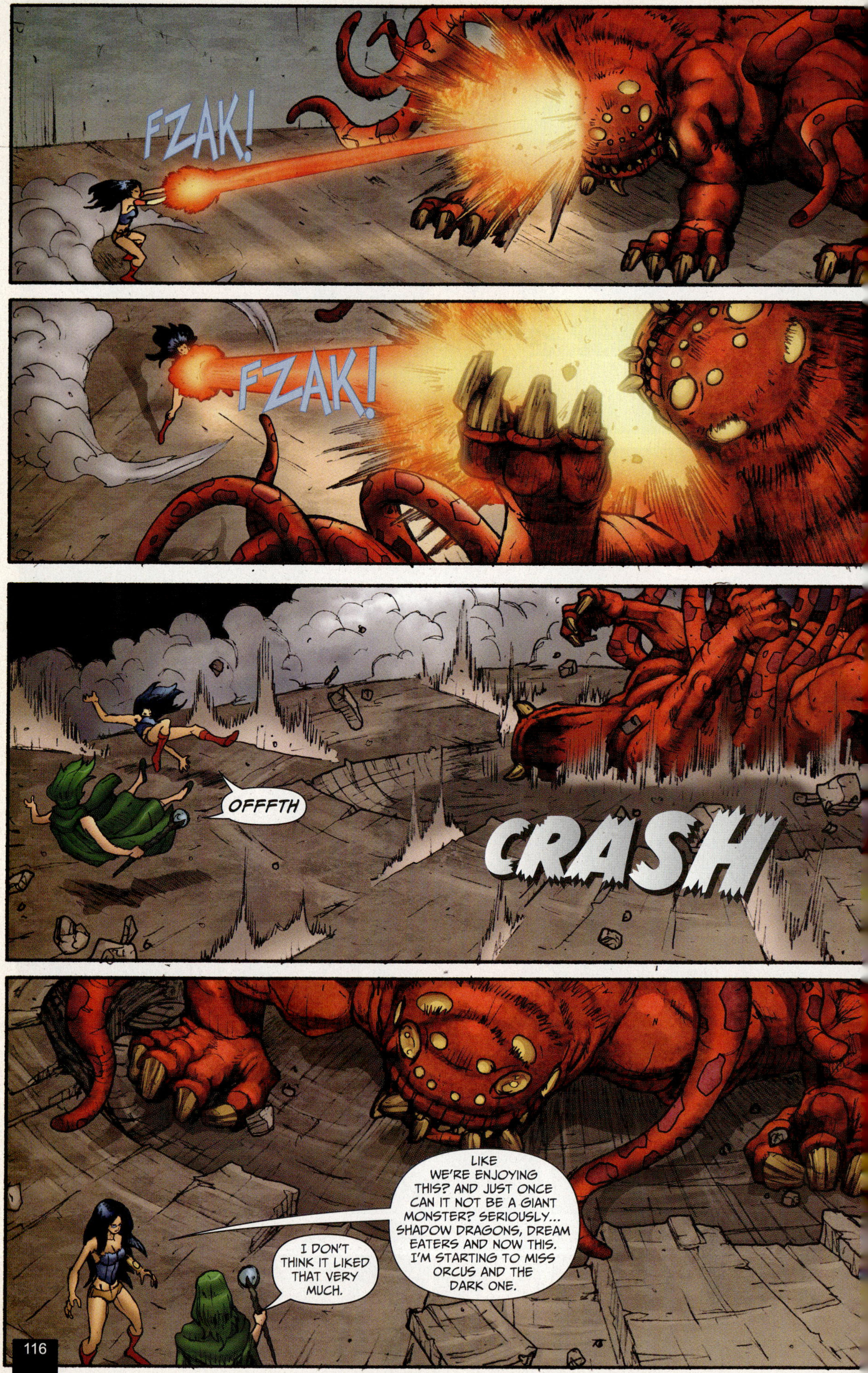
FZAK!
FZAK!
OFFFTH
CRASH
LIKE WE'RE ENJOYING THIS? AND JUST ONCE CAN IT NOT BE A GIANT MONSTER? SERIOUSLY... SHADOW DRAGONS, DREAM EATERS AND NOW THIS. I'M STARTING TO MISS ORCUS AND THE DARK ONE.
I DON'T THINK IT LIKED THAT VERY MUCH.

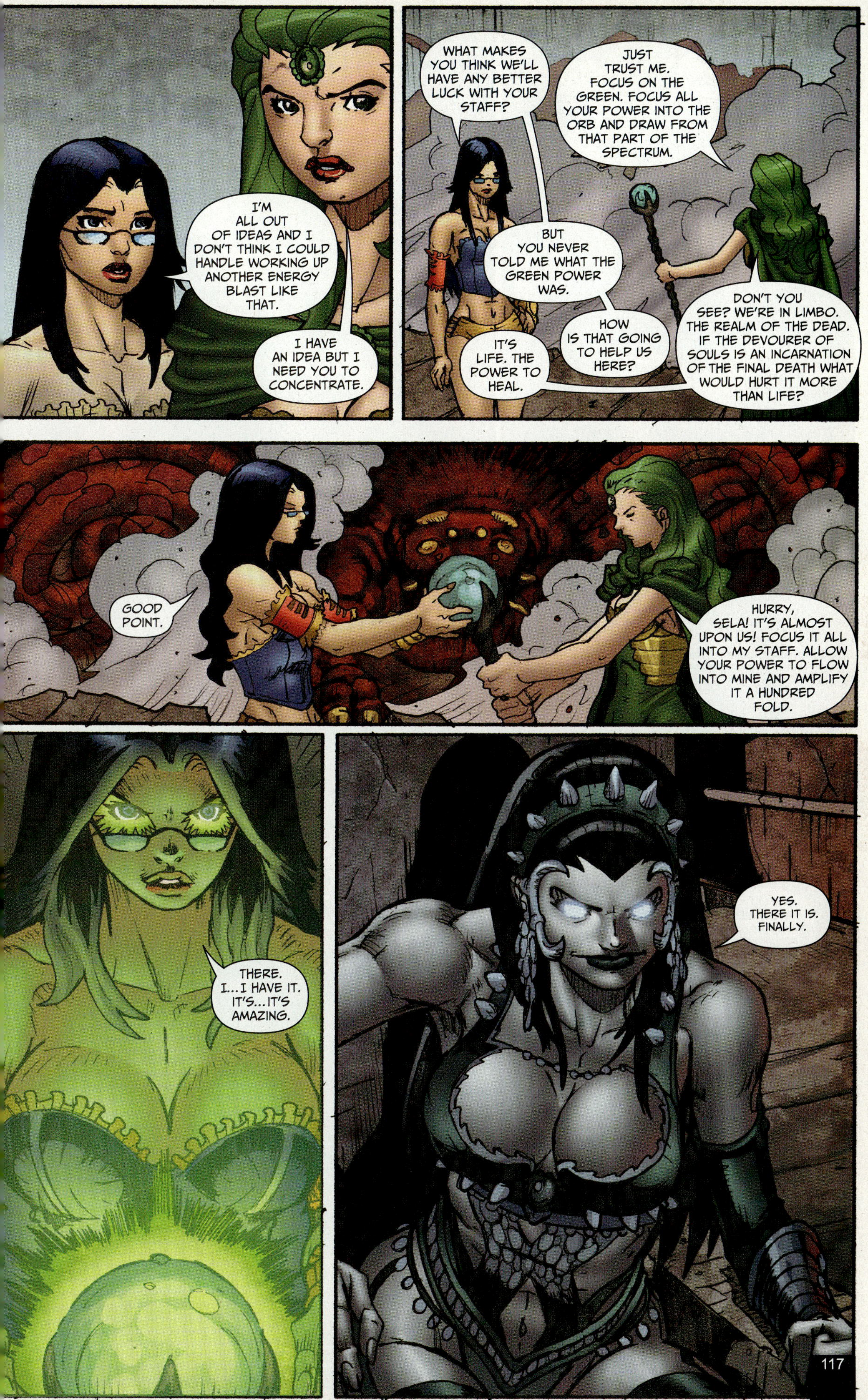
I'M ALL OUT OF IDEAS AND I DON'T THINK I COULD HANDLE WORKING UP ANOTHER ENERGY BLAST LIKE THAT.
I HAVE AN IDEA BUT I NEED YOU TO CONCENTRATE.
WHAT MAKES YOU THINK WE'LL HAVE ANY BETTER LUCK WITH YOUR STAFF?
JUST TRUST ME. FOCUS ON THE GREEN. FOCUS ALL YOUR POWER INTO THE ORB AND DRAW FROM THAT PART OF THE SPECTRUM.
BUT YOU NEVER TOLD ME WHAT THE GREEN POWER WAS.
IT'S LIFE. THE POWER TO HEAL.
HOW IS THAT GOING TO HELP US HERE?
DON'T YOU SEE? WE'RE IN LIMBO. THE REALM OF THE DEAD. IF THE DEVOURER OF SOULS IS AN INCARNATION OF THE FINAL DEATH WHAT WOULD HURT IT MORE THAN LIFE?
GOOD POINT.
HURRY, SELA! IT'S ALMOST UPON US! FOCUS IT ALL INTO MY STAFF. ALLOW YOUR POWER TO FLOW INTO MINE AND AMPLIFY IT A HUNDRED FOLD.
THERE. I...I HAVE IT. IT'S...IT'S AMAZING.
YES. THERE IT IS. FINALLY.

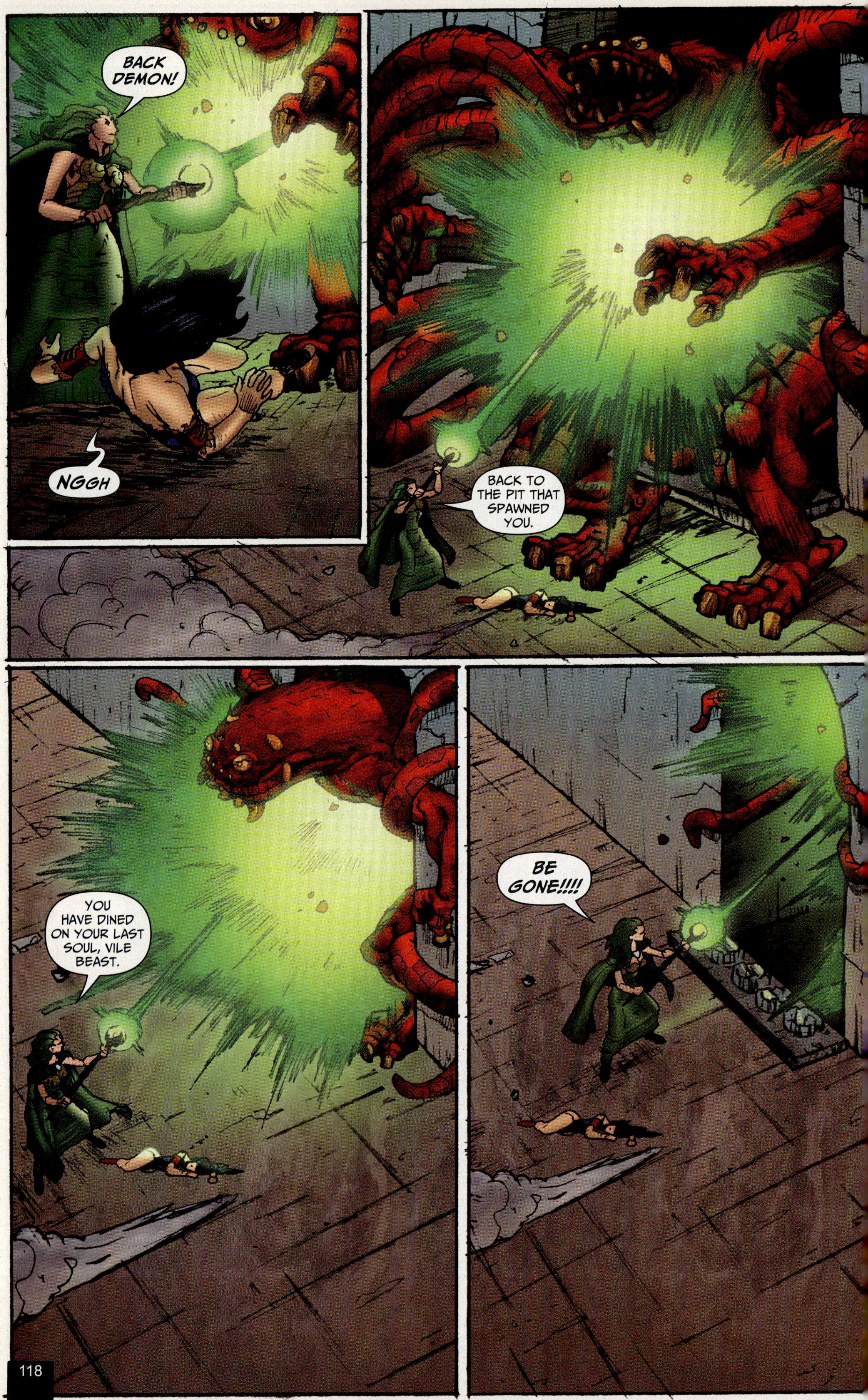
BACK DEMON!
NGGH
BACK TO THE PIT THAT SPAWNED YOU.
YOU HAVE DINED ON YOUR LAST SOUL, VILE BEAST.
BE GONE!!!!

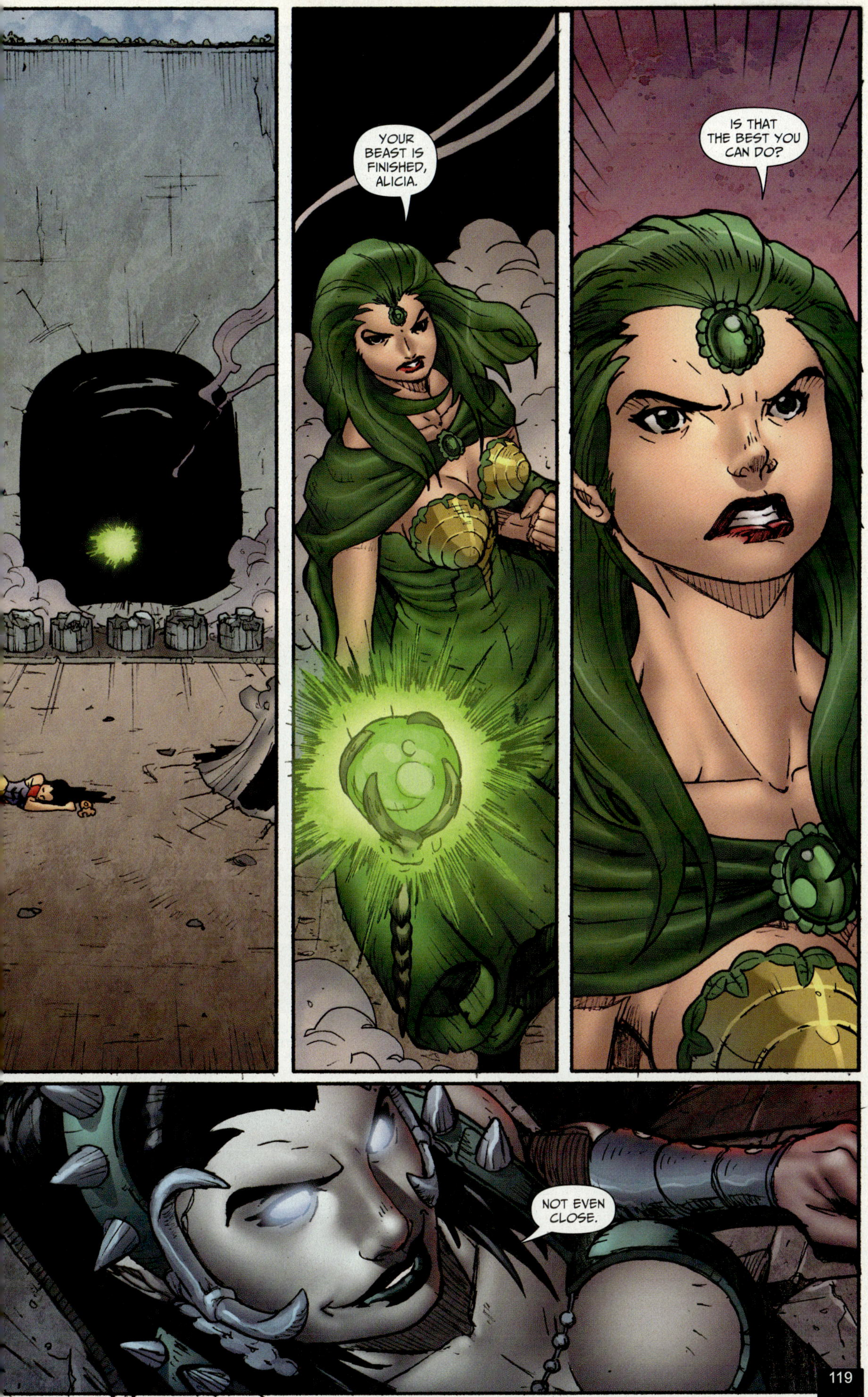
YOUR BEAST IS FINISHED, ALICIA.
IS THAT THE BEST YOU CAN DO?
NOT EVEN CLOSE.

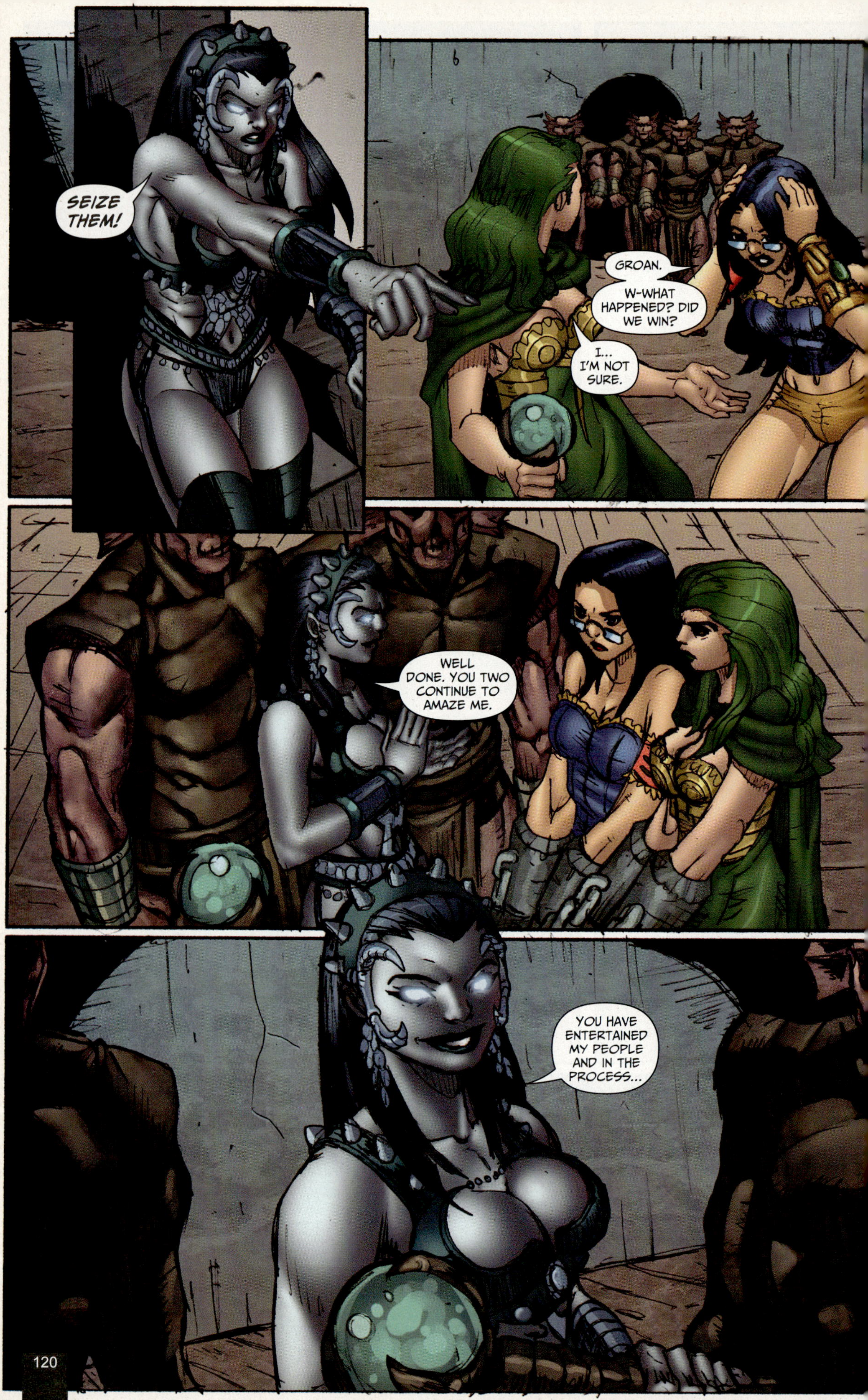
SEIZE THEM!
GROAN.
W-WHAT HAPPENED? DID WE WIN?
I... I'M NOT SURE.
WELL DONE. YOU TWO CONTINUE TO AMAZE ME.
YOU HAVE ENTERTAINED MY PEOPLE AND IN THE PROCESS...

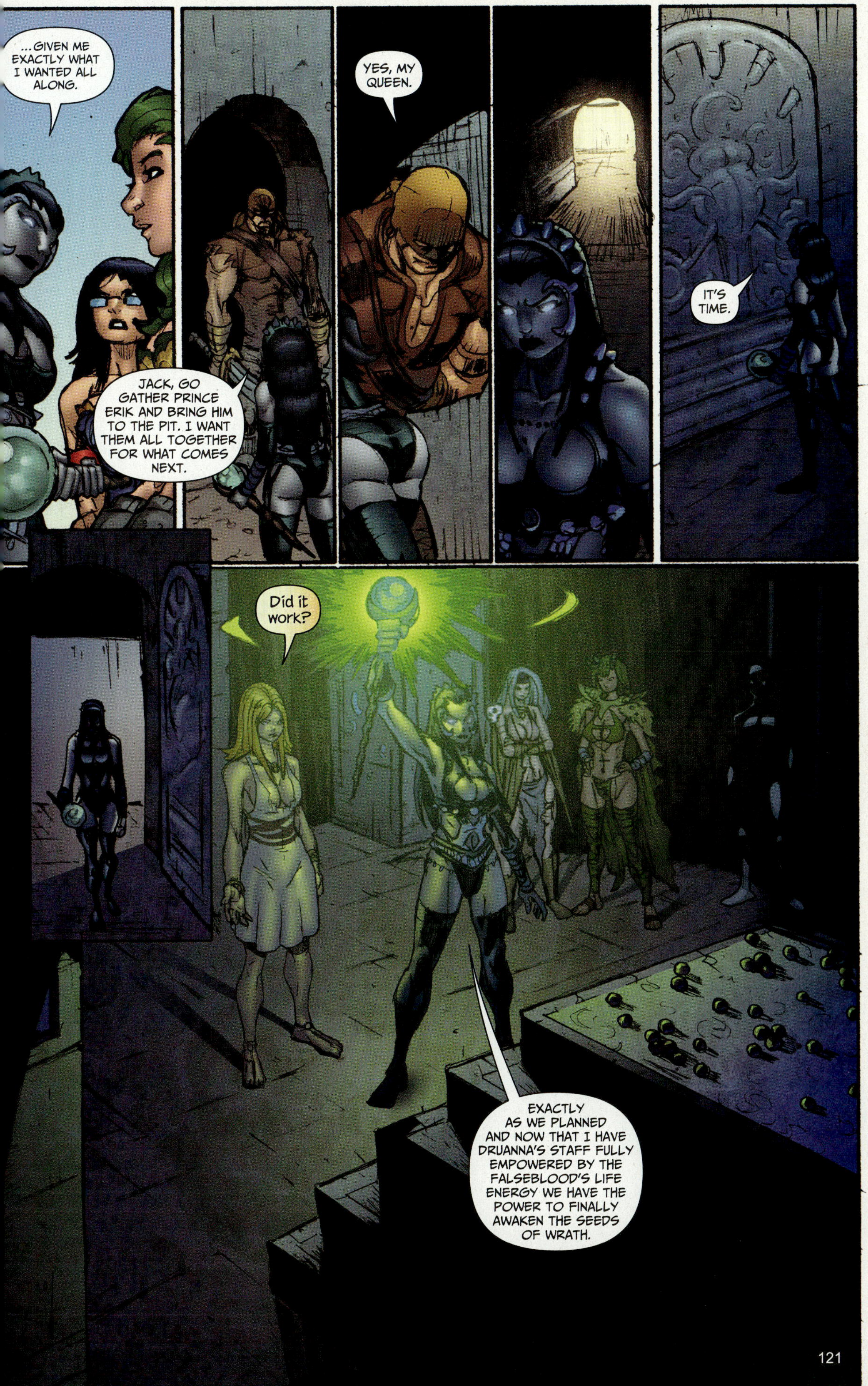

...GIVEN ME EXACTLY WHAT I WANTED ALL ALONG.
JACK, GO GATHER PRINCE ERIK AND BRING HIM TO THE PIT. I WANT THEM ALL TOGETHER FOR WHAT COMES NEXT.
YES, MY QUEEN.
IT'S TIME.
Did it work?
EXACTLY AS WE PLANNED AND NOW THAT I HAVE DRUANNA'S STAFF FULLY EMPOWERED BY THE FALSEBLOOD'S LIFE ENERGY WE HAVE THE POWER TO FINALLY AWAKEN THE SEEDS OF WRATH.

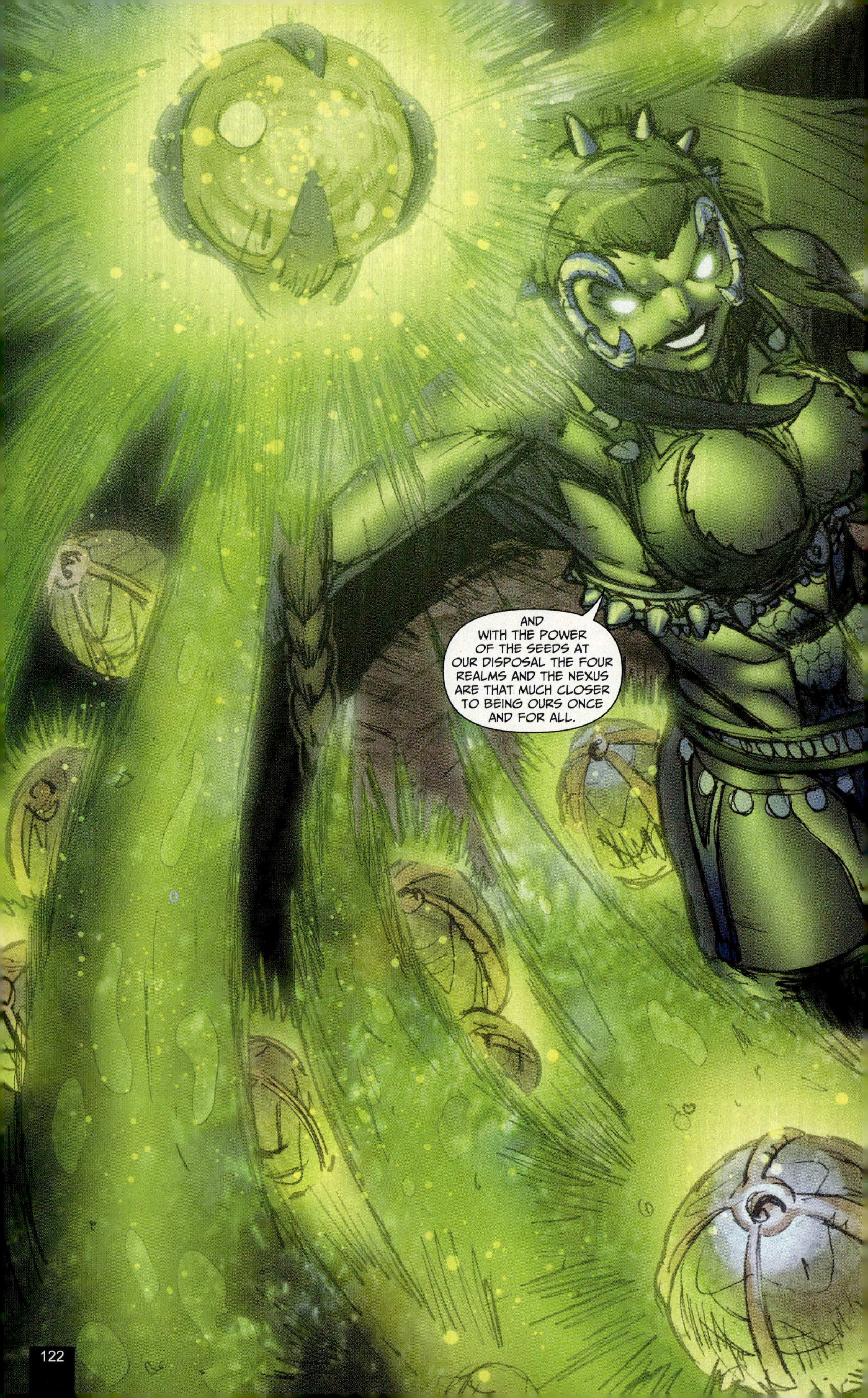
AND WITH THE POWER OF THE SEEDS AT OUR DISPOSAL THE FOUR REALMS AND THE NEXUS ARE THAT MUCH CLOSER TO BEING OURS ONCE AND FOR ALL.

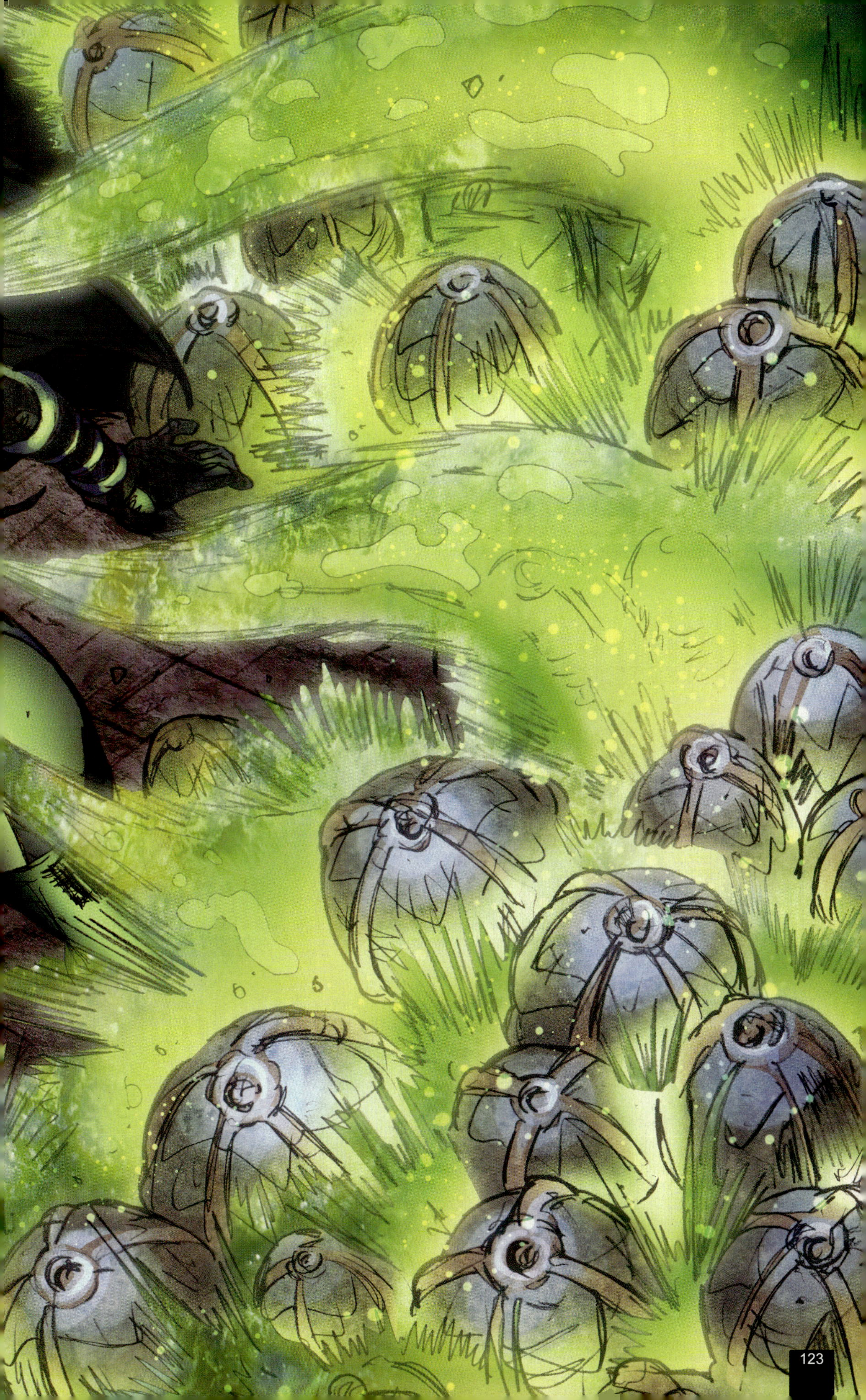

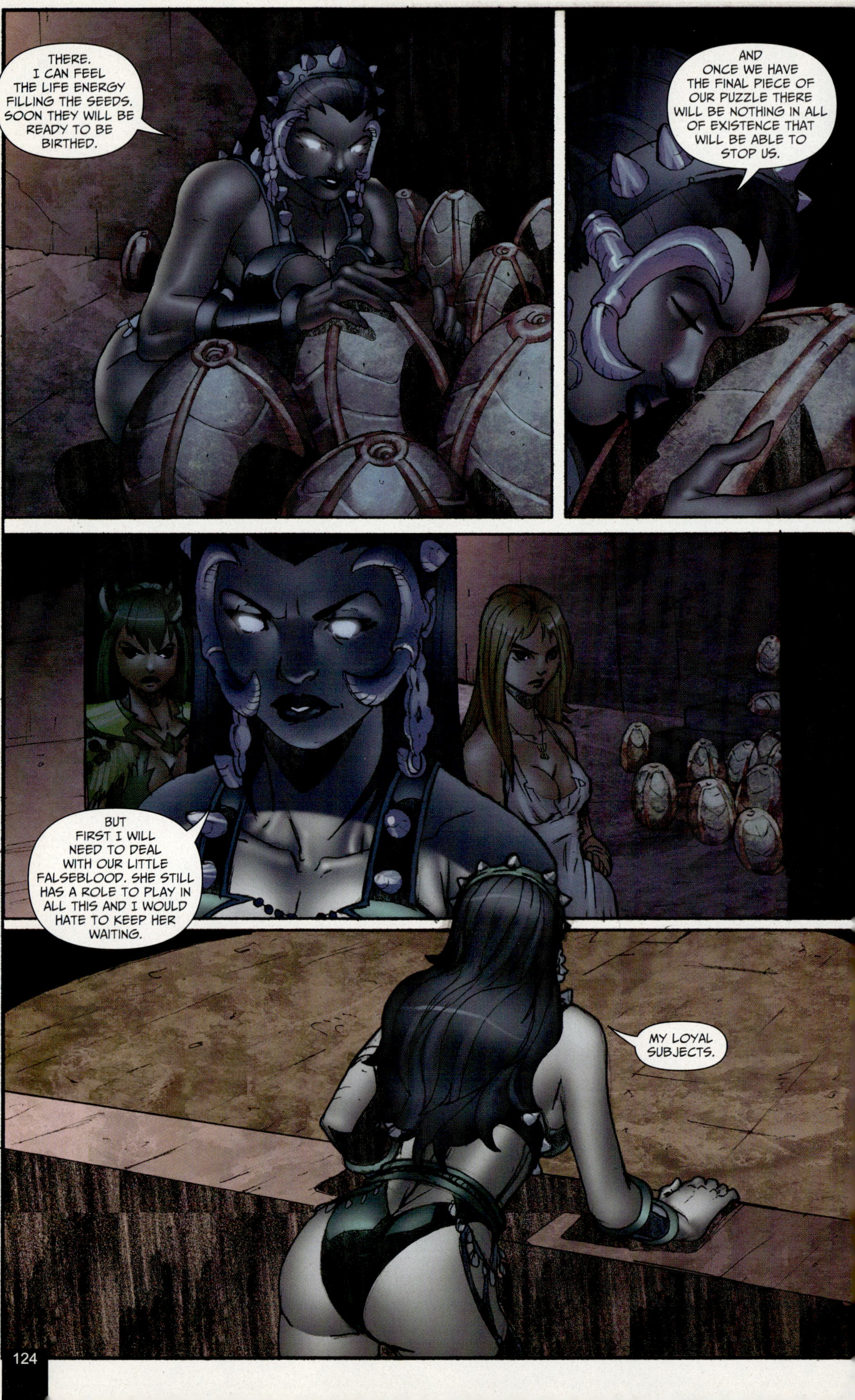
THERE. I CAN FEEL THE LIFE ENERGY FILLING THE SEEDS. SOON THEY WILL BE READY TO BE BIRTHED.
AND ONCE WE HAVE THE FINAL PIECE OF OUR PUZZLE THERE WILL BE NOTHING IN ALL OF EXISTENCE THAT WILL BE ABLE TO STOP US.
BUT FIRST I WILL NEED TO DEAL WITH OUR LITTLE FALSEBLOOD. SHE STILL HAS A ROLE TO PLAY IN ALL THIS AND I WOULD HATE TO KEEP HER WAITING.
MY LOYAL SUBJECTS.

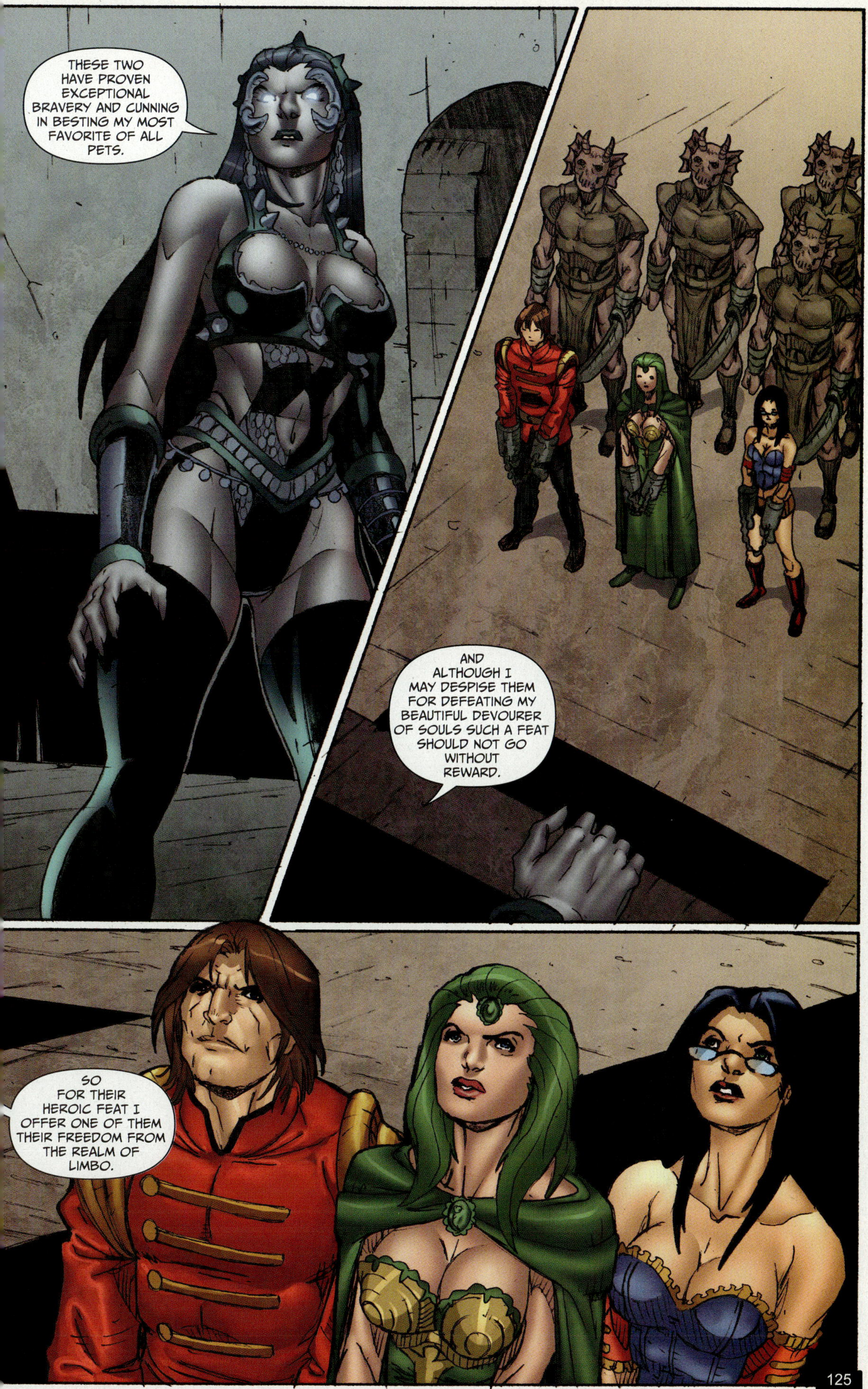
THESE TWO HAVE PROVEN EXCEPTIONAL BRAVERY AND CUNNING IN BESTING MY MOST FAVORITE OF ALL PETS.
AND ALTHOUGH I MAY DESPISE THEM FOR DEFEATING MY BEAUTIFUL DEVOURER OF SOULS SUCH A FEAT SHOULD NOT GO WITHOUT REWARD.
SO FOR THEIR HEROIC FEAT I OFFER ONE OF THEM THEIR FREEDOM FROM THE REALM OF LIMBO.

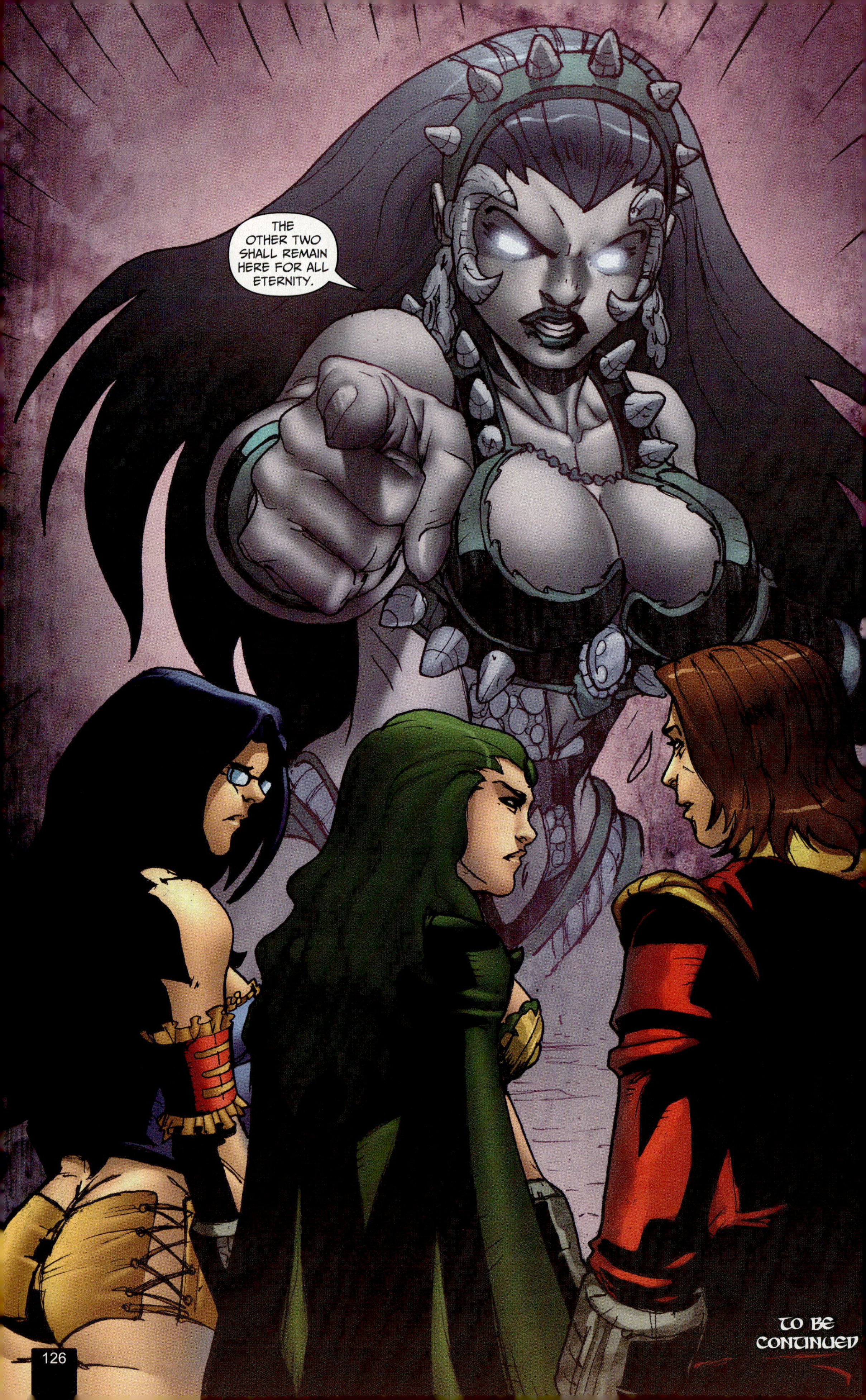
THE OTHER TWO SHALL REMAIN HERE FOR ALL ETERNITY.
TO BE CONTINUED

Grimm Fairy Tales
Volume 11

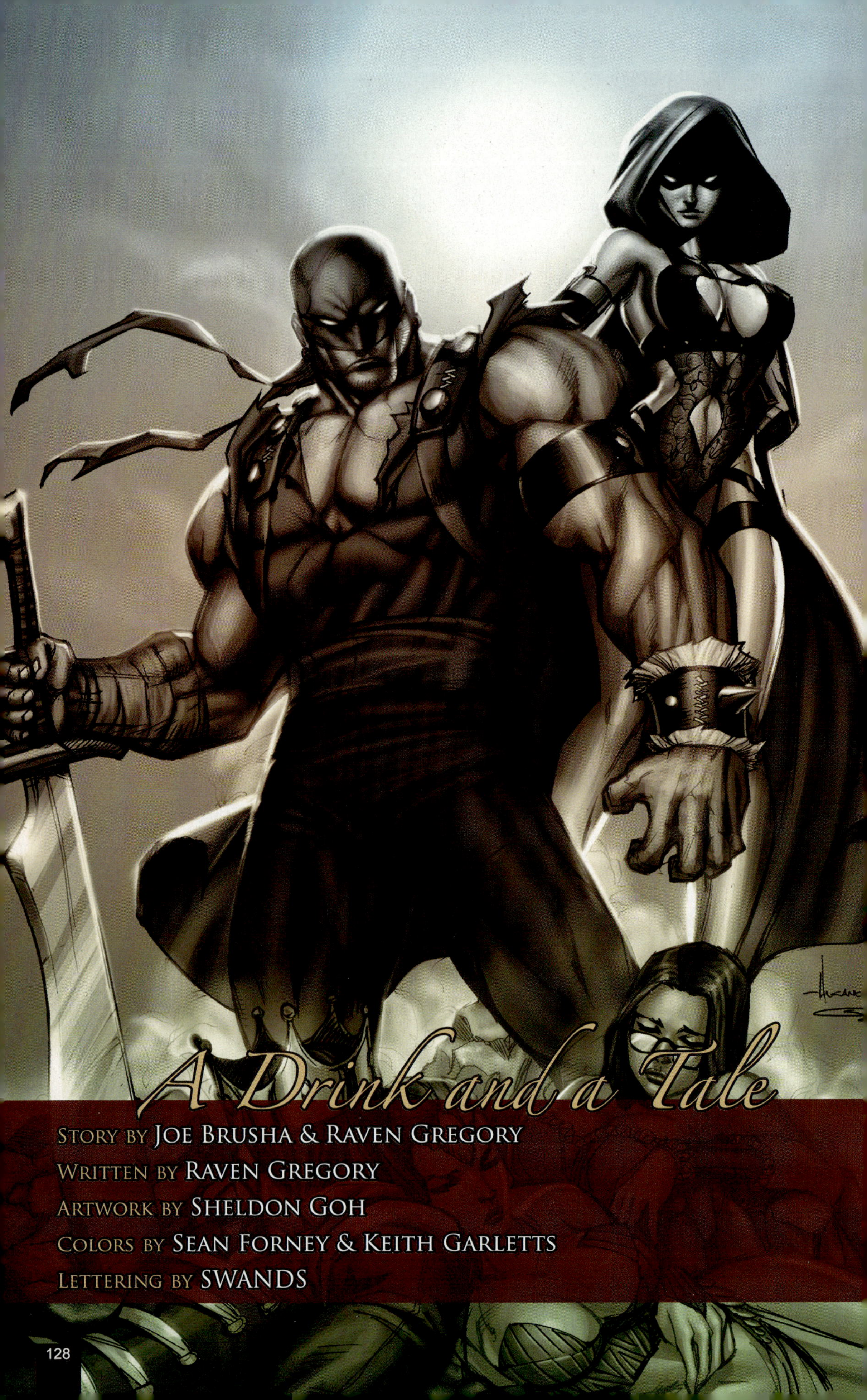

A Drink and a Tale

Story by Joe Brusha & Raven Gregory
Written by Raven Gregory
Artwork by Sheldon Goh
Colors by Sean Forney & Keith Garletts
Lettering by SWANDS

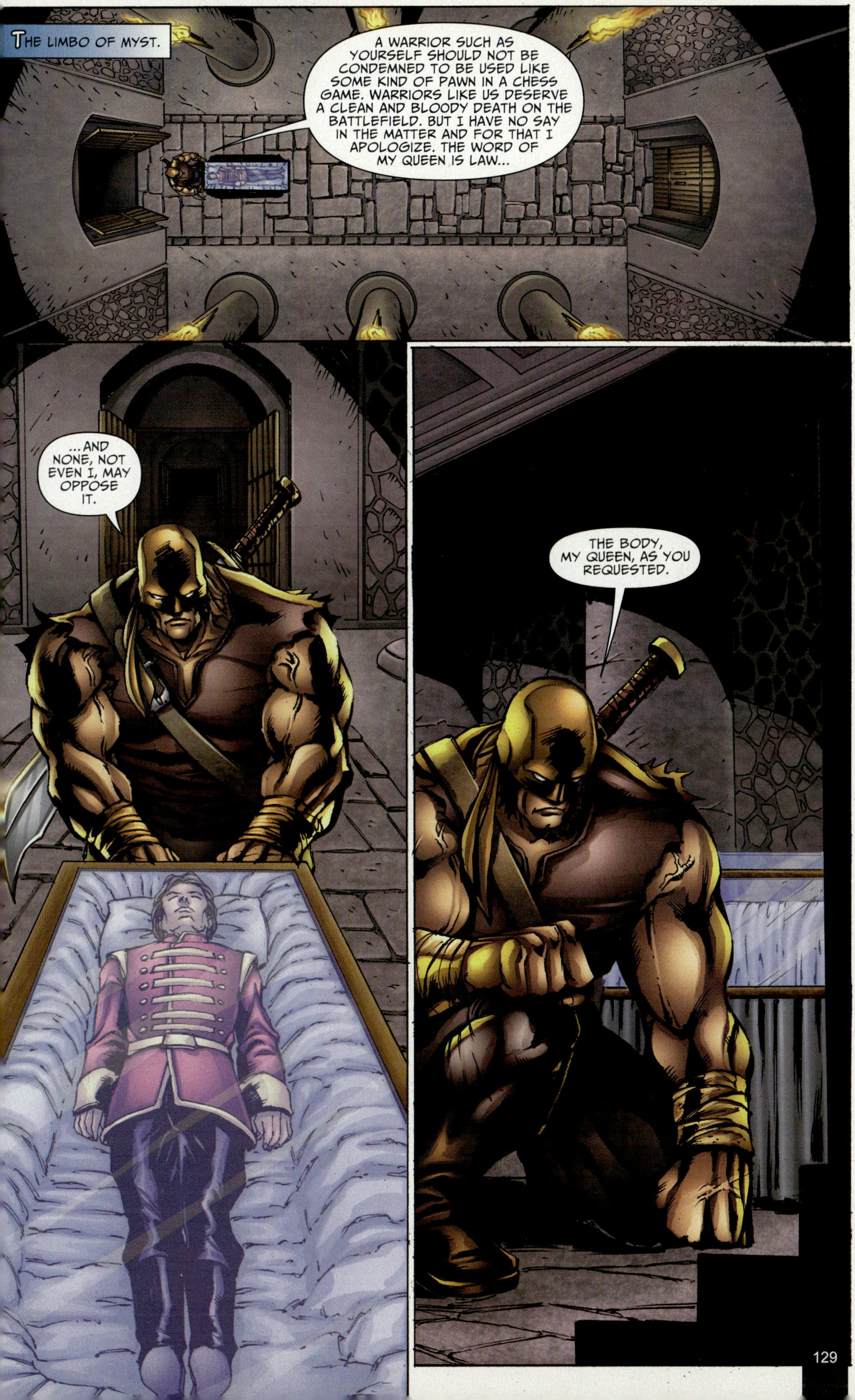
THE LIMBO OF MYST.
A WARRIOR SUCH AS YOURSELF SHOULD NOT BE CONDEMNED TO BE USED LIKE SOME KIND OF PAWN IN A CHESS GAME. WARRIORS LIKE US DESERVE A CLEAN AND BLOODY DEATH ON THE BATTLEFIELD. BUT I HAVE NO SAY IN THE MATTER AND FOR THAT I APOLOGIZE. THE WORD OF MY QUEEN IS LAW...
...AND NONE, NOT EVEN I, MAY OPPOSE IT.
THE BODY, MY QUEEN, AS YOU REQUESTED.

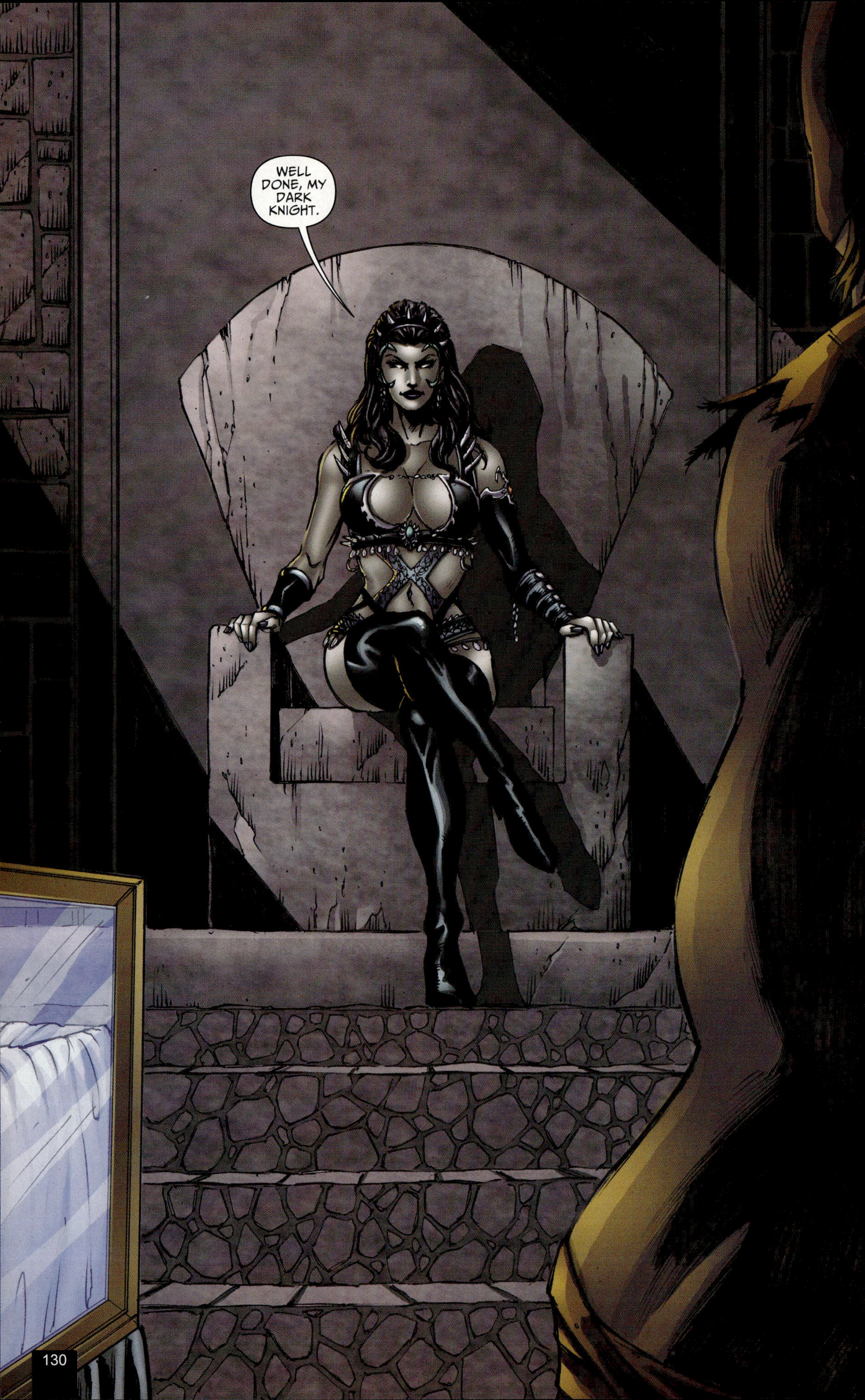
WELL DONE, MY DARK KNIGHT.

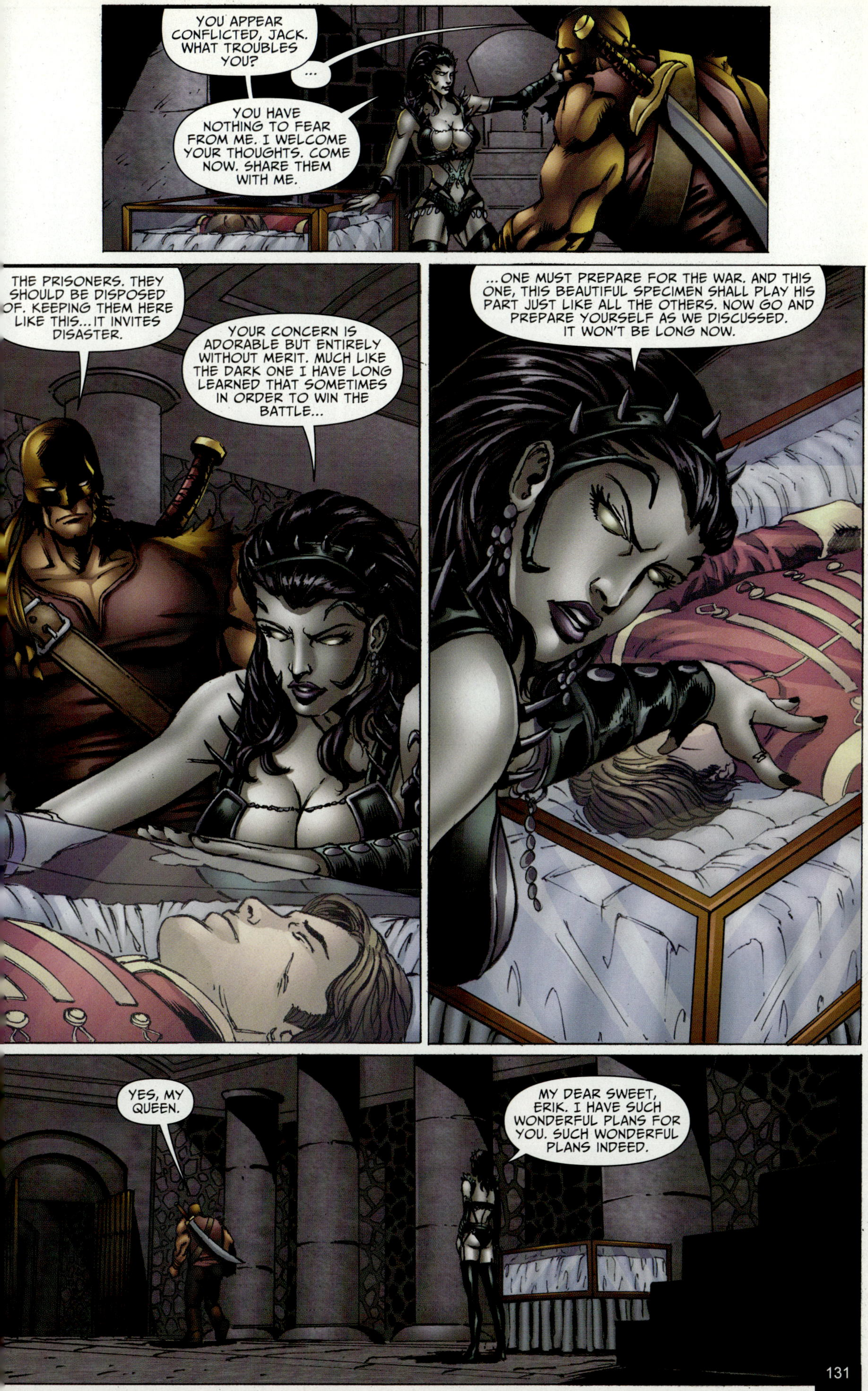
YOU APPEAR CONFLICTED, JACK. WHAT TROUBLES YOU?
...
YOU HAVE NOTHING TO FEAR FROM ME. I WELCOME YOUR THOUGHTS. COME NOW. SHARE THEM WITH ME.
THE PRISONERS. THEY SHOULD BE DISPOSED OF. KEEPING THEM HERE LIKE THIS... IT INVITES DISASTER.
YOUR CONCERN IS ADORABLE BUT ENTIRELY WITHOUT MERIT. MUCH LIKE THE DARK ONE I HAVE LONG LEARNED THAT SOMETIMES IN ORDER TO WIN THE BATTLE...
...ONE MUST PREPARE FOR THE WAR. AND THIS ONE, THIS BEAUTIFUL SPECIMEN SHALL PLAY HIS PART JUST LIKE ALL THE OTHERS. NOW GO AND PREPARE YOURSELF AS WE DISCUSSED. IT WON'T BE LONG NOW.
YES, MY QUEEN.
MY DEAR SWEET, ERIK. I HAVE SUCH WONDERFUL PLANS FOR YOU. SUCH WONDERFUL PLANS INDEED.

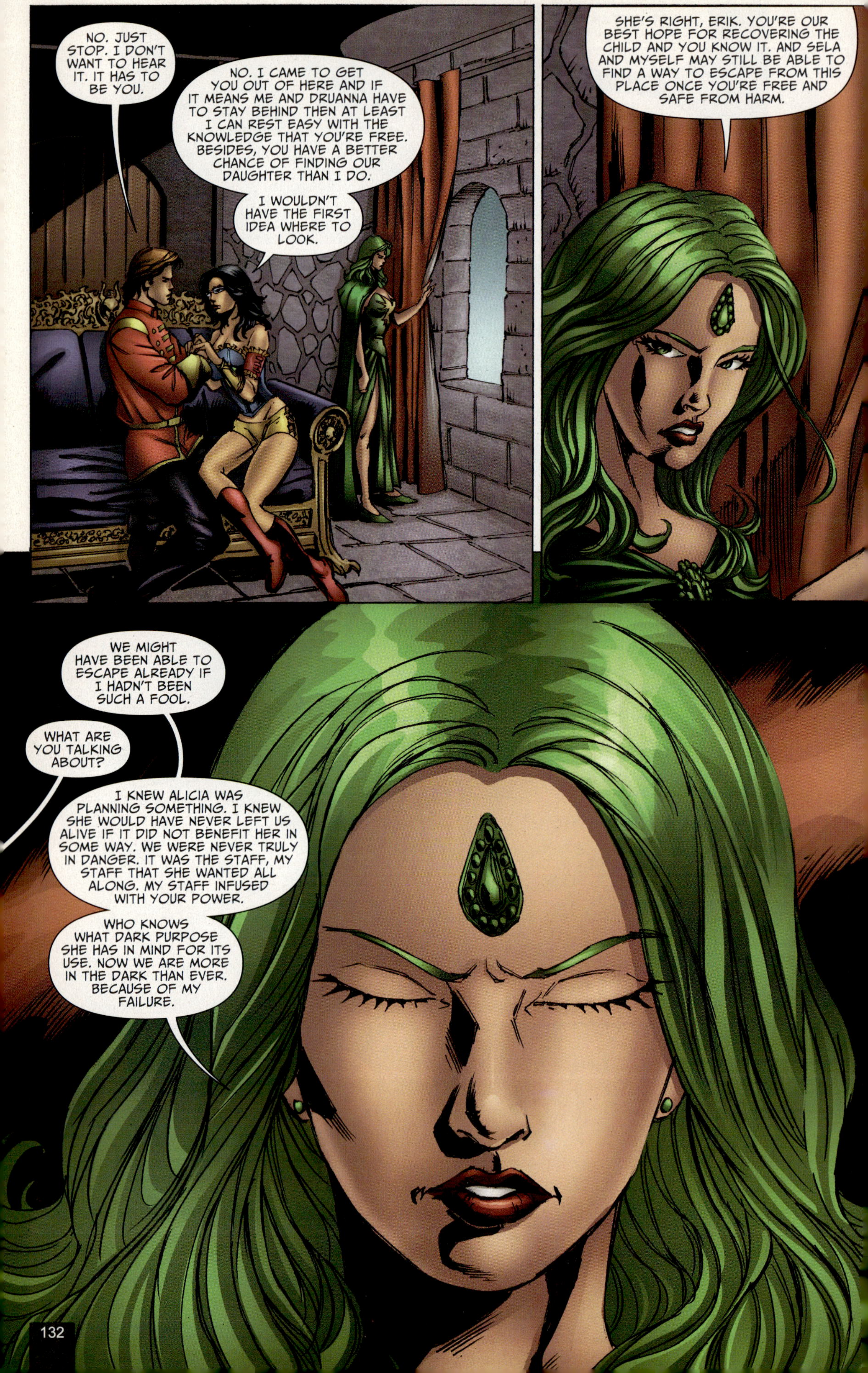
NO. JUST STOP. I DON'T WANT TO HEAR IT. IT HAS TO BE YOU.
NO. I CAME TO GET YOU OUT OF HERE AND IF IT MEANS ME AND DRUANNA HAVE TO STAY BEHIND THEN AT LEAST I CAN REST EASY WITH THE KNOWLEDGE THAT YOU'RE FREE. BESIDES, YOU HAVE A BETTER CHANCE OF FINDING OUR DAUGHTER THAN I DO.
I WOULDN'T HAVE THE FIRST IDEA WHERE TO LOOK.
SHE'S RIGHT, ERIK. YOU'RE OUR BEST HOPE FOR RECOVERING THE CHILD AND YOU KNOW IT. AND SELA AND MYSELF MAY STILL BE ABLE TO FIND A WAY TO ESCAPE FROM THIS PLACE ONCE YOU'RE FREE AND SAFE FROM HARM.
WE MIGHT HAVE BEEN ABLE TO ESCAPE ALREADY IF I HADN'T BEEN SUCH A FOOL.
WHAT ARE YOU TALKING ABOUT?
I KNEW ALICIA WAS PLANNING SOMETHING. I KNEW SHE WOULD HAVE NEVER LEFT US ALIVE IF IT DID NOT BENEFIT HER IN SOME WAY. WE WERE NEVER TRULY IN DANGER. IT WAS THE STAFF, MY STAFF THAT SHE WANTED ALL ALONG. MY STAFF INFUSED WITH YOUR POWER.
WHO KNOWS WHAT DARK PURPOSE SHE HAS IN MIND FOR ITS USE. NOW WE ARE MORE IN THE DARK THAN EVER. BECAUSE OF MY FAILURE.

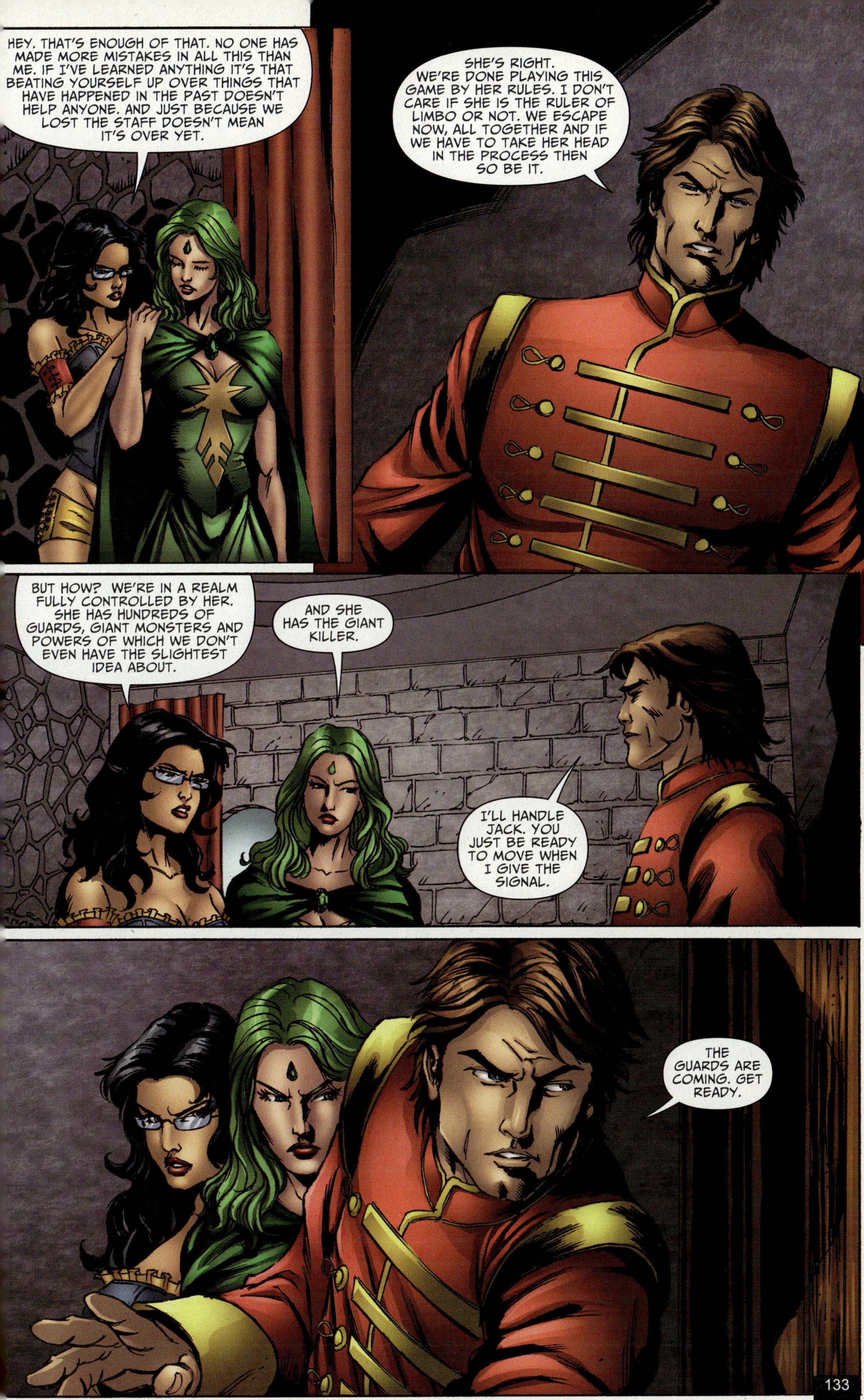
HEY. THAT'S ENOUGH OF THAT. NO ONE HAS MADE MORE MISTAKES IN ALL THIS THAN ME. IF I'VE LEARNED ANYTHING IT'S THAT BEATING YOURSELF UP OVER THINGS THAT HAVE HAPPENED IN THE PAST DOESN'T HELP ANYONE. AND JUST BECAUSE WE LOST THE STAFF DOESN'T MEAN IT'S OVER YET.
SHE'S RIGHT. WE'RE DONE PLAYING THIS GAME BY HER RULES. I DON'T CARE IF SHE IS THE RULER OF LIMBO OR NOT. WE ESCAPE NOW, ALL TOGETHER AND IF WE HAVE TO TAKE HER HEAD IN THE PROCESS THEN SO BE IT.
BUT HOW? WE'RE IN A REALM FULLY CONTROLLED BY HER. SHE HAS HUNDREDS OF GUARDS, GIANT MONSTERS AND POWERS OF WHICH WE DON'T EVEN HAVE THE SLIGHTEST IDEA ABOUT.
AND SHE HAS THE GIANT KILLER.
I'LL HANDLE JACK. YOU JUST BE READY TO MOVE WHEN I GIVE THE SIGNAL.
THE GUARDS ARE COMING. GET READY.

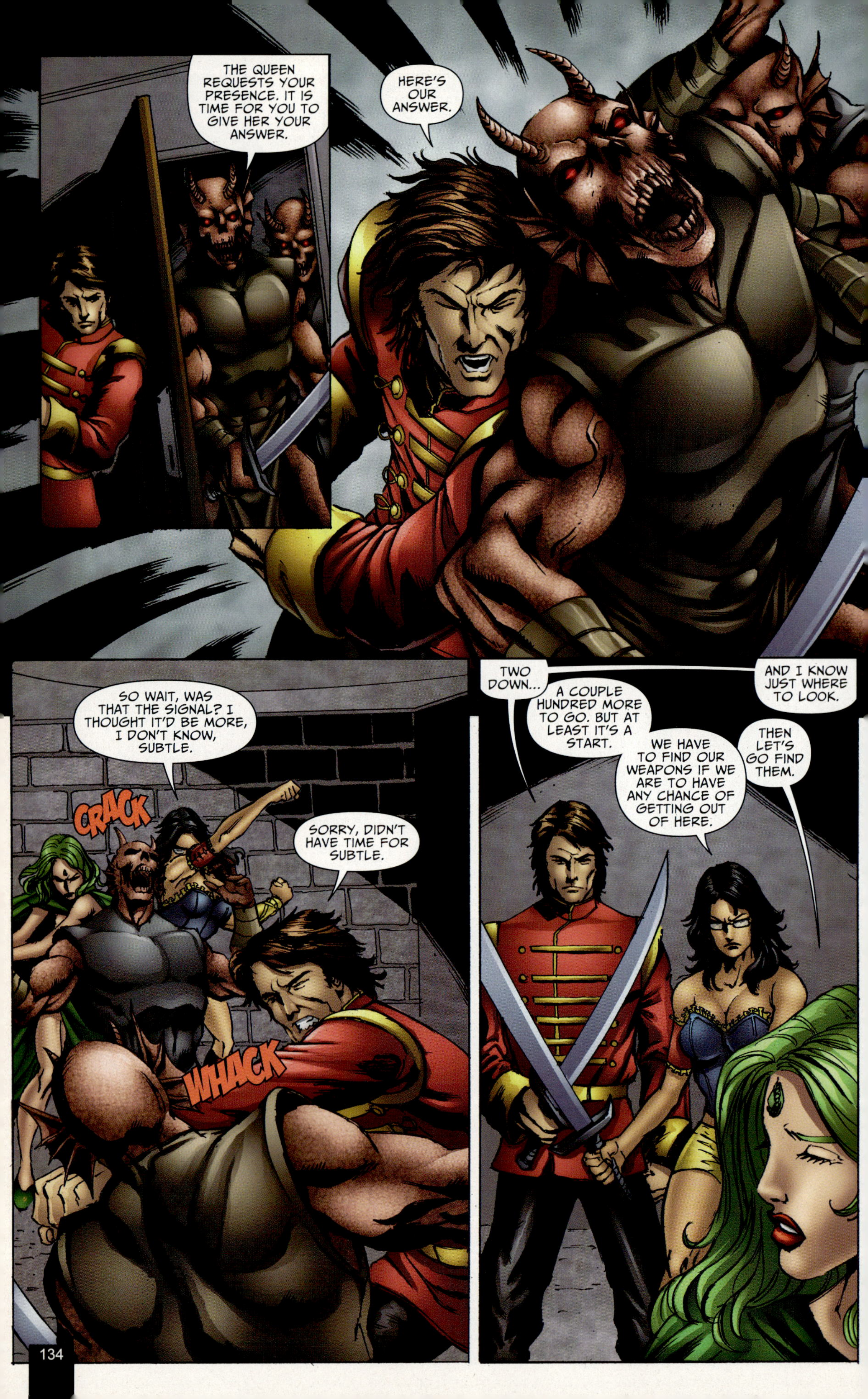

THE QUEEN REQUESTS YOUR PRESENCE. IT IS TIME FOR YOU TO GIVE HER YOUR ANSWER.
HERE'S OUR ANSWER.
SO WAIT, WAS THAT THE SIGNAL? I THOUGHT IT'D BE MORE, I DON'T KNOW, SUBTLE.
CRACK
SORRY, DIDN'T HAVE TIME FOR SUBTLE.
WHACK
TWO DOWN...
A COUPLE HUNDRED MORE TO GO. BUT AT LEAST IT'S A START.
AND I KNOW JUST WHERE TO LOOK.
WE HAVE TO FIND OUR WEAPONS IF WE ARE TO HAVE ANY CHANCE OF GETTING OUT OF HERE.
THEN LET'S GO FIND THEM.

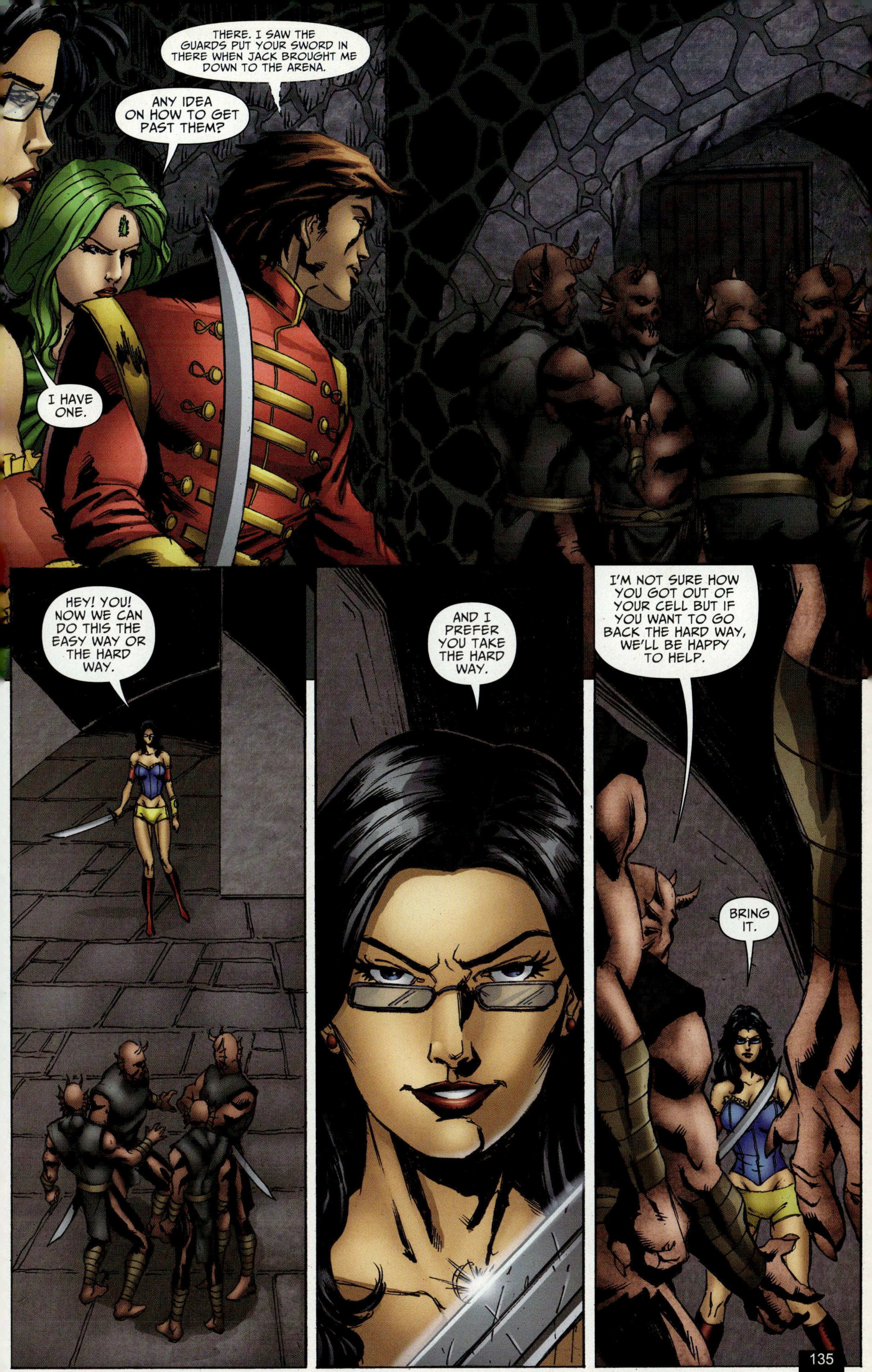

THERE. I SAW THE GUARDS PUT YOUR SWORD IN THERE WHEN JACK BROUGHT ME DOWN TO THE ARENA.
ANY IDEA ON HOW TO GET PAST THEM?
I HAVE ONE.
HEY! YOU! NOW WE CAN DO THIS THE EASY WAY OR THE HARD WAY.
AND I PREFER YOU TAKE THE HARD WAY.
I'M NOT SURE HOW YOU GOT OUT OF YOUR CELL BUT IF YOU WANT TO GO BACK THE HARD WAY, WE'LL BE HAPPY TO HELP.
BRING IT.

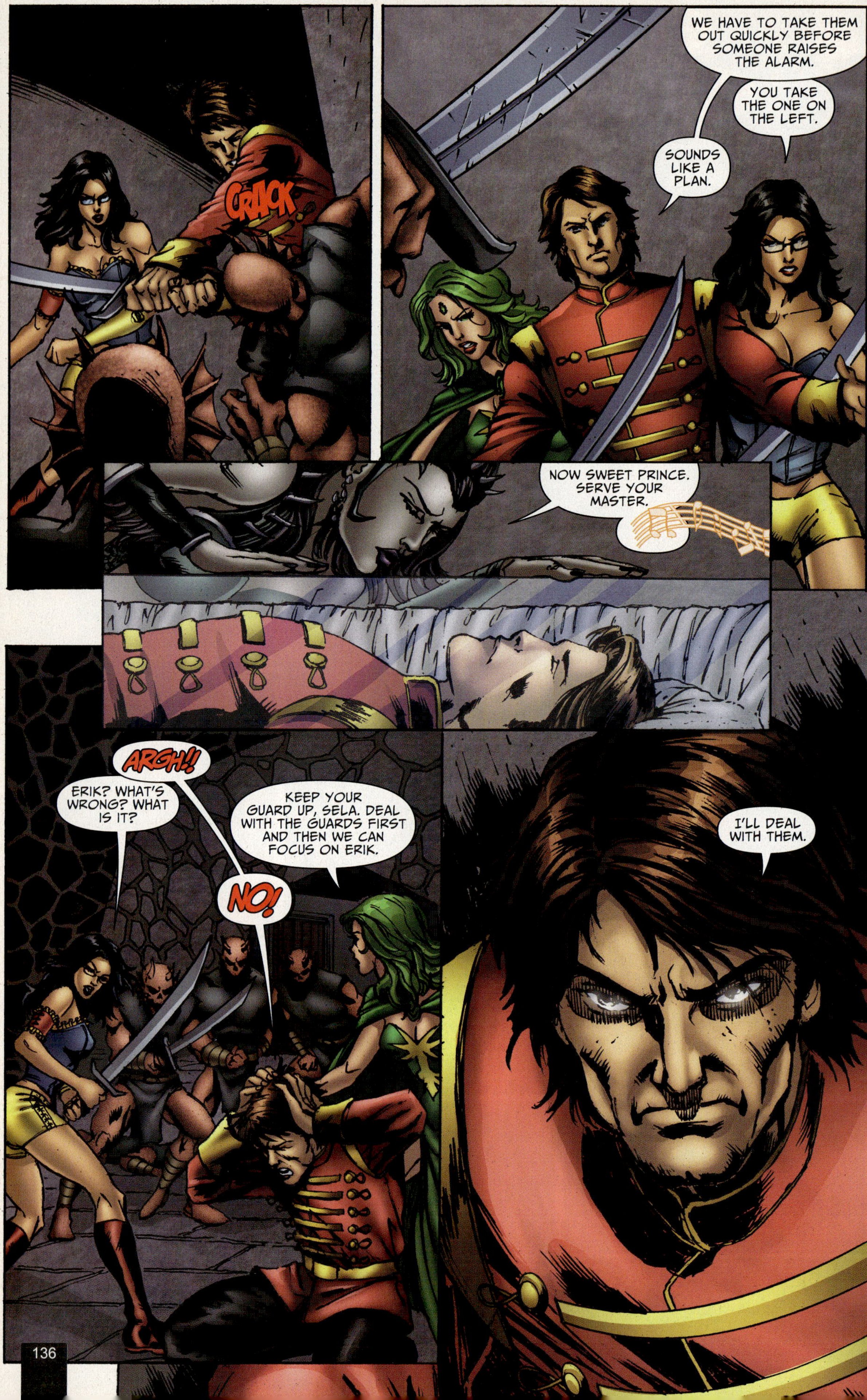
CRACK
WE HAVE TO TAKE THEM OUT QUICKLY BEFORE SOMEONE RAISES THE ALARM.
YOU TAKE THE ONE ON THE LEFT.
SOUNDS LIKE A PLAN.
NOW SWEET PRINCE. SERVE YOUR MASTER.
ARGH!!
ERIK? WHAT'S WRONG? WHAT IS IT?
KEEP YOUR GUARD UP, SELA. DEAL WITH THE GUARDS FIRST AND THEN WE CAN FOCUS ON ERIK.
NO!
I'LL DEAL WITH THEM.

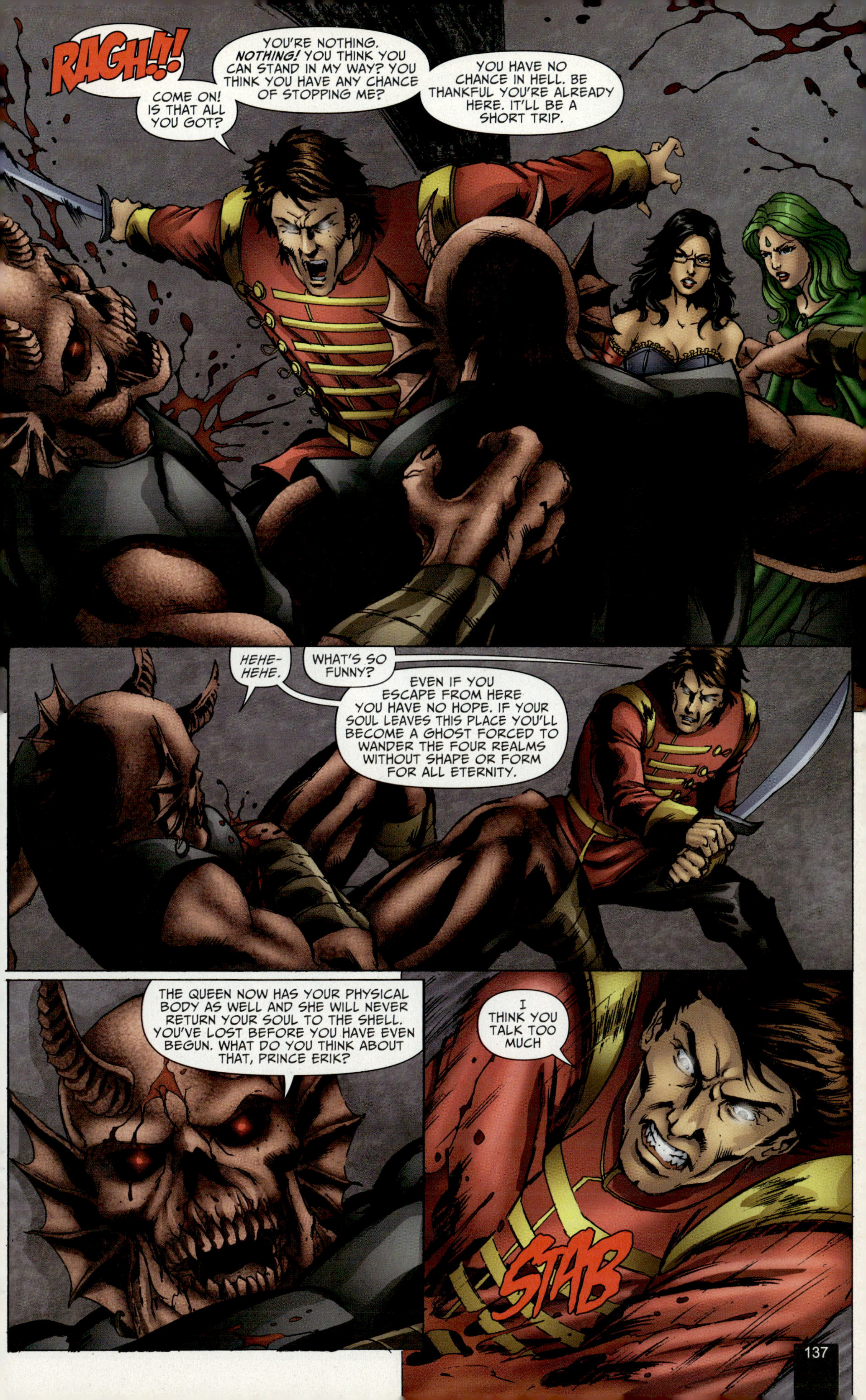
RAGH!!!
COME ON! IS THAT ALL YOU GOT?
YOU'RE NOTHING. *NOTHING!* YOU THINK YOU CAN STAND IN MY WAY? YOU THINK YOU HAVE ANY CHANCE OF STOPPING ME?
YOU HAVE NO CHANCE IN HELL. BE THANKFUL YOU'RE ALREADY HERE. IT'LL BE A SHORT TRIP.
HEHE-HEHE.
WHAT'S SO FUNNY?
EVEN IF YOU ESCAPE FROM HERE YOU HAVE NO HOPE. IF YOUR SOUL LEAVES THIS PLACE YOU'LL BECOME A GHOST FORCED TO WANDER THE FOUR REALMS WITHOUT SHAPE OR FORM FOR ALL ETERNITY.
THE QUEEN NOW HAS YOUR PHYSICAL BODY AS WELL AND SHE WILL NEVER RETURN YOUR SOUL TO THE SHELL. YOU'VE LOST BEFORE YOU HAVE EVEN BEGUN. WHAT DO YOU THINK ABOUT THAT, PRINCE ERIK?
I THINK YOU TALK TOO MUCH
STAB

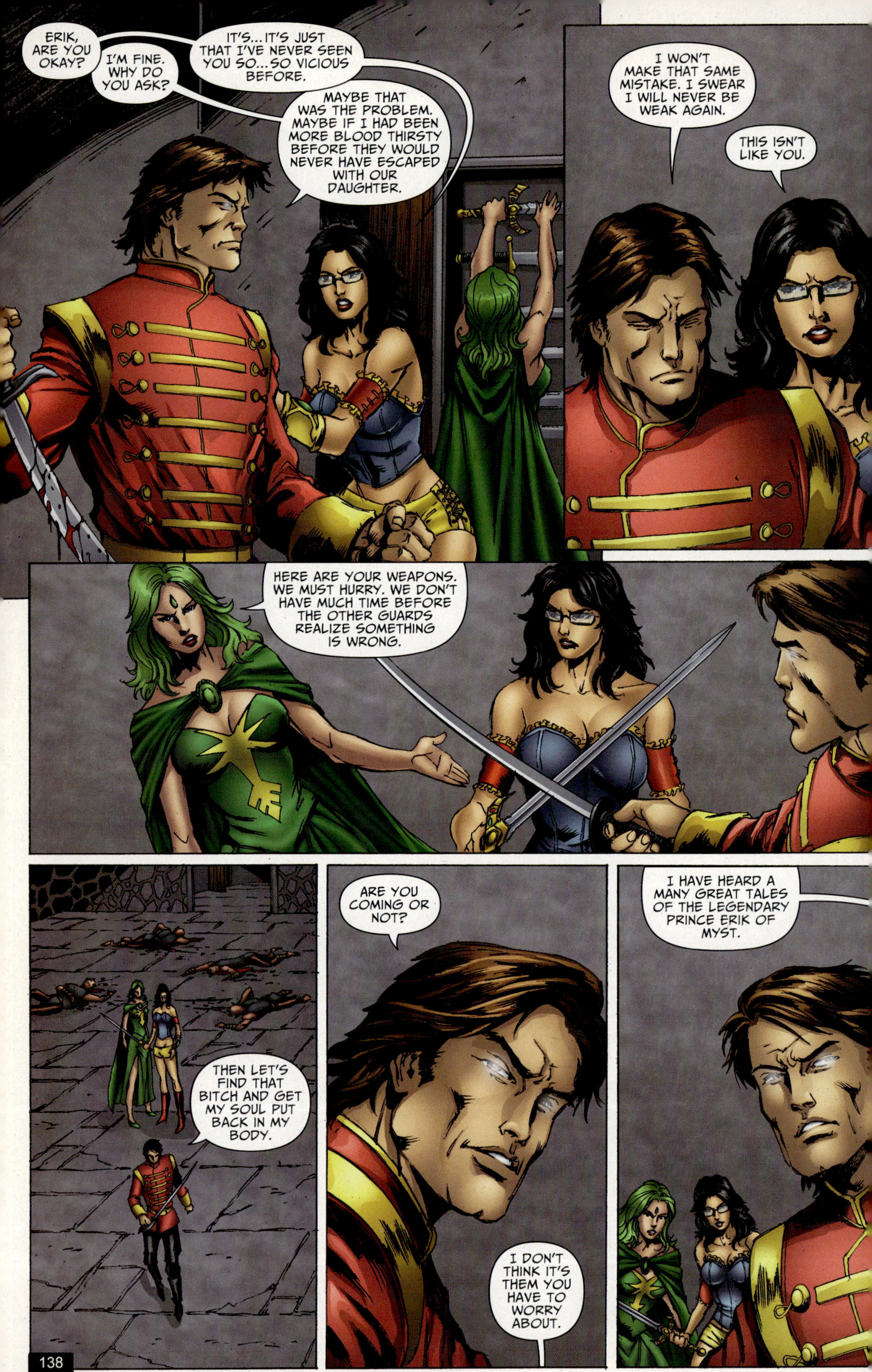
ERIK, ARE YOU OKAY?
I'M FINE. WHY DO YOU ASK?
IT'S... IT'S JUST THAT I'VE NEVER SEEN YOU SO... SO VICIOUS BEFORE.
MAYBE THAT WAS THE PROBLEM. MAYBE IF I HAD BEEN MORE BLOOD THIRSTY BEFORE THEY WOULD NEVER HAVE ESCAPED WITH OUR DAUGHTER.
I WON'T MAKE THAT SAME MISTAKE. I SWEAR I WILL NEVER BE WEAK AGAIN.
THIS ISN'T LIKE YOU.
HERE ARE YOUR WEAPONS. WE MUST HURRY. WE DON'T HAVE MUCH TIME BEFORE THE OTHER GUARDS REALIZE SOMETHING IS WRONG.
THEN LET'S FIND THAT BITCH AND GET MY SOUL PUT BACK IN MY BODY.
ARE YOU COMING OR NOT?
I DON'T THINK IT'S THEM YOU HAVE TO WORRY ABOUT.
I HAVE HEARD A MANY GREAT TALES OF THE LEGENDARY PRINCE ERIK OF MYST.

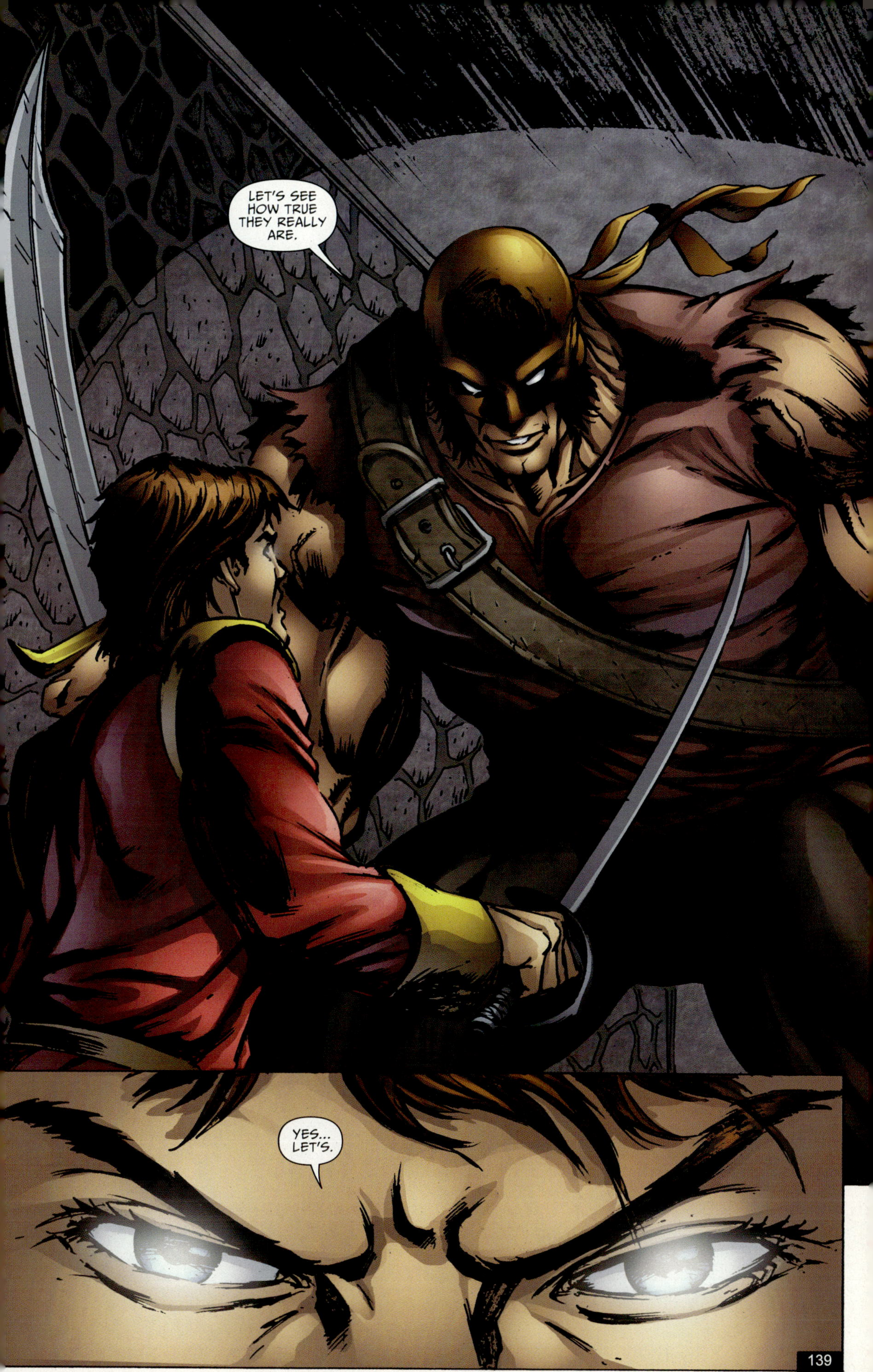
LET'S SEE HOW TRUE THEY REALLY ARE.
YES... LET'S.

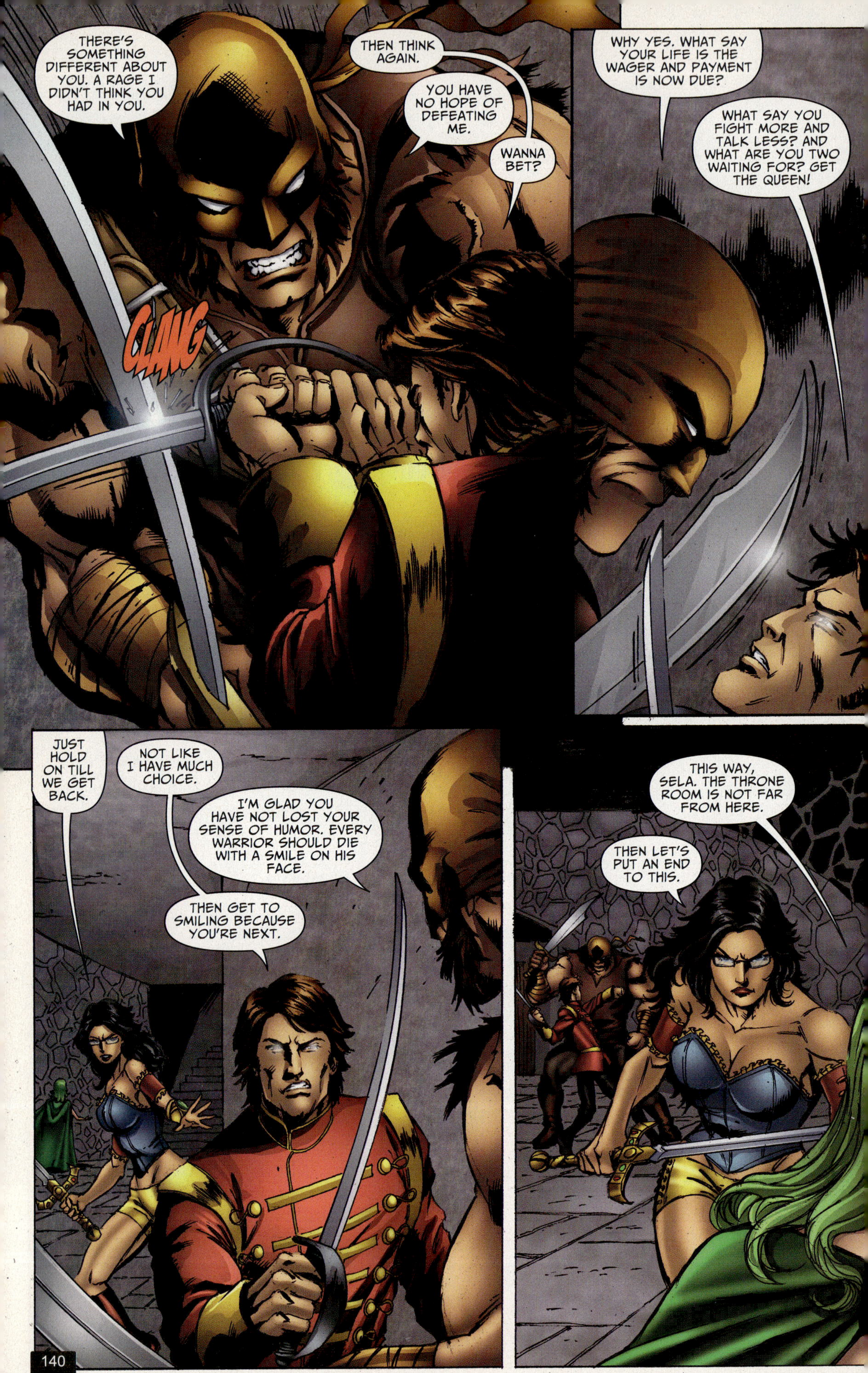
THERE'S SOMETHING DIFFERENT ABOUT YOU. A RAGE I DIDN'T THINK YOU HAD IN YOU.
THEN THINK AGAIN.
YOU HAVE NO HOPE OF DEFEATING ME.
WANNA BET?
CLANG
WHY YES. WHAT SAY YOUR LIFE IS THE WAGER AND PAYMENT IS NOW DUE?
WHAT SAY YOU FIGHT MORE AND TALK LESS? AND WHAT ARE YOU TWO WAITING FOR? GET THE QUEEN!
JUST HOLD ON TILL WE GET BACK.
NOT LIKE I HAVE MUCH CHOICE.
I'M GLAD YOU HAVE NOT LOST YOUR SENSE OF HUMOR. EVERY WARRIOR SHOULD DIE WITH A SMILE ON HIS FACE.
THEN GET TO SMILING BECAUSE YOU'RE NEXT.
THIS WAY, SELA. THE THRONE ROOM IS NOT FAR FROM HERE.
THEN LET'S PUT AN END TO THIS.

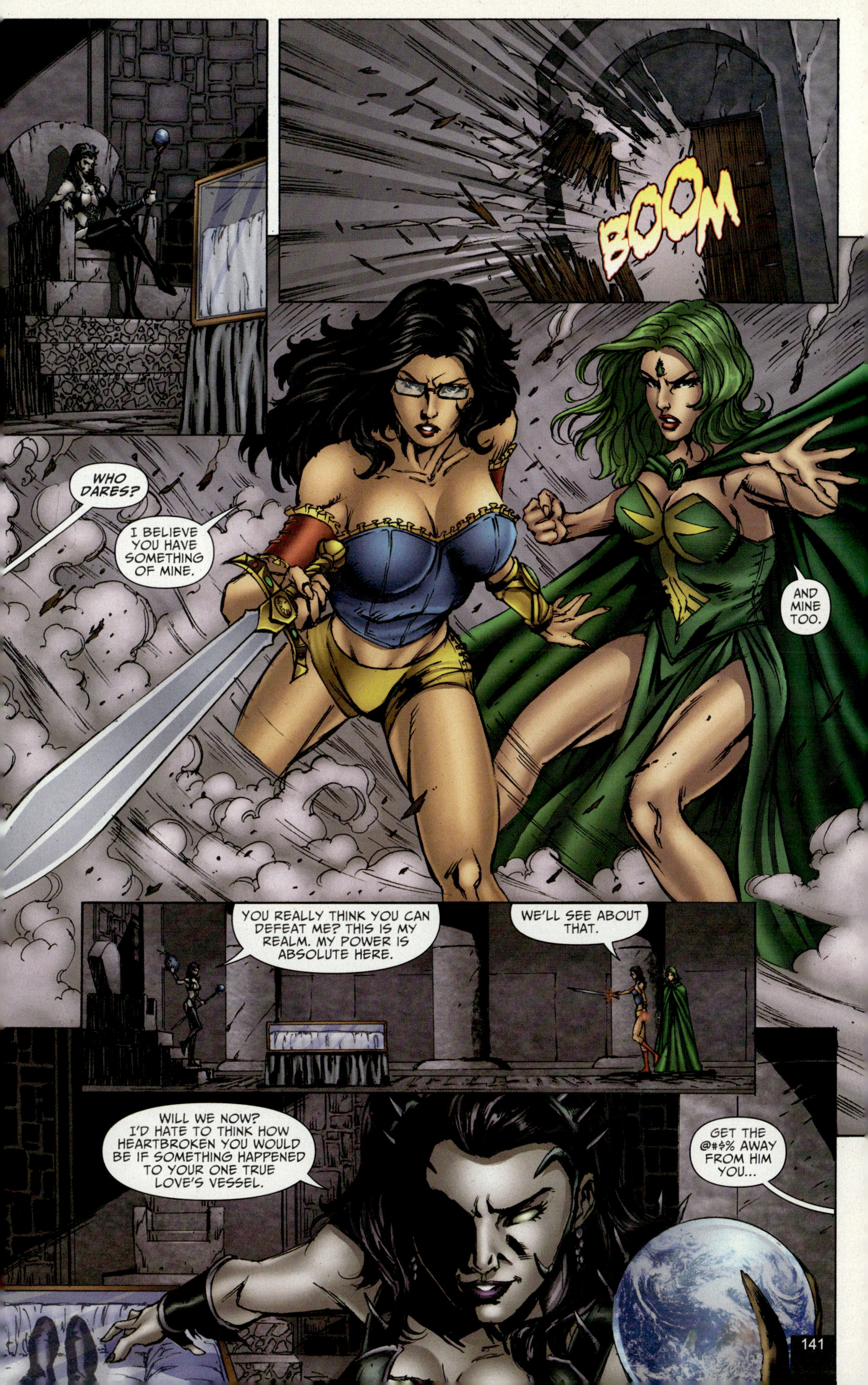
BOOM
WHO DARES?
I BELIEVE YOU HAVE SOMETHING OF MINE.
AND MINE TOO.
YOU REALLY THINK YOU CAN DEFEAT ME? THIS IS MY REALM. MY POWER IS ABSOLUTE HERE.
WE'LL SEE ABOUT THAT.
WILL WE NOW? I'D HATE TO THINK HOW HEARTBROKEN YOU WOULD BE IF SOMETHING HAPPENED TO YOUR ONE TRUE LOVE'S VESSEL.
GET THE @#$% AWAY FROM HIM YOU...

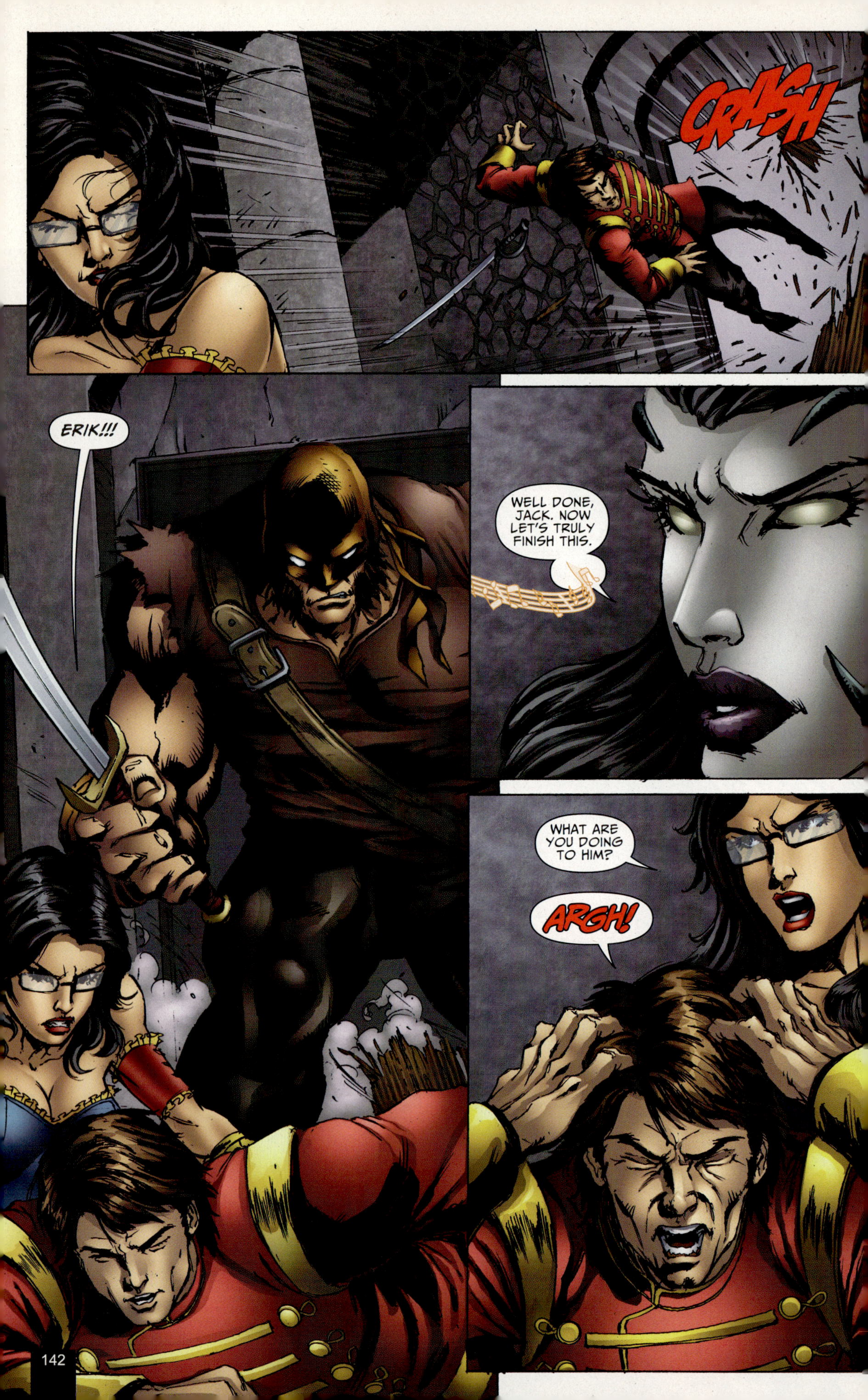
CRASH
ERIK!!!
WELL DONE, JACK. NOW LET'S TRULY FINISH THIS.
WHAT ARE YOU DOING TO HIM?
ARGH!

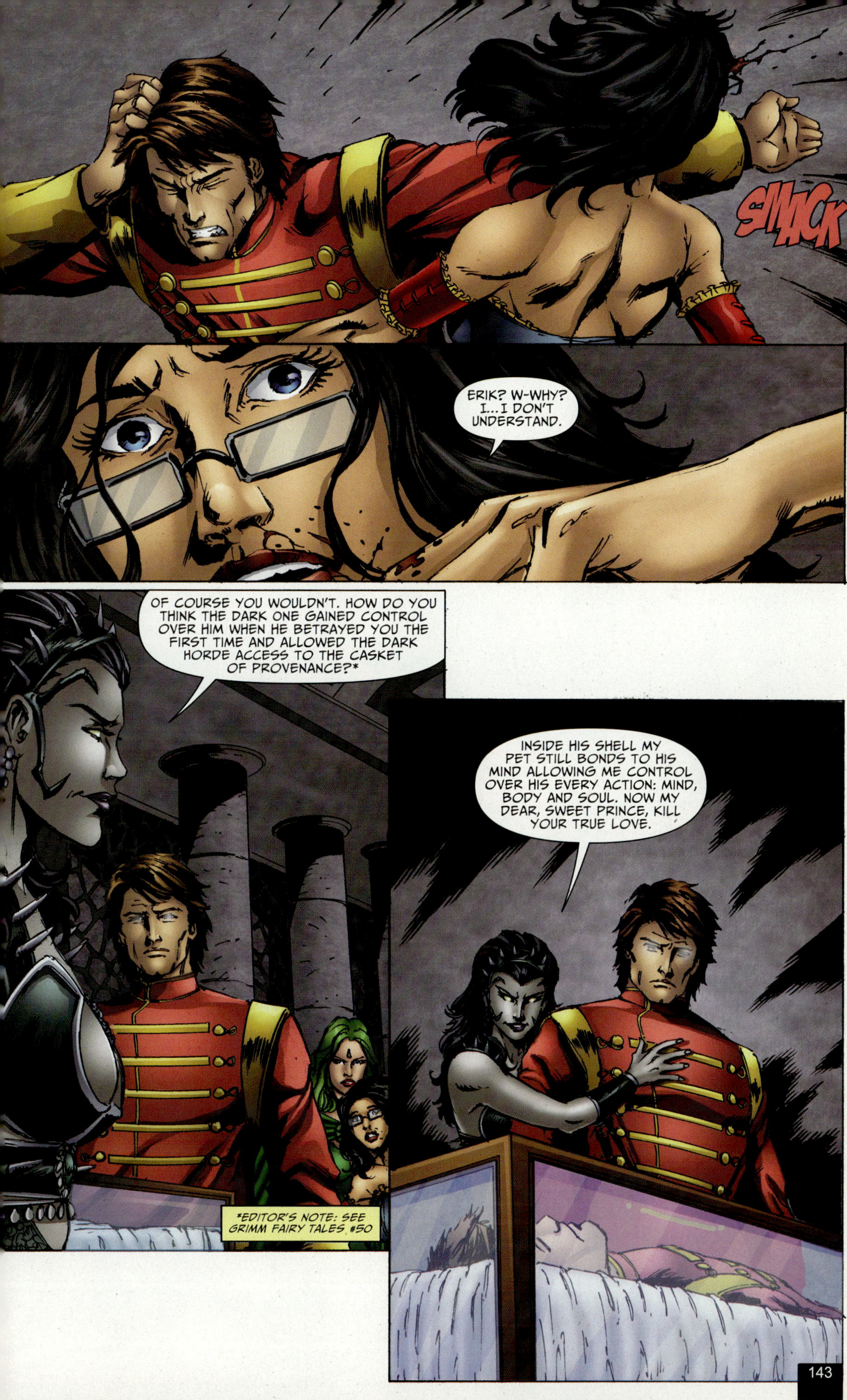
SMACK
ERIK? W-WHY? I...I DON'T UNDERSTAND.
OF COURSE YOU WOULDN'T. HOW DO YOU THINK THE DARK ONE GAINED CONTROL OVER HIM WHEN HE BETRAYED YOU THE FIRST TIME AND ALLOWED THE DARK HORDE ACCESS TO THE CASKET OF PROVENANCE?*
*EDITOR'S NOTE: SEE GRIMM FAIRY TALES #50
INSIDE HIS SHELL MY PET STILL BONDS TO HIS MIND ALLOWING ME CONTROL OVER HIS EVERY ACTION: MIND, BODY AND SOUL. NOW MY DEAR, SWEET PRINCE, KILL YOUR TRUE LOVE.

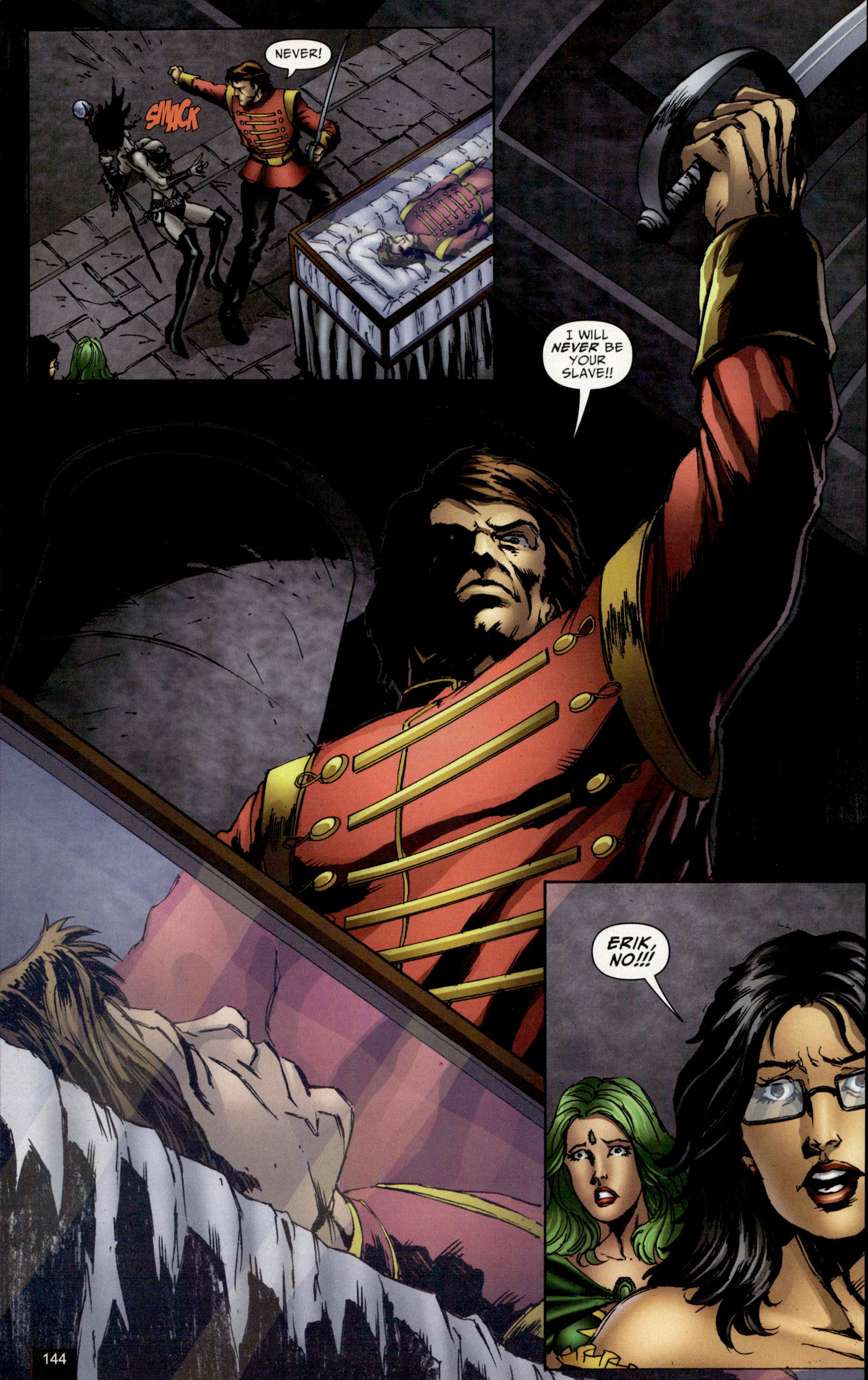
NEVER!
SMACK
I WILL NEVER BE YOUR SLAVE!!
ERIK, NO!!!

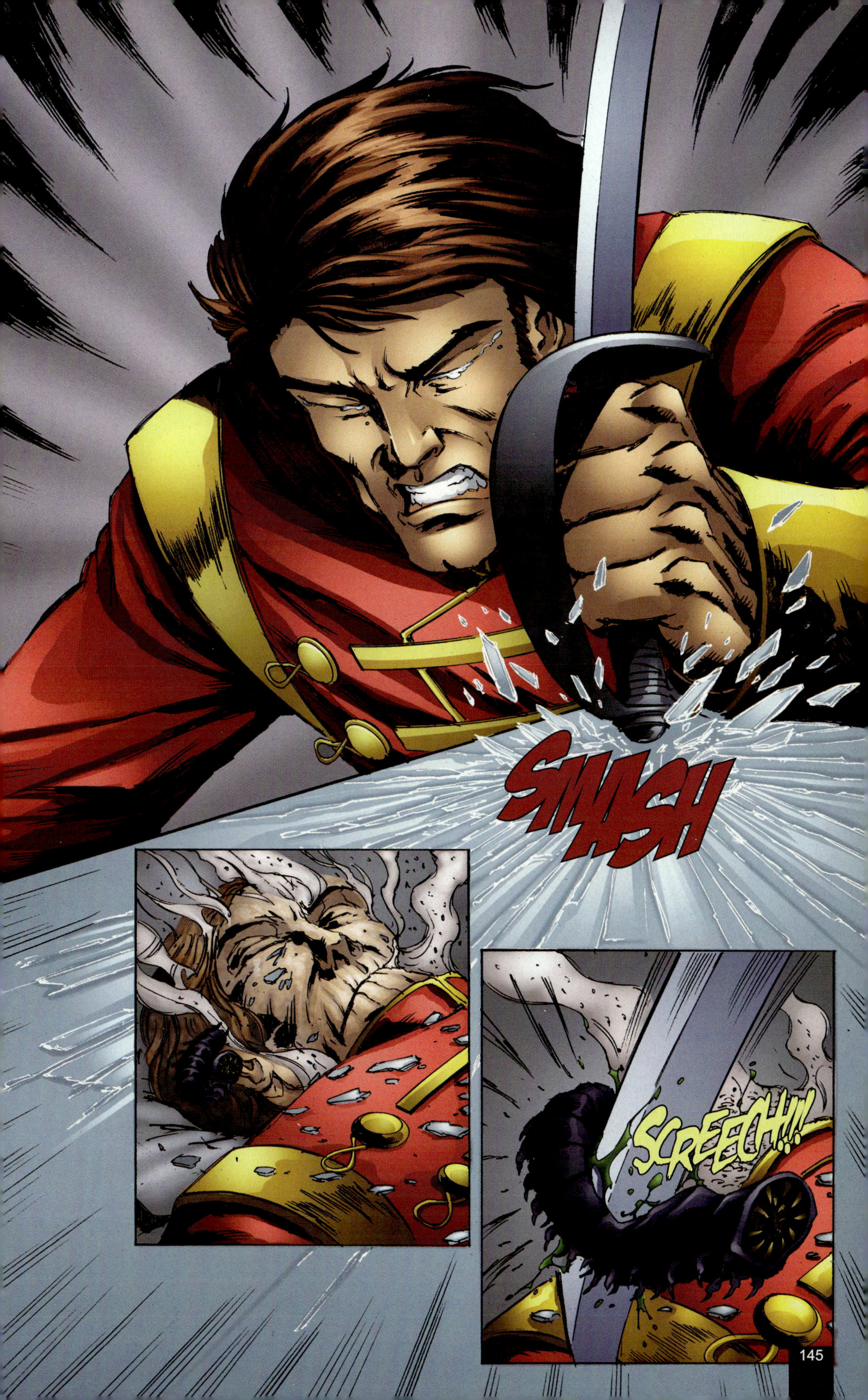
SMASH
SCREECH!!!

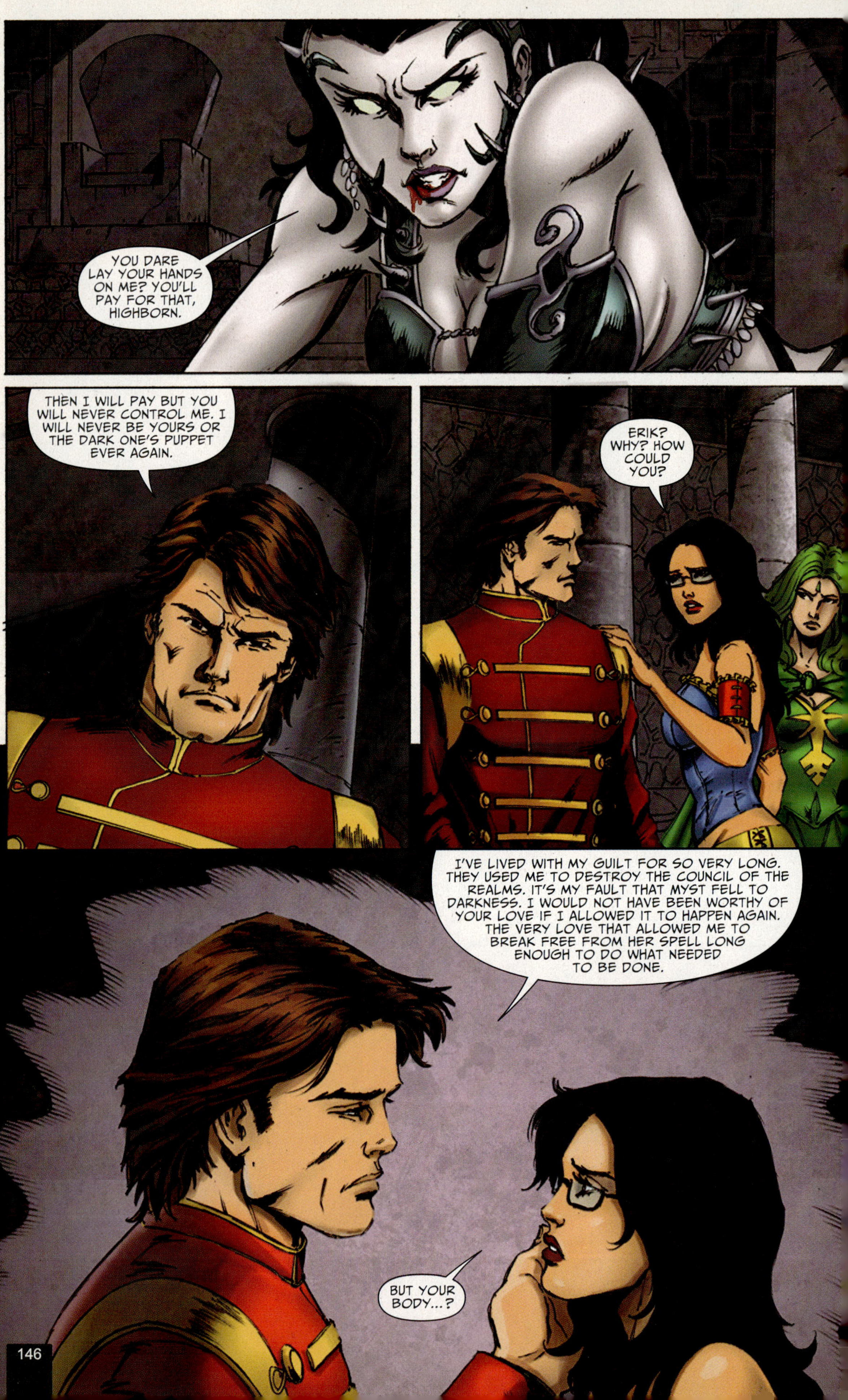
YOU DARE LAY YOUR HANDS ON ME? YOU'LL PAY FOR THAT, HIGHBORN.
THEN I WILL PAY BUT YOU WILL NEVER CONTROL ME. I WILL NEVER BE YOURS OR THE DARK ONE'S PUPPET EVER AGAIN.
ERIK? WHY? HOW COULD YOU?
I'VE LIVED WITH MY GUILT FOR SO VERY LONG. THEY USED ME TO DESTROY THE COUNCIL OF THE REALMS. IT'S MY FAULT THAT MYST FELL TO DARKNESS. I WOULD NOT HAVE BEEN WORTHY OF YOUR LOVE IF I ALLOWED IT TO HAPPEN AGAIN. THE VERY LOVE THAT ALLOWED ME TO BREAK FREE FROM HER SPELL LONG ENOUGH TO DO WHAT NEEDED TO BE DONE.
BUT YOUR BODY...?

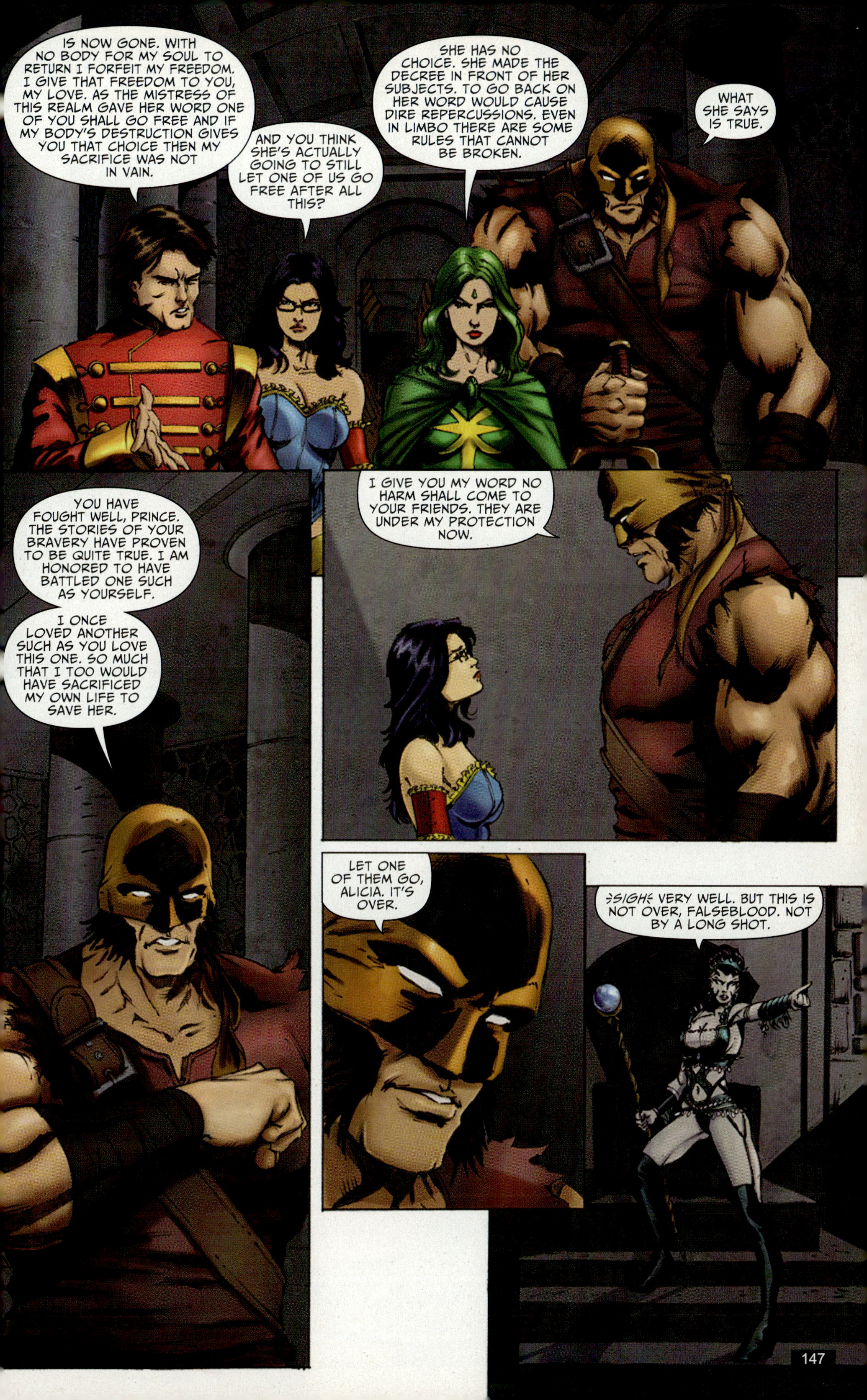

IS NOW GONE. WITH NO BODY FOR MY SOUL TO RETURN I FORFEIT MY FREEDOM. I GIVE THAT FREEDOM TO YOU, MY LOVE. AS THE MISTRESS OF THIS REALM GAVE HER WORD ONE OF YOU SHALL GO FREE AND IF MY BODY'S DESTRUCTION GIVES YOU THAT CHOICE THEN MY SACRIFICE WAS NOT IN VAIN.
AND YOU THINK SHE'S ACTUALLY GOING TO STILL LET ONE OF US GO FREE AFTER ALL THIS?
SHE HAS NO CHOICE. SHE MADE THE DECREE IN FRONT OF HER SUBJECTS. TO GO BACK ON HER WORD WOULD CAUSE DIRE REPERCUSSIONS. EVEN IN LIMBO THERE ARE SOME RULES THAT CANNOT BE BROKEN.
WHAT SHE SAYS IS TRUE.
YOU HAVE FOUGHT WELL, PRINCE. THE STORIES OF YOUR BRAVERY HAVE PROVEN TO BE QUITE TRUE. I AM HONORED TO HAVE BATTLED ONE SUCH AS YOURSELF.
I ONCE LOVED ANOTHER SUCH AS YOU LOVE THIS ONE. SO MUCH THAT I TOO WOULD HAVE SACRIFICED MY OWN LIFE TO SAVE HER.
I GIVE YOU MY WORD NO HARM SHALL COME TO YOUR FRIENDS. THEY ARE UNDER MY PROTECTION NOW.
LET ONE OF THEM GO, ALICIA. IT'S OVER.
SIGH VERY WELL. BUT THIS IS NOT OVER, FALSEBLOOD. NOT BY A LONG SHOT.

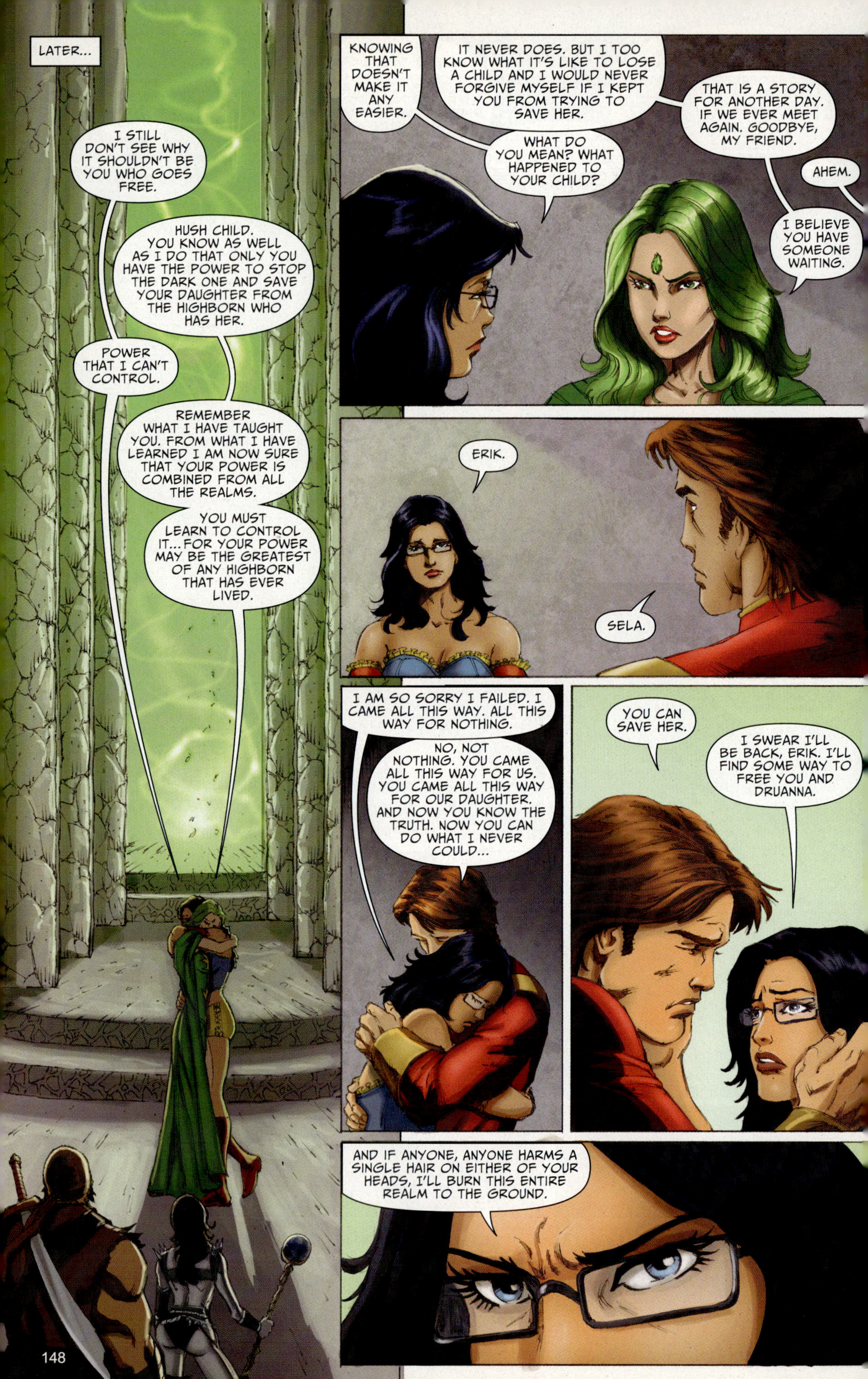
LATER...
I STILL DON'T SEE WHY IT SHOULDN'T BE YOU WHO GOES FREE.
HUSH CHILD. AS YOU KNOW AS WELL AS I DO THAT ONLY YOU HAVE THE POWER TO STOP THE DARK ONE AND SAVE YOUR DAUGHTER FROM THE HIGHBORN WHO HAS HER.
POWER THAT I CAN'T CONTROL.
REMEMBER WHAT I HAVE TAUGHT YOU. FROM WHAT I HAVE LEARNED I AM NOW SURE THAT YOUR POWER IS COMBINED FROM ALL THE REALMS.
YOU MUST LEARN TO CONTROL IT...FOR YOUR POWER MAY BE THE GREATEST OF ANY HIGHBORN THAT HAS EVER LIVED.
KNOWING THAT DOESN'T MAKE IT ANY EASIER.
IT NEVER DOES. BUT I TOO KNOW WHAT IT'S LIKE TO LOSE A CHILD AND I WOULD NEVER FORGIVE MYSELF IF I KEPT YOU FROM TRYING TO SAVE HER.
WHAT DO YOU MEAN? WHAT HAPPENED TO YOUR CHILD?
THAT IS A STORY FOR ANOTHER DAY. IF WE EVER MEET AGAIN. GOODBYE, MY FRIEND.
AHEM.
I BELIEVE YOU HAVE SOMEONE WAITING.
ERIK.
SELA.
I AM SO SORRY I FAILED. I CAME ALL THIS WAY. ALL THIS WAY FOR NOTHING.
NO, NOT NOTHING. YOU CAME ALL THIS WAY FOR US. YOU CAME ALL THIS WAY FOR OUR DAUGHTER. AND NOW YOU KNOW THE TRUTH. NOW YOU CAN DO WHAT I NEVER COULD...
YOU CAN SAVE HER.
I SWEAR I'LL BE BACK, ERIK. I'LL FIND SOME WAY TO FREE YOU AND DRUANNA.
AND IF ANYONE, ANYONE HARMS A SINGLE HAIR ON EITHER OF YOUR HEADS, I'LL BURN THIS ENTIRE REALM TO THE GROUND.

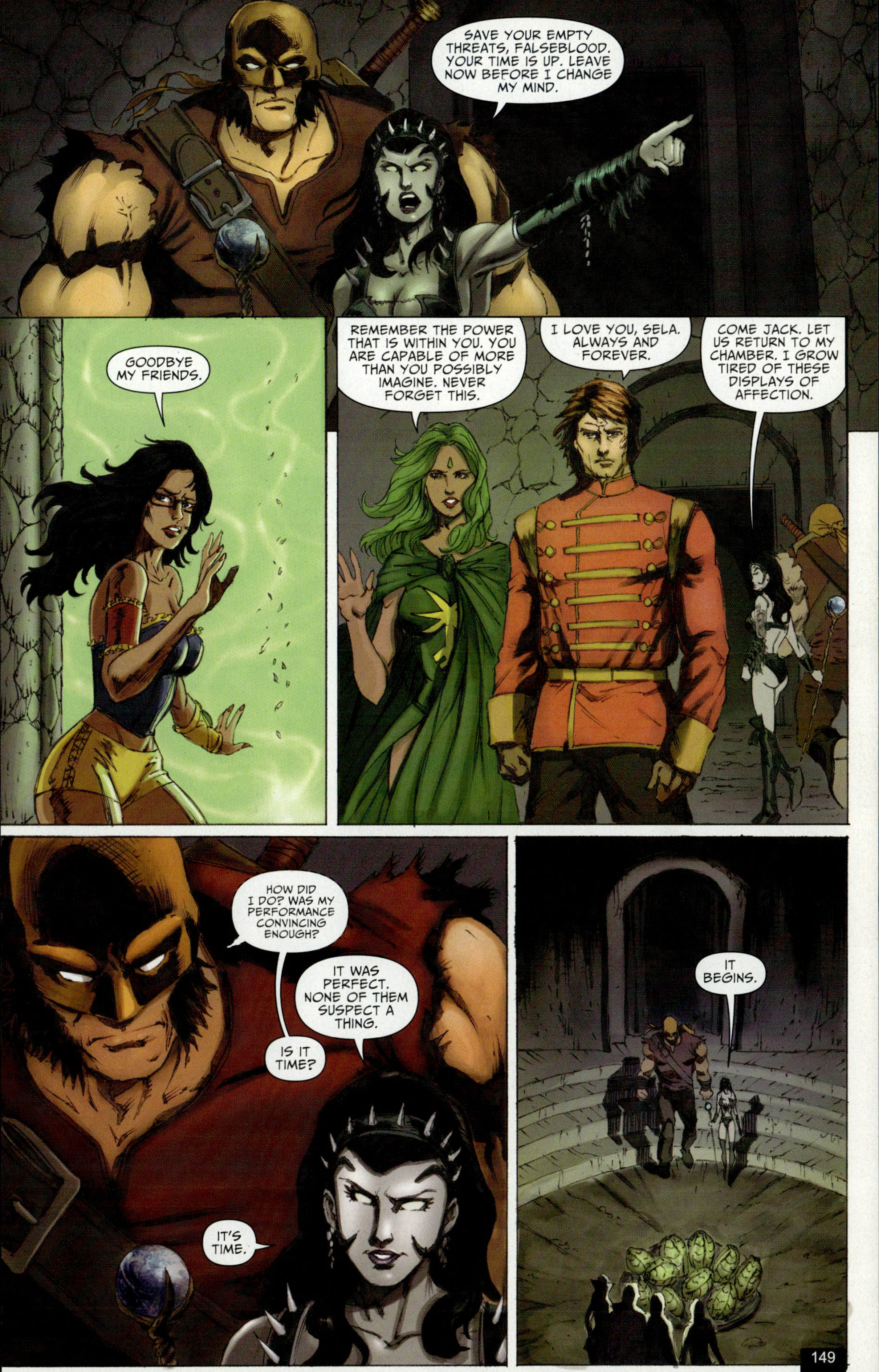
SAVE YOUR EMPTY THREATS, FALSEBLOOD. YOUR TIME IS UP. LEAVE NOW BEFORE I CHANGE MY MIND.
GOODBYE MY FRIENDS.
REMEMBER THE POWER THAT IS WITHIN YOU. YOU ARE CAPABLE OF MORE THAN YOU POSSIBLY IMAGINE. NEVER FORGET THIS.
I LOVE YOU, SELA. ALWAYS AND FOREVER.
COME JACK. LET US RETURN TO MY CHAMBER. I GROW TIRED OF THESE DISPLAYS OF AFFECTION.
HOW DID I DO? WAS MY PERFORMANCE CONVINCING ENOUGH?
IT WAS PERFECT. NONE OF THEM SUSPECT A THING.
IS IT TIME?
IT'S TIME.
IT BEGINS.

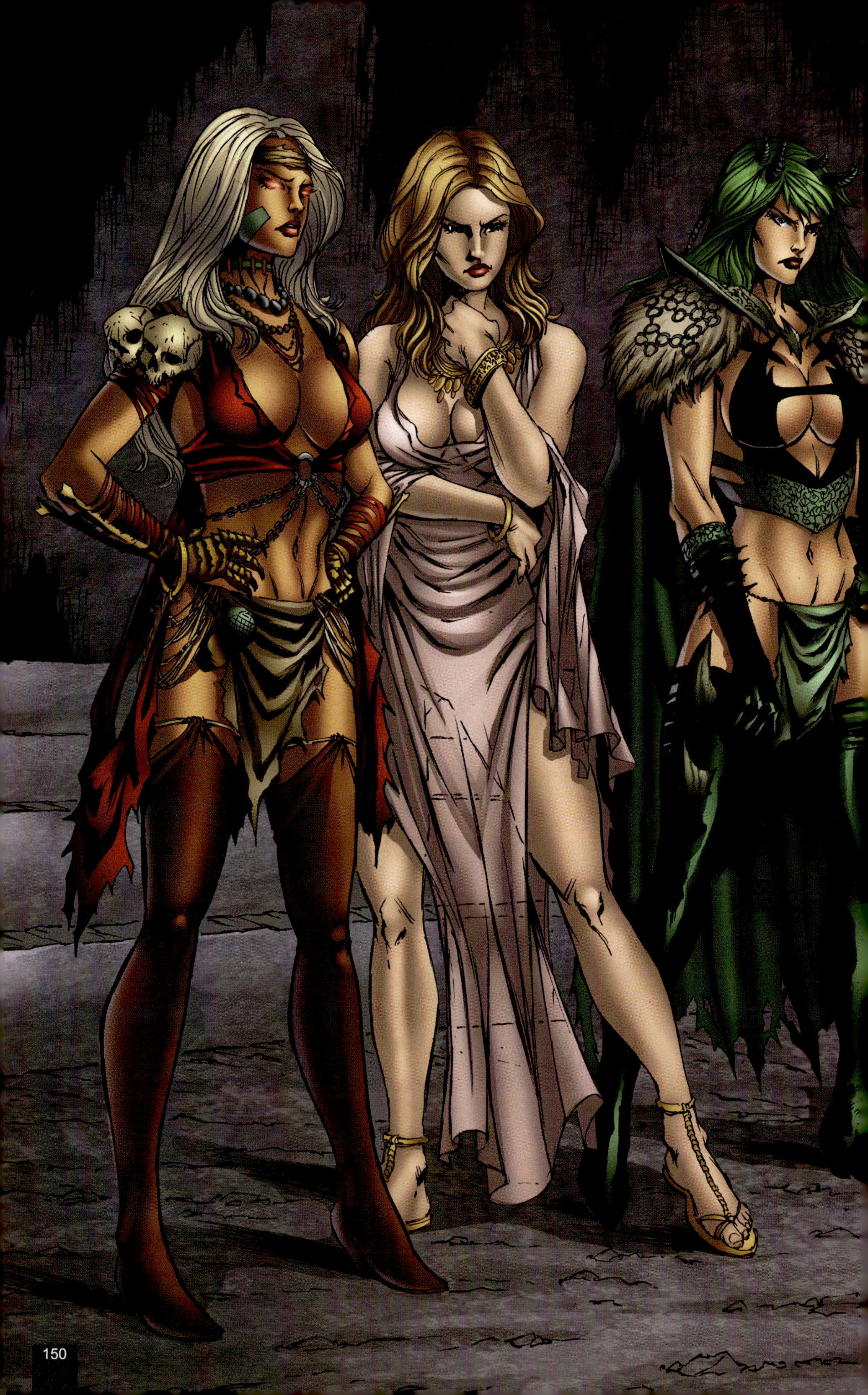

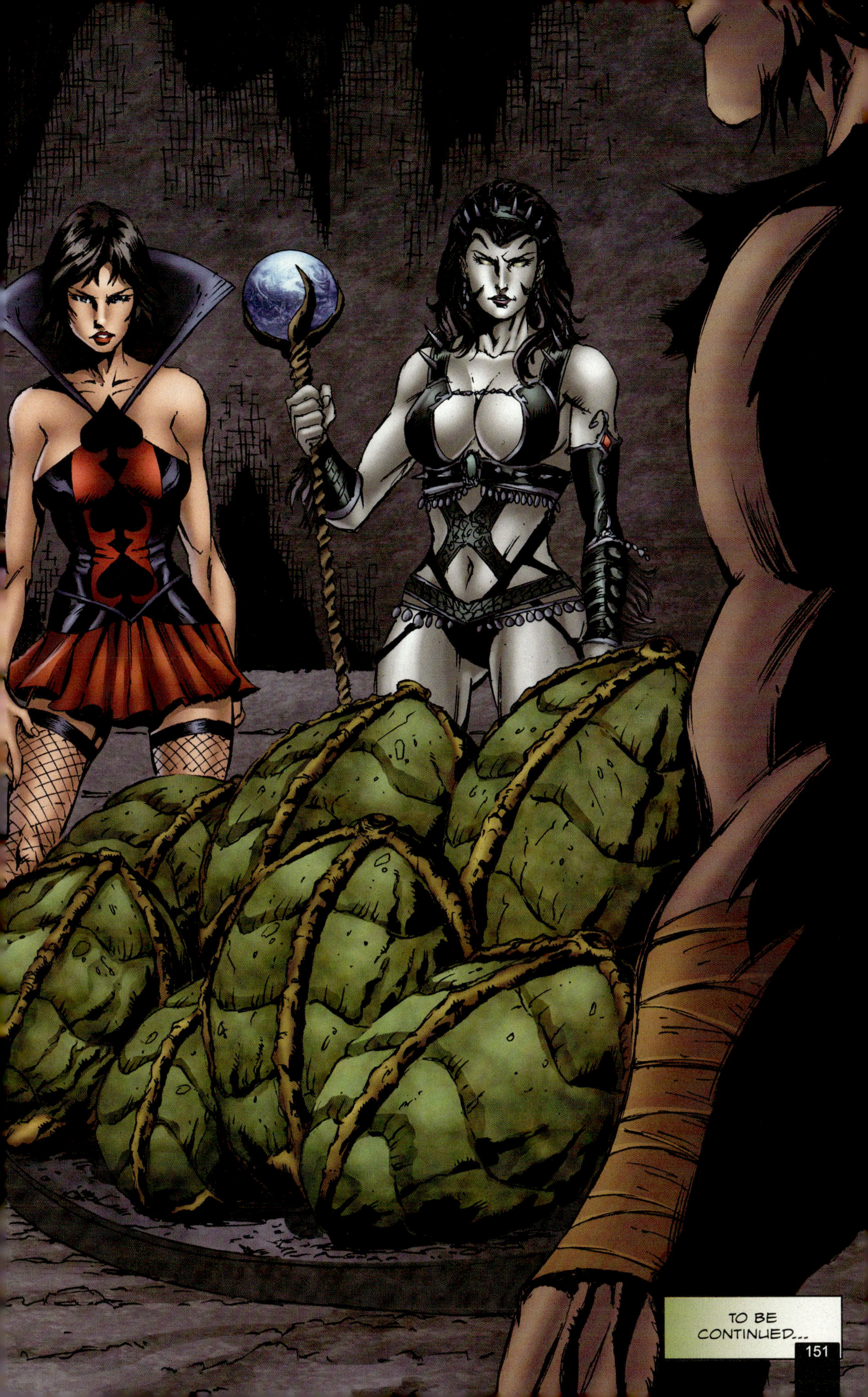
TO BE CONTINUED...

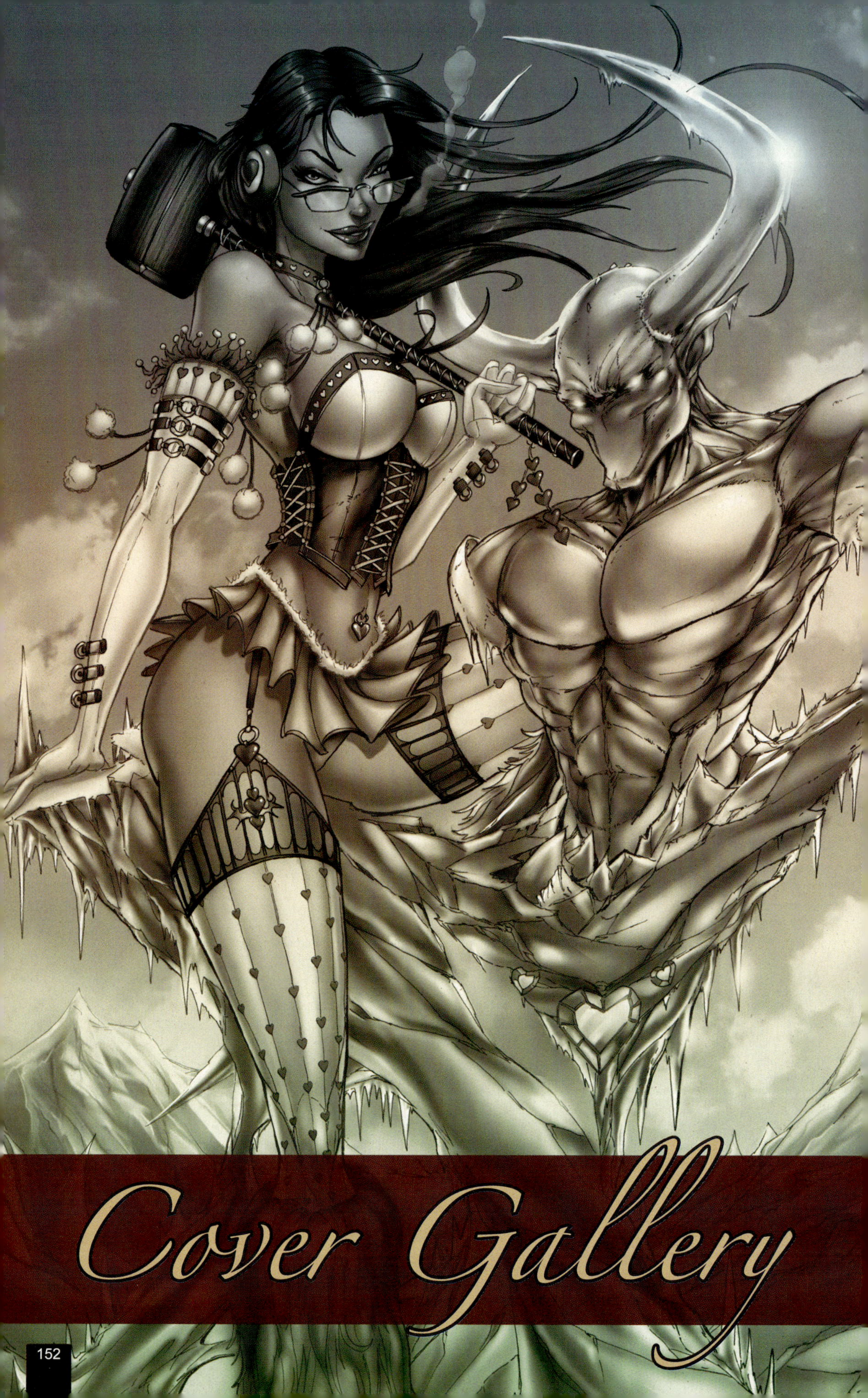

Cover Gallery

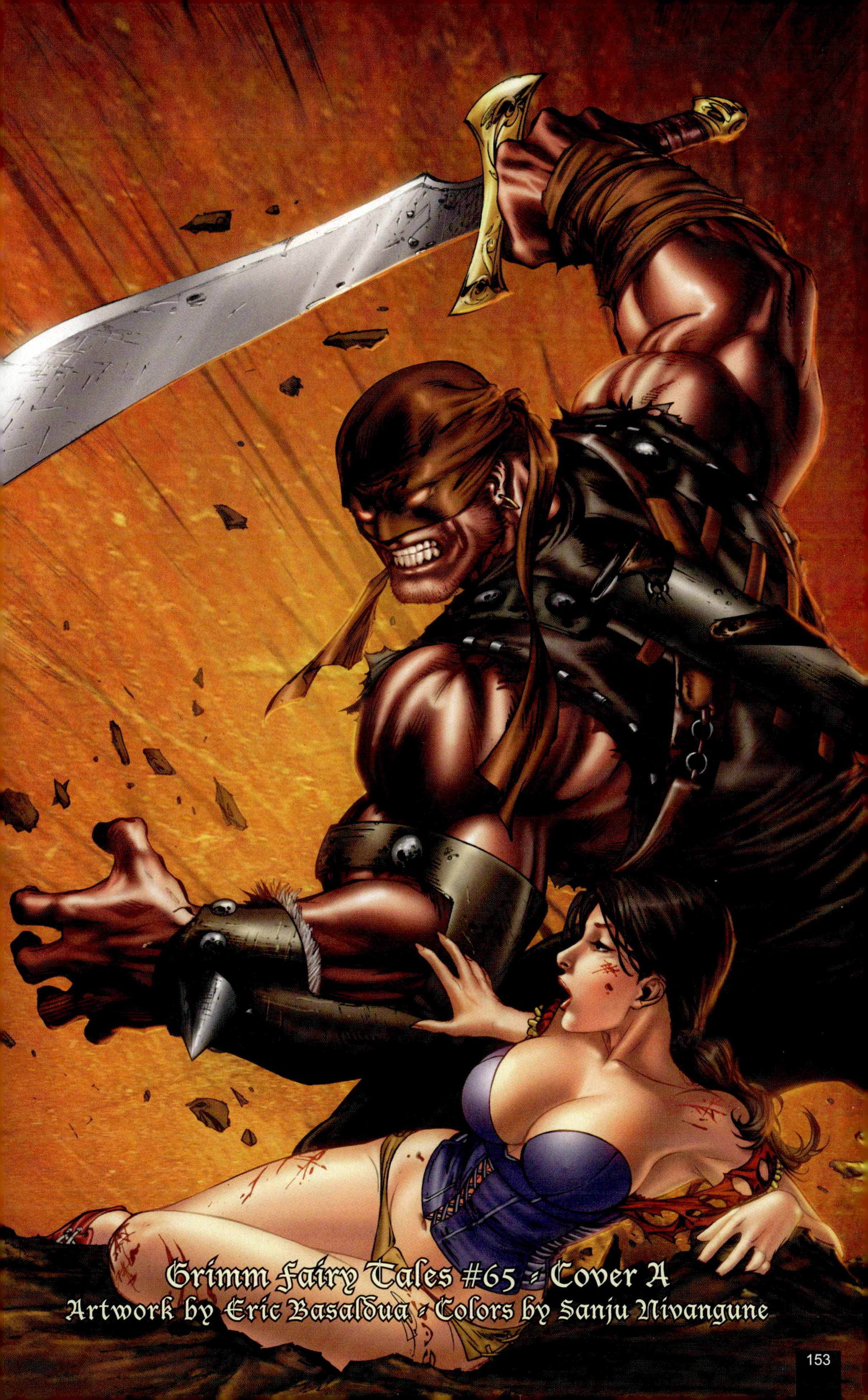

Grimm Fairy Tales #65 - Cover A
Artwork by Eric Basaldua - Colors by Sanju Nivangune

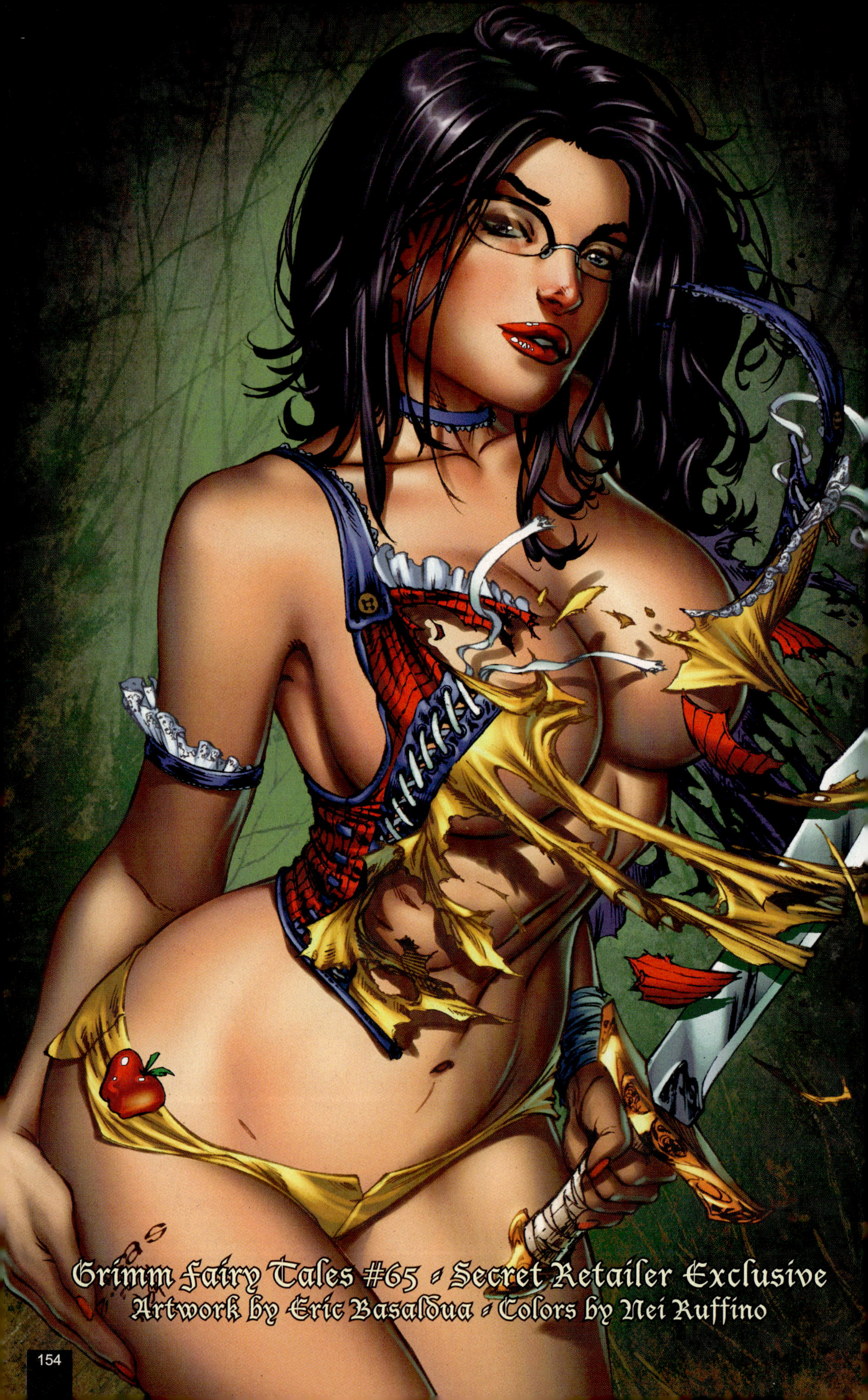

Grimm Fairy Tales #65 - Secret Retailer Exclusive
Artwork by Eric Basaldua - Colors by Nei Ruffino

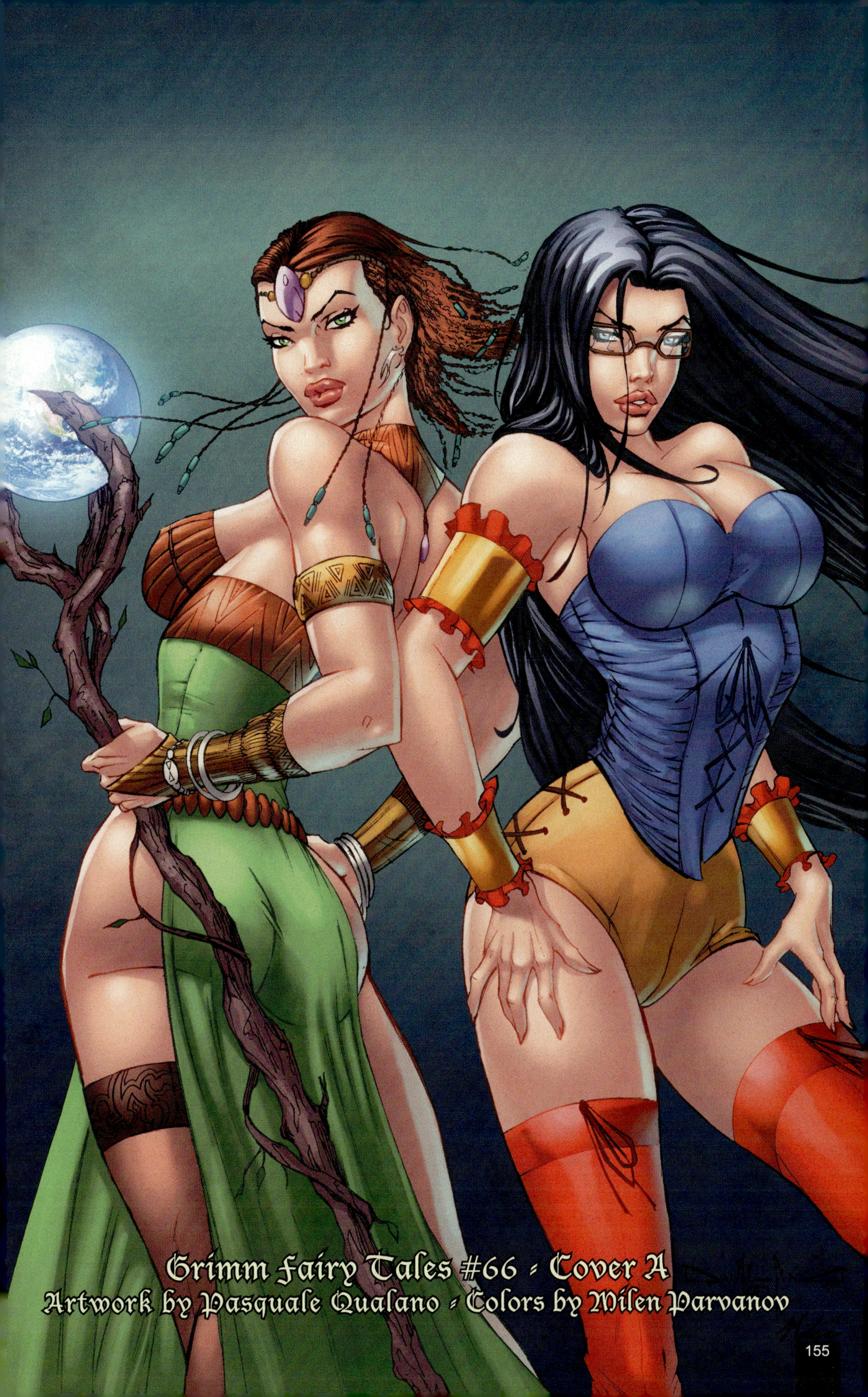

Grimm Fairy Tales #66 - Cover A
Artwork by Pasquale Qualano - Colors by Milen Parvanov

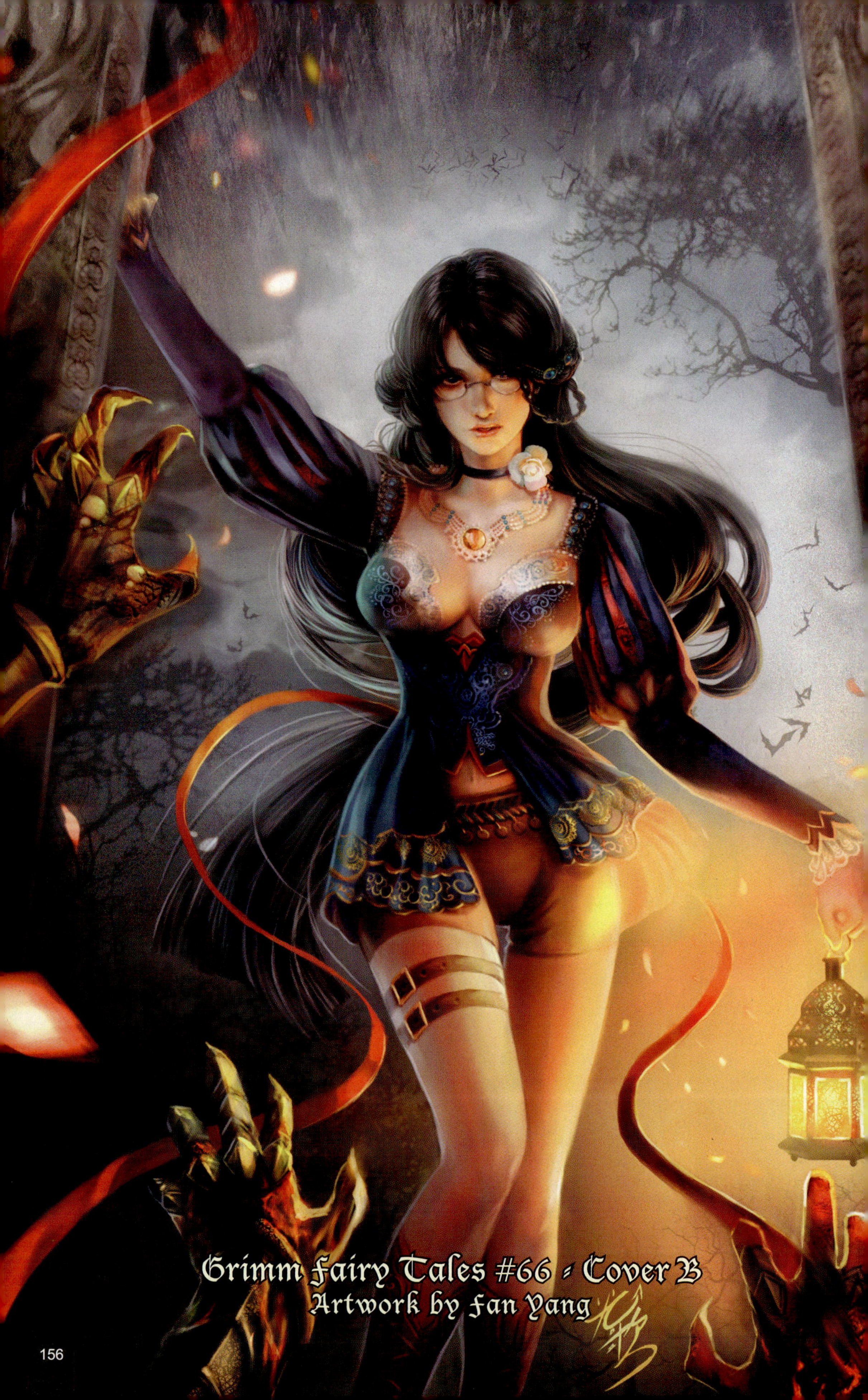

Grimm Fairy Tales #66 - Cover B
Artwork by Fan Yang

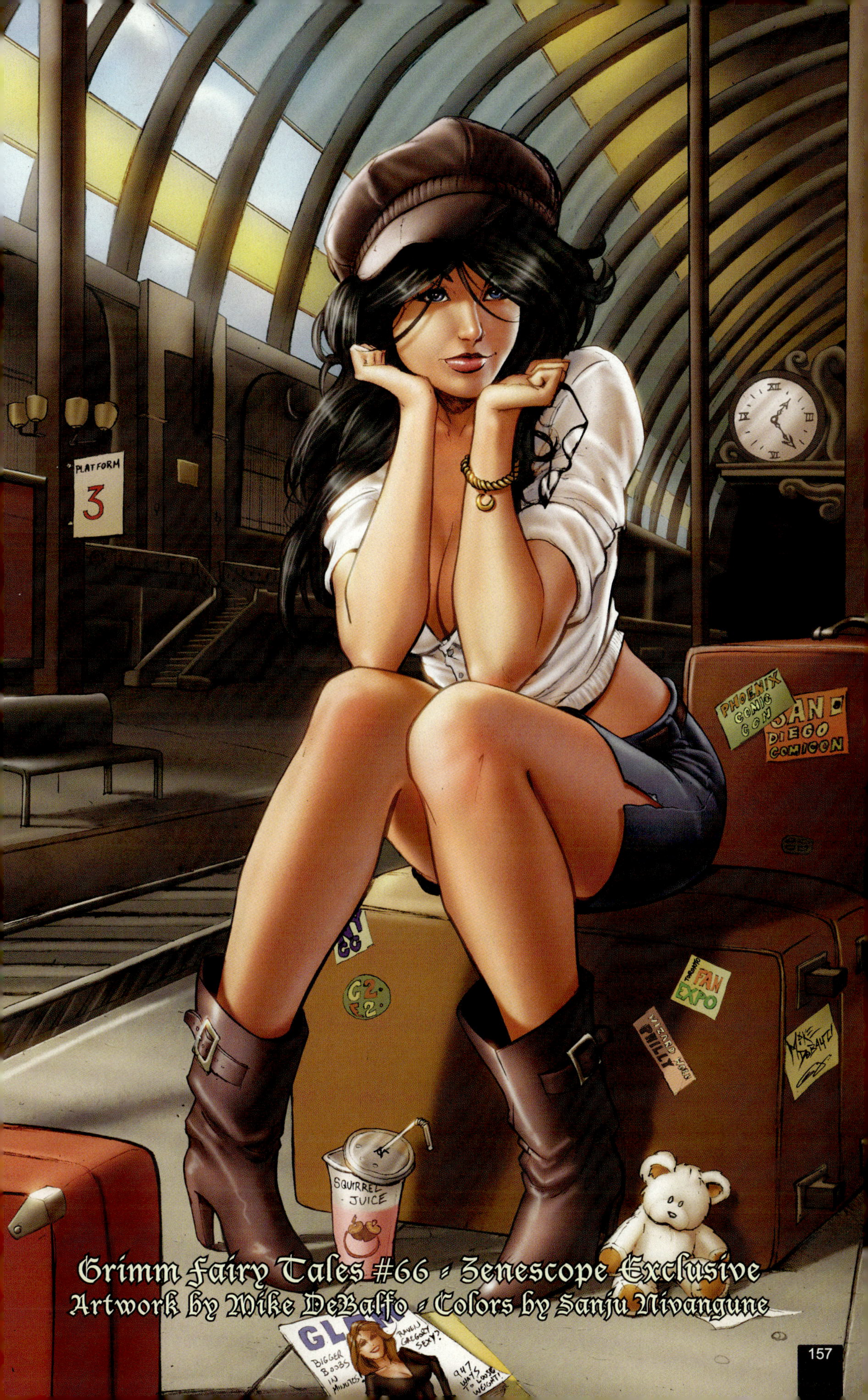
PLATFORM
3
PHOENIX COMIC CON
SAN DIEGO COMICON
FAN EXPO
PHILLY
SQUIRREL JUICE
BIGGER BOOBS IN MINUTES

Grimm Fairy Tales #66 - Zenescope Exclusive
Artwork by Mike DeBalfo - Colors by Sanju Nivangune

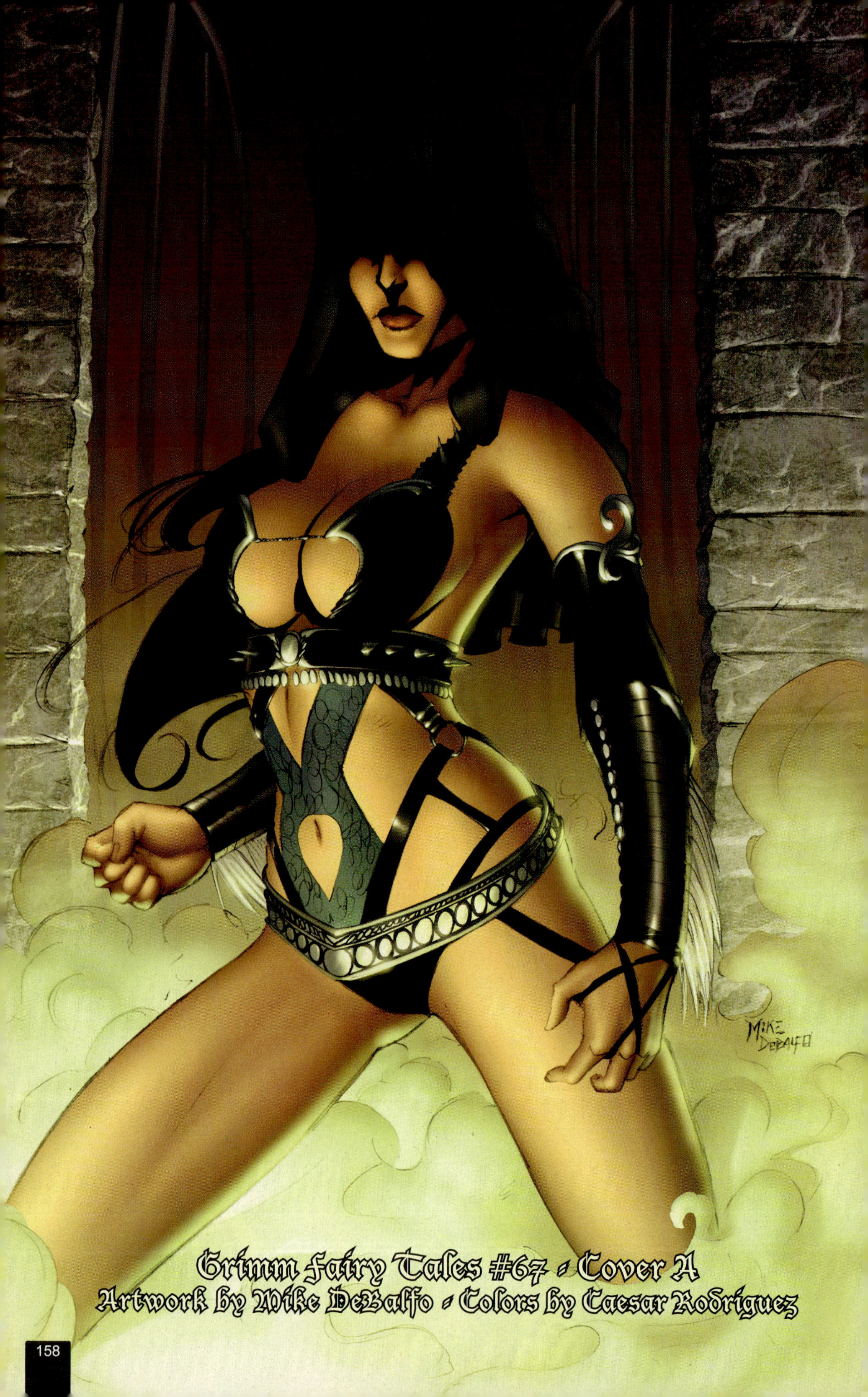
MIKE DEBALFO

Grimm Fairy Tales #67 - Cover A
Artwork by Mike DeBalfo - Colors by Caesar Rodriguez

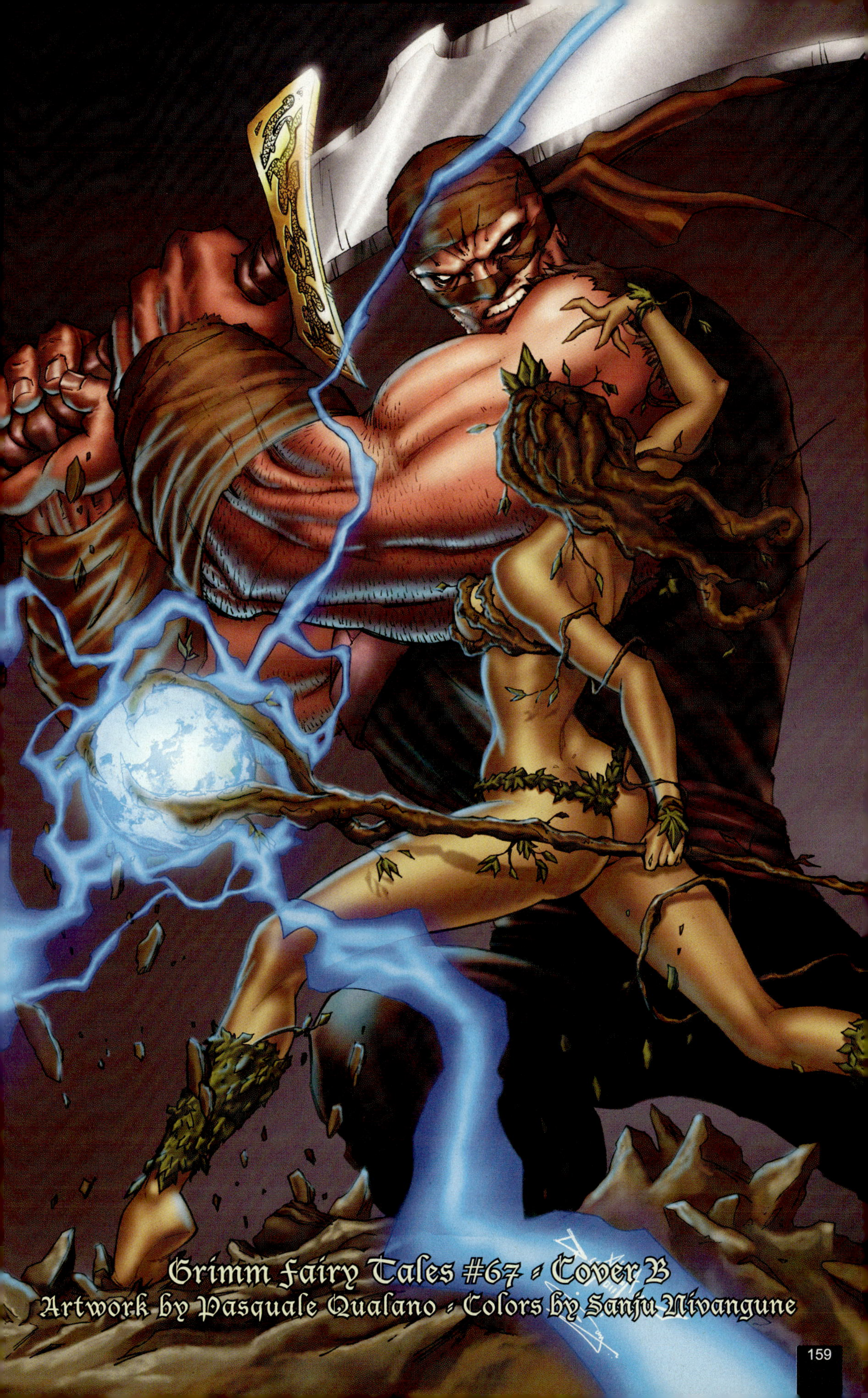

Grimm Fairy Tales #67 - Cover B
Artwork by Pasquale Qualano - Colors by Sanju Nivangune

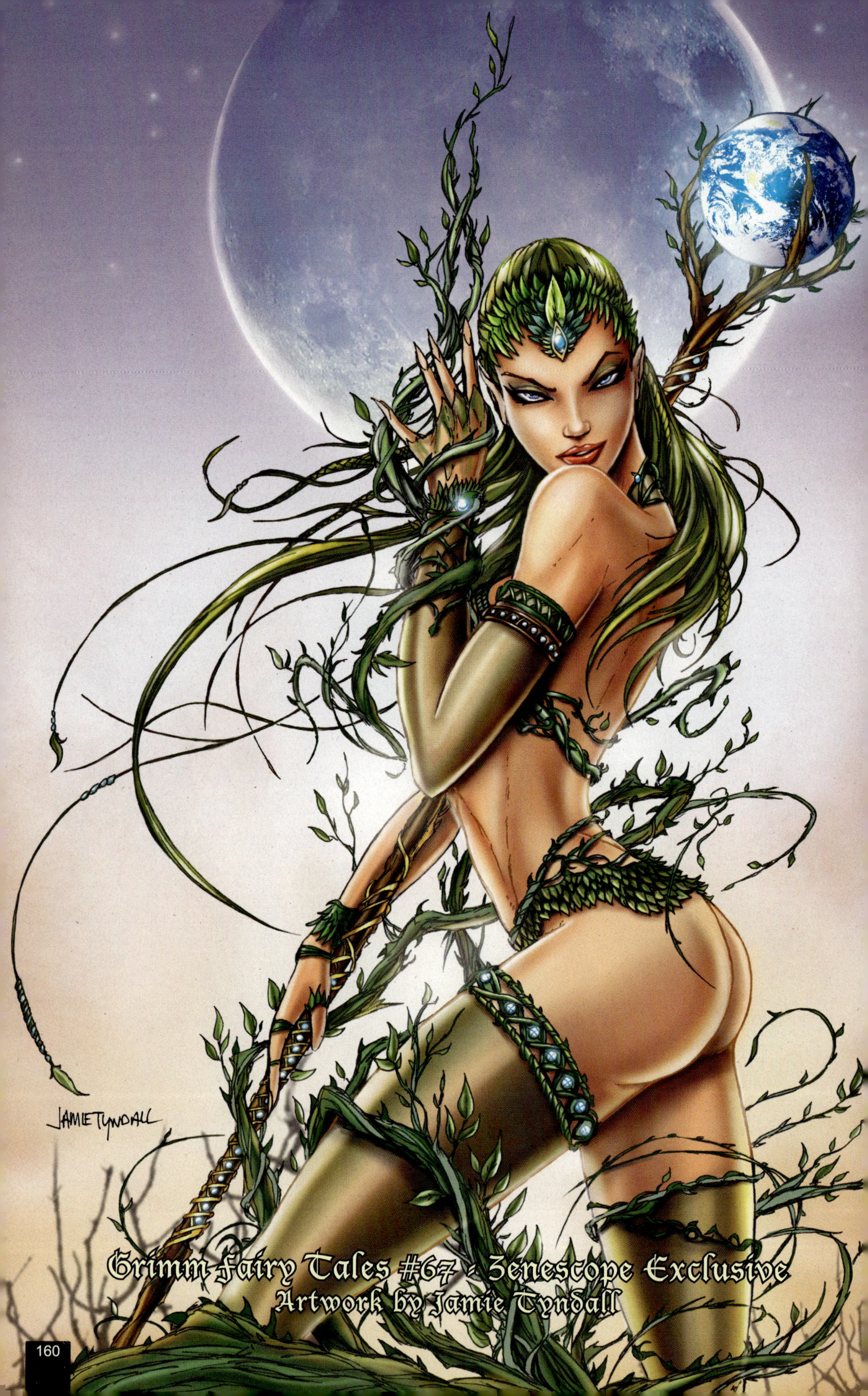
JAMIE TYNDALL

Grimm Fairy Tales #67 - Zenescope Exclusive
Artwork by Jamie Tyndall

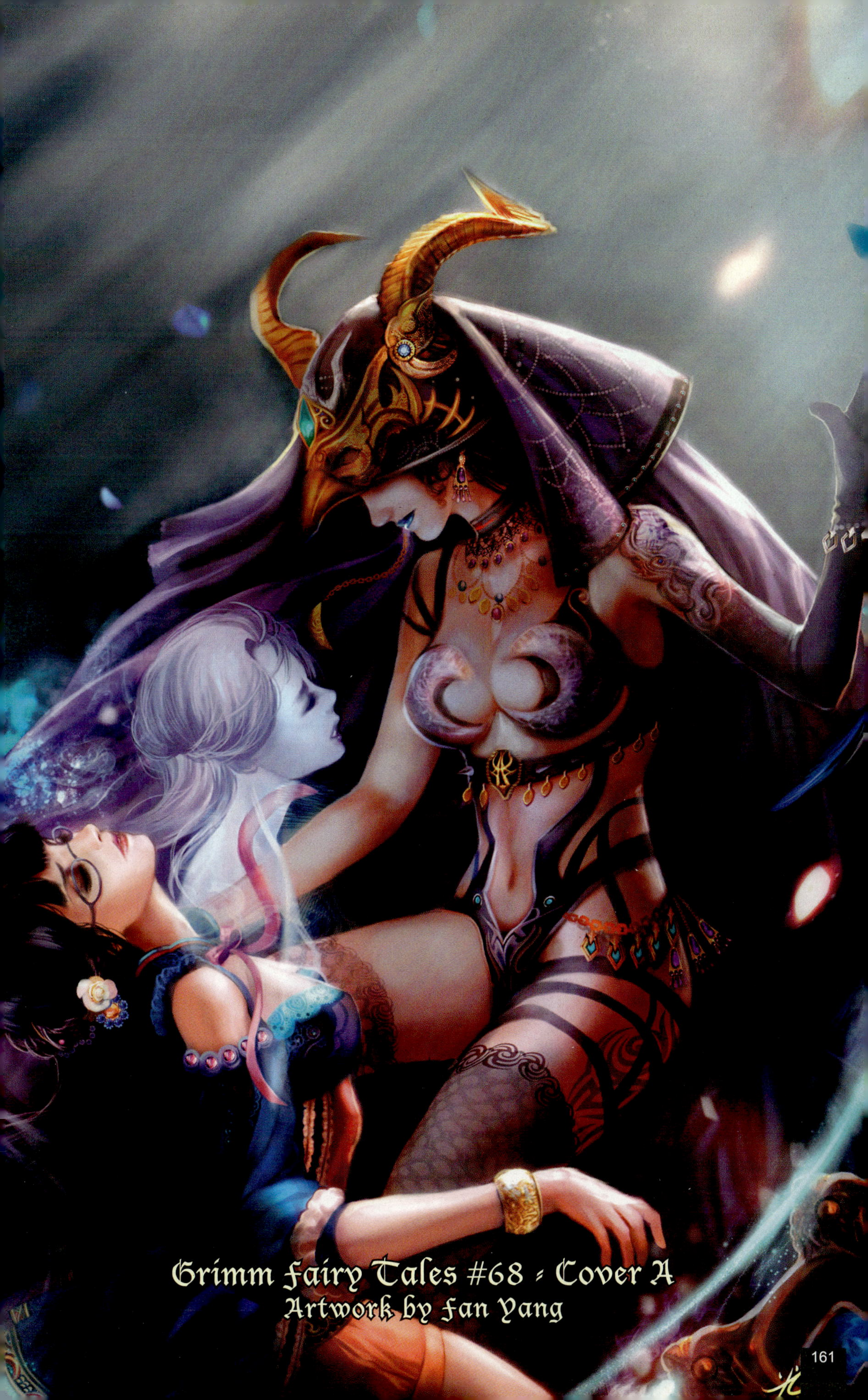

Grimm Fairy Tales #68 - Cover A
Artwork by Fan Yang

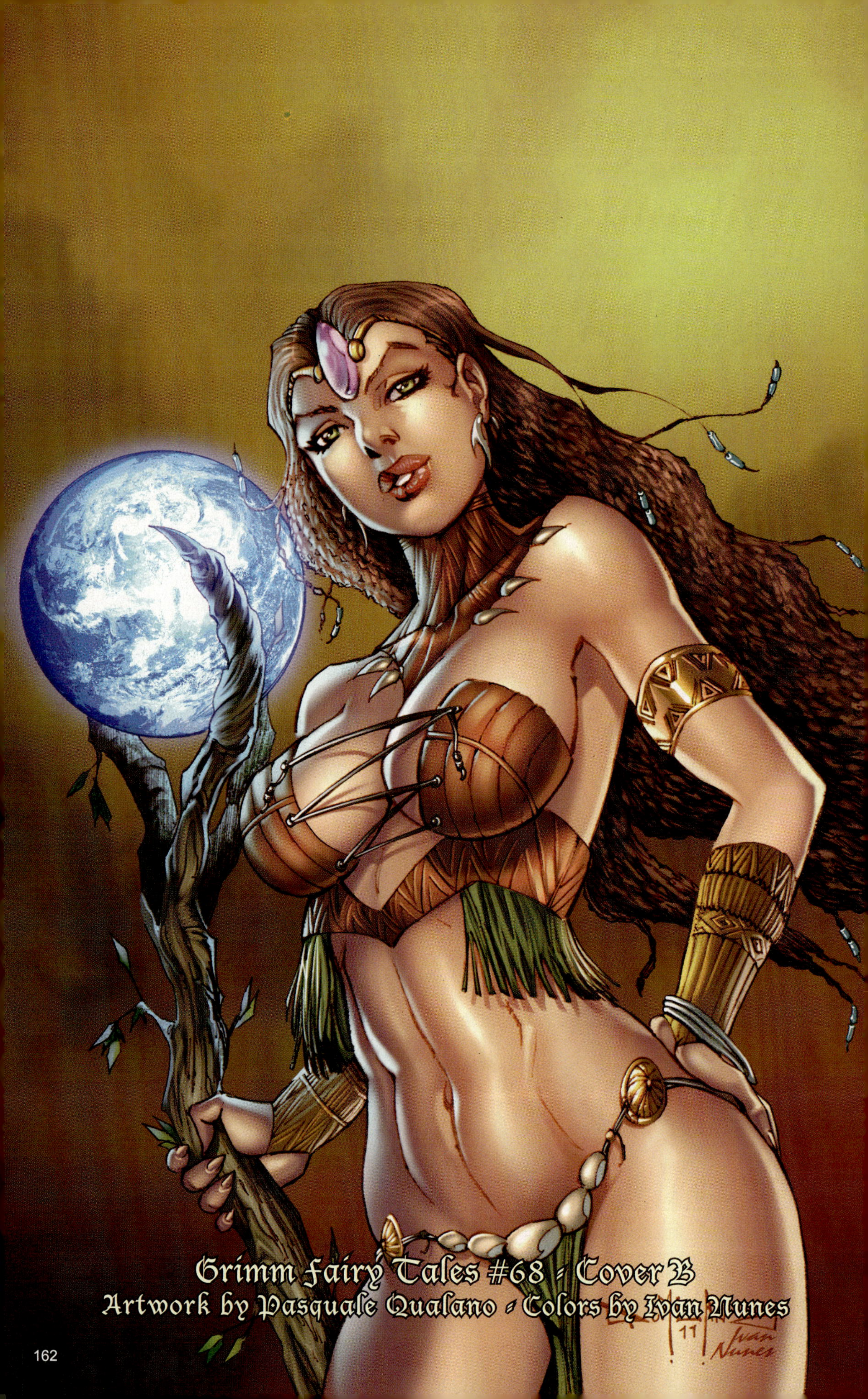

Grimm Fairy Tales #68 - Cover B
Artwork by Pasquale Qualano - Colors by Ivan Nunes

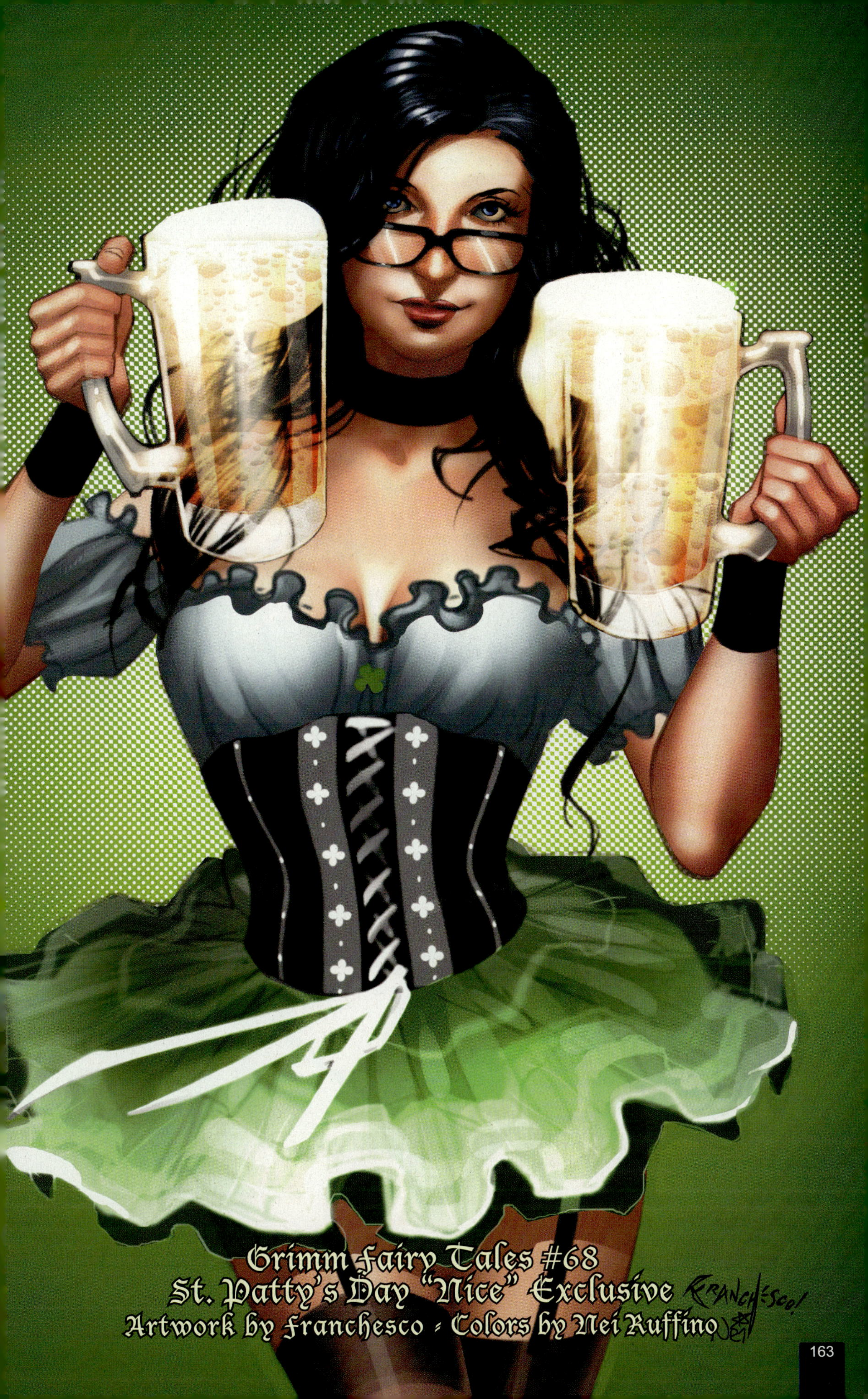
FRANCHESCO!
NEI

Grimm Fairy Tales #68
St. Patty's Day "Nice" Exclusive
Artwork by Franchesco - Colors by Nei Ruffino

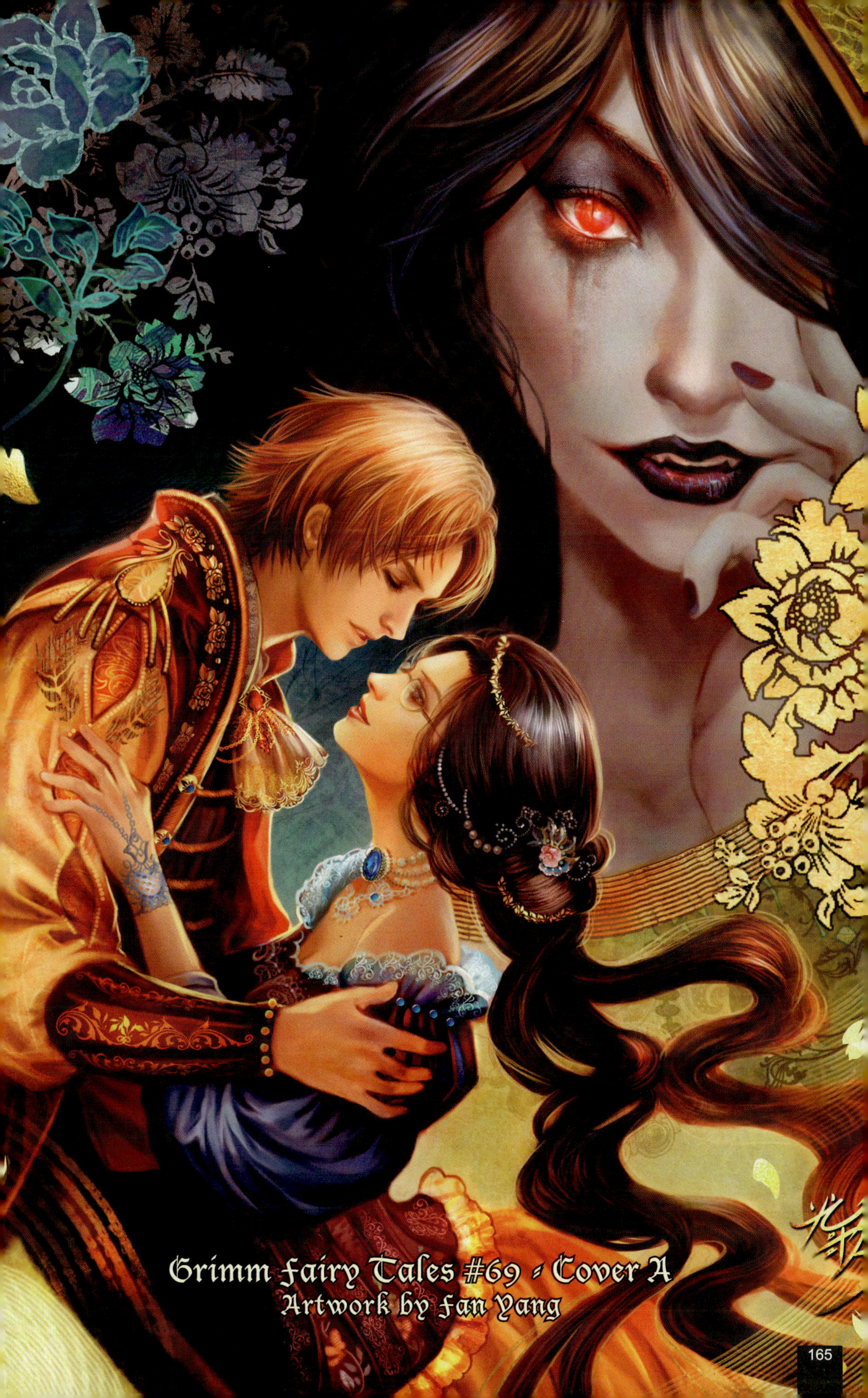

Grimm Fairy Tales #69 - Cover A
Artwork by Fan Yang

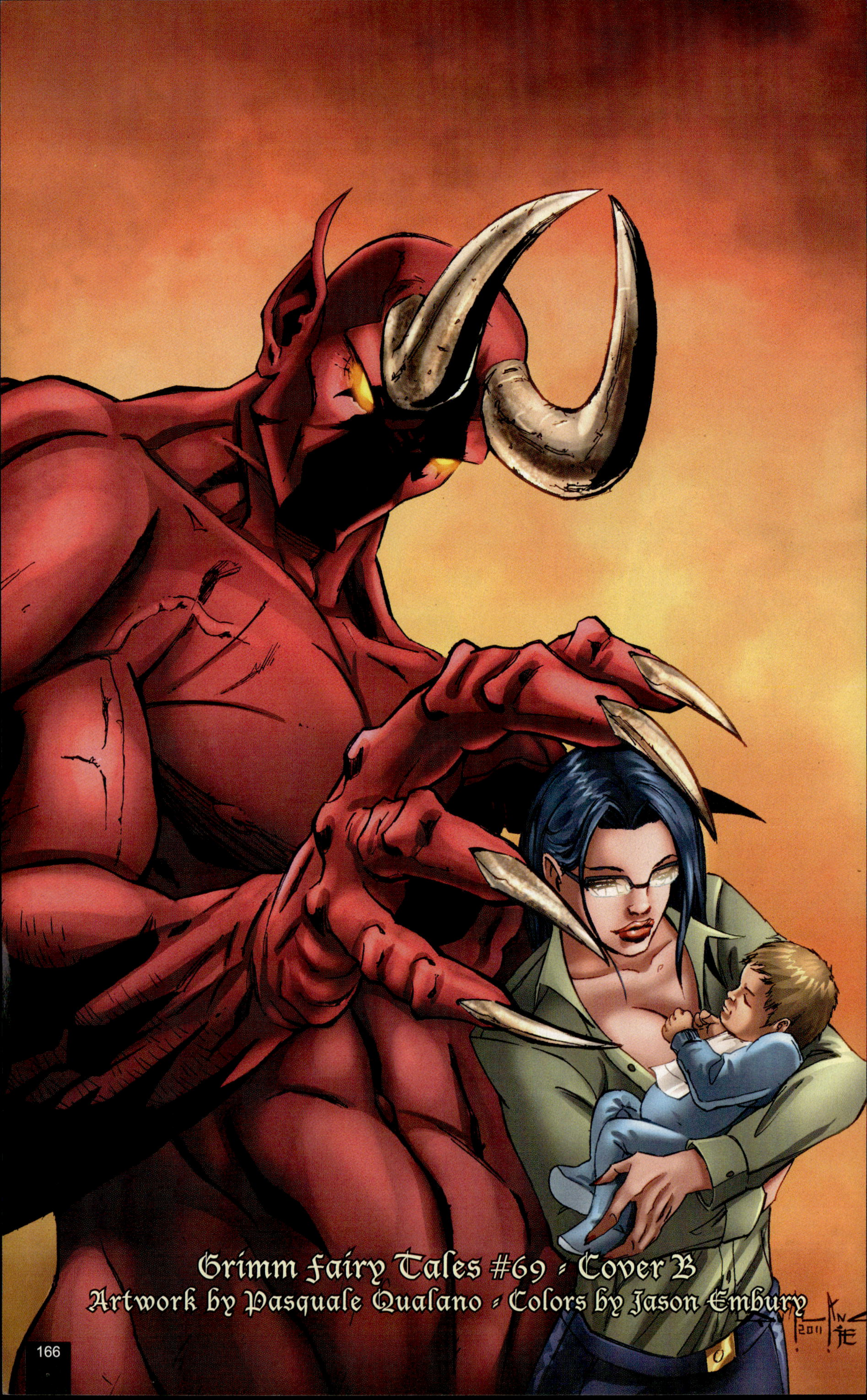

Grimm Fairy Tales #69 - Cover B
Artwork by Pasquale Qualano - Colors by Jason Embury

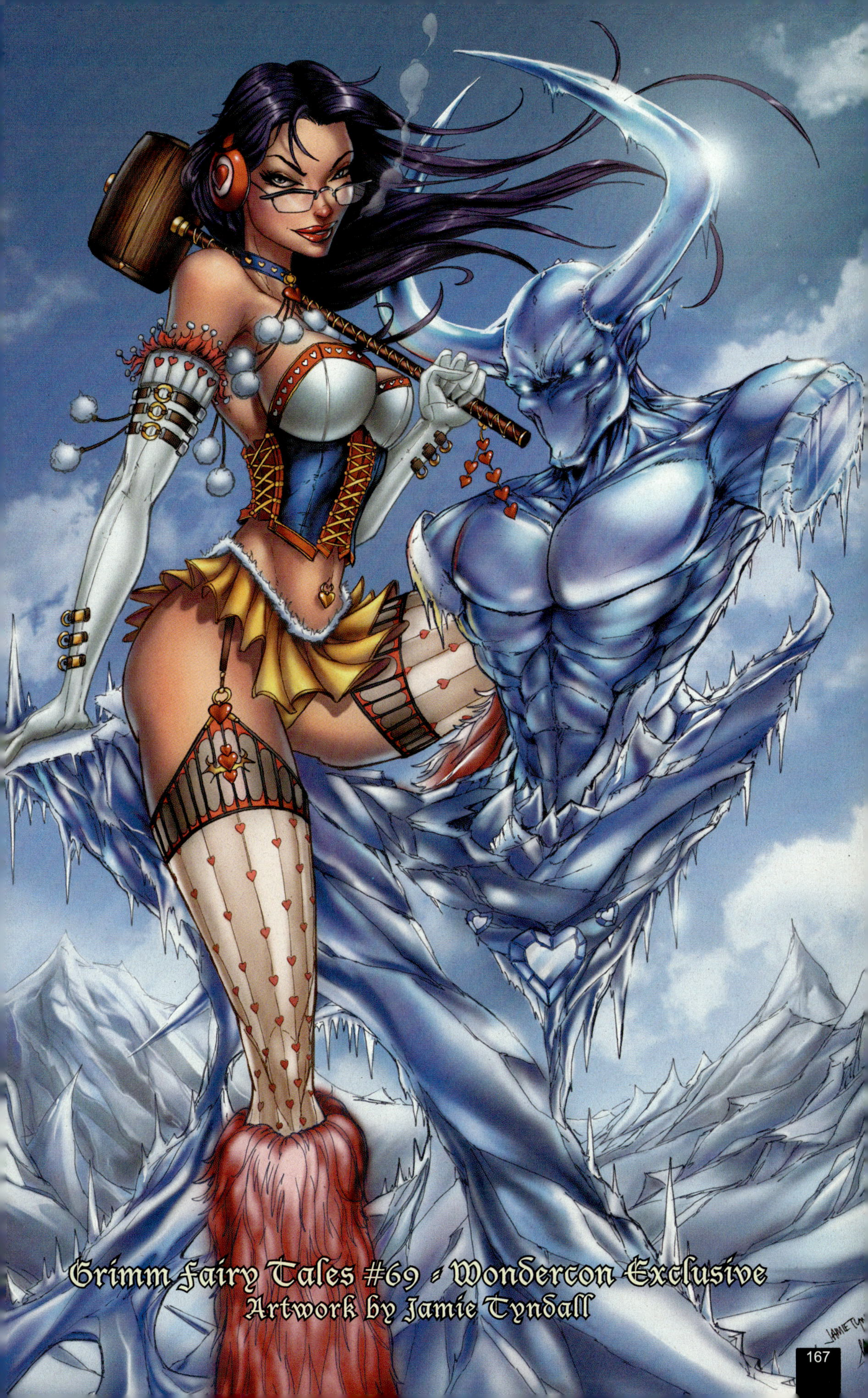

Grimm Fairy Tales #69 - Wondercon Exclusive
Artwork by Jamie Tyndall

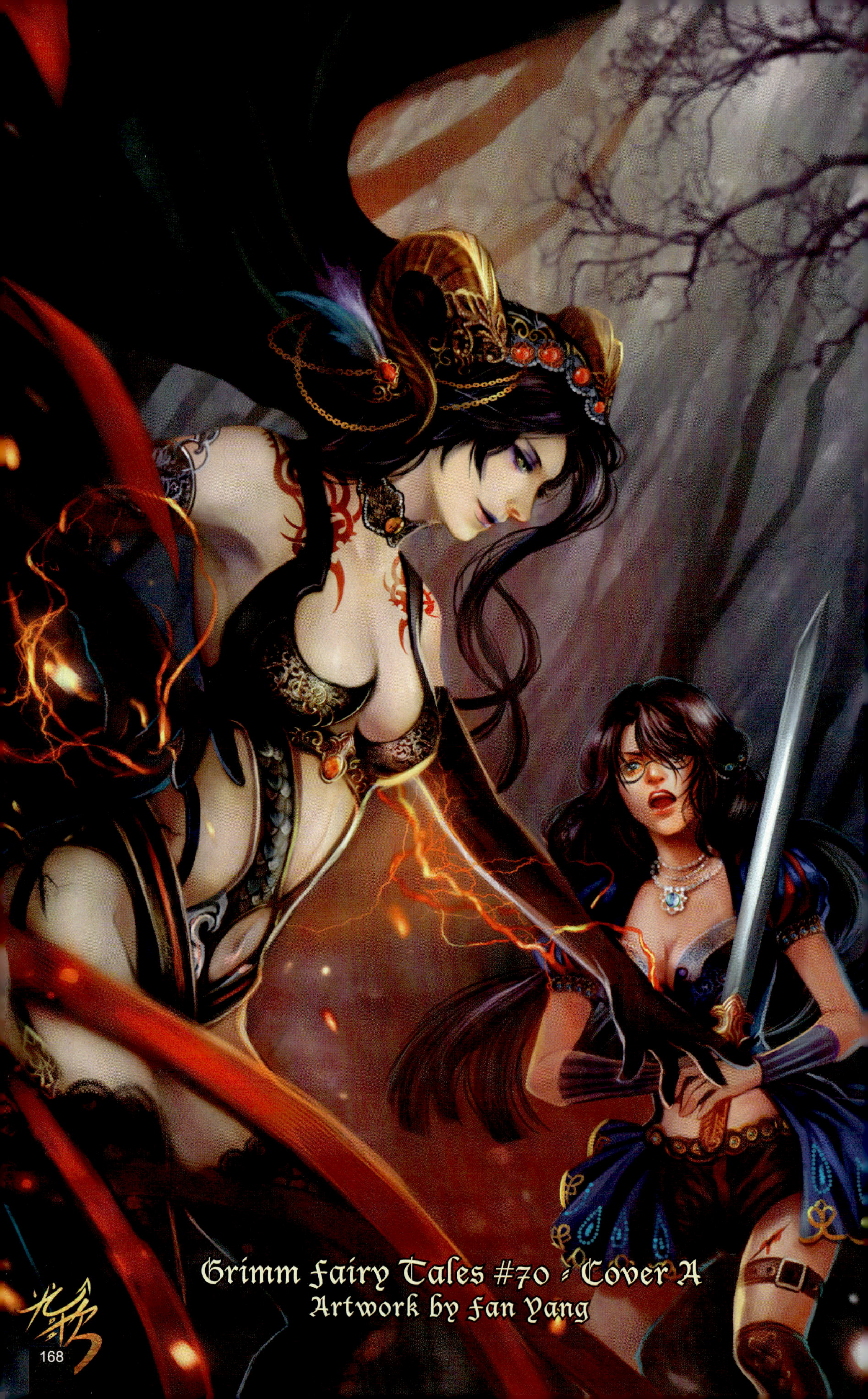

Grimm Fairy Tales #70 - Cover A
Artwork by Fan Yang

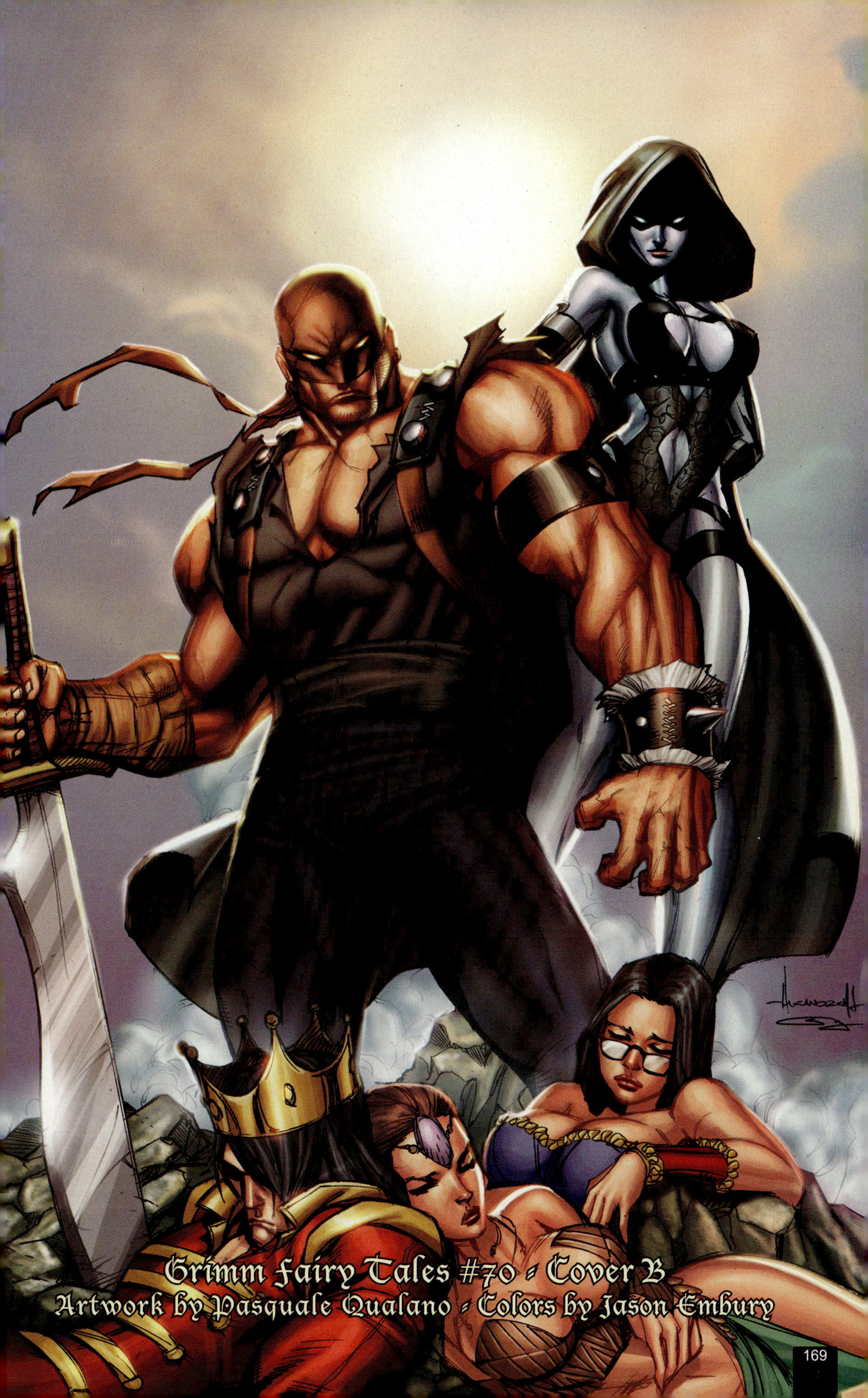

Grimm Fairy Tales #70 - Cover B
Artwork by Pasquale Qualano - Colors by Jason Embury

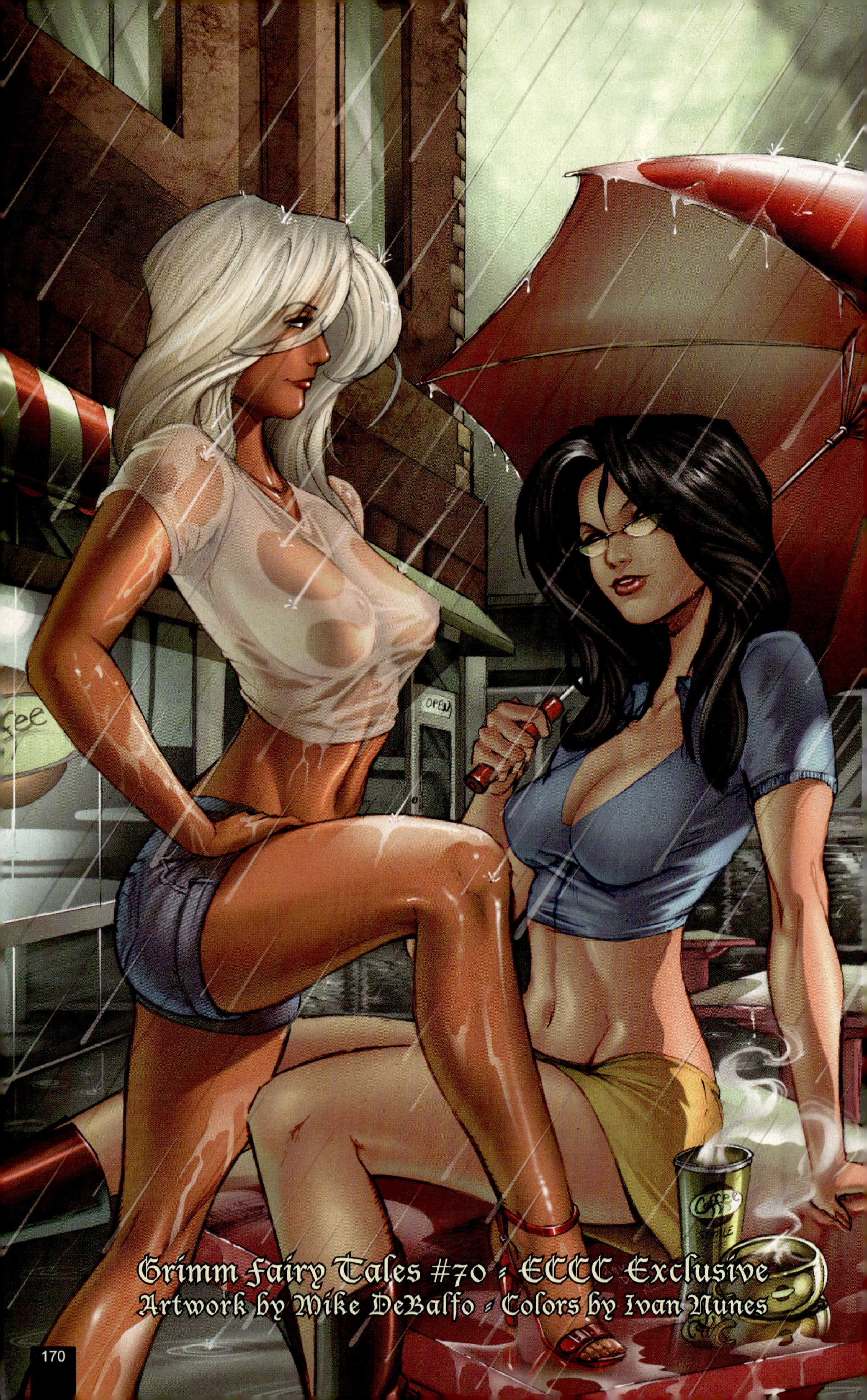
OPEN

Grimm Fairy Tales #70 - ECCC Exclusive
Artwork by Mike DeBalfo - Colors by Ivan Nunes

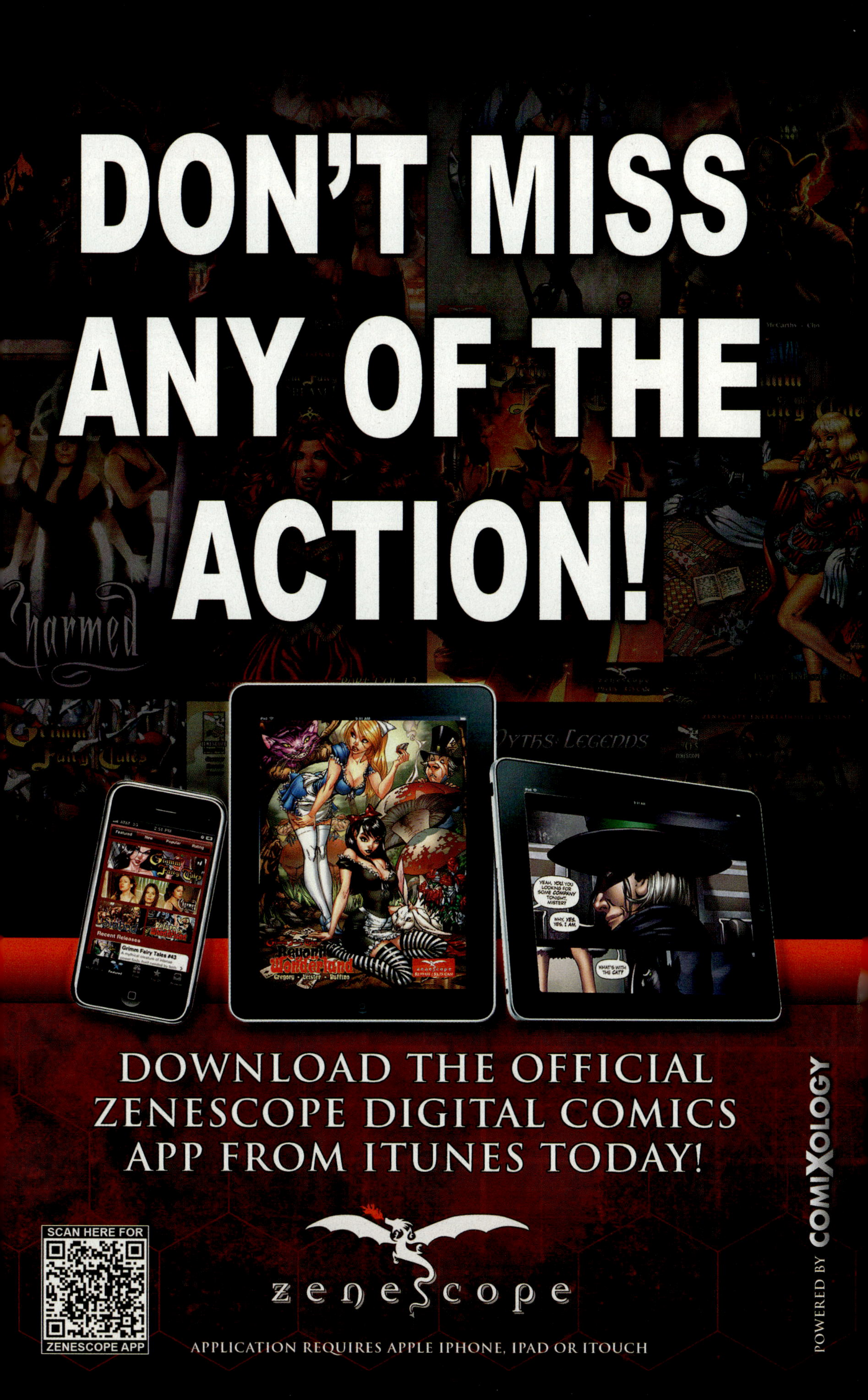

DON'T MISS ANY OF THE ACTION!
YEAH, YOU. YOU LOOKING FOR SOME COMPANY TONIGHT, MISTER?
WHY, YES. YES, I AM.
WHAT'S WITH THE CAT?
DOWNLOAD THE OFFICIAL ZENESCOPE DIGITAL COMICS APP FROM ITUNES TODAY!
SCAN HERE FOR ZENESCOPE APP
zenescope
APPLICATION REQUIRES APPLE IPHONE, IPAD OR ITOUCH
POWERED BY COMIXOLOGY

ENTER THE GRIMM FAIRY TALES UNIVERSE WITH THESE EPIC TRADE COLLECTIONS!

GRIMM FAIRY TALES
VOLUME ONE
COLLECTING ISSUES #1-6

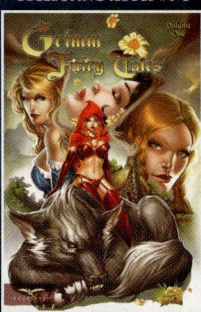

Grimm Fairy Tales

DIAMOND
ORDER CODE:
MAY063495

GRIMM FAIRY TALES
VOLUME TWO
COLLECTING ISSUES #7-12

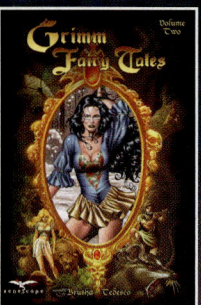

Volume Two
Grimm Fairy Tales

DIAMOND
ORDER CODE:
MAY073862

GRIMM FAIRY TALES
VOLUME THREE
COLLECTING ISSUES #13-18

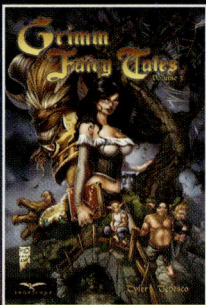

Grimm Fairy Tales

DIAMOND
ORDER CODE:
JAN084010

GRIMM FAIRY TALES
VOLUME FOUR
COLLECTING ISSUES #19-24

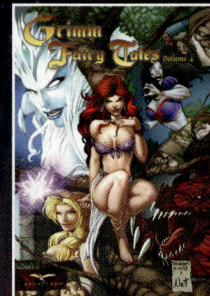

Grimm Fairy Tales

DIAMOND
ORDER CODE:
JUN084376

GRIMM FAIRY TALES
VOLUME FIVE
COLLECTING ISSUES #25-30

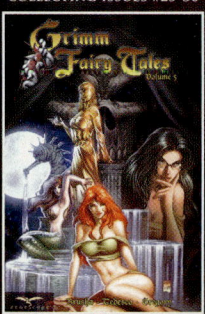

Grimm Fairy Tales

DIAMOND
ORDER CODE:
DEC084356

GRIMM FAIRY TALES
VOLUME SIX
COLLECTING ISSUES #31-36

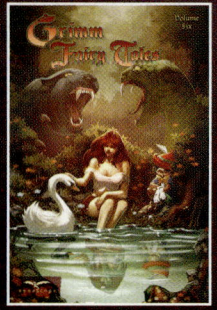

Grimm Fairy Tales

DIAMOND
ORDER CODE:
APR091068

GRIMM FAIRY TALES
VOLUME SEVEN
COLLECTING ISSUES #37-42

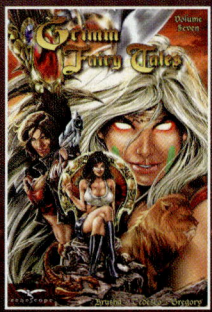

Volume Seven
Grimm Fairy Tales

DIAMOND
ORDER CODE:
NOV091001

GRIMM FAIRY TALES
VOLUME EIGHT
COLLECTING ISSUES #43-50

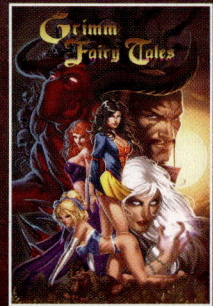

Grimm Fairy Tales

DIAMOND
ORDER CODE:
MAY101211

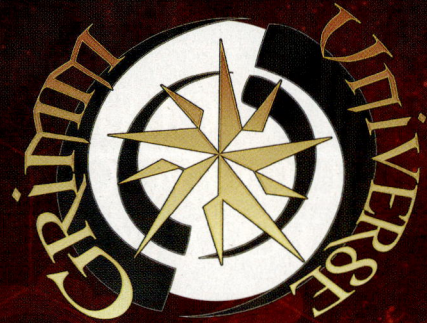

GRIMM UNIVERSE

GRIMM FAIRY TALES
VOLUME NINE
COLLECTING ISSUES #51-56

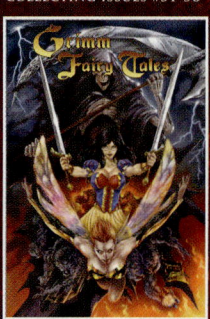

Grimm Fairy Tales

DIAMOND
ORDER CODE:
DEC101123

GRIMM FAIRY TALES
VOLUME TEN
COLLECTING ISSUES #57-62

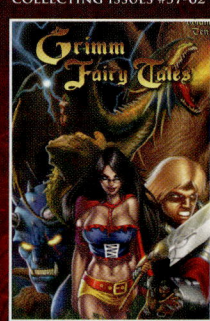

Grimm Fairy Tales

DIAMOND
ORDER CODE:
JUN111309

COLLECT THEM ALL AT ZENESCOPE.COM OR YOUR LOCAL COMIC RETAILER!

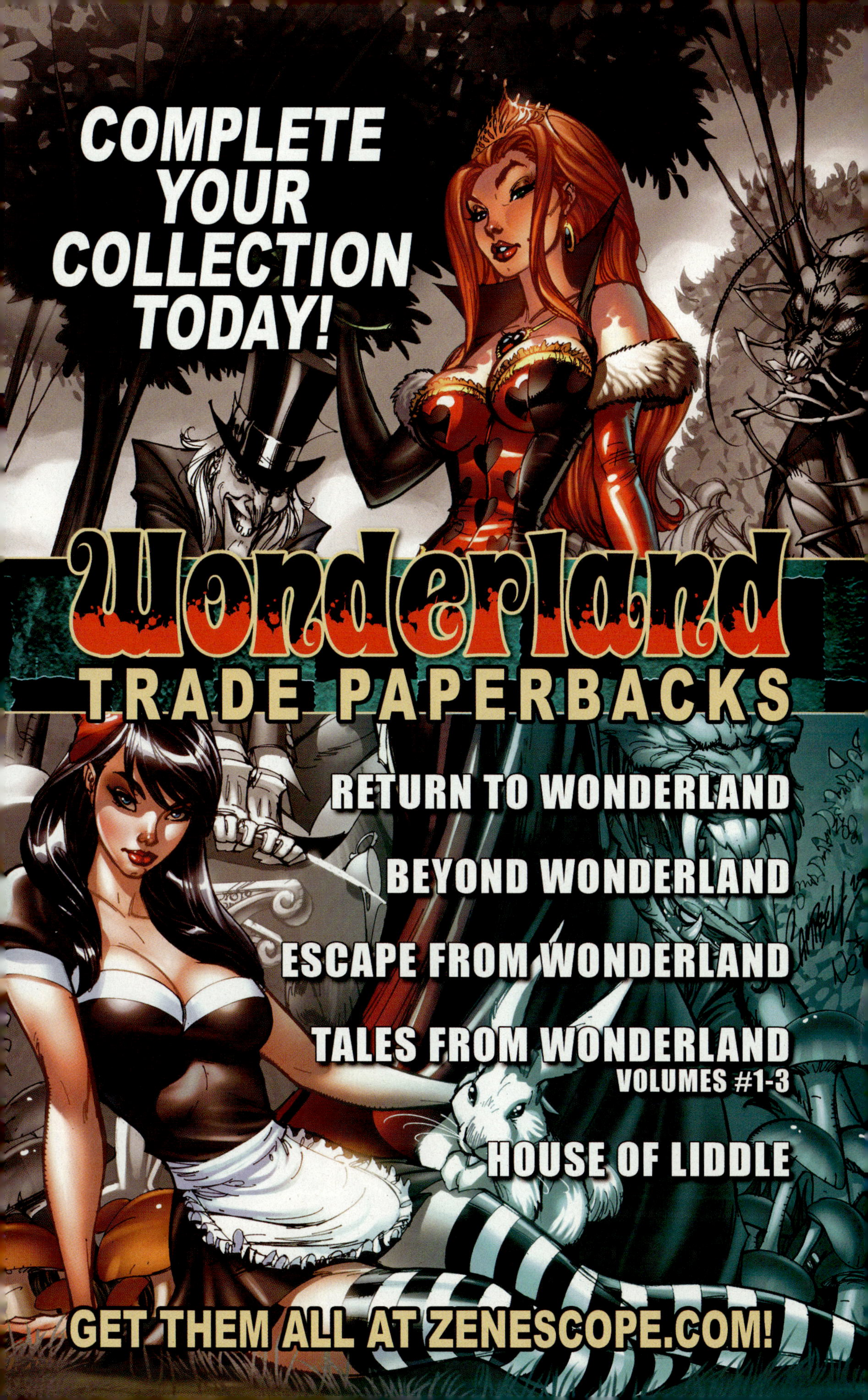
COMPLETE YOUR COLLECTION TODAY!
Wonderland
TRADE PAPERBACKS
RETURN TO WONDERLAND
BEYOND WONDERLAND
ESCAPE FROM WONDERLAND
TALES FROM WONDERLAND
VOLUMES #1-3
HOUSE OF LIDDLE
GET THEM ALL AT ZENESCOPE.COM!

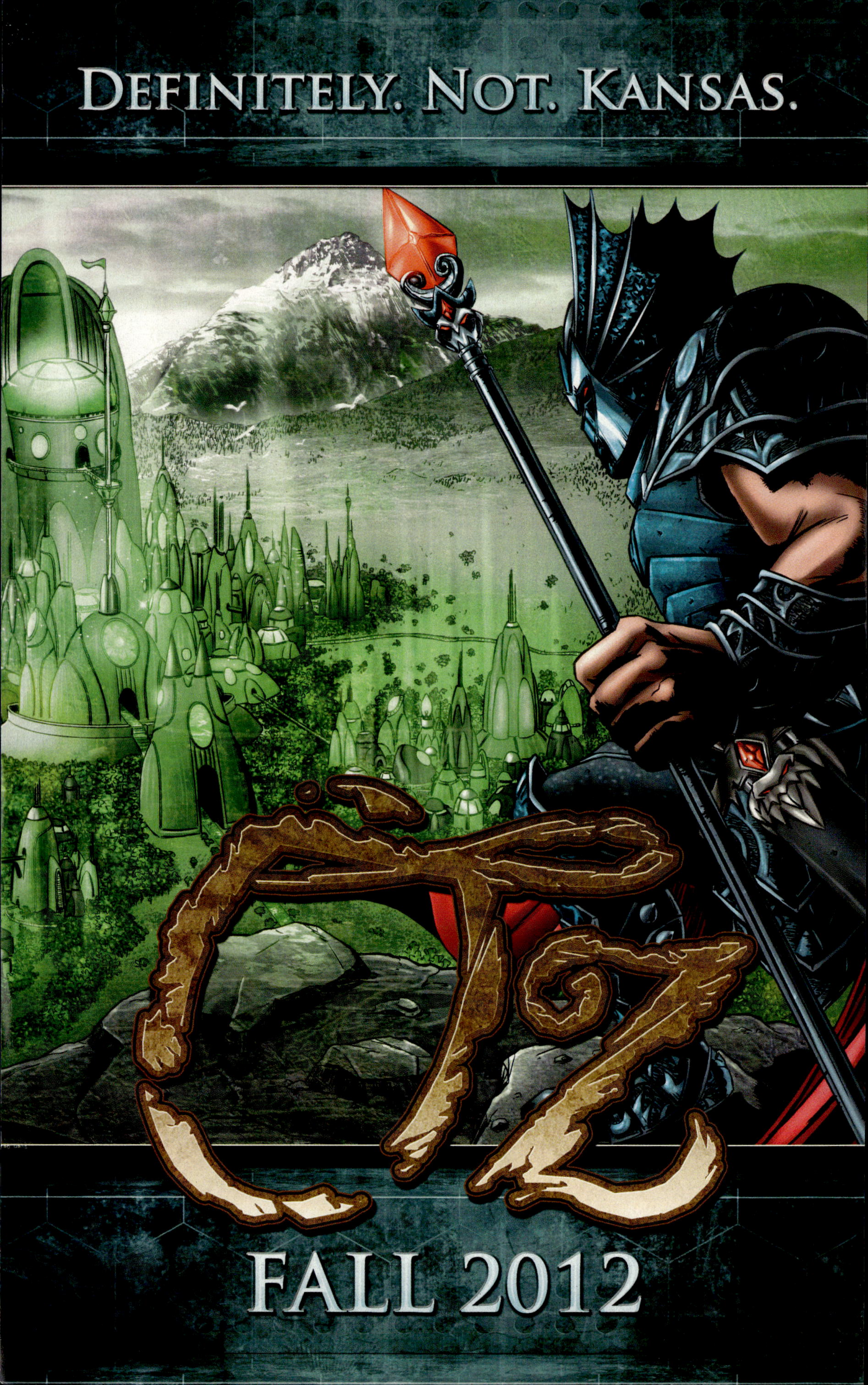
DEFINITELY. NOT. KANSAS.
OZ
FALL 2012

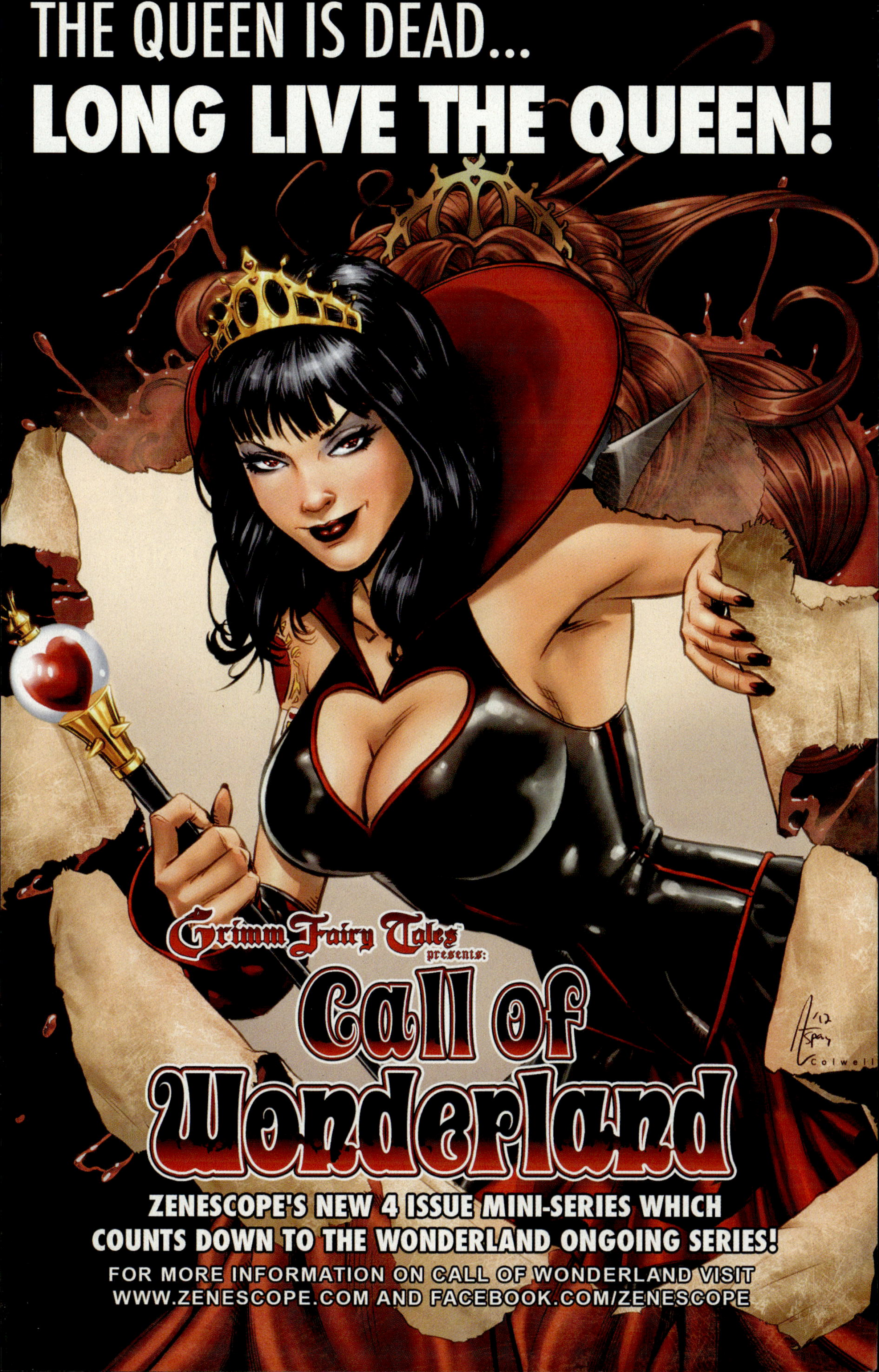

Grimm Fairy Tales

Volume 11